THE WAR OF THE WORLDS

COLLECTION

Featuring writing from
H. G. Wells
Tony Wright
Bayne MacGregor

And artwork by
Peter Fussey
Brendan Perkins
Richard Daborn
Michael Grote
George Jones

A Wild Wolf Publication

Published by Wild Wolf Publishing in 2017

First print

All Characters appearing in this work are fictitious or fictitious interpretations of historical figures.

ISBN: 978-1-907954-47-4

Also available as an E-Book

www.wildwolfpublishing.com

Contents

Stunning new and previously unseen artwork throughout

Foreword

A group of avid *The War of the Worlds* fanatics decided to create the ultimate collection of writing and artwork relating to H. G. Wells' original classic. This huge tome is the result. We hope you enjoy it and hope that the great man himself would approve. Thank you, Herbert George Wells.

The War of the Worlds
By H. G. Wells

Book One
The Coming of the Martians

Chapter One
The Eve of the War

But who shall dwell in these worlds if they be inhabited? . . .
Are we or they Lords of the World? . . .
And how are all things made for man?
~ Kepler (quoted in *The Anatomy of Melancholy*)

No one would have believed in the last years of the nineteenth century that this world was being watched keenly and closely by intelligences greater than man's and yet as mortal as his own; that as men busied themselves about their various concerns they were scrutinised and studied, perhaps almost as narrowly as a man with a microscope might scrutinise the transient creatures that swarm and multiply in a drop of water. With infinite complacency men went to and fro over this globe about their little affairs, serene in their assurance of their empire over matter. It is possible that the infusoria under the microscope do the same. No one gave a thought to the older worlds of space as sources of human danger, or thought of them only to dismiss the idea of life upon them as impossible or improbable. It is curious to recall some of the mental habits of those departed days. At most terrestrial men fancied there might be other men upon Mars, perhaps inferior to themselves and ready to welcome a missionary enterprise. Yet across the gulf of space, minds that are to our minds as ours are to those of the beasts that perish, intellects vast and cool and unsympathetic, regarded this earth with envious eyes, and slowly and surely drew their plans against us. And early in the twentieth century came the great disillusionment.

The planet Mars, I scarcely need remind the reader, revolves about the sun at a mean distance of 140,000,000 miles, and the light and heat it receives from the sun is barely half of that received by this world. It must be, if the nebular hypothesis has any truth, older than our world; and long before this earth ceased to be molten, life upon its surface must have begun its course. The fact that it is scarcely one seventh of the volume of the earth must have accelerated its cooling to the temperature at which life could begin. It has air and water and all that is necessary for the support of animated existence.

Yet so vain is man, and so blinded by his vanity, that no writer, up to the very end of the nineteenth century, expressed any idea that intelligent life might have developed there far, or indeed at all, beyond its earthly level. Nor was it generally understood that since Mars is older than our earth, with scarcely a quarter of the superficial area and remoter from the sun, it necessarily follows that it is not only more distant from time's beginning but nearer its end.

The secular cooling that must someday overtake our planet has already gone far indeed with our neighbour. Its physical condition is still largely a mystery, but we know now that even in its equatorial region the midday temperature barely approaches that of our coldest winter. Its air is much more attenuated than ours, its oceans have shrunk until they cover but a third of its surface, and as its slow seasons change huge snowcaps gather and melt about either pole and periodically inundate its temperate zones. That last stage of exhaustion, which to us is still incredibly remote, has become a present-day problem for the inhabitants of Mars. The immediate pressure of necessity has brightened their intellects, enlarged their powers, and hardened their hearts. And looking across space with instruments, and intelligences such as we have scarcely dreamed of, they see, at its nearest distance only 35,000,000 of miles sunward of them, a morning star of hope, our own warmer planet, green with vegetation and grey with water, with a cloudy atmosphere eloquent of fertility, with glimpses through its drifting cloud wisps of broad stretches of populous country and narrow, navy-crowded seas.

And we men, the creatures who inhabit this earth, must be to them at least as alien and lowly as are the monkeys and lemurs to us. The intellectual side of man already admits that life is an incessant struggle for existence, and it would seem that this too is the belief of the minds upon Mars. Their world is far gone in its cooling and this world is still crowded with life, but crowded only with what they regard as inferior animals. To carry warfare sunward is, indeed, their only escape from the destruction that, generation after generation, creeps upon them.

And before we judge of them too harshly we must remember what ruthless and utter destruction our own species has wrought, not only upon animals, such as the vanished bison and the dodo, but upon its inferior races. The Tasmanians, in spite of their human likeness, were entirely swept out of existence in a war of extermination waged by European immigrants, in the space of fifty years. Are we such apostles of mercy as to complain if the Martians warred in the same spirit?

The Martians seem to have calculated their descent with amazing subtlety--their mathematical learning is evidently far in excess of ours--and to have carried out their preparations with a well-nigh perfect unanimity. Had our instruments permitted it, we might have seen the gathering trouble far back in the nineteenth century. Men like Schiaparelli watched the red planet--it is odd, by-the-bye, that for countless centuries Mars has been the star of war--but failed to interpret the fluctuating appearances of the markings they mapped so well. All that time the Martians must have been getting ready.

During the opposition of 1894 a great light was seen on the illuminated part of the disk, first at the Lick Observatory, then by Perrotin of Nice, and then by other observers. English readers heard of it first in the issue of *Nature* dated August 2. I am inclined to think that this blaze may have been the casting of the huge gun, in the vast pit sunk into their planet, from which their shots were fired at us. Peculiar markings, as yet unexplained, were seen near the site of that outbreak during the next two oppositions.

The storm burst upon us six years ago now. As Mars approached opposition, Lavelle of Java set the wires of the astronomical exchange palpitating with the amazing intelligence of a huge outbreak of incandescent gas upon the planet. It had occurred towards midnight of the twelfth; and the spectroscope, to which he had at once resorted, indicated a mass of flaming gas, chiefly hydrogen, moving with an enormous velocity towards this earth. This jet of fire had become invisible about a quarter past twelve. He compared it to a colossal puff of flame suddenly and violently squirted out of the planet, "as flaming gases rushed out of a gun."

A singularly appropriate phrase it proved. Yet the next day there was nothing of this in the papers except a little note in the *Daily Telegraph*, and the world went in ignorance of one of the gravest dangers that ever threatened the human race. I might not have heard of the eruption at all had I not met Ogilvy, the well-known astronomer, at Ottershaw. He was immensely excited at the news, and in the excess of his feelings invited me up to take a turn with him that night in a scrutiny of the red planet.

In spite of all that has happened since, I still remember that vigil very distinctly: the black and silent observatory, the shadowed lantern throwing a feeble glow upon the floor in the corner, the steady ticking of the clockwork of the telescope, the little slit in the roof--an oblong profundity with the stardust streaked across it. Ogilvy moved about, invisible but audible. Looking through the telescope, one saw a circle of deep blue and the little round planet swimming in the field. It seemed such a little thing, so bright and small and still, faintly marked with transverse stripes, and slightly flattened from the perfect round. But so little it was, so silvery warm--a pin's-head of light! It was as if it quivered, but really this was the telescope vibrating with the activity of the clockwork that kept the planet in view.

As I watched, the planet seemed to grow larger and smaller and to advance and recede, but that was simply that my eye was tired. Forty millions of miles it was from us--more than forty millions of miles of void. Few people realise the immensity of vacancy in which the dust of the material universe swims. Near it in the field, I remember, were three faint points of light, three telescopic stars infinitely remote, and all around it was the unfathomable darkness of empty space. You know how that blackness looks on a frosty starlight night. In a telescope it seems far profounder. And invisible to me because it was so remote and small, flying swiftly and steadily towards me across that incredible distance, drawing nearer every minute by so many thousands of miles, came the Thing they were sending us, the Thing that was to bring so much struggle and calamity and death to the earth. I never dreamed of it then as I watched; no one on earth dreamed of that unerring missile.

That night, too, there was another jetting out of gas from the distant planet. I saw it. A reddish flash at the edge, the slightest projection of the outline just as the chronometer struck midnight; and at that I told Ogilvy and he took my place. The night was warm and I was thirsty, and I went stretching my legs clumsily and feeling my way in the darkness, to the little table where the siphon stood, while Ogilvy exclaimed at the streamer of gas that came out towards us.

That night another invisible missile started on its way to the earth from Mars, just a second or so under twenty-four hours after the first one. I remember how I sat on the table there in the blackness, with patches of green and crimson swimming before my eyes. I wished I had a light to smoke by, little suspecting the meaning of the minute gleam I had seen and all that it would presently bring me. Ogilvy watched till one, and then gave it up; and we lit the lantern and walked over to his house. Down below in the darkness were Ottershaw and Chertsey and all their hundreds of people, sleeping in peace.

He was full of speculation that night about the condition of Mars, and scoffed at the vulgar idea of its having inhabitants who were signalling us. His idea was that meteorites might be falling in a heavy shower upon the planet, or that a huge volcanic explosion was in progress. He pointed out to me how unlikely it was that organic evolution had taken the same direction in the two adjacent planets.

"The chances against anything manlike on Mars are a million to one," he said.

Hundreds of observers saw the flame that night and the night after about midnight, and again the night after; and so for ten nights, a flame each night. Why the shots ceased after the tenth no one on earth has attempted to explain. It may be the gases of the firing caused the Martians inconvenience. Dense clouds of smoke or dust, visible through a powerful telescope on earth as little grey, fluctuating patches, spread through the clearness of the planet's atmosphere and obscured its more familiar features.

Even the daily papers woke up to the disturbances at last, and popular notes appeared here, there, and everywhere concerning the volcanoes upon Mars. The seriocomic periodical *Punch*, I remember, made a happy use of it in the political cartoon. And, all unsuspected, those missiles the Martians had fired at us drew earthward, rushing now at a pace of many miles a second through the empty gulf of space, hour by hour and day by day, nearer and nearer. It seems to me now almost incredibly wonderful that, with that swift fate hanging over us, men could go about their petty concerns as they did. I remember how jubilant Markham was at securing a new photograph of the planet for the illustrated paper he edited in those days. People in these latter times scarcely realise the abundance and enterprise of our nineteenth-century papers. For my own part, I was much occupied in learning to ride the bicycle, and busy upon a series of papers discussing the probable developments of moral ideas as civilisation progressed.

One night (the first missile then could scarcely have been 10,000,000 miles away) I went for a walk with my wife. It was starlight and I explained the Signs of the Zodiac to her, and pointed out Mars, a bright dot of light creeping zenithward, towards which so many telescopes were pointed. It was a warm night. Coming home, a party of excursionists from Chertsey or Isleworth passed us singing and playing music. There were lights in the upper windows of the houses as the people went to bed. From the railway station in the distance came the sound of shunting trains, ringing and rumbling, softened almost into melody by the distance. My wife pointed out to me the brightness of the red, green, and yellow signal lights hanging in a framework against the sky. It seemed so safe and tranquil.

Chapter Two
The Falling Star

Then came the night of the first falling star. It was seen early in the morning, rushing over Winchester eastward, a line of flame high in the atmosphere. Hundreds must have seen it, and taken it for an ordinary falling star. Albin described it as leaving a greenish streak behind it that glowed for some seconds. Denning, our greatest authority on meteorites, stated that the height of its first appearance was about ninety or one hundred miles. It seemed to him that it fell to earth about one hundred miles east of him.

I was at home at that hour and writing in my study; and although my French windows face towards Ottershaw and the blind was up (for I loved in those days to look up at the night sky), I saw nothing of it. Yet this strangest of all things that ever came to earth from outer space must have fallen while I was sitting there, visible to me had I only looked up as it passed. Some of those who saw its flight say it travelled with a hissing sound. I myself heard nothing of that. Many people in Berkshire, Surrey, and Middlesex must have seen the fall of it, and, at most, have thought that another meteorite had descended. No one seems to have troubled to look for the fallen mass that night.

But very early in the morning poor Ogilvy, who had seen the shooting star and who was persuaded that a meteorite lay somewhere on the common between Horsell, Ottershaw, and Woking, rose early with the idea of finding it. Find it he did, soon after dawn, and not far from the sand pits. An enormous hole had been made by the impact of the projectile, and the sand and gravel had been flung violently in every direction over the heath, forming heaps visible a mile and a half away. The heather was on fire eastward, and a thin blue smoke rose against the dawn.

The Thing itself lay almost entirely buried in sand, amidst the scattered splinters of a fir tree it had shivered to fragments in its descent. The uncovered part had the appearance of a huge cylinder, caked over and its outline softened by a thick scaly dun-coloured incrustation. It had a diameter of about thirty yards. He approached the mass, surprised at the size and more so at the shape, since most meteorites are rounded more or less completely. It was, however, still so hot from its flight through the air as to forbid his near approach. A stirring noise within its cylinder he ascribed to the unequal cooling of its surface; for at that time it had not occurred to him that it might be hollow.

He remained standing at the edge of the pit that the Thing had made for itself, staring at its strange appearance, astonished chiefly at its unusual shape and colour, and dimly perceiving even then some evidence of design in its arrival. The early morning was wonderfully still, and the sun, just clearing the pine trees towards Weybridge, was already warm. He did not remember hearing any birds that morning, there was certainly no breeze stirring, and the only sounds were the faint movements from within the cindery cylinder. He was all alone on the common.

Then suddenly he noticed with a start that some of the grey clinker, the ashy incrustation that covered the meteorite, was falling off the circular edge of the end. It was dropping off in flakes and raining down upon the sand. A large piece suddenly came off and fell with a sharp noise that brought his heart into his mouth.

For a minute he scarcely realised what this meant, and, although the heat was excessive, he clambered down into the pit close to the bulk to see the Thing more clearly. He fancied even then that the cooling of the body might account for this, but what disturbed that idea was the fact that the ash was falling only from the end of the cylinder.

And then he perceived that, very slowly, the circular top of the cylinder was rotating on its body. It was such a gradual movement that he discovered it only through noticing that a black mark that had been near him five minutes ago was now at the other side of the circumference. Even then he scarcely understood what this indicated, until he heard a muffled grating sound and saw the black mark jerk forward an inch or so. Then the thing came upon him in a flash. The cylinder was artificial--hollow--with an end that screwed out! Something within the cylinder was unscrewing the top!

"Good heavens!" said Ogilvy. "There's a man in it--men in it! Half roasted to death! Trying to escape!"

At once, with a quick mental leap, he linked the Thing with the flash upon Mars.

The thought of the confined creature was so dreadful to him that he forgot the heat and went forward to the cylinder to help turn. But luckily the dull radiation arrested him before he could burn his hands on the still-glowing metal. At that he stood irresolute for a moment, then turned, scrambled out of the pit, and set off running wildly into Woking. The time then must have been somewhere about six o'clock. He met a waggoner and tried to make him understand, but the tale he told and his appearance were so wild--his hat had fallen off in the pit--that the man simply drove on. He was equally unsuccessful with the potman who was just unlocking the doors of the public-house by Horsell Bridge. The fellow thought he was a lunatic at large and made an unsuccessful attempt to shut him into the taproom. That sobered him a little; and when he saw Henderson, the London journalist, in his garden, he called over the palings and made himself understood.

"Henderson," he called, "you saw that shooting star last night?"

"Well?" said Henderson.

"It's out on Horsell Common now."

"Good Lord!" said Henderson. "Fallen meteorite! That's good."

"But it's something more than a meteorite. It's a cylinder--an artificial cylinder, man! And there's something inside."

Henderson stood up with his spade in his hand.

"What's that?" he said. He was deaf in one ear.

Ogilvy told him all that he had seen. Henderson was a minute or so taking it in. Then he dropped his spade, snatched up his jacket, and came out into the road. The two men hurried back at once to the common, and found the cylinder still lying in the same position. But now the sounds inside had ceased, and a thin circle of bright metal showed between the top and the body of the cylinder. Air was either entering or escaping at the rim with a thin, sizzling sound.

They listened, rapped on the scaly burnt metal with a stick, and, meeting with no response, they both concluded the man or men inside must be insensible or dead.

Of course the two were quite unable to do anything. They shouted consolation and promises, and went off back to the town again to get help. One can imagine them, covered with sand, excited and disordered, running up the little street in the bright sunlight just as the shop folks were taking down their shutters and people were opening their bedroom windows. Henderson went into the railway station at once, in order to telegraph the news to London. The newspaper articles had prepared men's minds for the reception of the idea.

By eight o'clock a number of boys and unemployed men had already started for the common to see the "dead men from Mars." That was the form the story took. I heard of it first from my newspaper boy about a quarter to nine when I went out to get my *Daily Chronicle*. I was naturally startled, and lost no time in going out and across the Ottershaw bridge to the sand pits.

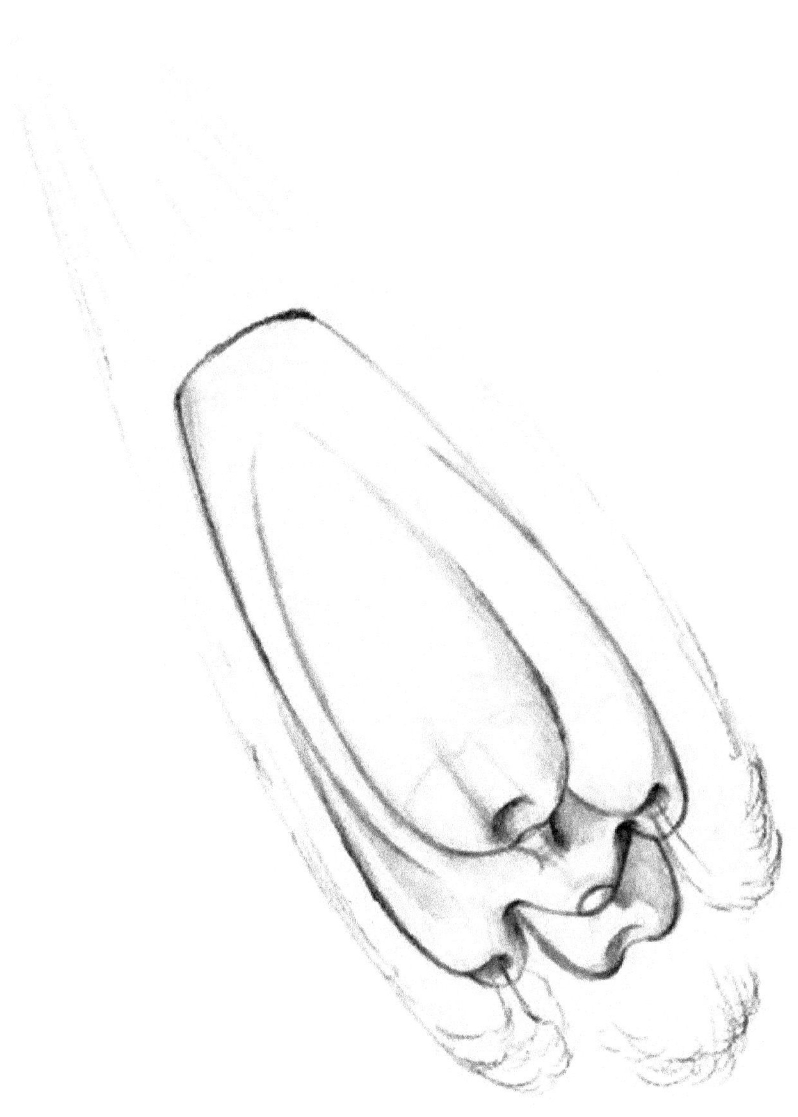

The Cylinder by Peter Fussey

Chapter Three
On Horsell Common

I found a little crowd of perhaps twenty people surrounding the huge hole in which the cylinder lay. I have already described the appearance of that colossal bulk, embedded in the ground. The turf and gravel about it seemed charred as if by a sudden explosion. No doubt its impact had caused a flash of fire. Henderson and Ogilvy were not there. I think they perceived that nothing was to be done for the present, and had gone away to breakfast at Henderson's house.

There were four or five boys sitting on the edge of the Pit, with their feet dangling, and amusing themselves--until I stopped them--by throwing stones at the giant mass. After I had spoken to them about it, they began playing at "touch" in and out of the group of bystanders.

Among these were a couple of cyclists, a jobbing gardener I employed sometimes, a girl carrying a baby, Gregg the butcher and his little boy, and two or three loafers and golf caddies who were accustomed to hang about the railway station. There was very little talking. Few of the common people in England had anything but the vaguest astronomical ideas in those days. Most of them were staring quietly at the big tablelike end of the cylinder, which was still as Ogilvy and Henderson had left it. I fancy the popular expectation of a heap of charred corpses was disappointed at this inanimate bulk. Some went away while I was there, and other people came. I clambered into the pit and fancied I heard a faint movement under my feet. The top had certainly ceased to rotate.

It was only when I got thus close to it that the strangeness of this object was at all evident to me. At the first glance it was really no more exciting than an overturned carriage or a tree blown across the road. Not so much so, indeed. It looked like a rusty gas float. It required a certain amount of scientific education to perceive that the grey scale of the Thing was no common oxide, that the yellowish-white metal that gleamed in the crack between the lid and the cylinder had an unfamiliar hue. "Extra-terrestrial" had no meaning for most of the onlookers.

At that time it was quite clear in my own mind that the Thing had come from the planet Mars, but I judged it improbable that it contained any living creature. I thought the unscrewing might be automatic. In spite of Ogilvy, I still believed that there were men in Mars. My mind ran fancifully on the possibilities of its containing manuscript, on the difficulties in translation that might arise, whether we should find coins and models in it, and so forth. Yet it was a little too large for assurance on this idea. I felt an impatience to see it opened. About eleven, as nothing seemed happening, I walked back, full of such thought, to my home in Maybury. But I found it difficult to get to work upon my abstract investigations.

In the afternoon the appearance of the common had altered very much. The early editions of the evening papers had startled London with enormous headlines:

"A MESSAGE RECEIVED FROM MARS."

"REMARKABLE STORY FROM WOKING,"

and so forth. In addition, Ogilvy's wire to the Astronomical Exchange had roused every observatory in the three kingdoms.

There were half a dozen flies or more from the Woking station standing in the road by the sand pits, a basket-chaise from Chobham, and a rather lordly carriage. Besides that, there was quite a heap of bicycles. In addition, a large number of people must have walked, in spite of the heat of the day, from Woking and Chertsey, so that there was altogether quite a considerable crowd--one or two gaily dressed ladies among the others.

It was glaringly hot, not a cloud in the sky nor a breath of wind, and the only shadow was that of the few scattered pine trees. The burning heather had been extinguished, but the level ground towards Ottershaw was blackened as far as one could see, and still giving off vertical streamers of smoke. An enterprising sweet-stuff dealer in the Chobham Road had sent up his son with a barrow-load of green apples and ginger beer.

Going to the edge of the pit, I found it occupied by a group of about half a dozen men--Henderson, Ogilvy, and a tall, fair-haired man that I afterwards learned was Stent, the Astronomer Royal, with several workmen wielding spades and pickaxes. Stent was giving directions in a clear, high-pitched voice. He was standing on the cylinder, which was now evidently much cooler; his face was crimson and streaming with perspiration, and something seemed to have irritated him.

A large portion of the cylinder had been uncovered, though its lower end was still embedded. As soon as Ogilvy saw me among the staring crowd on the edge of the pit he called to me to come down, and asked me if I would mind going over to see Lord Hilton, the lord of the manor.

The growing crowd, he said, was becoming a serious impediment to their excavations, especially the boys. They wanted a light railing put up, and help to keep the people back. He told me that a faint stirring was occasionally still audible within the case, but that the workmen had failed to unscrew the top, as it afforded no grip to them. The case appeared to be enormously thick, and it was possible that the faint sounds we heard represented a noisy tumult in the interior.

I was very glad to do as he asked, and so become one of the privileged spectators within the contemplated enclosure. I failed to find Lord Hilton at his house, but I was told he was expected from London by the six o'clock train from Waterloo; and as it was then about a quarter past five, I went home, had some tea, and walked up to the station to waylay him.

The Cylinder on Horsell Common by Peter Fussey

Chapter Four
The Cylinder Opens

When I returned to the common the sun was setting. Scattered groups were hurrying from the direction of Woking, and one or two persons were returning. The crowd about the pit had increased, and stood out black against the lemon yellow of the sky--a couple of hundred people, perhaps. There were raised voices, and some sort of struggle appeared to be going on about the pit. Strange imaginings passed through my mind. As I drew nearer I heard Stent's voice:

"Keep back! Keep back!"

A boy came running towards me.

"It's a-movin'," he said to me as he passed; "a-screwin' and a-screwin' out. I don't like it. I'm a-goin' 'ome, I am."

I went on to the crowd. There were really, I should think, two or three hundred people elbowing and jostling one another, the one or two ladies there being by no means the least active.

"He's fallen in the pit!" cried some one.

"Keep back!" said several.

The crowd swayed a little, and I elbowed my way through. Every one seemed greatly excited. I heard a peculiar humming sound from the pit.

"I say!" said Ogilvy; "help keep these idiots back. We don't know what's in the confounded thing, you know!"

I saw a young man, a shop assistant in Woking I believe he was, standing on the cylinder and trying to scramble out of the hole again. The crowd had pushed him in.

The end of the cylinder was being screwed out from within. Nearly two feet of shining screw projected. Somebody blundered against me, and I narrowly missed being pitched onto the top of the screw. I turned, and as I did so the screw must have come out, for the lid of the cylinder fell upon the gravel with a ringing concussion. I stuck my elbow into the person behind me, and turned my head towards the Thing again. For a moment that circular cavity seemed perfectly black. I had the sunset in my eyes.

I think everyone expected to see a man emerge--possibly something a little unlike us terrestrial men, but in all essentials a man. I know I did. But, looking, I presently saw something stirring within the shadow: greyish billowy movements, one above another, and then two luminous disks--like eyes. Then something resembling a little grey snake, about the thickness of a walking stick, coiled up out of the writhing middle, and wriggled in the air towards me--and then another.

A sudden chill came over me. There was a loud shriek from a woman behind. I half turned, keeping my eyes fixed upon the cylinder still, from which other tentacles were now projecting, and began pushing my way back from the edge of the pit. I saw astonishment giving place to horror on the faces of the people about me. I heard inarticulate exclamations on all sides. There was a general movement backwards. I saw the shopman struggling still on the edge of the pit. I found myself alone, and saw the people on the other side of the pit running off, Stent among them. I looked again at the cylinder, and ungovernable terror gripped me. I stood petrified and staring.

A big greyish rounded bulk, the size, perhaps, of a bear, was rising slowly and painfully out of the cylinder. As it bulged up and caught the light, it glistened like wet leather.

Two large dark-coloured eyes were regarding me steadfastly. The mass that framed them, the head of the thing, was rounded, and had, one might say, a face. There was a mouth under the eyes, the lipless brim of which quivered and panted, and dropped saliva. The whole creature heaved and pulsated convulsively. A lank tentacular appendage gripped the edge of the cylinder, another swayed in the air.

Those who have never seen a living Martian can scarcely imagine the strange horror of its appearance. The peculiar V-shaped mouth with its pointed upper lip, the absence of brow ridges, the absence of a chin beneath the wedgelike lower lip, the incessant quivering of this mouth, the Gorgon groups of tentacles, the tumultuous breathing of the lungs in a strange atmosphere, the evident heaviness and painfulness of movement due to the greater gravitational energy of the earth--above all, the extraordinary intensity of the immense eyes--were at once vital, intense, inhuman, crippled and monstrous. There was something fungoid in the oily brown skin, something in the clumsy deliberation of the tedious movements unspeakably nasty. Even at this first encounter, this first glimpse, I was overcome with disgust and dread.

Suddenly the monster vanished. It had toppled over the brim of the cylinder and fallen into the pit, with a thud like the fall of a great mass of leather. I heard it give a peculiar thick cry, and forthwith another of these creatures appeared darkly in the deep shadow of the aperture.

I turned and, running madly, made for the first group of trees, perhaps a hundred yards away; but I ran slantingly and stumbling, for I could not avert my face from these things.

There, among some young pine trees and furze bushes, I stopped, panting, and waited further developments. The common round the sand pits was dotted with people, standing like myself in a half-fascinated terror, staring at these creatures, or rather at the heaped gravel at the edge of the pit in which they lay. And then, with a renewed horror, I saw a round, black object bobbing up and down on the edge of the pit. It was the head of the shopman who had fallen in, but showing as a little black object against the hot western sun. Now he got his shoulder and knee up, and again he seemed to slip back until only his head was visible. Suddenly he vanished, and I could have fancied a faint shriek had reached me. I had a momentary impulse to go back and help him that my fears overruled.

Everything was then quite invisible, hidden by the deep pit and the heap of sand that the fall of the cylinder had made. Anyone coming along the road from Chobham or Woking would have been amazed at the sight--a dwindling multitude of perhaps a hundred people or more standing in a great irregular circle, in ditches, behind bushes, behind gates and hedges, saying little to one another and that in short, excited shouts, and staring, staring hard at a few heaps of sand. The barrow of ginger beer stood, a queer derelict, black against the burning sky, and in the sand pits was a row of deserted vehicles with their horses feeding out of nosebags or pawing the ground.

The Martian by Peter Fussey

Chapter Five
The Heat-Ray

After the glimpse I had had of the Martians emerging from the cylinder in which they had come to the earth from their planet, a kind of fascination paralysed my actions. I remained standing knee-deep in the heather, staring at the mound that hid them. I was a battleground of fear and curiosity.

I did not dare to go back towards the pit, but I felt a passionate longing to peer into it. I began walking, therefore, in a big curve, seeking some point of vantage and continually looking at the sand heaps that hid these new-comers to our earth. Once a leash of thin black whips, like the arms of an octopus, flashed across the sunset and was immediately withdrawn, and afterwards a thin rod rose up, joint by joint, bearing at its apex a circular disk that spun with a wobbling motion. What could be going on there?

Most of the spectators had gathered in one or two groups--one a little crowd towards Woking, the other a knot of people in the direction of Chobham. Evidently they shared my mental conflict. There were few near me. One man I approached--he was, I perceived, a neighbour of mine, though I did not know his name--and accosted. But it was scarcely a time for articulate conversation.

"What ugly brutes!" he said. "Good God! What ugly brutes!" He repeated this over and over again.

"Did you see a man in the pit?" I said; but he made no answer to that. We became silent, and stood watching for a time side by side, deriving, I fancy, a certain comfort in one another's company. Then I shifted my position to a little knoll that gave me the advantage of a yard or more of elevation and when I looked for him presently he was walking towards Woking.

The sunset faded to twilight before anything further happened. The crowd far away on the left, towards Woking, seemed to grow, and I heard now a faint murmur from it. The little knot of people towards Chobham dispersed. There was scarcely an intimation of movement from the pit.

It was this, as much as anything, that gave people courage, and I suppose the new arrivals from Woking also helped to restore confidence. At any rate, as the dusk came on a slow, intermittent movement upon the sand pits began, a movement that seemed to gather force as the stillness of the evening about the cylinder remained unbroken. Vertical black figures in twos and threes would advance, stop, watch, and advance again, spreading out as they did so in a thin irregular crescent that promised to enclose the pit in its attenuated horns. I, too, on my side began to move towards the pit.

Then I saw some cabmen and others had walked boldly into the sand pits, and heard the clatter of hoofs and the gride of wheels. I saw a lad trundling off the barrow of apples. And then, within thirty yards of the pit, advancing from the direction of Horsell, I noted a little black knot of men, the foremost of whom was waving a white flag.

This was the Deputation. There had been a hasty consultation, and since the Martians were evidently, in spite of their repulsive forms, intelligent creatures, it had been resolved to show them, by approaching them with signals, that we too were intelligent.

Flutter, flutter, went the flag, first to the right, then to the left. It was too far for me to recognise anyone there, but afterwards I learned that Ogilvy, Stent, and Henderson were with others in this attempt at communication. This little group had in its advance dragged inward, so to speak, the circumference of the now almost complete circle of people, and a number of dim black figures followed it at discreet distances.

Suddenly there was a flash of light, and a quantity of luminous greenish smoke came out of the pit in three distinct puffs, which drove up, one after the other, straight into the still air.

This smoke (or flame, perhaps, would be the better word for it) was so bright that the deep blue sky overhead and the hazy stretches of brown common towards Chertsey, set with black pine trees, seemed to darken abruptly as these puffs arose, and to remain the darker after their dispersal. At the same time a faint hissing sound became audible.

Beyond the pit stood the little wedge of people with the white flag at its apex, arrested by these phenomena, a little knot of small vertical black shapes upon the black ground. As the green smoke arose, their faces flashed out pallid green, and faded again as it vanished. Then slowly the hissing passed into a humming, into a long, loud, droning noise. Slowly a humped shape rose out of the pit, and the ghost of a beam of light seemed to flicker out from it.

Forthwith flashes of actual flame, a bright glare leaping from one to another, sprang from the scattered group of men. It was as if some invisible jet impinged upon them and flashed into white flame. It was as if each man were suddenly and momentarily turned to fire.

Then, by the light of their own destruction, I saw them staggering and falling, and their supporters turning to run.

I stood staring, not as yet realising that this was death leaping from man to man in that little distant crowd. All I felt was that it was something very strange. An almost noiseless and blinding flash of light, and a man fell headlong and lay still; and as the unseen shaft of heat passed over them, pine trees burst into fire, and every dry furze bush became with one dull thud a mass of flames. And far away towards Knaphill I saw the flashes of trees and hedges and wooden buildings suddenly set alight.

It was sweeping round swiftly and steadily, this flaming death, this invisible, inevitable sword of heat. I perceived it coming towards me by the flashing bushes it touched, and was too astounded and stupefied to stir. I heard the crackle of fire in the sand pits and the sudden squeal of a horse that was as suddenly stilled. Then it was as if an invisible yet intensely heated finger were drawn through the heather between me and the Martians, and all along a curving line beyond the sand pits the dark ground smoked and crackled. Something fell with a crash far away to the left where the road from Woking station opens out on the common. Forthwith the hissing and humming ceased, and the black, domelike object sank slowly out of sight into the pit.

All this had happened with such swiftness that I had stood motionless, dumbfounded and dazzled by the flashes of light.

Had that death swept through a full circle, it must inevitably have slain me in my surprise. But it passed and spared me, and left the night about me suddenly dark and unfamiliar.

The undulating common seemed now dark almost to blackness, except where its roadways lay grey and pale under the deep blue sky of the early night. It was dark, and suddenly void of men. Overhead the stars were mustering, and in the west the sky was still a pale, bright, almost greenish blue. The tops of the pine trees and the roofs of Horsell came out sharp and black against the western afterglow. The Martians and their appliances were altogether invisible, save for that thin mast upon which their restless mirror wobbled. Patches of bush and isolated trees here and there smoked and glowed still, and the houses towards Woking station were sending up spires of flame into the stillness of the evening air.

Nothing was changed save for that and a terrible astonishment. The little group of black specks with the flag of white had been swept out of existence, and the stillness of the evening, so it seemed to me, had scarcely been broken.

It came to me that I was upon this dark common, helpless, unprotected, and alone. Suddenly, like a thing falling upon me from without, came--fear.

With an effort I turned and began a stumbling run through the heather.

The fear I felt was no rational fear, but a panic terror not only of the Martians, but of the dusk and stillness all about me. Such an extraordinary effect in unmanning me it had that I ran weeping silently as a child might do. Once I had turned, I did not dare to look back.

I remember I felt an extraordinary persuasion that I was being played with, that presently, when I was upon the very verge of safety, this mysterious death--as swift as the passage of light--would leap after me from the pit about the cylinder and strike me down.

Chapter Six
The Heat-Ray in the Chobham Road

It is still a matter of wonder how the Martians are able to slay men so swiftly and so silently. Many think that in some way they are able to generate an intense heat in a chamber of practically absolute non-conductivity. This intense heat they project in a parallel beam against any object they choose, by means of a polished parabolic mirror of unknown composition, much as the parabolic mirror of a lighthouse projects a beam of light. But no one has absolutely proved these details. However it is done, it is certain that a beam of heat is the essence of the matter. Heat, and invisible, instead of visible, light. Whatever is combustible flashes into flame at its touch, lead runs like water, it softens iron, cracks and melts glass, and when it falls upon water, incontinently that explodes into steam.

That night nearly forty people lay under the starlight about the pit, charred and distorted beyond recognition, and all night long the common from Horsell to Maybury was deserted and brightly ablaze.

The news of the massacre probably reached Chobham, Woking, and Ottershaw about the same time. In Woking the shops had closed when the tragedy happened, and a number of people, shop people and so forth, attracted by the stories they had heard, were walking over the Horsell Bridge and along the road between the hedges that runs out at last upon the common. You may imagine the young people brushed up after the labours of the day, and making this novelty, as they would make any novelty, the excuse for walking together and enjoying a trivial flirtation. You may figure to yourself the hum of voices along the road in the gloaming....

As yet, of course, few people in Woking even knew that the cylinder had opened, though poor Henderson had sent a messenger on a bicycle to the post office with a special wire to an evening paper.

As these folks came out by twos and threes upon the open, they found little knots of people talking excitedly and peering at the spinning mirror over the sand pits, and the new-comers were, no doubt, soon infected by the excitement of the occasion.

By half past eight, when the Deputation was destroyed, there may have been a crowd of three hundred people or more at this place, besides those who had left the road to approach the Martians nearer. There were three policemen too, one of whom was mounted, doing their best, under instructions from Stent, to keep the people back and deter them from approaching the cylinder. There was some booing from those more thoughtless and excitable souls to whom a crowd is always an occasion for noise and horse-play.

Stent and Ogilvy, anticipating some possibilities of a collision, had telegraphed from Horsell to the barracks as soon as the Martians emerged, for the help of a company of soldiers to protect these strange creatures from violence. After that they returned to lead that ill-fated advance. The description of their death, as it was seen by the crowd, tallies very closely with my own impressions: the three puffs of green smoke, the deep humming note, and the flashes of flame.

But that crowd of people had a far narrower escape than mine. Only the fact that a hummock of heathery sand intercepted the lower part of the Heat-Ray saved them. Had the elevation of the parabolic mirror been a few yards higher, none could have lived to tell the tale. They saw the flashes and the men falling and an invisible hand, as it were, lit the bushes as it hurried towards them through the twilight. Then, with a whistling note that rose above the droning of the pit, the beam swung close over their heads, lighting the tops of the beech trees that line the road, and splitting the bricks, smashing the windows, firing the window frames, and bringing down in crumbling ruin a portion of the gable of the house nearest the corner.

In the sudden thud, hiss, and glare of the igniting trees, the panic-stricken crowd seems to have swayed hesitatingly for some moments. Sparks and burning twigs began to fall into the road, and single leaves like puffs of flame. Hats and dresses caught fire. Then came a crying from the common. There were shrieks and shouts, and suddenly a mounted policeman came galloping through the confusion with his hands clasped over his head, screaming.

"They're coming!" a woman shrieked, and incontinently everyone was turning and pushing at those behind, in order to clear their way to Woking again. They must have bolted as blindly as a flock of sheep. Where the road grows narrow and black between the high banks the crowd jammed, and a desperate struggle occurred. All that crowd did not escape; three persons at least, two women and a little boy, were crushed and trampled there, and left to die amid the terror and the darkness.

Chapter Seven
How I Reached Home

For my own part, I remember nothing of my flight except the stress of blundering against trees and stumbling through the heather. All about me gathered the invisible terrors of the Martians; that pitiless sword of heat seemed whirling to and fro, flourishing overhead before it descended and smote me out of life. I came into the road between the crossroads and Horsell, and ran along this to the crossroads.

At last I could go no further; I was exhausted with the violence of my emotion and of my flight, and I staggered and fell by the wayside. That was near the bridge that crosses the canal by the gasworks. I fell and lay still.

I must have remained there some time.

I sat up, strangely perplexed. For a moment, perhaps, I could not clearly understand how I came there. My terror had fallen from me like a garment. My hat had gone, and my collar had burst away from its fastener. A few minutes before, there had only been three real things before me--the immensity of the night and space and nature, my own feebleness and anguish, and the near approach of death. Now it was as if something turned over, and the point of view altered abruptly. There was no sensible transition from one state of mind to the other. I was immediately the self of every day again--a decent, ordinary citizen. The silent common, the impulse of my flight, the starting flames, were as if they had been in a dream. I asked myself had these latter things indeed happened? I could not credit it.

I rose and walked unsteadily up the steep incline of the bridge. My mind was blank wonder. My muscles and nerves seemed drained of their strength. I dare say I staggered drunkenly. A head rose over the arch, and the figure of a workman carrying a basket appeared. Beside him ran a little boy. He passed me, wishing me good night. I was minded to speak to him, but did not. I answered his greeting with a meaningless mumble and went on over the bridge.

Over the Maybury arch a train, a billowing tumult of white, firelit smoke, and a long caterpillar of lighted windows, went flying south--clatter, clatter, clap, rap, and it had gone. A dim group of people talked in the gate of one of the houses in the pretty little row of gables that was called Oriental Terrace. It was all so real and so familiar. And that behind me! It was frantic, fantastic! Such things, I told myself, could not be.

Perhaps I am a man of exceptional moods. I do not know how far my experience is common. At times I suffer from the strangest sense of detachment from myself and the world about me; I seem to watch it all from the outside, from somewhere inconceivably remote, out of time, out of space, out of the stress and tragedy of it all. This feeling was very strong upon me that night. Here was another side to my dream.

But the trouble was the blank incongruity of this serenity and the swift death flying yonder, not two miles away. There was a noise of business from the gasworks, and the electric lamps were all alight. I stopped at the group of people.

"What news from the common?" said I.

There were two men and a woman at the gate.

"Eh?" said one of the men, turning.

"What news from the common?" I said. "'Ain't yer just *been* there?" asked the men.

"People seem fair silly about the common," said the woman over the gate. "What's it all abart?"

"Haven't you heard of the men from Mars?" said I; "the creatures from Mars?"

"Quite enough," said the woman over the gate. "Thenks"; and all three of them laughed.

I felt foolish and angry. I tried and found I could not tell them what I had seen. They laughed again at my broken sentences.

"You'll hear more yet," I said, and went on to my home.

I startled my wife at the doorway, so haggard was I. I went into the dining room, sat down, drank some wine, and so soon as I could collect myself sufficiently I told her the things I had seen. The dinner, which was a cold one, had already been served, and remained neglected on the table while I told my story.

"There is one thing," I said, to allay the fears I had aroused; "they are the most sluggish things I ever saw crawl. They may keep the pit and kill people who come near them, but they cannot get out of it ... But the horror of them!"

"Don't, dear!" said my wife, knitting her brows and putting her hand on mine.

"Poor Ogilvy!" I said. "To think he may be lying dead there!"

My wife at least did not find my experience incredible. When I saw how deadly white her face was, I ceased abruptly.

"They may come here," she said again and again.

I pressed her to take wine, and tried to reassure her.

"They can scarcely move," I said.

I began to comfort her and myself by repeating all that Ogilvy had told me of the impossibility of the Martians establishing themselves on the earth. In particular I laid stress on the gravitational difficulty. On the surface of the earth the force of gravity is three times what it is on the surface of Mars. A Martian, therefore, would weigh three times more than on Mars, albeit his muscular strength would be the same. His own body would be a cope of lead to him. That, indeed, was the general opinion. Both *The Times* and the *Daily Telegraph*, for instance, insisted on it the next morning, and both overlooked, just as I did, two obvious modifying influences.

The atmosphere of the earth, we now know, contains far more oxygen or far less argon (whichever way one likes to put it) than does Mars. The invigorating influences of this excess of oxygen upon the Martians indisputably did much to counterbalance the increased weight of their bodies. And, in the second place, we all overlooked the fact that such mechanical intelligence as the Martian possessed was quite able to dispense with muscular exertion at a pinch.

But I did not consider these points at the time, and so my reasoning was dead against the chances of the invaders. With wine and food, the confidence of my own table, and the necessity of reassuring my wife, I grew by insensible degrees courageous and secure.

"They have done a foolish thing," said I, fingering my wineglass. "They are dangerous because, no doubt, they are mad with terror. Perhaps they expected to find no living things--certainly no intelligent living things.

"A shell in the pit" said I, "if the worst comes to the worst will kill them all."

The intense excitement of the events had no doubt left my perceptive powers in a state of erethism. I remember that dinner table with extraordinary vividness even now. My dear wife's sweet anxious face peering at me from under the pink lamp shade, the white cloth with its silver and glass table furniture--for in those days even philosophical writers had many little luxuries--the crimson-purple wine in my glass, are photographically distinct. At the end of it I sat, tempering nuts with a cigarette, regretting Ogilvy's rashness, and denouncing the shortsighted timidity of the Martians.

So some respectable dodo in the Mauritius might have lorded it in his nest, and discussed the arrival of that shipful of pitiless sailors in want of animal food. "We will peck them to death tomorrow, my dear."

I did not know it, but that was the last civilised dinner I was to eat for very many strange and terrible days.

Chapter Eight
Friday Night

The most extraordinary thing to my mind, of all the strange and wonderful things that happened upon that Friday, was the dovetailing of the commonplace habits of our social order with the first beginnings of the series of events that was to topple that social order headlong. If on Friday night you had taken a pair of compasses and drawn a circle with a radius of five miles round the Woking sand pits, I doubt if you would have had one human being outside it, unless it were some relation of Stent or of the three or four cyclists or London people lying dead on the common, whose emotions or habits were at all affected by the new-comers. Many people had heard of the cylinder, of course, and talked about it in their leisure, but it certainly did not make the sensation that an ultimatum to Germany would have done.

In London that night poor Henderson's telegram describing the gradual unscrewing of the shot was judged to be a canard, and his evening paper, after wiring for authentication from him and receiving no reply--the man was killed--decided not to print a special edition.

Even within the five-mile circle the great majority of people were inert. I have already described the behaviour of the men and women to whom I spoke. All over the district people were dining and supping; working men were gardening after the labours of the day, children were being put to bed, young people were wandering through the lanes love-making, students sat over their books.

Maybe there was a murmur in the village streets, a novel and dominant topic in the public-houses, and here and there a messenger, or even an eye-witness of the later occurrences, caused a whirl of excitement, a shouting, and a running to and fro; but for the most part the daily routine of working, eating, drinking, sleeping, went on as it had done for countless years--as though no planet Mars existed in the sky. Even at Woking station and Horsell and Chobham that was the case.

In Woking junction, until a late hour, trains were stopping and going on, others were shunting on the sidings, passengers were alighting and waiting, and everything was proceeding in the most ordinary way. A boy from the town, trenching on Smith's monopoly, was selling papers with the afternoon's news. The ringing impact of trucks, the sharp whistle of the engines from the junction, mingled with their shouts of "Men from Mars!" Excited men came into the station about nine o'clock with incredible tidings, and caused no more disturbance than drunkards might have done. People rattling Londonwards peered into the darkness outside the carriage windows, and saw only a rare, flickering, vanishing spark dance up from the direction of Horsell, a red glow and a thin veil of smoke driving across the stars, and thought that nothing more serious than a heath fire was happening. It was only round the edge of the common that any disturbance was perceptible. There were half a dozen villas burning on the Woking border. There were lights in all the houses on the common side of the three villages, and the people there kept awake till dawn.

A curious crowd lingered restlessly, people coming and going but the crowd remaining, both on the Chobham and Horsell bridges. One or two adventurous souls, it was afterwards found, went into the darkness and crawled quite near the Martians; but they never returned, for now and again a light-ray, like the beam of a warship's searchlight swept the common, and the Heat-Ray was ready to follow. Save for such, that big area of common was silent and desolate, and the charred bodies lay about on it all night under the stars, and all the next day. A noise of hammering from the pit was heard by many people.

So you have the state of things on Friday night. In the centre, sticking into the skin of our old planet Earth like a poisoned dart, was this cylinder. But the poison was scarcely working yet. Around it was a patch of silent common, smouldering in places, and with a few dark, dimly seen objects lying in contorted attitudes here and there. Here and there was a burning bush or tree. Beyond was a fringe of excitement, and farther than that fringe the inflammation had not crept as yet. In the rest of the world the stream of life still flowed as it had flowed for immemorial years. The fever of war that would presently clog vein and artery, deaden nerve and destroy brain, had still to develop.

All night long the Martians were hammering and stirring, sleepless, indefatigable, at work upon the machines they were making ready, and ever and again a puff of greenish-white smoke whirled up to the starlit sky.

About eleven a company of soldiers came through Horsell, and deployed along the edge of the common to form a cordon. Later a second company marched through Chobham to deploy on the north side of the common. Several officers from the Inkerman barracks had been on the common earlier in the day, and one, Major Eden, was reported to be missing. The colonel of the regiment came to the Chobham bridge and was busy questioning the crowd at midnight. The military authorities were certainly alive to the seriousness of the business. About eleven, the next morning's papers were able to say, a squadron of hussars, two Maxims, and about four hundred men of the Cardigan regiment started from Aldershot.

A few seconds after midnight the crowd in the Chertsey road, Woking, saw a star fall from heaven into the pine woods to the northwest. It had a greenish colour, and caused a silent brightness like summer lightning. This was the second cylinder.

Chapter Nine
The Fighting Begins

Saturday lives in my memory as a day of suspense. It was a day of lassitude too, hot and close, with, I am told, a rapidly fluctuating barometer. I had slept but little, though my wife had succeeded in sleeping, and I rose early. I went into my garden before breakfast and stood listening, but towards the common there was nothing stirring but a lark.

The milkman came as usual. I heard the rattle of his chariot and I went round to the side gate to ask the latest news. He told me that during the night the Martians had been surrounded by troops, and that guns were expected. Then--a familiar, reassuring note--I heard a train running towards Woking.

"They aren't to be killed," said the milkman, "if that can possibly be avoided."

I saw my neighbour gardening, chatted with him for a time, and then strolled in to breakfast. It was a most unexceptional morning. My neighbour was of opinion that the troops would be able to capture or to destroy the Martians during the day.

"It's a pity they make themselves so unapproachable," he said. "It would be curious to know how they live on another planet; we might learn a thing or two."

He came up to the fence and extended a handful of strawberries, for his gardening was as generous as it was enthusiastic. At the same time he told me of the burning of the pine woods about the Byfleet Golf Links.

"They say," said he, "that there's another of those blessed things fallen there--number two. But one's enough, surely. This lot'll cost the insurance people a pretty penny before everything's settled." He laughed with an air of the greatest good humour as he said this. The woods, he said, were still burning, and pointed out a haze of smoke to me. "They will be hot under foot for days, on account of the thick soil of pine needles and turf," he said, and then grew serious over "poor Ogilvy."

After breakfast, instead of working, I decided to walk down towards the common. Under the railway bridge I found a group of soldiers--sappers, I think, men in small round caps, dirty red jackets unbuttoned, and showing their blue shirts, dark trousers, and boots coming to the calf. They told me no one was allowed over the canal, and, looking along the road towards the bridge, I saw one of the Cardigan men standing sentinel there. I talked with these soldiers for a time; I told them of my sight of the Martians on the previous evening. None of them had seen the Martians, and they had but the vaguest ideas of them, so that they plied me with questions. They said that they did not know who had authorised the movements of the troops; their idea was that a dispute had arisen at the Horse Guards. The ordinary sapper is a great deal better educated than the common soldier, and they discussed the peculiar conditions of the possible fight with some acuteness. I described the Heat-Ray to them, and they began to argue among themselves.

"Crawl up under cover and rush 'em, say I," said one.

"Get aht!," said another. "What's cover against this 'ere 'eat? Sticks to cook yer! What we got to do is to go as near as the ground'll let us, and then drive a trench."

"Blow yer trenches! You always want trenches; you ought to ha' been born a rabbit Snippy."

"'Ain't they got any necks, then?" said a third, abruptly--a little, contemplative, dark man, smoking a pipe.

I repeated my description.

"Octopuses," said he, "that's what I calls 'em. Talk about fishers of men--fighters of fish it is this time!"

"It ain't no murder killing beasts like that," said the first speaker.

"Why not shell the darned things strite off and finish 'em?" said the little dark man. "You carn tell what they might do."

"Where's your shells?" said the first speaker. "There ain't no time. Do it in a rush, that's my tip, and do it at once."

So they discussed it. After a while I left them, and went on to the railway station to get as many morning papers as I could.

But I will not weary the reader with a description of that long morning and of the longer afternoon. I did not succeed in getting a glimpse of the common, for even Horsell and Chobham church towers were in the hands of the military authorities. The soldiers I addressed didn't know anything; the officers were mysterious as well as busy. I found people in the town quite secure again in the presence of the military, and I heard for the first time from Marshall, the tobacconist, that his son was among the dead on the common. The soldiers had made the people on the outskirts of Horsell lock up and leave their houses.

I got back to lunch about two, very tired for, as I have said, the day was extremely hot and dull; and in order to refresh myself I took a cold bath in the afternoon. About half past four I went up to the railway station to get an evening paper, for the morning papers had contained only a very inaccurate description of the killing of Stent, Henderson, Ogilvy, and the others. But there was little I didn't know. The Martians did not show an inch of themselves. They seemed busy in their pit, and there was a sound of hammering and an almost continuous streamer of smoke. Apparently they were busy getting ready for a struggle. "Fresh attempts have been made to signal, but without success," was the stereotyped formula of the papers. A sapper told me it was done by a man in a ditch with a flag on a long pole. The Martians took as much notice of such advances as we should of the lowing of a cow.

I must confess the sight of all this armament, all this preparation, greatly excited me. My imagination became belligerent, and defeated the invaders in a dozen striking ways; something of my schoolboy dreams of battle and heroism came back. It hardly seemed a fair fight to me at that time. They seemed very helpless in that pit of theirs.

About three o'clock there began the thud of a gun at measured intervals from Chertsey or Addlestone. I learned that the smouldering pine wood into which the second cylinder had fallen was being shelled, in the hope of destroying that object before it opened. It was only about five, however, that a field gun reached Chobham for use against the first body of Martians.

About six in the evening, as I sat at tea with my wife in the summerhouse talking vigorously about the battle that was lowering upon us, I heard a muffled detonation from the common, and immediately after a gust of firing. Close on the heels of that came a violent rattling crash, quite close to us, that shook the ground; and, starting out upon the lawn, I saw the tops of the trees about the Oriental College burst into smoky red flame, and the tower of the little church beside it slide down into ruin. The pinnacle of the mosque had vanished, and the roof line of the college itself looked as if a hundred-ton gun had been at work upon it. One of our chimneys cracked as if a shot had hit it, flew, and a piece of it came clattering down the tiles and made a heap of broken red fragments upon the flower bed by my study window.

I and my wife stood amazed. Then I realised that the crest of Maybury Hill must be within range of the Martians' Heat-Ray now that the college was cleared out of the way.

At that I gripped my wife's arm, and without ceremony ran her out into the road. Then I fetched out the servant, telling her I would go upstairs myself for the box she was clamouring for.

"We can't possibly stay here," I said; and as I spoke the firing reopened for a moment upon the common.

"But where are we to go?" said my wife in terror.

I thought perplexed. Then I remembered her cousins at Leatherhead.

"Leatherhead!" I shouted above the sudden noise.

She looked away from me downhill. The people were coming out of their houses, astonished.

"How are we to get to Leatherhead?" she said.

Down the hill I saw a bevy of hussars ride under the railway bridge; three galloped through the open gates of the Oriental College; two others dismounted, and began running from house to house. The sun, shining through the smoke that drove up from the tops of the trees, seemed blood red, and threw an unfamiliar lurid light upon everything.

"Stop here," said I; "you are safe here"; and I started off at once for the Spotted Dog, for I knew the landlord had a horse and dog cart. I ran, for I perceived that in a moment everyone upon this side of the hill would be moving. I found him in his bar, quite unaware of what was going on behind his house. A man stood with his back to me, talking to him.

"I must have a pound," said the landlord, "and I've no one to drive it."

"I'll give you two," said I, over the stranger's shoulder.

"What for?"

"And I'll bring it back by midnight," I said.

"Lord!" said the landlord; "what's the hurry? I'm selling my bit of a pig. Two pounds, and you bring it back? What's going on now?"

I explained hastily that I had to leave my home, and so secured the dog cart. At the time it did not seem to me nearly so urgent that the landlord should leave his. I took care to have the cart there and then, drove it off down the road, and, leaving it in charge of my wife and servant, rushed into my house and packed a few valuables, such plate as we had, and so forth. The beech trees below the house were burning while I did this, and the palings up the road glowed red. While I was occupied in this way, one of the dismounted hussars came running up. He was going from house to house, warning people to leave. He was going on as I came out of my front door, lugging my treasures, done up in a tablecloth. I shouted after him:

"What news?"

He turned, stared, bawled something about "crawling out in a thing like a dish cover," and ran on to the gate of the house at the crest. A sudden whirl of black smoke driving across the road hid him for a moment. I ran to my neighbour's door and rapped to satisfy myself of what I already knew, that his wife had gone to London with him and had locked up their house. I went in again, according to my promise, to get my servant's box, lugged it out, clapped it beside her on the tail of the dog cart, and then caught the reins and jumped up into the driver's seat beside my wife. In another moment we were clear of the smoke and noise, and spanking down the opposite slope of Maybury Hill towards Old Woking.

In front was a quiet sunny landscape, a wheat field ahead on either side of the road, and the Maybury Inn with its swinging sign. I saw the doctor's cart ahead of me. At the bottom of the hill I turned my head to look at the hillside I was leaving. Thick streamers of black smoke shot with threads of red fire were driving up into the still air, and throwing dark shadows upon the green treetops eastward. The smoke already extended far away to the east and west--to the Byfleet pine woods eastward, and to

Woking on the west. The road was dotted with people running towards us. And very faint now, but very distinct through the hot, quiet air, one heard the whirr of a machine-gun that was presently stilled, and an intermittent cracking of rifles. Apparently the Martians were setting fire to everything within range of their Heat-Ray.

I am not an expert driver, and I had immediately to turn my attention to the horse. When I looked back again the second hill had hidden the black smoke. I slashed the horse with the whip, and gave him a loose rein until Woking and Send lay between us and that quivering tumult. I overtook and passed the doctor between Woking and Send.

Martians by Brendan Perkins

Chapter Ten
In the Storm

Leatherhead is about twelve miles from Maybury Hill. The scent of hay was in the air through the lush meadows beyond Pyrford, and the hedges on either side were sweet and gay with multitudes of dog-roses. The heavy firing that had broken out while we were driving down Maybury Hill ceased as abruptly as it began, leaving the evening very peaceful and still. We got to Leatherhead without misadventure about nine o'clock, and the horse had an hour's rest while I took supper with my cousins and commended my wife to their care.

My wife was curiously silent throughout the drive, and seemed oppressed with forebodings of evil. I talked to her reassuringly, pointing out that the Martians were tied to the Pit by sheer heaviness, and at the utmost could but crawl a little out of it; but she answered only in monosyllables. Had it not been for my promise to the innkeeper, she would, I think, have urged me to stay in Leatherhead that night. Would that I had! Her face, I remember, was very white as we parted.

For my own part, I had been feverishly excited all day. Something very like the war fever that occasionally runs through a civilised community had got into my blood, and in my heart I was not so very sorry that I had to return to Maybury that night. I was even afraid that that last fusillade I had heard might mean the extermination of our invaders from Mars. I can best express my state of mind by saying that I wanted to be in at the death.

It was nearly eleven when I started to return. The night was unexpectedly dark; to me, walking out of the lighted passage of my cousins' house, it seemed indeed black, and it was as hot and close as the day. Overhead the clouds were driving fast, albeit not a breath stirred the shrubs about us. My cousins' man lit both lamps. Happily, I knew the road intimately. My wife stood in the light of the doorway, and watched me until I jumped up into the dog cart. Then abruptly she turned and went in, leaving my cousins side by side wishing me good hap.

I was a little depressed at first with the contagion of my wife's fears, but very soon my thoughts reverted to the Martians.

At that time I was absolutely in the dark as to the course of the evening's fighting. I did not know even the circumstances that had precipitated the conflict. As I came through Ockham (for that was the way I returned, and not through Send and Old Woking) I saw along the western horizon a blood-red glow, which as I drew nearer, crept slowly up the sky. The driving clouds of the gathering thunderstorm mingled there with masses of black and red smoke.

Ripley Street was deserted, and except for a lighted window or so the village showed not a sign of life; but I narrowly escaped an accident at the corner of the road to Pyrford, where a knot of people stood with their backs to me. They said nothing to me as I passed. I do not know what they knew of the things happening beyond the hill, nor do I know if the silent houses I passed on my way were sleeping securely, or deserted and empty, or harassed and watching against the terror of the night.

From Ripley until I came through Pyrford I was in the valley of the Wey, and the red glare was hidden from me. As I ascended the little hill beyond Pyrford Church the glare came into view again, and the trees about me shivered with the first intimation of the storm that was upon me. Then I heard midnight pealing out from Pyrford Church behind me, and then came the silhouette of Maybury Hill, with its treetops and roofs black and sharp against the red.

Even as I beheld this a lurid green glare lit the road about me and showed the distant woods towards Addlestone. I felt a tug at the reins. I saw that the driving clouds had been pierced as it were by a thread of green fire, suddenly lighting their confusion and falling into the field to my left. It was the third falling star!

Close on its apparition, and blindingly violet by contrast, danced out the first lightning of the gathering storm, and the thunder burst like a rocket overhead. The horse took the bit between his teeth and bolted.

A moderate incline runs towards the foot of Maybury Hill, and down this we clattered. Once the lightning had begun, it went on in as rapid a succession of flashes as I have ever seen. The thunderclaps, treading one on the heels of another and with a strange crackling accompaniment, sounded more like the working of a gigantic electric machine than the usual detonating reverberations. The flickering light was blinding and confusing, and a thin hail smote gustily at my face as I drove down the slope.

At first I regarded little but the road before me, and then abruptly my attention was arrested by something that was moving rapidly down the opposite slope of Maybury Hill. At first I took it for the wet roof of a house, but one flash following another showed it to be in swift rolling movement. It was an elusive vision--a moment of bewildering darkness, and then, in a flash like daylight, the red masses of the Orphanage near the crest of the hill, the green tops of the pine trees, and this problematical object came out clear and sharp and bright.

And this Thing I saw! How can I describe it? A monstrous tripod, higher than many houses, striding over the young pine trees, and smashing them aside in its career; a walking engine of glittering metal, striding now across the heather; articulate ropes of steel dangling from it, and the clattering tumult of its passage mingling with the riot of the thunder. A flash, and it came out vividly, heeling over one way with two feet in the air, to vanish and reappear almost instantly as it seemed, with the next flash, a hundred yards nearer. Can you imagine a milking stool tilted and bowled violently along the ground? That was the impression those instant flashes gave. But instead of a milking stool imagine it a great body of machinery on a tripod stand.

Then suddenly the trees in the pine wood ahead of me were parted, as brittle reeds are parted by a man thrusting through them; they were snapped off and driven headlong, and a second huge tripod appeared, rushing, as it seemed, headlong towards me. And I was galloping hard to meet it! At the sight of the second monster my nerve went altogether. Not stopping to look again, I wrenched the horse's head hard round to the right and in another moment the dog cart had heeled over upon the horse; the shafts smashed noisily, and I was flung sideways and fell heavily into a shallow pool of water.

I crawled out almost immediately, and crouched, my feet still in the water, under a clump of furze. The horse lay motionless (his neck was broken, poor brute!) and by the lightning flashes I saw the black bulk of the overturned dog cart and the silhouette of the wheel still spinning slowly. In another moment the colossal mechanism went striding by me, and passed uphill towards Pyrford.

Seen nearer, the Thing was incredibly strange, for it was no mere insensate machine driving on its way. Machine it was, with a ringing metallic pace, and long, flexible, glittering tentacles (one of which gripped a young pine tree) swinging and rattling about its strange body. It picked its road as it went striding along, and the brazen hood that surmounted it moved to and fro with the inevitable suggestion of a head looking about. Behind the main body was a huge mass of white metal like a gigantic fisherman's basket, and puffs of green smoke squirted out from the joints of the limbs as the monster swept by me. And in an instant it was gone.

So much I saw then, all vaguely for the flickering of the lightning, in blinding highlights and dense black shadows.

As it passed it set up an exultant deafening howl that drowned the thunder--"Aloo! Aloo!"--and in another minute it was with its companion, half a mile away, stooping over something in the field. I have no doubt this Thing in the field was the third of the ten cylinders they had fired at us from Mars.

For some minutes I lay there in the rain and darkness watching, by the intermittent light, these monstrous beings of metal moving about in the distance over the hedge tops. A thin hail was now beginning, and as it came and went their figures grew misty and then flashed into clearness again. Now and then came a gap in the lightning, and the night swallowed them up.

I was soaked with hail above and puddle water below. It was some time before my blank astonishment would let me struggle up the bank to a drier position, or think at all of my imminent peril.

Not far from me was a little one-roomed squatter's hut of wood, surrounded by a patch of potato garden. I struggled to my feet at last, and, crouching and making use of every chance of cover, I made a run for this. I hammered at the door, but I could not make the people hear (if there were any people inside), and after a time I desisted, and, availing myself of a ditch for the greater part of the way, succeeded in crawling, unobserved by these monstrous machines, into the pine woods towards Maybury.

Under cover of this I pushed on, wet and shivering now, towards my own house. I walked among the trees trying to find the footpath. It was very dark indeed in the wood, for the lightning was now becoming infrequent, and the hail, which was pouring down in a torrent, fell in columns through the gaps in the heavy foliage.

If I had fully realised the meaning of all the things I had seen I should have immediately worked my way round through Byfleet to Street Cobham, and so gone back to rejoin my wife at Leatherhead. But that night the strangeness of things about me, and my physical wretchedness, prevented me, for I was bruised, weary, wet to the skin, deafened and blinded by the storm.

I had a vague idea of going on to my own house, and that was as much motive as I had. I staggered through the trees, fell into a ditch and bruised my knees against a plank, and finally splashed out into the lane that ran down from the College Arms. I say splashed, for the storm water was sweeping the sand down the hill in a muddy torrent. There in the darkness a man blundered into me and sent me reeling back.

He gave a cry of terror, sprang sideways, and rushed on before I could gather my wits sufficiently to speak to him. So heavy was the stress of the storm just at this place that I had the hardest task to win my way up the hill. I went close up to the fence on the left and worked my way along its palings.

Near the top I stumbled upon something soft, and, by a flash of lightning, saw between my feet a heap of black broadcloth and a pair of boots. Before I could distinguish clearly how the man lay, the flicker of light had passed. I stood over him waiting for the next flash. When it came, I saw that he was a sturdy man, cheaply but not shabbily dressed; his head was bent under his body, and he lay crumpled up close to the fence, as though he had been flung violently against it.

Overcoming the repugnance natural to one who had never before touched a dead body, I stooped and turned him over to feel for his heart. He was quite dead. Apparently his neck had been broken. The lightning flashed for a third time, and his face leaped upon me. I sprang to my feet. It was the landlord of the Spotted Dog, whose conveyance I had taken.

I stepped over him gingerly and pushed on up the hill. I made my way by the police station and the College Arms towards my own house. Nothing was burning on the hillside, though from the common there still came a red glare and a rolling tumult of ruddy smoke beating up against the drenching hail. So far as I could see by the flashes, the houses about me were mostly uninjured. By the College Arms a dark heap lay in the road.

Down the road towards Maybury Bridge there were voices and the sound of feet, but I had not the courage to shout or to go to them. I let myself in with my latchkey, closed, locked and bolted the door, staggered to the foot of the staircase, and sat down. My imagination was full of those striding metallic monsters, and of the dead body smashed against the fence.

I crouched at the foot of the staircase with my back to the wall, shivering violently.

In The Storm by Peter Fussey

Chapter Eleven
At the Window

I have already said that my storms of emotion have a trick of exhausting themselves. After a time I discovered that I was cold and wet, and with little pools of water about me on the stair carpet. I got up almost mechanically, went into the dining room and drank some whiskey, and then I was moved to change my clothes.

After I had done that I went upstairs to my study, but why I did so I do not know. The window of my study looks over the trees and the railway towards Horsell Common. In the hurry of our departure this window had been left open. The passage was dark, and, by contrast with the picture the window frame enclosed, the side of the room seemed impenetrably dark. I stopped short in the doorway.

The thunderstorm had passed. The towers of the Oriental College and the pine trees about it had gone, and very far away, lit by a vivid red glare, the common about the sand pits was visible. Across the light huge black shapes, grotesque and strange, moved busily to and fro.

It seemed indeed as if the whole country in that direction was on fire--a broad hillside set with minute tongues of flame, swaying and writhing with the gusts of the dying storm, and throwing a red reflection upon the cloud scud above. Every now and then a haze of smoke from some nearer conflagration drove across the window and hid the Martian shapes. I could not see what they were doing, nor the clear form of them, nor recognise the black objects they were busied upon. Neither could I see the nearer fire, though the reflections of it danced on the wall and ceiling of the study. A sharp, resinous tang of burning was in the air.

I closed the door noiselessly and crept towards the window. As I did so, the view opened out until, on the one hand, it reached to the houses about Woking station, and on the other to the charred and blackened pine woods of Byfleet. There was a light down below the hill, on the railway, near the arch, and several of the houses along the Maybury road and the streets near the station were glowing ruins. The light upon the railway puzzled me at first; there were a black heap and a vivid glare, and to the right of that a row of yellow oblongs. Then I perceived this was a wrecked train, the fore part smashed and on fire, the hinder carriages still upon the rails.

Between these three main centres of light--the houses, the train, and the burning county towards Chobham--stretched irregular patches of dark country, broken here and there by intervals of dimly glowing and smoking ground. It was the strangest spectacle, that black expanse set with fire. It reminded me, more than anything else, of the Potteries at night. At first I could distinguish no people at all, though I peered intently for them. Later I saw against the light of Woking station a number of black figures hurrying one after the other across the line.

And this was the little world in which I had been living securely for years, this fiery chaos! What had happened in the last seven hours I still did not know; nor did I know, though I was beginning to guess, the relation between these mechanical colossi and the sluggish lumps I had seen disgorged from the cylinder. With a queer feeling of impersonal interest I turned my desk chair to the window, sat down, and stared at the blackened country, and particularly at the three gigantic black things that were going to and fro in the glare about the sand pits.

They seemed amazingly busy. I began to ask myself what they could be. Were they intelligent mechanisms? Such a thing I felt was impossible. Or did a Martian sit within each, ruling, directing, using, much as a man's brain sits and rules in his body? I began to compare the things to human machines, to ask myself for the first time in my life how an ironclad or a steam engine would seem to an intelligent lower animal.

The storm had left the sky clear, and over the smoke of the burning land the little fading pinpoint of Mars was dropping into the west, when a soldier came into my garden. I heard a slight scraping at the fence, and rousing myself from the lethargy that had fallen upon me, I looked down and saw him dimly, clambering over the palings. At the sight of another human being my torpor passed, and I leaned out of the window eagerly.

"Hist!" said I, in a whisper.

He stopped astride of the fence in doubt. Then he came over and across the lawn to the corner of the house. He bent down and stepped softly.

"Who's there?" he said, also whispering, standing under the window and peering up.

"Where are you going?" I asked.

"God knows."

"Are you trying to hide?"

"That's it."

"Come into the house," I said.

I went down, unfastened the door, and let him in, and locked the door again. I could not see his face. He was hatless, and his coat was unbuttoned.

"My God!" he said, as I drew him in.

"What has happened?" I asked.

"What hasn't?" In the obscurity I could see he made a gesture of despair. "They wiped us out--simply wiped us out," he repeated again and again.

He followed me, almost mechanically, into the dining room.

"Take some whiskey," I said, pouring out a stiff dose.

He drank it. Then abruptly he sat down before the table, put his head on his arms, and began to sob and weep like a little boy, in a perfect passion of emotion, while I, with a curious forgetfulness of my own recent despair, stood beside him, wondering.

It was a long time before he could steady his nerves to answer my questions, and then he answered perplexingly and brokenly. He was a driver in the artillery, and had only come into action about seven. At that time firing was going on across the common, and it was said the first party of Martians were crawling slowly towards their second cylinder under cover of a metal shield.

Later this shield staggered up on tripod legs and became the first of the fighting-machines I had seen. The gun he drove had been unlimbered near Horsell, in order to command the sand pits, and its arrival it was that had precipitated the action. As the limber gunners went to the rear, his horse trod in a rabbit hole and came down, throwing him into a depression of the ground. At the same moment the gun exploded behind him, the ammunition blew up, there was fire all about him, and he found himself lying under a heap of charred dead men and dead horses.

"I lay still," he said, "scared out of my wits, with the fore quarter of a horse atop of me. We'd been wiped out. And the smell--good God! Like burnt meat! I was hurt across the back by the fall of the horse, and there I had to lie until I felt better. Just like parade it had been a minute before--then stumble, bang, swish!"

"Wiped out!" he said.

He had hid under the dead horse for a long time, peeping out furtively across the common. The Cardigan men had tried a rush, in skirmishing order, at the pit, simply to be swept out of existence. Then the monster had risen to its feet and had begun to walk leisurely to and fro across the common among the few fugitives, with its headlike hood turning about exactly like the head of a cowled human being. A kind of arm carried a complicated metallic case, about which green flashes scintillated, and out of the funnel of this there smoked the Heat-Ray.

In a few minutes there was, so far as the soldier could see, not a living thing left upon the common, and every bush and tree upon it that was not already a blackened skeleton was burning. The hussars had been on the road beyond the curvature of the ground, and he saw nothing of them. He heard the Martians rattle for a time and then become still. The giant saved Woking station and its cluster of houses until the last; then in a moment the Heat-Ray was brought to bear, and the town became a heap of fiery ruins. Then the Thing shut off the Heat-Ray, and turning its back upon the artilleryman, began to waddle away towards the smouldering pine woods that sheltered the second cylinder. As it did so a second glittering Titan built itself up out of the pit.

The second monster followed the first, and at that the artilleryman began to crawl very cautiously across the hot heather ash towards Horsell. He managed to get alive into the ditch by the side of the road, and so escaped to Woking. There his story became ejaculatory. The place was impassable. It seems there were a few people alive there, frantic for the most part and many burned and scalded. He was turned aside by the fire, and hid among some almost scorching heaps of broken wall as one of the Martian giants returned. He saw this one pursue a man, catch him up in one of its steely tentacles, and knock his head against the trunk of a pine tree. At last, after nightfall, the artilleryman made a rush for it and got over the railway embankment.

Since then he had been skulking along towards Maybury, in the hope of getting out of danger Londonward. People were hiding in trenches and cellars, and many of the survivors had made off towards Woking village and Send. He had been consumed with thirst until he found one of the water mains near the railway arch smashed, and the water bubbling out like a spring upon the road.

That was the story I got from him, bit by bit. He grew calmer telling me and trying to make me see the things he had seen. He had eaten no food since midday, he told me early in his narrative, and I found some mutton and bread in the pantry and brought it into the room. We lit no lamp for fear of attracting the Martians, and ever and again our hands would touch upon bread or meat. As he talked, things about us came darkly out of the darkness, and the trampled bushes and broken rose trees outside the window grew distinct. It would seem that a number of men or animals had rushed across the lawn. I began to see his face, blackened and haggard, as no doubt mine was also.

When we had finished eating we went softly upstairs to my study, and I looked again out of the open window. In one night the valley had become a valley of ashes. The fires had dwindled now. Where flames had been there were now streamers of smoke; but the countless ruins of shattered and gutted houses and blasted and blackened trees that the night had hidden stood out now gaunt and terrible in the pitiless light of dawn. Yet here and there some object had had the luck to escape--a white railway signal here, the end of a greenhouse there, white and fresh amid the wreckage. Never before in the history of warfare had destruction been so indiscriminate and so universal. And shining with the growing light of the east, three of the metallic giants stood about the pit, their cowls rotating as though they were surveying the desolation they had made.

It seemed to me that the pit had been enlarged, and ever and again puffs of vivid green vapour streamed up and out of it towards the brightening dawn--streamed up, whirled, broke, and vanished.

Beyond were the pillars of fire about Chobham. They became pillars of bloodshot smoke at the first touch of day.

Chapter Twelve
What I Saw of the Destruction of Weybridge and Shepperton

As the dawn grew brighter we withdrew from the window from which we had watched the Martians, and went very quietly downstairs.

The artilleryman agreed with me that the house was no place to stay in. He proposed, he said, to make his way Londonward, and thence rejoin his battery--No. 12, of the Horse Artillery. My plan was to return at once to Leatherhead; and so greatly had the strength of the Martians impressed me that I had determined to take my wife to Newhaven, and go with her out of the country forthwith. For I already perceived clearly that the country about London must inevitably be the scene of a disastrous struggle before such creatures as these could be destroyed.

Between us and Leatherhead, however, lay the third cylinder, with its guarding giants. Had I been alone, I think I should have taken my chance and struck across country. But the artilleryman dissuaded me: "It's no kindness to the right sort of wife," he said, "to make her a widow"; and in the end I agreed to go with him, under cover of the woods, northward as far as Street Cobham before I parted with him. Thence I would make a big detour by Epsom to reach Leatherhead.

I should have started at once, but my companion had been in active service and he knew better than that. He made me ransack the house for a flask, which he filled with whiskey; and we lined every available pocket with packets of biscuits and slices of meat. Then we crept out of the house, and ran as quickly as we could down the ill-made road by which I had come overnight. The houses seemed deserted. In the road lay a group of three charred bodies close together, struck dead by the Heat-Ray; and here and there were things that people had dropped--a clock, a slipper, a silver spoon, and the like poor valuables. At the corner turning up towards the post office a little cart, filled with boxes and furniture, and horseless, heeled over on a broken wheel. A cash box had been hastily smashed open and thrown under the debris.

Except the lodge at the Orphanage, which was still on fire, none of the houses had suffered very greatly here. The Heat-Ray had shaved the chimney tops and passed. Yet, save ourselves, there did not seem to be a living soul on Maybury Hill. The majority of the inhabitants had escaped, I suppose, by way of the Old Woking road--the road I had taken when I drove to Leatherhead--or they had hidden.

We went down the lane, by the body of the man in black, sodden now from the overnight hail, and broke into the woods at the foot of the hill. We pushed through these towards the railway without meeting a soul. The woods across the line were but the scarred and blackened ruins of woods; for the most part the trees had fallen, but a certain proportion still stood, dismal grey stems, with dark brown foliage instead of green.

On our side the fire had done no more than scorch the nearer trees; it had failed to secure its footing. In one place the woodmen had been at work on Saturday; trees, felled and freshly trimmed, lay in a clearing, with heaps of sawdust by the sawing-machine and its engine. Hard by was a temporary hut, deserted. There was not a breath of wind this morning, and everything was strangely still. Even the birds were hushed, and as we hurried along I and the artilleryman talked in whispers and looked now and again over our shoulders. Once or twice we stopped to listen.

After a time we drew near the road, and as we did so we heard the clatter of hoofs and saw through the tree stems three cavalry soldiers riding slowly towards Woking. We hailed them, and they halted while we hurried towards them. It was a lieutenant and a couple of privates of the 8th Hussars, with a stand like a theodolite, which the artilleryman told me was a heliograph.

"You are the first men I've seen coming this way this morning," said the lieutenant. "What's brewing?"

His voice and face were eager. The men behind him stared curiously. The artilleryman jumped down the bank into the road and saluted. "Gun destroyed last night, sir. Have been hiding.

Trying to rejoin battery, sir. You'll come in sight of the Martians, I expect, about half a mile along this road."

"What the dickens are they like?" asked the lieutenant.

"Giants in armour, sir. Hundred feet high. Three legs and a body like 'luminium, with a mighty great head in a hood, sir."

"Get out!" said the lieutenant. "What confounded nonsense!"

"You'll see, sir. They carry a kind of box, sir, that shoots fire and strikes you dead."

"What d'ye mean--a gun?"

"No, sir," and the artilleryman began a vivid account of the Heat-Ray. Halfway through, the lieutenant interrupted him and looked up at me. I was still standing on the bank by the side of the road.

"It's perfectly true," I said.

"Well," said the lieutenant, "I suppose it's my business to see it too. Look here"--to the artilleryman--"we're detailed here clearing people out of their houses. You'd better go along and report yourself to Brigadier-General Marvin, and tell him all you know. He's at Weybridge. Know the way?"

"I do," I said; and he turned his horse southward again.

"Half a mile, you say?" said he.

"At most," I answered, and pointed over the treetops southward. He thanked me and rode on, and we saw them no more.

Farther along we came upon a group of three women and two children in the road, busy clearing out a labourer's cottage. They had got hold of a little hand truck, and were piling it up with unclean-looking bundles and shabby furniture. They were all too assiduously engaged to talk to us as we passed.

By Byfleet station we emerged from the pine trees, and found the country calm and peaceful under the morning sunlight. We were far beyond the range of the Heat-Ray there, and had it not been for the silent desertion of some of the houses, the stirring movement of packing in others, and the knot of soldiers standing on the bridge over the railway and staring down the line towards Woking, the day would have seemed very like any other Sunday.

Several farm waggons and carts were moving creakily along the road to Addlestone, and suddenly through the gate of a field we saw, across a stretch of flat meadow, six twelve-pounders standing neatly at equal distances pointing towards Woking. The gunners stood by the guns waiting, and the ammunition waggons were at a business-like distance. The men stood almost as if under inspection.

"That's good!" said I. "They will get one fair shot, at any rate."

The artilleryman hesitated at the gate.

"I shall go on," he said.

Farther on towards Weybridge, just over the bridge, there were a number of men in white fatigue jackets throwing up a long rampart, and more guns behind.

"It's bows and arrows against the lightning, anyhow," said the artilleryman. "They 'aven't seen that fire-beam yet."

The officers who were not actively engaged stood and stared over the treetops southwestward, and the men digging would stop every now and again to stare in the same direction.

Byfleet was in a tumult; people packing, and a score of hussars, some of them dismounted, some on horseback, were hunting them about. Three or four black government waggons, with crosses in white circles, and an old omnibus, among other vehicles, were being loaded in the village street. There were scores of people, most of them sufficiently sabbatical to have assumed their best clothes. The soldiers were having the greatest difficulty in making them realise the gravity of their position. We saw one shrivelled old fellow with a huge box and a score or more of flower pots containing orchids, angrily expostulating with the corporal who would leave them behind. I stopped and gripped his arm.

"Do you know what's over there?" I said, pointing at the pine tops that hid the Martians.

"Eh?" said he, turning. "I was explainin' these is vallyble."

"Death!" I shouted. "Death is coming! Death!" and leaving him to digest that if he could, I hurried on after the artilleryman. At the corner I looked back. The soldier had left him, and he was still standing by his box, with the pots of orchids on the lid of it, and staring vaguely over the trees.

No one in Weybridge could tell us where the headquarters were established; the whole place was in such confusion as I had never seen in any town before. Carts, carriages everywhere, the most astonishing miscellany of conveyances and horseflesh. The respectable inhabitants of the place, men in golf and boating costumes, wives prettily dressed, were packing, river-side loafers energetically helping, children excited, and, for the most part, highly delighted at this astonishing variation of their Sunday experiences. In the midst of it all the worthy vicar was very pluckily holding an early celebration, and his bell was jangling out above the excitement.

I and the artilleryman, seated on the step of the drinking fountain, made a very passable meal upon what we had brought with us. Patrols of soldiers--here no longer hussars, but grenadiers in white--were warning people to move now or to take refuge in their cellars as soon as the firing began. We saw as we crossed the railway bridge that a growing crowd of people had assembled in and about the railway station, and the swarming platform was piled with boxes and packages. The ordinary traffic had been stopped, I believe, in order to allow of the passage of troops and guns to Chertsey, and I have heard since that a savage struggle occurred for places in the special trains that were put on at a later hour.

We remained at Weybridge until midday, and at that hour we found ourselves at the place near Shepperton Lock where the Wey and Thames join. Part of the time we spent helping two old women to pack a little cart. The Wey has a treble mouth, and at this point boats are to be hired, and there was a ferry across the river. On the Shepperton side was an inn with a lawn, and beyond that the tower of Shepperton Church--it has been replaced by a spire--rose above the trees.

Here we found an excited and noisy crowd of fugitives. As yet the flight had not grown to a panic, but there were already far more people than all the boats going to and fro could enable to cross. People came panting along under heavy burdens; one husband and wife were even carrying a small outhouse door between them, with some of their household goods piled thereon. One man told us he meant to try to get away from Shepperton station.

There was a lot of shouting, and one man was even jesting. The idea people seemed to have here was that the Martians were simply formidable human beings, who might attack and sack the town, to be certainly destroyed in the end. Every now and then people would glance nervously across the Wey, at the meadows towards Chertsey, but everything over there was still.

Across the Thames, except just where the boats landed, everything was quiet, in vivid contrast with the Surrey side. The people who landed there from the boats went tramping off down the lane. The big ferryboat had just made a journey. Three or four soldiers stood on the lawn of the inn, staring and jesting at the fugitives, without offering to help. The inn was closed, as it was now within prohibited hours.

"What's that?" cried a boatman, and "Shut up, you fool!" said a man near me to a yelping dog. Then the sound came again, this time from the direction of Chertsey, a muffled thud--the sound of a gun.

The fighting was beginning. Almost immediately unseen batteries across the river to our right, unseen because of the trees, took up the chorus, firing heavily one after the other. A woman screamed. Everyone stood arrested by the sudden stir of battle, near us and yet invisible to us. Nothing was to be seen save flat meadows, cows feeding unconcernedly for the most part, and silvery pollard willows motionless in the warm sunlight.

"The sojers'll stop 'em," said a woman beside me, doubtfully. A haziness rose over the treetops.

Then suddenly we saw a rush of smoke far away up the river, a puff of smoke that jerked up into the air and hung; and forthwith the ground heaved under foot and a heavy explosion shook the air, smashing two or three windows in the houses near, and leaving us astonished.

"Here they are!" shouted a man in a blue jersey. "Yonder! D'yer see them? Yonder!"

Quickly, one after the other, one, two, three, four of the armoured Martians appeared, far away over the little trees, across the flat meadows that stretched towards Chertsey, and striding hurriedly towards the river. Little cowled figures they seemed at first, going with a rolling motion and as fast as flying birds.

Then, advancing obliquely towards us, came a fifth. Their armoured bodies glittered in the sun as they swept swiftly forward upon the guns, growing rapidly larger as they drew nearer. One on the extreme left, the remotest that is, flourished a huge case high in the air, and the ghostly, terrible Heat-Ray I had already seen on Friday night smote towards Chertsey, and struck the town.

At sight of these strange, swift, and terrible creatures the crowd near the water's edge seemed to me to be for a moment horror-struck. There was no screaming or shouting, but a silence. Then a hoarse murmur and a movement of feet--a splashing from the water. A man, too frightened to drop the portmanteau he carried on his shoulder, swung round and sent me staggering with a blow from the corner of his burden. A woman thrust at me with her hand and rushed past me. I turned with the rush of the people, but I was not too terrified for thought. The terrible Heat-Ray was in my mind. To get under water! That was it!

"Get under water!" I shouted, unheeded.

I faced about again, and rushed towards the approaching Martian, rushed right down the gravelly beach and headlong into the water. Others did the same. A boatload of people putting back came leaping out as I rushed past. The stones under my feet were muddy and slippery, and the river was so low that I ran perhaps twenty feet scarcely waist-deep. Then, as the Martian towered overhead scarcely a couple of hundred yards away, I flung myself forward under the surface. The splashes of the people in the boats leaping into the river sounded like thunderclaps in my ears. People were landing hastily on both sides of the river.

But the Martian machine took no more notice for the moment of the people running this way and that than a man would of the confusion of ants in a nest against which his foot has kicked. When, half suffocated, I raised my head above water, the Martian's hood pointed at the batteries that were still firing across the river, and as it advanced it swung loose what must have been the generator of the Heat-Ray.

In another moment it was on the bank, and in a stride wading halfway across. The knees of its foremost legs bent at the farther bank, and in another moment it had raised itself to its full height again, close to the village of Shepperton. Forthwith the six guns which, unknown to anyone on the right bank, had been hidden behind the outskirts of that village, fired simultaneously. The sudden near concussion, the last close upon the first, made my heart jump. The monster was already raising the case generating the Heat-Ray as the first shell burst six yards above the hood.

I gave a cry of astonishment. I saw and thought nothing of the other four Martian monsters; my attention was riveted upon the nearer incident. Simultaneously two other shells burst in the air near the body as the hood twisted round in time to receive, but not in time to dodge, the fourth shell.

The shell burst clean in the face of the Thing. The hood bulged, flashed, was whirled off in a dozen tattered fragments of red flesh and glittering metal.

"Hit!" shouted I, with something between a scream and a cheer.

I heard answering shouts from the people in the water about me. I could have leaped out of the water with that momentary exultation.

The decapitated colossus reeled like a drunken giant; but it did not fall over. It recovered its balance by a miracle, and, no longer heeding its steps and with the camera that fired the Heat-Ray now rigidly upheld, it reeled swiftly upon Shepperton. The living intelligence, the Martian within the hood, was slain and splashed to the four winds of heaven, and the Thing was now but a mere intricate device of metal whirling to destruction. It drove along in a straight line, incapable of guidance. It struck the tower of Shepperton Church, smashing it down as the impact of a battering ram might have done, swerved aside, blundered on and collapsed with tremendous force into the river out of my sight.

A violent explosion shook the air, and a spout of water, steam, mud, and shattered metal shot far up into the sky. As the camera of the Heat-Ray hit the water, the latter had immediately flashed into steam. In another moment a huge wave, like a muddy tidal bore but almost scaldingly hot, came sweeping round the bend upstream. I saw people struggling shorewards, and heard their screaming and shouting faintly above the seething and roar of the Martian's collapse.

For a moment I heeded nothing of the heat, forgot the patent need of self-preservation. I splashed through the tumultuous water, pushing aside a man in black to do so, until I could see round the bend. Half a dozen deserted boats pitched aimlessly upon the confusion of the waves. The fallen Martian came into sight downstream, lying across the river, and for the most part submerged.

Thick clouds of steam were pouring off the wreckage, and through the tumultuously whirling wisps I could see, intermittently and vaguely, the gigantic limbs churning the water and flinging a splash and spray of mud and froth into the air. The tentacles swayed and struck like living arms, and, save for the helpless purposelessness of these movements, it was as if some wounded thing were struggling for its life amid the waves. Enormous quantities of a ruddy-brown fluid were spurting up in noisy jets out of the machine.

My attention was diverted from this death flurry by a furious yelling, like that of the thing called a siren in our manufacturing towns. A man, knee-deep near the towing path, shouted inaudibly to me and pointed. Looking back, I saw the other Martians advancing with gigantic strides down the riverbank from the direction of Chertsey. The Shepperton guns spoke this time unavailingly.

At that I ducked at once under water, and, holding my breath until movement was an agony, blundered painfully ahead under the surface as long as I could. The water was in a tumult about me, and rapidly growing hotter.

When for a moment I raised my head to take breath and throw the hair and water from my eyes, the steam was rising in a whirling white fog that at first hid the Martians altogether. The noise was deafening. Then I saw them dimly, colossal figures of grey, magnified by the mist. They had passed by me, and two were stooping over the frothing, tumultuous ruins of their comrade.

The third and fourth stood beside him in the water, one perhaps two hundred yards from me, the other towards Laleham. The generators of the Heat-Rays waved high, and the hissing beams smote down this way and that.

The air was full of sound, a deafening and confusing conflict of noises--the clangorous din of the Martians, the crash of falling houses, the thud of trees, fences, sheds flashing into flame, and the crackling and roaring of fire. Dense black smoke was leaping up to mingle with the steam from the river, and as the Heat-Ray went to and fro over Weybridge its impact was marked by flashes of incandescent white, that gave place at once to a smoky dance of lurid flames. The nearer houses still stood intact, awaiting their fate, shadowy, faint and pallid in the steam, with the fire behind them going to and fro.

For a moment perhaps I stood there, breast-high in the almost boiling water, dumbfounded at my position, hopeless of escape. Through the reek I could see the people who had been with me in the river scrambling out of the water through the reeds, like little frogs hurrying through grass from the advance of a man, or running to and fro in utter dismay on the towing path.

Then suddenly the white flashes of the Heat-Ray came leaping towards me. The houses caved in as they dissolved at its touch, and darted out flames; the trees changed to fire with a roar. The Ray flickered up and down the towing path, licking off the people who ran this way and that, and came down to the water's edge not fifty yards from where I stood. It swept across the river to Shepperton, and the water in its track rose in a boiling weal crested with steam. I turned shoreward.

In another moment the huge wave, well-nigh at the boiling-point had rushed upon me. I screamed aloud, and scalded, half blinded, agonised, I staggered through the leaping, hissing water towards the shore. Had my foot stumbled, it would have been the end. I fell helplessly, in full sight of the Martians, upon the broad, bare gravelly spit that runs down to mark the angle of the Wey and Thames. I expected nothing but death.

I have a dim memory of the foot of a Martian coming down within a score of yards of my head, driving straight into the loose gravel, whirling it this way and that and lifting again; of a long suspense, and then of the four carrying the debris of their comrade between them, now clear and then presently faint through a veil of smoke, receding interminably, as it seemed to me, across a vast space of river and meadow. And then, very slowly, I realised that by a miracle I had escaped.

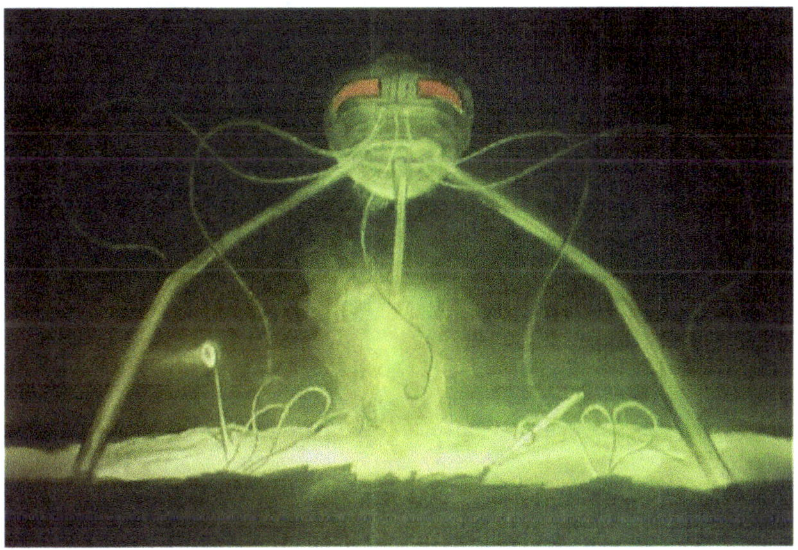

Sentinel by Brendan Perkins

Chapter Thirteen
How I Fell in with the Curate

After getting this sudden lesson in the power of terrestrial weapons, the Martians retreated to their original position upon Horsell Common; and in their haste, and encumbered with the débris of their smashed companion, they no doubt overlooked many such a stray and negligible victim as myself. Had they left their comrade and pushed on forthwith, there was nothing at that time between them and London but batteries of twelve-pounder guns, and they would certainly have reached the capital in advance of the tidings of their approach; as sudden, dreadful, and destructive their advent would have been as the earthquake that destroyed Lisbon a century ago.

But they were in no hurry. Cylinder followed cylinder on its interplanetary flight; every twenty-four hours brought them reinforcement. And meanwhile the military and naval authorities, now fully alive to the tremendous power of their antagonists, worked with furious energy. Every minute a fresh gun came into position until, before twilight, every copse, every row of suburban villas on the hilly slopes about Kingston and Richmond, masked an expectant black muzzle. And through the charred and desolated area--perhaps twenty square miles altogether--that encircled the Martian encampment on Horsell Common, through charred and ruined villages among the green trees, through the blackened and smoking arcades that had been but a day ago pine spinneys, crawled the devoted scouts with the heliographs that were presently to warn the gunners of the Martian approach. But the Martians now understood our command of artillery and the danger of human proximity, and not a man ventured within a mile of either cylinder, save at the price of his life.

It would seem that these giants spent the earlier part of the afternoon in going to and fro, transferring everything from the second and third cylinders--the second in Addlestone Golf Links and the third at Pyrford--to their original pit on Horsell Common. Over that, above the blackened heather and ruined buildings that stretched far and wide, stood one as sentinel, while the rest abandoned their vast fighting-machines and descended into the pit. They were hard at work there far into the night, and the towering pillar of dense green smoke that rose therefrom could be seen from the hills about Merrow, and even, it is said, from Banstead and Epsom Downs.

And while the Martians behind me were thus preparing for their next sally, and in front of me Humanity gathered for the battle, I made my way with infinite pains and labour from the fire and smoke of burning Weybridge towards London.

I saw an abandoned boat, very small and remote, drifting down-stream; and throwing off the most of my sodden clothes, I went after it, gained it, and so escaped out of that destruction. There were no oars in the boat, but I contrived to paddle, as well as my parboiled hands would allow, down the river towards Halliford and Walton, going very tediously and continually looking behind me, as you may well understand. I followed the river, because I considered that the water gave me my best chance of escape should these giants return.

The hot water from the Martian's overthrow drifted downstream with me, so that for the best part of a mile I could see little of either bank. Once, however, I made out a string of black figures hurrying across the meadows from the direction of Weybridge. Halliford, it seemed, was deserted, and several of the houses facing the river were on fire. It was strange to see the place quite tranquil, quite desolate under the hot blue sky, with the smoke and little threads of flame going straight up into the heat of the afternoon. Never before had I seen houses burning without the accompaniment of an obstructive crowd. A little farther on the dry reeds up the bank were smoking and glowing, and a line of fire inland was marching steadily across a late field of hay.

For a long time I drifted, so painful and weary was I after the violence I had been through, and so intense the heat upon the water. Then my fears got the better of me again, and I resumed my paddling. The sun scorched my bare back. At last, as the bridge at Walton was coming into sight round the bend, my fever and faintness overcame my fears, and I landed on the Middlesex bank and lay down, deadly sick, amid the long grass. I suppose the time was then about four or five o'clock. I got up presently, walked perhaps half a mile without meeting a soul, and then lay down again in the shadow of a hedge. I seem to remember talking, wanderingly, to myself during that last spurt. I was also very thirsty, and bitterly regretful I had drunk no more water. It is a curious thing that I felt angry with my wife; I cannot account for it, but my impotent desire to reach Leatherhead worried me excessively.

I do not clearly remember the arrival of the curate, so that probably I dozed. I became aware of him as a seated figure in soot-smudged shirt sleeves, and with his upturned, clean-shaven face staring at a faint flickering that danced over the sky. The sky was what is called a mackerel sky--rows and rows of faint down-plumes of cloud, just tinted with the midsummer sunset.

I sat up, and at the rustle of my motion he looked at me quickly.

"Have you any water?" I asked abruptly.

He shook his head.

"You have been asking for water for the last hour," he said.

For a moment we were silent, taking stock of each other. I dare say he found me a strange enough figure, naked, save for my water-soaked trousers and socks, scalded, and my face and shoulders blackened by the smoke. His face was a fair weakness, his chin retreated, and his hair lay in crisp, almost flaxen curls on his low forehead; his eyes were rather large, pale blue, and blankly staring. He spoke abruptly, looking vacantly away from me.

"What does it mean?" he said. "What do these things mean?"

I stared at him and made no answer.

He extended a thin white hand and spoke in almost a complaining tone.

"Why are these things permitted? What sins have we done? The morning service was over, I was walking through the roads to clear my brain for the afternoon, and then--fire, earthquake, death! As if it were Sodom and Gomorrah! All our work undone, all the work---- What are these Martians?"

"What are we?" I answered, clearing my throat.

He gripped his knees and turned to look at me again. For half a minute, perhaps, he stared silently.

"I was walking through the roads to clear my brain," he said. "And suddenly--fire, earthquake, death!"

He relapsed into silence, with his chin now sunken almost to his knees.

Presently he began waving his hand.

"All the work--all the Sunday schools---- What have we done--what has Weybridge done? Everything gone--everything destroyed. The church! We rebuilt it only three years ago. Gone! Swept out of existence! Why?"

Another pause, and he broke out again like one demented.

"The smoke of her burning goeth up for ever and ever!" he shouted.

His eyes flamed, and he pointed a lean finger in the direction of Weybridge.

By this time I was beginning to take his measure. The tremendous tragedy in which he had been involved--it was evident he was a fugitive from Weybridge--had driven him to the very verge of his reason.

"Are we far from Sunbury?" I said, in a matter-of-fact tone.

"What are we to do?" he asked. "Are these creatures everywhere? Has the earth been given over to them?"

"Are we far from Sunbury?"

"Only this morning I officiated at early celebration----"

"Things have changed," I said, quietly. "You must keep your head. There is still hope."

"Hope!"

"Yes. Plentiful hope--for all this destruction!"

I began to explain my view of our position. He listened at first, but as I went on the interest dawning in his eyes gave place to their former stare, and his regard wandered from me.

"This must be the beginning of the end," he said, interrupting me. "The end! The great and terrible day of the Lord! When men shall call upon the mountains and the rocks to fall upon them and hide them--hide them from the face of Him that sitteth upon the throne!"

I began to understand the position. I ceased my laboured reasoning, struggled to my feet, and, standing over him, laid my hand on his shoulder.

"Be a man!" said I. "You are scared out of your wits! What good is religion if it collapses under calamity? Think of what earthquakes and floods, wars and volcanoes, have done before to men! Did you think God had exempted Weybridge? He is not an insurance agent."

For a time he sat in blank silence.

"But how can we escape?" he asked, suddenly. "They are invulnerable, they are pitiless."

"Neither the one nor, perhaps, the other," I answered. "And the mightier they are the more sane and wary should we be. One of them was killed yonder not three hours ago."

"Killed!" he said, staring about him. "How can God's ministers be killed?"

"I saw it happen." I proceeded to tell him. "We have chanced to come in for the thick of it," said I, "and that is all."

"What is that flicker in the sky?" he asked abruptly.

I told him it was the heliograph signalling--that it was the sign of human help and effort in the sky.

"We are in the midst of it," I said, "quiet as it is. That flicker in the sky tells of the gathering storm. Yonder, I take it are the Martians, and Londonward, where those hills rise about Richmond and Kingston and the trees give cover, earthworks are being thrown up and guns are being placed. Presently the Martians will be coming this way again."

And even as I spoke he sprang to his feet and stopped me by a gesture.

"Listen!" he said.

From beyond the low hills across the water came the dull resonance of distant guns and a remote weird crying. Then everything was still. A cockchafer came droning over the hedge and past us. High in the west the crescent moon hung faint and pale above the smoke of Weybridge and Shepperton and the hot, still splendour of the sunset.

"We had better follow this path," I said, "northward."

Chapter Fourteen
In London

My younger brother was in London when the Martians fell at Woking. He was a medical student working for an imminent examination, and he heard nothing of the arrival until Saturday morning. The morning papers on Saturday contained, in addition to lengthy special articles on the planet Mars, on life in the planets, and so forth, a brief and vaguely worded telegram, all the more striking for its brevity.

The Martians, alarmed by the approach of a crowd, had killed a number of people with a quick-firing gun, so the story ran. The telegram concluded with the words: "Formidable as they seem to be, the Martians have not moved from the pit into which they have fallen, and, indeed, seem incapable of doing so. Probably this is due to the relative strength of the earth's gravitational energy." On that last text their leader-writer expanded very comfortingly.

Of course all the students in the crammer's biology class, to which my brother went that day, were intensely interested, but there were no signs of any unusual excitement in the streets. The afternoon papers puffed scraps of news under big headlines. They had nothing to tell beyond the movements of troops about the common, and the burning of the pine woods between Woking and Weybridge, until eight. Then the **St. James's Gazette**, in an extra-special edition, announced the bare fact of the interruption of telegraphic communication. This was thought to be due to the falling of burning pine trees across the line. Nothing more of the fighting was known that night, the night of my drive to Leatherhead and back.

My brother felt no anxiety about us, as he knew from the description in the papers that the cylinder was a good two miles from my house. He made up his mind to run down that night to me, in order, as he says, to see the Things before they were killed. He despatched a telegram, which never reached me, about four o'clock, and spent the evening at a music hall.

In London, also, on Saturday night there was a thunderstorm, and my brother reached Waterloo in a cab. On the platform from which the midnight train usually starts he learned, after some waiting, that an accident prevented trains from reaching Woking that night. The nature of the accident he could not ascertain; indeed, the railway authorities did not clearly know at that time. There was very little excitement in the station, as the officials, failing to realise that anything further than a breakdown between Byfleet and Woking junction had occurred, were running the theatre trains which usually passed through Woking round by Virginia Water or Guildford. They were busy making the necessary arrangements to alter the route of the Southampton and Portsmouth Sunday League excursions. A nocturnal newspaper reporter, mistaking my brother for the traffic manager, to whom he bears a slight resemblance, waylaid and tried to interview him. Few people, excepting the railway officials, connected the breakdown with the Martians.

I have read, in another account of these events, that on Sunday morning "all London was electrified by the news from Woking." As a matter of fact, there was nothing to justify that very extravagant phrase. Plenty of Londoners did not hear of the Martians until the panic of Monday morning. Those who did took some time to realise all that the hastily worded telegrams in the Sunday papers conveyed. The majority of people in London do not read Sunday papers.

The habit of personal security, moreover, is so deeply fixed in the Londoner's mind, and startling intelligence so much a matter of course in the papers, that they could read without any personal tremors: "About seven o'clock last night the Martians came out of the cylinder, and, moving about under an armour of metallic shields, have completely wrecked Woking station with the adjacent houses, and massacred an entire battalion of the Cardigan Regiment. No details are known. Maxims have been absolutely useless against their armour; the field guns have been disabled by them. Flying hussars have been galloping into Chertsey. The Martians appear to be moving slowly towards Chertsey or Windsor. Great anxiety prevails in West Surrey, and earthworks are being thrown up to check the advance Londonward." That was how the Sunday *Sun* put it, and a clever and remarkably prompt "handbook" article in the *Referee* compared the affair to a menagerie suddenly let loose in a village.

No one in London knew positively of the nature of the armoured Martians, and there was still a fixed idea that these monsters must be sluggish: "crawling," "creeping painfully"--such expressions occurred in almost all the earlier reports. None of the telegrams could have been written by an eyewitness of their advance. The Sunday papers printed separate editions as further news came to hand, some even in default of it. But there was practically nothing more to tell people until late in the afternoon, when the authorities gave the press agencies the news in their possession. It was stated that the people of Walton and Weybridge, and all the district were pouring along the roads Londonward, and that was all.

My brother went to church at the Foundling Hospital in the morning, still in ignorance of what had happened on the previous night. There he heard allusions made to the invasion, and a special prayer for peace. Coming out, he bought a *Referee*. He became alarmed at the news in this, and went again to Waterloo station to find out if communication were restored. The omnibuses, carriages, cyclists, and innumerable people walking in their best clothes seemed scarcely affected by the strange intelligence that the news venders were disseminating. People were interested, or, if alarmed, alarmed only on account of the local residents. At the station he heard for the first time that the Windsor and Chertsey lines were now interrupted. The porters told him that several remarkable telegrams had been received in the morning from Byfleet and Chertsey stations, but that these had abruptly ceased. My brother could get very little precise detail out of them.

"There's fighting going on about Weybridge" was the extent of their information.

The train service was now very much disorganised. Quite a number of people who had been expecting friends from places on the South-Western network were standing about the station. One grey-headed old gentleman came and abused the South-Western Company bitterly to my brother. "It wants showing up," he said.

One or two trains came in from Richmond, Putney, and Kingston, containing people who had gone out for a day's boating and found the locks closed and a feeling of panic in the air. A man in a blue and white blazer addressed my brother, full of strange tidings.

"There's hosts of people driving into Kingston in traps and carts and things, with boxes of valuables and all that," he said. "They come from Molesey and Weybridge and Walton, and they say there's been guns heard at Chertsey, heavy firing, and that mounted soldiers have told them to get off at once because the Martians are coming. We heard guns firing at Hampton Court station, but we thought it was thunder. What the dickens does it all mean? The Martians can't get out of their pit, can they?"

My brother could not tell him.

Afterwards he found that the vague feeling of alarm had spread to the clients of the underground railway, and that the Sunday excursionists began to return from all over the South-Western "lung"--Barnes, Wimbledon, Richmond Park, Kew, and so forth--at unnaturally early hours; but not a soul had anything more than vague hearsay to tell of. Everyone connected with the terminus seemed ill-tempered.

About five o'clock the gathering crowd in the station was immensely excited by the opening of the line of communication, which is almost invariably closed, between the South-Eastern and the South-Western stations, and the passage of carriage trucks bearing huge guns and carriages crammed with soldiers. These were the guns that were brought up from Woolwich and Chatham to cover Kingston. There was an exchange of pleasantries: "You'll get eaten!" "We're the beast-tamers!" and so forth. A little while after that a squad of police came into the station and began to clear the public off the platforms, and my brother went out into the street again.

The church bells were ringing for evensong, and a squad of Salvation Army lassies came singing down Waterloo Road. On the bridge a number of loafers were watching a curious brown scum that came drifting down the stream in patches. The sun was just setting, and the Clock Tower and the Houses of Parliament rose against one of the most peaceful skies it is possible to imagine, a sky of gold, barred with long transverse stripes of reddish-purple cloud. There was talk of a floating body. One of the men there, a reservist he said he was, told my brother he had seen the heliograph flickering in the west.

In Wellington Street my brother met a couple of sturdy roughs who had just been rushed out of Fleet Street with still-wet newspapers and staring placards. "Dreadful catastrophe!" they bawled one to the other down Wellington Street. "Fighting at Weybridge! Full description! Repulse of the Martians! London in Danger!" He had to give threepence for a copy of that paper.

Then it was, and then only, that he realised something of the full power and terror of these monsters. He learned that they were not merely a handful of small sluggish creatures, but that they were minds swaying vast mechanical bodies; and that they could move swiftly and smite with such power that even the mightiest guns could not stand against them.

They were described as "vast spiderlike machines, nearly a hundred feet high, capable of the speed of an express train, and able to shoot out a beam of intense heat." Masked batteries, chiefly of field guns, had been planted in the country about Horsell Common, and especially between the Woking district and London. Five of the machines had been seen moving towards the Thames, and one, by a happy chance, had been destroyed. In the other cases the shells had missed, and the batteries had been at once annihilated by the Heat-Rays. Heavy losses of soldiers were mentioned, but the tone of the despatch was optimistic.

The Martians had been repulsed; they were not invulnerable. They had retreated to their triangle of cylinders again, in the circle about Woking. Signallers with heliographs were pushing forward upon them from all sides. Guns were in rapid transit from Windsor, Portsmouth, Aldershot, Woolwich--even from the north; among others, long wire-guns of ninety-five tons from Woolwich. Altogether one hundred and sixteen were in position or being hastily placed, chiefly covering London. Never before in England had there been such a vast or rapid concentration of military material.

Any further cylinders that fell, it was hoped, could be destroyed at once by high explosives, which were being rapidly manufactured and distributed. No doubt, ran the report, the situation was of the strangest and gravest description, but the public was exhorted to avoid and discourage panic. No doubt the Martians were strange and terrible in the extreme, but at the outside there could not be more than twenty of them against our millions.

The authorities had reason to suppose, from the size of the cylinders, that at the outside there could not be more than five in each cylinder--fifteen altogether. And one at least was disposed of--perhaps more. The public would be fairly warned of the approach of danger, and elaborate measures were being taken for the protection of the people in the threatened southwestern suburbs. And so, with reiterated assurances of the safety of London and the ability of the authorities to cope with the difficulty, this quasi-proclamation closed.

This was printed in enormous type on paper so fresh that it was still wet, and there had been no time to add a word of comment. It was curious, my brother said, to see how ruthlessly the usual contents of the paper had been hacked and taken out to give this place.

All down Wellington Street people could be seen fluttering out the pink sheets and reading, and the Strand was suddenly noisy with the voices of an army of hawkers following these pioneers. Men came scrambling off buses to secure copies. Certainly this news excited people intensely, whatever their previous apathy. The shutters of a map shop in the Strand were being taken down, my brother said, and a man in his Sunday raiment, lemon-yellow gloves even, was visible inside the window hastily fastening maps of Surrey to the glass.

Going on along the Strand to Trafalgar Square, the paper in his hand, my brother saw some of the fugitives from West Surrey. There was a man with his wife and two boys and some articles of furniture in a cart such as greengrocers use. He was driving from the direction of Westminster Bridge; and close behind him came a hay waggon with five or six respectable-looking people in it, and some boxes and bundles. The faces of these people were haggard, and their entire appearance contrasted conspicuously with the Sabbath-best appearance of the people on the omnibuses. People in fashionable clothing peeped at them out of cabs. They stopped at the Square as if undecided which way to take, and finally turned eastward along the Strand. Some way behind these came a man in workday clothes, riding one of those old-fashioned tricycles with a small front wheel. He was dirty and white in the face.

My brother turned down towards Victoria, and met a number of such people. He had a vague idea that he might see something of me. He noticed an unusual number of police regulating the traffic. Some of the refugees were exchanging news with the people on the omnibuses. One was professing to have seen the Martians. "Boilers on stilts, I tell you, striding along like men." Most of them were excited and animated by their strange experience.

Beyond Victoria the public-houses were doing a lively trade with these arrivals. At all the street corners groups of people were reading papers, talking excitedly, or staring at these unusual Sunday visitors. They seemed to increase as night drew on, until at last the roads, my brother said, were like Epsom High Street on a Derby Day. My brother addressed several of these fugitives and got unsatisfactory answers from most.

None of them could tell him any news of Woking except one man, who assured him that Woking had been entirely destroyed on the previous night.

"I come from Byfleet," he said; "man on a bicycle came through the place in the early morning, and ran from door to door warning us to come away. Then came soldiers. We went out to look, and there were clouds of smoke to the south--nothing but smoke, and not a soul coming that way. Then we heard the guns at Chertsey, and folks coming from Weybridge. So I've locked up my house and come on."

At the time there was a strong feeling in the streets that the authorities were to blame for their incapacity to dispose of the invaders without all this inconvenience.

About eight o'clock a noise of heavy firing was distinctly audible all over the south of London. My brother could not hear it for the traffic in the main thoroughfares, but by striking through the quiet back streets to the river he was able to distinguish it quite plainly.

He walked from Westminster to his apartments near Regent's Park, about two. He was now very anxious on my account, and disturbed at the evident magnitude of the trouble. His mind was inclined to run, even as mine had run on Saturday, on military details. He thought of all those silent, expectant guns, of the suddenly nomadic countryside; he tried to imagine "boilers on stilts" a hundred feet high.

There were one or two cartloads of refugees passing along Oxford Street, and several in the Marylebone Road, but so slowly was the news spreading that Regent Street and Portland Place were full of their usual Sunday-night promenaders, albeit they talked in groups, and along the edge of Regent's Park there were as many silent couples "walking out" together under the scattered gas lamps as ever there had been. The night was warm and still, and a little oppressive; the sound of guns continued intermittently, and after midnight there seemed to be sheet lightning in the south.

He read and re-read the paper, fearing the worst had happened to me. He was restless, and after supper prowled out again aimlessly. He returned and tried in vain to divert his attention to his examination notes. He went to bed a little after midnight, and was awakened from lurid dreams in the small hours of Monday by the sound of door knockers, feet running in the street, distant drumming, and a clamour of bells. Red reflections danced on the ceiling. For a moment he lay astonished, wondering whether day had come or the world gone mad. Then he jumped out of bed and ran to the window.

His room was an attic and as he thrust his head out, up and down the street there were a dozen echoes to the noise of his window sash, and heads in every kind of night disarray appeared. Enquiries were being shouted. "They are coming!" bawled a policeman, hammering at the door; "the Martians are coming!" and hurried to the next door.

The sound of drumming and trumpeting came from the Albany Street Barracks, and every church within earshot was hard at work killing sleep with a vehement disorderly tocsin. There was a noise of doors opening, and window after window in the houses opposite flashed from darkness into yellow illumination.

Up the street came galloping a closed carriage, bursting abruptly into noise at the corner, rising to a clattering climax under the window, and dying away slowly in the distance. Close on the rear of this came a couple of cabs, the forerunners of a long procession of flying vehicles, going for the most part to Chalk Farm station, where the North-Western special trains were loading up, instead of coming down the gradient into Euston.

For a long time my brother stared out of the window in blank astonishment, watching the policemen hammering at door after door, and delivering their incomprehensible message. Then the door behind him opened, and the man who lodged across the landing came in, dressed only in shirt, trousers, and slippers, his braces loose about his waist, his hair disordered from his pillow.

"What the devil is it?" he asked. "A fire? What a devil of a row!"

They both craned their heads out of the window, straining to hear what the policemen were shouting. People were coming out of the side streets, and standing in groups at the corners talking.

"What the devil is it all about?" said my brother's fellow lodger.

My brother answered him vaguely and began to dress, running with each garment to the window in order to miss nothing of the growing excitement. And presently men selling unnaturally early newspapers came bawling into the street:

"London in danger of suffocation! The Kingston and Richmond defences forced! Fearful massacres in the Thames Valley!"

And all about him--in the rooms below, in the houses on each side and across the road, and behind in the Park Terraces and in the hundred other streets of that part of Marylebone, and the Westbourne Park district and St. Pancras, and westward and northward in Kilburn and St. John's Wood and Hampstead, and eastward in Shoreditch and Highbury and Haggerston and

Hoxton, and, indeed, through all the vastness of London from Ealing to East Ham--people were rubbing their eyes, and opening windows to stare out and ask aimless questions, dressing hastily as the first breath of the coming storm of Fear blew through the streets. It was the dawn of the great panic. London, which had gone to bed on Sunday night oblivious and inert, was awakened, in the small hours of Monday morning, to a vivid sense of danger.

Unable from his window to learn what was happening, my brother went down and out into the street, just as the sky between the parapets of the houses grew pink with the early dawn. The flying people on foot and in vehicles grew more numerous every moment. "Black Smoke!" he heard people crying, and again "Black Smoke!" The contagion of such a unanimous fear was inevitable. As my brother hesitated on the door-step, he saw another news vender approaching, and got a paper forthwith. The man was running away with the rest, and selling his papers for a shilling each as he ran--a grotesque mingling of profit and panic.

And from this paper my brother read that catastrophic despatch of the Commander-in-Chief:

"The Martians are able to discharge enormous clouds of a black and poisonous vapour by means of rockets. They have smothered our batteries, destroyed Richmond, Kingston, and Wimbledon, and are advancing slowly towards London, destroying everything on the way. It is impossible to stop them. There is no safety from the Black Smoke but in instant flight."

That was all, but it was enough. The whole population of the great six-million city was stirring, slipping, running; presently it would be pouring en masse northward.

"Black Smoke!" the voices cried. "Fire!"

The bells of the neighbouring church made a jangling tumult, a cart carelessly driven smashed, amid shrieks and curses, against the water trough up the street. Sickly yellow lights went to and fro in the houses, and some of the passing cabs flaunted unextinguished lamps. And overhead the dawn was growing brighter, clear and steady and calm.

He heard footsteps running to and fro in the rooms, and up and down stairs behind him. His landlady came to the door, loosely wrapped in dressing gown and shawl; her husband followed ejaculating.

As my brother began to realise the import of all these things, he turned hastily to his own room, put all his available money--some ten pounds altogether--into his pockets, and went out again into the streets.

Subjugation by Brendan Perkins

Chapter Fifteen
What Had Happened in Surrey

It was while the curate had sat and talked so wildly to me under the hedge in the flat meadows near Halliford, and while my brother was watching the fugitives stream over Westminster Bridge, that the Martians had resumed the offensive. So far as one can ascertain from the conflicting accounts that have been put forth, the majority of them remained busied with preparations in the Horsell pit until nine that night, hurrying on some operation that disengaged huge volumes of green smoke.

But three certainly came out about eight o'clock and, advancing slowly and cautiously, made their way through Byfleet and Pyrford towards Ripley and Weybridge, and so came in sight of the expectant batteries against the setting sun. These Martians did not advance in a body, but in a line, each perhaps a mile and a half from his nearest fellow. They communicated with one another by means of sirenlike howls, running up and down the scale from one note to another.

It was this howling and firing of the guns at Ripley and St. George's Hill that we had heard at Upper Halliford. The Ripley gunners, unseasoned artillery volunteers who ought never to have been placed in such a position, fired one wild, premature, ineffectual volley, and bolted on horse and foot through the deserted village, while the Martian, without using his Heat-Ray, walked serenely over their guns, stepped gingerly among them, passed in front of them, and so came unexpectedly upon the guns in Painshill Park, which he destroyed.

The St. George's Hill men, however, were better led or of a better mettle. Hidden by a pine wood as they were, they seem to have been quite unsuspected by the Martian nearest to them. They laid their guns as deliberately as if they had been on parade, and fired at about a thousand yards' range.

The shells flashed all round him, and he was seen to advance a few paces, stagger, and go down. Everybody yelled together, and the guns were reloaded in frantic haste. The overthrown Martian set up a prolonged ululation, and immediately a second glittering giant, answering him, appeared over the trees to the south. It would seem that a leg of the tripod had been smashed by one of the shells. The whole of the second volley flew wide of the Martian on the ground, and, simultaneously, both his companions brought their Heat-Rays to bear on the battery. The ammunition blew up, the pine trees all about the guns flashed into fire, and only one or two of the men who were already running over the crest of the hill escaped.

After this it would seem that the three took counsel together and halted, and the scouts who were watching them report that they remained absolutely stationary for the next half hour. The Martian who had been overthrown crawled tediously out of his hood, a small brown figure, oddly suggestive from that distance of a speck of blight, and apparently engaged in the repair of his support. About nine he had finished, for his cowl was then seen above the trees again.

It was a few minutes past nine that night when these three sentinels were joined by four other Martians, each carrying a thick black tube. A similar tube was handed to each of the three, and the seven proceeded to distribute themselves at equal distances along a curved line between St. George's Hill, Weybridge, and the village of Send, southwest of Ripley.

A dozen rockets sprang out of the hills before them so soon as they began to move, and warned the waiting batteries about Ditton and Esher. At the same time four of their fighting machines, similarly armed with tubes, crossed the river, and two of them, black against the western sky, came into sight of myself and the curate as we hurried wearily and painfully along the road that runs northward out of Halliford. They moved, as it seemed to us, upon a cloud, for a milky mist covered the fields and rose to a third of their height.

At this sight the curate cried faintly in his throat, and began running; but I knew it was no good running from a Martian, and I turned aside and crawled through dewy nettles and brambles into the broad ditch by the side of the road. He looked back, saw what I was doing, and turned to join me.

The two halted, the nearer to us standing and facing Sunbury, the remoter being a grey indistinctness towards the evening star, away towards Staines.

The occasional howling of the Martians had ceased; they took up their positions in the huge crescent about their cylinders in absolute silence. It was a crescent with twelve miles between its horns. Never since the devising of gunpowder was the beginning of a battle so still. To us and to an observer about Ripley it would have had precisely the same effect--the Martians seemed in solitary possession of the darkling night, lit only as it was by the slender moon, the stars, the afterglow of the daylight, and the ruddy glare from St. George's Hill and the woods of Painshill.

But facing that crescent everywhere--at Staines, Hounslow, Ditton, Esher, Ockham, behind hills and woods south of the river, and across the flat grass meadows to the north of it, wherever a cluster of trees or village houses gave sufficient cover--the guns were waiting. The signal rockets burst and rained their sparks through the night and vanished, and the spirit of all those watching batteries rose to a tense expectation. The Martians had but to advance into the line of fire, and instantly those motionless black forms of men, those guns glittering so darkly in the early night, would explode into a thunderous fury of battle.

No doubt the thought that was uppermost in a thousand of those vigilant minds, even as it was uppermost in mine, was the riddle--how much they understood of us. Did they grasp that we in our millions were organized, disciplined, working together? Or did they interpret our spurts of fire, the sudden stinging of our shells, our steady investment of their encampment, as we should the furious unanimity of onslaught in a disturbed hive of bees? Did they dream they might exterminate us? (At that time no one knew what food they needed.) A hundred such questions struggled together in my mind as I watched that vast sentinel shape. And in the back of my mind was the sense of all the huge unknown and hidden forces Londonward. Had they prepared pitfalls? Were the powder mills at Hounslow ready as a snare? Would the Londoners have the heart and courage to make a greater Moscow of their mighty province of houses?

Then, after an interminable time, as it seemed to us, crouching and peering through the hedge, came a sound like the distant concussion of a gun. Another nearer, and then another. And then the Martian beside us raised his tube on high and discharged it, gunwise, with a heavy report that made the ground heave. The one towards Staines answered him. There was no flash, no smoke, simply that loaded detonation.

I was so excited by these heavy minute-guns following one another that I so far forgot my personal safety and my scalded hands as to clamber up into the hedge and stare towards Sunbury. As I did so a second report followed, and a big projectile hurtled overhead towards Hounslow. I expected at least to see smoke or fire, or some such evidence of its work. But all I saw was the deep blue sky above, with one solitary star, and the white mist spreading wide and low beneath. And there had been no crash, no answering explosion. The silence was restored; the minute lengthened to three.

"What has happened?" said the curate, standing up beside me.

"Heaven knows!" said I.

A bat flickered by and vanished. A distant tumult of shouting began and ceased. I looked again at the Martian, and saw he was now moving eastward along the riverbank, with a swift, rolling motion,

Every moment I expected the fire of some hidden battery to spring upon him; but the evening calm was unbroken. The figure of the Martian grew smaller as he receded, and presently the mist and the gathering night had swallowed him up. By a common impulse we clambered higher. Towards Sunbury was a dark appearance, as though a conical hill had suddenly come into being there, hiding our view of the farther country; and then, remoter across the river, over Walton, we saw another such summit. These hill-like forms grew lower and broader even as we stared.

Moved by a sudden thought, I looked northward, and there I perceived a third of these cloudy black kopjes had risen.

Everything had suddenly become very still. Far away to the southeast, marking the quiet, we heard the Martians hooting to one another, and then the air quivered again with the distant thud of their guns. But the earthly artillery made no reply.

Now at the time we could not understand these things, but later I was to learn the meaning of these ominous kopjes that gathered in the twilight. Each of the Martians, standing in the great crescent I have described, had discharged, by means of the gunlike tube he carried, a huge canister over whatever hill, copse, cluster of houses, or other possible cover for guns, chanced to be in front of him. Some fired only one of these, some two--as in the case of the one we had seen; the one at Ripley is said to have discharged no fewer than five at that time. These canisters smashed on striking the ground--they did not explode--and incontinently disengaged an enormous volume of heavy, inky vapour, coiling and pouring upward in a huge and ebony cumulus cloud, a gaseous hill that sank and spread itself slowly over the surrounding country. And the touch of that vapour, the inhaling of its pungent wisps, was death to all that breathes.

It was heavy, this vapour, heavier than the densest smoke, so that, after the first tumultuous uprush and outflow of its impact, it sank down through the air and poured over the ground in a manner rather liquid than gaseous, abandoning the hills, and streaming into the valleys and ditches and watercourses even as I have heard the carbonic-acid gas that pours from volcanic clefts is wont to do. And where it came upon water some chemical action occurred, and the surface would be instantly covered with a powdery scum that sank slowly and made way for more. The scum was absolutely insoluble, and it is a strange thing, seeing the instant effect of the gas, that one could drink without hurt the water from which it had been strained. The vapour did not diffuse as a true gas would do. It hung together in banks, flowing sluggishly down the slope of the land and driving reluctantly before the wind, and very slowly it combined with the mist and moisture of the air, and sank to the earth in the form of dust. Save that an unknown element giving a group of four lines in the blue of the spectrum is concerned, we are still entirely ignorant of the nature of this substance.

Once the tumultuous upheaval of its dispersion was over, the black smoke clung so closely to the ground, even before its precipitation, that fifty feet up in the air, on the roofs and upper stories of high houses and on great trees, there was a chance of escaping its poison altogether, as was proved even that night at Street Cobham and Ditton.

The man who escaped at the former place tells a wonderful story of the strangeness of its coiling flow, and how he looked down from the church spire and saw the houses of the village rising like ghosts out of its inky nothingness. For a day and a half he remained there, weary, starving and sun-scorched, the earth under the blue sky and against the prospect of the distant hills a velvet-black expanse, with red roofs, green trees, and, later, black-veiled shrubs and gates, barns, outhouses, and walls, rising here and there into the sunlight.

But that was at Street Cobham, where the black vapour was allowed to remain until it sank of its own accord into the ground. As a rule the Martians, when it had served its purpose, cleared the air of it again by wading into it and directing a jet of steam upon it.

This they did with the vapour banks near us, as we saw in the starlight from the window of a deserted house at Upper Halliford, whither we had returned. From there we could see the searchlights on Richmond Hill and Kingston Hill going to and fro, and about eleven the windows rattled, and we heard the sound of the huge siege guns that had been put in position there. These continued intermittently for the space of a quarter of an hour, sending chance shots at the invisible Martians at Hampton and Ditton, and then the pale beams of the electric light vanished, and were replaced by a bright red glow.

Then the fourth cylinder fell--a brilliant green meteor--as I learned afterwards, in Bushey Park. Before the guns on the Richmond and Kingston line of hills began, there was a fitful cannonade far away in the southwest, due, I believe, to guns being fired haphazard before the black vapour could overwhelm the gunners.

So, setting about it as methodically as men might smoke out a wasps' nest, the Martians spread this strange stifling vapour over the Londonward country. The horns of the crescent slowly moved apart, until at last they formed a line from Hanwell to Coombe and Malden. All night through their destructive tubes advanced. Never once, after the Martian at St. George's Hill was brought down, did they give the artillery the ghost of a chance against them. Wherever there was a possibility of guns being laid for them unseen, a fresh canister of the black vapour was discharged, and where the guns were openly displayed the Heat-Ray was brought to bear.

By midnight the blazing trees along the slopes of Richmond Park and the glare of Kingston Hill threw their light upon a network of black smoke, blotting out the whole valley of the Thames and extending as far as the eye could reach. And through this two Martians slowly waded, and turned their hissing steam jets this way and that.

They were sparing of the Heat-Ray that night, either because they had but a limited supply of material for its production or because they did not wish to destroy the country but only to crush and overawe the opposition they had aroused. In the latter aim they certainly succeeded. Sunday night was the end of the organised opposition to their movements. After that no body of men would stand against them, so hopeless was the enterprise. Even the crews of the torpedo-boats and destroyers that had brought their quick-firers up the Thames refused to stop, mutinied, and went down again. The only offensive operation men ventured upon after that night was the preparation of mines and pitfalls, and even in that their energies were frantic and spasmodic.

One has to imagine, as well as one may, the fate of those batteries towards Esher, waiting so tensely in the twilight. Survivors there were none. One may picture the orderly expectation, the officers alert and watchful, the gunners ready, the ammunition piled to hand, the limber gunners with their horses and waggons, the groups of civilian spectators standing as near as they were permitted, the evening stillness, the ambulances and hospital tents with the burned and wounded from Weybridge; then the dull resonance of the shots the Martians fired, and the clumsy projectile whirling over the trees and houses and smashing amid the neighbouring fields.

One may picture, too, the sudden shifting of the attention, the swiftly spreading coils and bellyings of that blackness advancing headlong, towering heavenward, turning the twilight to a palpable darkness, a strange and horrible antagonist of vapour striding upon its victims, men and horses near it seen dimly, running, shrieking, falling headlong, shouts of dismay, the guns suddenly abandoned, men choking and writhing on the ground, and the swift broadening-out of the opaque cone of smoke. And then night and extinction--nothing but a silent mass of impenetrable vapour hiding its dead.

Before dawn the black vapour was pouring through the streets of Richmond, and the disintegrating organism of government was, with a last expiring effort, rousing the population of London to the necessity of flight.

Smoke by Brendan Perkins

Chapter Sixteen
The Exodus from London

So you understand the roaring wave of fear that swept through the greatest city in the world just as Monday was dawning--the stream of flight rising swiftly to a torrent, lashing in a foaming tumult round the railway stations, banked up into a horrible struggle about the shipping in the Thames, and hurrying by every available channel northward and eastward. By ten o'clock the police organisation, and by midday even the railway organisations, were losing coherency, losing shape and efficiency, guttering, softening, running at last in that swift liquefaction of the social body.

All the railway lines north of the Thames and the South-Eastern people at Cannon Street had been warned by midnight on Sunday, and trains were being filled. People were fighting savagely for standing-room in the carriages even at two o'clock. By three, people were being trampled and crushed even in Bishopsgate Street, a couple of hundred yards or more from Liverpool Street station; revolvers were fired, people stabbed, and the policemen who had been sent to direct the traffic, exhausted and infuriated, were breaking the heads of the people they were called out to protect.

And as the day advanced and the engine drivers and stokers refused to return to London, the pressure of the flight drove the people in an ever-thickening multitude away from the stations and along the northward-running roads. By midday a Martian had been seen at Barnes, and a cloud of slowly sinking black vapour drove along the Thames and across the flats of Lambeth, cutting off all escape over the bridges in its sluggish advance. Another bank drove over Ealing, and surrounded a little island of survivors on Castle Hill, alive, but unable to escape.

After a fruitless struggle to get aboard a North-Western train at Chalk Farm--the engines of the trains that had loaded in the goods yard there ploughed through shrieking people, and a dozen stalwart men fought to keep the crowd from crushing the driver against his furnace--my brother emerged upon the Chalk Farm road, dodged across through a hurrying swarm of vehicles, and had the luck to be foremost in the sack of a cycle shop. The front tire of the machine he got was punctured in dragging it through the window, but he got up and off, notwithstanding, with no further injury than a cut wrist. The steep foot of Haverstock Hill was impassable owing to several overturned horses, and my brother struck into Belsize Road.

So he got out of the fury of the panic, and, skirting the Edgware Road, reached Edgware about seven, fasting and wearied, but well ahead of the crowd. Along the road people were standing in the roadway, curious, wondering. He was passed by a number of cyclists, some horsemen, and two motor cars. A mile from Edgware the rim of the wheel broke, and the machine became unridable. He left it by the roadside and trudged through the village. There were shops half opened in the main street of the place, and people crowded on the pavement and in the doorways and windows, staring astonished at this extraordinary procession of fugitives that was beginning. He succeeded in getting some food at an inn.

For a time he remained in Edgware not knowing what next to do. The flying people increased in number. Many of them, like my brother, seemed inclined to loiter in the place. There was no fresh news of the invaders from Mars.

At that time the road was crowded, but as yet far from congested. Most of the fugitives at that hour were mounted on cycles, but there were soon motor cars, hansom cabs, and carriages hurrying along, and the dust hung in heavy clouds along the road to St. Albans.

It was perhaps a vague idea of making his way to Chelmsford, where some friends of his lived, that at last induced my brother to strike into a quiet lane running eastward. Presently he came upon a stile, and, crossing it, followed a footpath northeastward. He passed near several farmhouses and some little places whose names he did not learn. He saw few fugitives until, in a grass lane towards High Barnet, he happened upon two ladies who became his fellow travellers. He came upon them just in time to save them.

He heard their screams, and, hurrying round the corner, saw a couple of men struggling to drag them out of the little pony-chaise in which they had been driving, while a third with difficulty held the frightened pony's head. One of the ladies, a short woman dressed in white, was simply screaming; the other, a dark, slender figure, slashed at the man who gripped her arm with a whip she held in her disengaged hand.

My brother immediately grasped the situation, shouted, and hurried towards the struggle. One of the men desisted and turned towards him, and my brother, realising from his antagonist's face that a fight was unavoidable, and being an expert boxer, went into him forthwith and sent him down against the wheel of the chaise.

It was no time for pugilistic chivalry and my brother laid him quiet with a kick, and gripped the collar of the man who pulled at the slender lady's arm. He heard the clatter of hoofs, the whip stung across his face, a third antagonist struck him between the eyes, and the man he held wrenched himself free and made off down the lane in the direction from which he had come.

Partly stunned, he found himself facing the man who had held the horse's head, and became aware of the chaise receding from him down the lane, swaying from side to side, and with the women in it looking back. The man before him, a burly rough, tried to close, and he stopped him with a blow in the face. Then, realising that he was deserted, he dodged round and made off down the lane after the chaise, with the sturdy man close behind him, and the fugitive, who had turned now, following remotely.

Suddenly he stumbled and fell; his immediate pursuer went headlong, and he rose to his feet to find himself with a couple of antagonists again. He would have had little chance against them had not the slender lady very pluckily pulled up and returned to his help. It seems she had had a revolver all this time, but it had been under the seat when she and her companion were attacked. She fired at six yards' distance, narrowly missing my brother. The less courageous of the robbers made off, and his companion followed him, cursing his cowardice. They both stopped in sight down the lane, where the third man lay insensible.

"Take this!" said the slender lady, and she gave my brother her revolver.

"Go back to the chaise," said my brother, wiping the blood from his split lip.

She turned without a word--they were both panting--and they went back to where the lady in white struggled to hold back the frightened pony.

The robbers had evidently had enough of it. When my brother looked again they were retreating.

"I'll sit here," said my brother, "if I may"; and he got upon the empty front seat. The lady looked over her shoulder.

"Give me the reins," she said, and laid the whip along the pony's side. In another moment a bend in the road hid the three men from my brother's eyes.

So, quite unexpectedly, my brother found himself, panting, with a cut mouth, a bruised jaw, and bloodstained knuckles, driving along an unknown lane with these two women.

He learned they were the wife and the younger sister of a surgeon living at Stanmore, who had come in the small hours from a dangerous case at Pinner, and heard at some railway station on his way of the Martian advance. He had hurried home, roused the women--their servant had left them two days before--packed some provisions, put his revolver under the seat--luckily for my brother--and told them to drive on to Edgware, with the idea of getting a train there. He stopped behind to tell the neighbours. He would overtake them, he said, at about half past four in the morning, and now it was nearly nine and they had seen nothing of him. They could not stop in Edgware because of the growing traffic through the place, and so they had come into this side lane.

That was the story they told my brother in fragments when presently they stopped again, nearer to New Barnet. He promised to stay with them, at least until they could determine what to do, or until the missing man arrived, and professed to be an expert shot with the revolver--a weapon strange to him--in order to give them confidence.

They made a sort of encampment by the wayside, and the pony became happy in the hedge. He told them of his own escape out of London, and all that he knew of these Martians and their ways. The sun crept higher in the sky, and after a time their talk died out and gave place to an uneasy state of anticipation. Several wayfarers came along the lane, and of these my brother gathered such news as he could. Every broken answer he had deepened his impression of the great disaster that had come on humanity, deepened his persuasion of the immediate necessity for prosecuting this flight. He urged the matter upon them.

"We have money," said the slender woman, and hesitated.

Her eyes met my brother's, and her hesitation ended.

"So have I," said my brother.

She explained that they had as much as thirty pounds in gold, besides a five-pound note, and suggested that with that they might get upon a train at St. Albans or New Barnet. My brother thought that was hopeless, seeing the fury of the Londoners to crowd upon the trains, and broached his own idea of striking across Essex towards Harwich and thence escaping from the country altogether.

Mrs. Elphinstone--that was the name of the woman in white--would listen to no reasoning, and kept calling upon "George"; but her sister-in-law was astonishingly quiet and deliberate, and at last agreed to my brother's suggestion. So, designing to cross the Great North Road, they went on towards Barnet, my brother leading the pony to save it as much as possible.

As the sun crept up the sky the day became excessively hot, and under foot a thick, whitish sand grew burning and blinding, so that they travelled only very slowly. The hedges were grey with dust. And as they advanced towards Barnet a tumultuous murmuring grew stronger.

They began to meet more people. For the most part these were staring before them, murmuring indistinct questions, jaded, haggard, unclean. One man in evening dress passed them on foot, his eyes on the ground. They heard his voice, and, looking back at him, saw one hand clutched in his hair and the other beating invisible things. His paroxysm of rage over, he went on his way without once looking back.

As my brother's party went on towards the crossroads to the south of Barnet they saw a woman approaching the road across some fields on their left, carrying a child and with two other children; and then passed a man in dirty black, with a thick stick in one hand and a small portmanteau in the other. Then round the corner of the lane, from between the villas that guarded it at its confluence with the high road, came a little cart drawn by a sweating black pony and driven by a sallow youth in a bowler hat, grey with dust. There were three girls, East End factory girls, and a couple of little children crowded in the cart.

"This'll tike us rahnd Edgware?" asked the driver, wild-eyed, white-faced; and when my brother told him it would if he turned to the left, he whipped up at once without the formality of thanks.

My brother noticed a pale grey smoke or haze rising among the houses in front of them, and veiling the white facade of a terrace beyond the road that appeared between the backs of the villas. Mrs. Elphinstone suddenly cried out at a number of tongues of smoky red flame leaping up above the houses in front of them against the hot, blue sky. The tumultuous noise resolved itself now into the disorderly mingling of many voices, the gride of many wheels, the creaking of waggons, and the staccato of hoofs. The lane came round sharply not fifty yards from the crossroads.

"Good heavens!" cried Mrs. Elphinstone. "What is this you are driving us into?"

My brother stopped.

For the main road was a boiling stream of people, a torrent of human beings rushing northward, one pressing on another. A great bank of dust, white and luminous in the blaze of the sun, made everything within twenty feet of the ground grey and indistinct and was perpetually renewed by the hurrying feet of a dense crowd of horses and of men and women on foot, and by the wheels of vehicles of every description.

"Way!" my brother heard voices crying. "Make way!"

It was like riding into the smoke of a fire to approach the meeting point of the lane and road; the crowd roared like a fire, and the dust was hot and pungent. And, indeed, a little way up the road a villa was burning and sending rolling masses of black smoke across the road to add to the confusion.

Two men came past them. Then a dirty woman, carrying a heavy bundle and weeping. A lost retriever dog, with hanging tongue, circled dubiously round them, scared and wretched, and fled at my brother's threat.

So much as they could see of the road Londonward between the houses to the right was a tumultuous stream of dirty, hurrying people, pent in between the villas on either side; the black heads, the crowded forms, grew into distinctness as they rushed towards the corner, hurried past, and merged their individuality again in a receding multitude that was swallowed up at last in a cloud of dust.

"Go on! Go on!" cried the voices. "Way! Way!"

One man's hands pressed on the back of another. My brother stood at the pony's head. Irresistibly attracted, he advanced slowly, pace by pace, down the lane.

Edgware had been a scene of confusion, Chalk Farm a riotous tumult, but this was a whole population in movement. It is hard to imagine that host. It had no character of its own. The figures poured out past the corner, and receded with their backs to the group in the lane. Along the margin came those who were on foot threatened by the wheels, stumbling in the ditches, blundering into one another.

The carts and carriages crowded close upon one another, making little way for those swifter and more impatient vehicles that darted forward every now and then when an opportunity showed itself of doing so, sending the people scattering against the fences and gates of the villas.

"Push on!" was the cry. "Push on! They are coming!"

In one cart stood a blind man in the uniform of the Salvation Army, gesticulating with his crooked fingers and bawling, "Eternity! Eternity!" His voice was hoarse and very loud so that my brother could hear him long after he was lost to sight in the dust. Some of the people who crowded in the carts whipped stupidly at their horses and quarrelled with other drivers; some sat motionless, staring at nothing with miserable eyes; some gnawed their hands with thirst, or lay prostrate in the bottoms of their conveyances. The horses' bits were covered with foam, their eyes bloodshot.

There were cabs, carriages, shop cars, waggons, beyond counting; a mail cart, a road-cleaner's cart marked "Vestry of St. Pancras," a huge timber waggon crowded with roughs. A brewer's dray rumbled by with its two near wheels splashed with fresh blood.

"Clear the way!" cried the voices. "Clear the way!"

"Eter-nity! Eter-nity!" came echoing down the road.

There were sad, haggard women tramping by, well dressed, with children that cried and stumbled, their dainty clothes smothered in dust, their weary faces smeared with tears. With many of these came men, sometimes helpful, sometimes lowering and savage. Fighting side by side with them pushed some weary street outcast in faded black rags, wide-eyed, loud-voiced, and foul-mouthed. There were sturdy workmen thrusting their way along, wretched, unkempt men, clothed like clerks or shopmen, struggling spasmodically; a wounded soldier my brother noticed, men dressed in the clothes of railway porters, one wretched creature in a nightshirt with a coat thrown over it.

But varied as its composition was, certain things all that host had in common. There were fear and pain on their faces, and fear behind them. A tumult up the road, a quarrel for a place in a waggon, sent the whole host of them quickening their pace; even a man so scared and broken that his knees bent under him was galvanised for a moment into renewed activity. The heat and dust had already been at work upon this multitude. Their skins were dry, their lips black and cracked. They were all thirsty, weary, and footsore. And amid the various cries one heard disputes, reproaches, groans of weariness and fatigue; the voices of most of them were hoarse and weak. Through it all ran a refrain:

"Way! Way! The Martians are coming!"

Few stopped and came aside from that flood. The lane opened slantingly into the main road with a narrow opening, and had a delusive appearance of coming from the direction of London. Yet a kind of eddy of people drove into its mouth; weaklings elbowed out of the stream, who for the most part rested but a moment before plunging into it again. A little way down the lane, with two friends bending over him, lay a man with a bare leg, wrapped about with bloody rags. He was a lucky man to have friends.

A little old man, with a grey military moustache and a filthy black frock coat, limped out and sat down beside the trap, removed his boot--his sock was blood-stained--shook out a pebble, and hobbled on again; and then a little girl of eight or nine, all alone, threw herself under the hedge close by my brother, weeping.

"I can't go on! I can't go on!"

My brother woke from his torpor of astonishment and lifted her up, speaking gently to her, and carried her to Miss Elphinstone. So soon as my brother touched her she became quite still, as if frightened.

"Ellen!" shrieked a woman in the crowd, with tears in her voice--"Ellen!" And the child suddenly darted away from my brother, crying "Mother!"

"They are coming," said a man on horseback, riding past along the lane.

"Out of the way, there!" bawled a coachman, towering high; and my brother saw a closed carriage turning into the lane.

The people crushed back on one another to avoid the horse. My brother pushed the pony and chaise back into the hedge, and the man drove by and stopped at the turn of the way. It was a carriage, with a pole for a pair of horses, but only one was in the traces. My brother saw dimly through the dust that two men lifted out something on a white stretcher and put it gently on the grass beneath the privet hedge.

One of the men came running to my brother.

"Where is there any water?" he said. "He is dying fast, and very thirsty. It is Lord Garrick."

"Lord Garrick!" said my brother; "the Chief Justice?"

"The water?" he said.

"There may be a tap," said my brother, "in some of the houses. We have no water. I dare not leave my people."

The man pushed against the crowd towards the gate of the corner house.

"Go on!" said the people, thrusting at him. "They are coming! Go on!"

Then my brother's attention was distracted by a bearded, eagle-faced man lugging a small handbag, which split even as my brother's eyes rested on it and disgorged a mass of sovereigns that seemed to break up into separate coins as it struck the ground. They rolled hither and thither among the struggling feet of men and horses. The man stopped and looked stupidly at the heap, and the shaft of a cab struck his shoulder and sent him reeling. He gave a shriek and dodged back, and a cartwheel shaved him narrowly.

"Way!" cried the men all about him. "Make way!"

So soon as the cab had passed, he flung himself, with both hands open, upon the heap of coins, and began thrusting handfuls in his pocket. A horse rose close upon him, and in another moment, half rising, he had been borne down under the horse's hoofs.

"Stop!" screamed my brother, and pushing a woman out of his way, tried to clutch the bit of the horse.

Before he could get to it, he heard a scream under the wheels, and saw through the dust the rim passing over the poor wretch's back. The driver of the cart slashed his whip at my brother, who ran round behind the cart. The multitudinous shouting confused his ears. The man was writhing in the dust among his scattered money, unable to rise, for the wheel had broken his back, and his lower limbs lay limp and dead. My brother stood up and yelled at the next driver, and a man on a black horse came to his assistance.

"Get him out of the road," said he; and, clutching the man's collar with his free hand, my brother lugged him sideways. But he still clutched after his money, and regarded my brother fiercely, hammering at his arm with a handful of gold. "Go on! Go on!" shouted angry voices behind.

"Way! Way!"

There was a smash as the pole of a carriage crashed into the cart that the man on horseback stopped. My brother looked up, and the man with the gold twisted his head round and bit the wrist that held his collar. There was a concussion, and the black horse came staggering sideways, and the carthorse pushed beside it. A hoof missed my brother's foot by a hair's breadth. He released his grip on the fallen man and jumped back. He saw anger change to terror on the face of the poor wretch on the ground, and in a moment he was hidden and my brother was borne backward and carried past the entrance of the lane, and had to fight hard in the torrent to recover it.

He saw Miss Elphinstone covering her eyes, and a little child, with all a child's want of sympathetic imagination, staring with dilated eyes at a dusty something that lay black and still, ground and crushed under the rolling wheels. "Let us go back!" he shouted, and began turning the pony round. "We cannot cross this--hell," he said and they went back a hundred yards the way they had come, until the fighting crowd was hidden. As they passed the bend in the lane my brother saw the face of the dying man in the ditch under the privet, deadly white and drawn, and shining with perspiration. The two women sat silent, crouching in their seat and shivering.

Then beyond the bend my brother stopped again. Miss Elphinstone was white and pale, and her sister-in-law sat weeping, too wretched even to call upon "George." My brother was horrified and perplexed. So soon as they had retreated he realised how urgent and unavoidable it was to attempt this crossing. He turned to Miss Elphinstone, suddenly resolute.

"We must go that way," he said, and led the pony round again.

For the second time that day this girl proved her quality. To force their way into the torrent of people, my brother plunged into the traffic and held back a cab horse, while she drove the pony across its head. A waggon locked wheels for a moment and ripped a long splinter from the chaise. In another moment they were caught and swept forward by the stream. My brother, with the cabman's whip marks red across his face and hands, scrambled into the chaise and took the reins from her.

"Point the revolver at the man behind," he said, giving it to her, "if he presses us too hard. No!--point it at his horse."

Then he began to look out for a chance of edging to the right across the road. But once in the stream he seemed to lose volition, to become a part of that dusty rout. They swept through Chipping Barnet with the torrent; they were nearly a mile beyond the centre of the town before they had fought across to the opposite side of the way. It was din and confusion indescribable; but in and beyond the town the road forks repeatedly, and this to some extent relieved the stress.

They struck eastward through Hadley, and there on either side of the road, and at another place farther on they came upon a great multitude of people drinking at the stream, some fighting to come at the water. And farther on, from a lull near East Barnet, they saw two trains running slowly one after the other without signal or order--trains swarming with people, with men even among the coals behind the engines--going northward along the Great Northern Railway. My brother supposes they must have filled outside London, for at that time the furious terror of the people had rendered the central termini impossible.

Near this place they halted for the rest of the afternoon, for the violence of the day had already utterly exhausted all three of them. They began to suffer the beginnings of hunger; the night was cold, and none of them dared to sleep. And in the evening many people came hurrying along the road nearby their stopping place, fleeing from unknown dangers before them, and going in the direction from which my brother had come.

Chapter Seventeen
The Thunder Child

Had the Martians aimed only at destruction, they might on Monday have annihilated the entire population of London, as it spread itself slowly through the home counties. Not only along the road through Barnet, but also through Edgware and Waltham Abbey, and along the roads eastward to Southend and Shoeburyness, and south of the Thames to Deal and Broadstairs, poured the same frantic rout. If one could have hung that June morning in a balloon in the blazing blue above London every northward and eastward road running out of the tangled maze of streets would have seemed stippled black with the streaming fugitives, each dot a human agony of terror and physical distress. I have set forth at length in the last chapter my brother's account of the road through Chipping Barnet, in order that my readers may realise how that swarming of black dots appeared to one of those concerned. Never before in the history of the world had such a mass of human beings moved and suffered together. The legendary hosts of Goths and Huns, the hugest armies Asia has ever seen, would have been but a drop in that current. And this was no disciplined march; it was a stampede--a stampede gigantic and terrible--without order and without a goal, six million people unarmed and unprovisioned, driving headlong. It was the beginning of the rout of civilisation, of the massacre of mankind.

Directly below him the balloonist would have seen the network of streets far and wide, houses, churches, squares, crescents, gardens--already derelict--spread out like a huge map, and in the southward **blotted**. Over Ealing, Richmond, Wimbledon, it would have seemed as if some monstrous pen had flung ink upon the chart. Steadily, incessantly, each black splash grew and spread, shooting out ramifications this way and that, now banking itself against rising ground, now pouring swiftly over a crest into a new-found valley, exactly as a gout of ink would spread itself upon blotting paper.

And beyond, over the blue hills that rise southward of the river, the glittering Martians went to and fro, calmly and methodically spreading their poison cloud over this patch of country and then over that, laying it again with their steam jets when it had served its purpose, and taking possession of the conquered country. They do not seem to have aimed at extermination so much as at complete demoralisation and the destruction of any opposition. They exploded any stores of powder they came upon, cut every telegraph, and wrecked the railways here and there. They were hamstringing mankind. They seemed in no hurry to extend the field of their operations, and did not come beyond the central part of London all that day. It is possible that a very considerable number of people in London stuck to their houses through Monday morning. Certain it is that many died at home suffocated by the Black Smoke.

Until about midday the Pool of London was an astonishing scene. Steamboats and shipping of all sorts lay there, tempted by the enormous sums of money offered by fugitives, and it is said that many who swam out to these vessels were thrust off with boathooks and drowned. About one o'clock in the afternoon the thinning remnant of a cloud of the black vapour appeared between the arches of Blackfriars Bridge. At that the Pool became a scene of mad confusion, fighting, and collision, and for some time a multitude of boats and barges jammed in the northern arch of the Tower Bridge, and the sailors and lightermen had to fight savagely against the people who swarmed upon them from the riverfront. People were actually clambering down the piers of the bridge from above.

When, an hour later, a Martian appeared beyond the Clock Tower and waded down the river, nothing but wreckage floated above Limehouse.

Of the falling of the fifth cylinder I have presently to tell. The sixth star fell at Wimbledon. My brother, keeping watch beside the women in the chaise in a meadow, saw the green flash of it far beyond the hills. On Tuesday the little party, still set upon getting across the sea, made its way through the swarming country towards Colchester. The news that the Martians were now in possession of the whole of London was confirmed. They had been seen at Highgate, and even, it was said, at Neasden. But they did not come into my brother's view until the morrow.

That day the scattered multitudes began to realise the urgent need of provisions. As they grew hungry the rights of property ceased to be regarded. Farmers were out to defend their cattle-sheds, granaries, and ripening root crops with arms in their hands. A number of people now, like my brother, had their faces eastward, and there were some desperate souls even going back towards London to get food. These were chiefly people from the northern suburbs, whose knowledge of the Black Smoke came by hearsay. He heard that about half the members of the government had gathered at Birmingham, and that enormous quantities of high explosives were being prepared to be used in automatic mines across the Midland counties.

He was also told that the Midland Railway Company had replaced the desertions of the first day's panic, had resumed traffic, and was running northward trains from St. Albans to relieve the congestion of the home counties. There was also a placard in Chipping Ongar announcing that large stores of flour were available in the northern towns and that within twenty-four hours bread would be distributed among the starving people in the neighbourhood. But this intelligence did not deter him from the plan of escape he had formed, and the three pressed eastward all day, and heard no more of the bread distribution than this promise. Nor, as a matter of fact, did anyone else hear more of it. That night fell the seventh star, falling upon Primrose Hill. It fell while Miss Elphinstone was watching, for she took that duty alternately with my brother. She saw it.

On Wednesday the three fugitives--they had passed the night in a field of unripe wheat--reached Chelmsford, and there a body of the inhabitants, calling itself the Committee of Public Supply, seized the pony as provisions, and would give nothing in exchange for it but the promise of a share in it the next day. Here there were rumours of Martians at Epping, and news of the destruction of Waltham Abbey Powder Mills in a vain attempt to blow up one of the invaders.

People were watching for Martians here from the church towers. My brother, very luckily for him as it chanced, preferred to push on at once to the coast rather than wait for food, although all three of them were very hungry. By midday they passed through Tillingham, which, strangely enough, seemed to be quite silent and deserted, save for a few furtive plunderers hunting for food. Near Tillingham they suddenly came in sight of the sea, and the most amazing crowd of shipping of all sorts that it is possible to imagine.

For after the sailors could no longer come up the Thames, they came on to the Essex coast, to Harwich and Walton and Clacton, and afterwards to Foulness and Shoebury, to bring off the people. They lay in a huge sickle-shaped curve that vanished into mist at last towards the Naze. Close inshore was a multitude of fishing smacks--English, Scotch, French, Dutch, and Swedish; steam launches from the Thames, yachts, electric boats; and beyond were ships of large burden, a multitude of filthy colliers, trim merchantmen, cattle ships, passenger boats, petroleum tanks, ocean tramps, an old white transport even, neat white and grey liners from Southampton and Hamburg; and along the blue coast across the Blackwater my brother could make out dimly a dense swarm of boats chaffering with the people on the beach, a swarm which also extended up the Blackwater almost to Maldon.

About a couple of miles out lay an ironclad, very low in the water, almost, to my brother's perception, like a waterlogged ship. This was the ram *Thunder Child.* It was the only warship in sight, but far away to the right over the smooth surface of the sea--for that day there was a dead calm--lay a serpent of black smoke to mark the next ironclads of the Channel Fleet, which hovered in an extended line, steam up and ready for action, across the Thames estuary during the course of the Martian conquest, vigilant and yet powerless to prevent it.

At the sight of the sea, Mrs. Elphinstone, in spite of the assurances of her sister-in-law, gave way to panic. She had never been out of England before, she would rather die than trust herself friendless in a foreign country, and so forth. She seemed, poor woman, to imagine that the French and the Martians might prove very similar. She had been growing increasingly hysterical, fearful, and depressed during the two days' journeyings. Her great idea was to return to Stanmore. Things had been always well and safe at Stanmore. They would find George at Stanmore.

It was with the greatest difficulty they could get her down to the beach, where presently my brother succeeded in attracting the attention of some men on a paddle steamer from the Thames. They sent a boat and drove a bargain for thirty-six pounds for the three. The steamer was going, these men said, to Ostend.

It was about two o'clock when my brother, having paid their fares at the gangway, found himself safely aboard the steamboat with his charges. There was food aboard, albeit at exorbitant prices, and the three of them contrived to eat a meal on one of the seats forward.

There were already a couple of score of passengers aboard, some of whom had expended their last money in securing a passage, but the captain lay off the Blackwater until five in the afternoon, picking up passengers until the seated decks were even dangerously crowded. He would probably have remained longer had it not been for the sound of guns that began about that hour in the south. As if in answer, the ironclad seaward fired a small gun and hoisted a string of flags. A jet of smoke sprang out of her funnels.

Some of the passengers were of opinion that this firing came from Shoeburyness, until it was noticed that it was growing louder. At the same time, far away in the southeast the masts and upperworks of three ironclads rose one after the other out of the sea, beneath clouds of black smoke. But my brother's attention speedily reverted to the distant firing in the south. He fancied he saw a column of smoke rising out of the distant grey haze.

The little steamer was already flapping her way eastward of the big crescent of shipping, and the low Essex coast was growing blue and hazy, when a Martian appeared, small and faint in the remote distance, advancing along the muddy coast from the direction of Foulness. At that the captain on the bridge swore at the top of his voice with fear and anger at his own delay, and the paddles seemed infected with his terror. Every soul aboard stood at the bulwarks or on the seats of the steamer and stared at that distant shape, higher than the trees or church towers inland, and advancing with a leisurely parody of a human stride.

It was the first Martian my brother had seen, and he stood, more amazed than terrified, watching this Titan advancing deliberately towards the shipping, wading farther and farther into the water as the coast fell away. Then, far away beyond the Crouch, came another, striding over some stunted trees, and then yet another, still farther off, wading deeply through a shiny mudflat that seemed to hang halfway up between sea and sky. They were all stalking seaward, as if to intercept the escape of the multitudinous vessels that were crowded between Foulness and the Naze. In spite of the throbbing exertions of the engines of the little paddleboat, and the pouring foam that her wheels flung behind her, she receded with terrifying slowness from this ominous advance.

Glancing northwestward, my brother saw the large crescent of shipping already writhing with the approaching terror; one ship passing behind another, another coming round from broadside to end on, steamships whistling and giving off volumes of steam, sails being let out, launches rushing hither and thither. He was so fascinated by this and by the creeping danger away to the left that he had no eyes for anything seaward. And then a swift movement of the steamboat (she had suddenly come round to avoid being run down) flung him headlong from the seat upon which he was standing. There was a shouting all about him, a trampling of feet, and a cheer that seemed to be answered faintly. The steamboat lurched and rolled him over upon his hands.

He sprang to his feet and saw to starboard, and not a hundred yards from their heeling, pitching boat, a vast iron bulk like the blade of a plough tearing through the water, tossing it on either side in huge waves of foam that leaped towards the steamer, flinging her paddles helplessly in the air, and then sucking her deck down almost to the waterline.

A douche of spray blinded my brother for a moment. When his eyes were clear again he saw the monster had passed and was rushing landward. Big iron upperworks rose out of this headlong structure, and from that twin funnels projected and spat a smoking blast shot with fire. It was the torpedo ram, *Thunder Child*, steaming headlong, coming to the rescue of the threatened shipping.

Keeping his footing on the heaving deck by clutching the bulwarks, my brother looked past this charging leviathan at the Martians again, and he saw the three of them now close together, and standing so far out to sea that their tripod supports were almost entirely submerged. Thus sunken, and seen in remote perspective, they appeared far less formidable than the huge iron bulk in whose wake the steamer was pitching so helplessly. It would seem they were regarding this new antagonist with astonishment. To their intelligence, it may be, the giant was even such another as themselves. The *Thunder Child* fired no gun, but simply drove full speed towards them. It was probably her not firing that enabled her to get so near the enemy as she did. They did not know what to make of her. One shell, and they would have sent her to the bottom forthwith with the Heat-Ray.

She was steaming at such a pace that in a minute she seemed halfway between the steamboat and the Martians--a diminishing black bulk against the receding horizontal expanse of the Essex coast.

Suddenly the foremost Martian lowered his tube and discharged a canister of the black gas at the ironclad. It hit her larboard side and glanced off in an inky jet that rolled away to seaward, an unfolding torrent of Black Smoke, from which the ironclad drove clear. To the watchers from the steamer, low in the water and with the sun in their eyes, it seemed as though she were already among the Martians.

They saw the gaunt figures separating and rising out of the water as they retreated shoreward, and one of them raised the camera-like generator of the Heat-Ray. He held it pointing obliquely downward, and a bank of steam sprang from the water at its touch. It must have driven through the iron of the ship's side like a white-hot iron rod through paper.

A flicker of flame went up through the rising steam, and then the Martian reeled and staggered. In another moment he was cut down, and a great body of water and steam shot high in the air. The guns of the *Thunder Child* sounded through the reek, going off one after the other, and one shot splashed the water high close by the steamer, ricocheted towards the other flying ships to the north, and smashed a smack to matchwood.

But no one heeded that very much. At the sight of the Martian's collapse the captain on the bridge yelled inarticulately, and all the crowding passengers on the steamer's stern shouted together. And then they yelled again. For, surging out beyond the white tumult, drove something long and black, the flames streaming from its middle parts, its ventilators and funnels spouting fire.

She was alive still; the steering gear, it seems, was intact and her engines working. She headed straight for a second Martian, and was within a hundred yards of him when the Heat-Ray came to bear. Then with a violent thud, a blinding flash, her decks, her funnels, leaped upward. The Martian staggered with the violence of her explosion, and in another moment the flaming wreckage, still driving forward with the impetus of its pace, had struck him and crumpled him up like a thing of cardboard. My brother shouted involuntarily. A boiling tumult of steam hid everything again.

"Two!," yelled the captain.

Everyone was shouting. The whole steamer from end to end rang with frantic cheering that was taken up first by one and then by all in the crowding multitude of ships and boats that was driving out to sea.

The steam hung upon the water for many minutes, hiding the third Martian and the coast altogether. And all this time the boat was paddling steadily out to sea and away from the fight; and when at last the confusion cleared, the drifting bank of black vapour intervened, and nothing of the *Thunder Child* could be made out, nor could the third Martian be seen. But the ironclads to seaward were now quite close and standing in towards shore past the steamboat.

The little vessel continued to beat its way seaward, and the ironclads receded slowly towards the coast, which was hidden still by a marbled bank of vapour, part steam, part black gas, eddying and combining in the strangest way. The fleet of refugees was scattering to the northeast; several smacks were sailing between the ironclads and the steamboat. After a time, and before they reached the sinking cloud bank, the warships turned northward, and then abruptly went about and passed into the thickening haze of evening southward. The coast grew faint, and at last indistinguishable amid the low banks of clouds that were gathering about the sinking sun.

Then suddenly out of the golden haze of the sunset came the vibration of guns, and a form of black shadows moving. Everyone struggled to the rail of the steamer and peered into the blinding furnace of the west, but nothing was to be distinguished clearly. A mass of smoke rose slanting and barred the face of the sun. The steamboat throbbed on its way through an interminable suspense.

The sun sank into grey clouds, the sky flushed and darkened, the evening star trembled into sight. It was deep twilight when the captain cried out and pointed. My brother strained his eyes. Something rushed up into the sky out of the greyness--rushed slantingly upward and very swiftly into the luminous clearness above the clouds in the western sky; something flat and broad, and very large, that swept round in a vast curve, grew smaller, sank slowly, and vanished again into the grey mystery of the night. And as it flew it rained down darkness upon the land.

The Thunder Child by Peter Fussey

Book Two
The Earth Under the Martians

Chapter One
Under Foot

In the first book I have wandered so much from my own adventures to tell of the experiences of my brother that all through the last two chapters I and the curate have been lurking in the empty house at Halliford whither we fled to escape the Black Smoke. There I will resume. We stopped there all Sunday night and all the next day--the day of the panic--in a little island of daylight, cut off by the Black Smoke from the rest of the world. We could do nothing but wait in aching inactivity during those two weary days.

My mind was occupied by anxiety for my wife. I figured her at Leatherhead, terrified, in danger, mourning me already as a dead man. I paced the rooms and cried aloud when I thought of how I was cut off from her, of all that might happen to her in my absence. My cousin I knew was brave enough for any emergency, but he was not the sort of man to realise danger quickly, to rise promptly. What was needed now was not bravery, but circumspection. My only consolation was to believe that the Martians were moving Londonward and away from her. Such vague anxieties keep the mind sensitive and painful. I grew very weary and irritable with the curate's perpetual ejaculations; I tired of the sight of his selfish despair. After some ineffectual remonstrance I kept away from him, staying in a room--evidently a children's schoolroom--containing globes, forms, and copybooks. When he followed me thither, I went to a box room at the top of the house and, in order to be alone with my aching miseries, locked myself in.

We were hopelessly hemmed in by the Black Smoke all that day and the morning of the next. There were signs of people in the next house on Sunday evening--a face at a window and moving lights, and later the slamming of a door. But I do not know who these people were, nor what became of them. We saw nothing of them next day. The Black Smoke drifted slowly riverward all through Monday morning, creeping nearer and nearer to us, driving at last along the roadway outside the house that hid us.

A Martian came across the fields about midday, laying the stuff with a jet of superheated steam that hissed against the walls, smashed all the windows it touched, and scalded the curate's hand as he fled out of the front room. When at last we crept across the sodden rooms and looked out again, the country northward was as though a black snowstorm had passed over it. Looking towards the river, we were astonished to see an unaccountable redness mingling with the black of the scorched meadows.

For a time we did not see how this change affected our position, save that we were relieved of our fear of the Black Smoke. But later I perceived that we were no longer hemmed in, that now we might get away. So soon as I realised that the way of escape was open, my dream of action returned. But the curate was lethargic, unreasonable.

"We are safe here," he repeated; "safe here."

I resolved to leave him--would that I had! Wiser now for the artilleryman's teaching, I sought out food and drink. I had found oil and rags for my burns, and I also took a hat and a flannel shirt that I found in one of the bedrooms. When it was clear to him that I meant to go alone--had reconciled myself to going alone--he suddenly roused himself to come. And all being quiet throughout the afternoon, we started about five o'clock, as I should judge, along the blackened road to Sunbury.

In Sunbury, and at intervals along the road, were dead bodies lying in contorted attitudes, horses as well as men, overturned carts and luggage, all covered thickly with black dust. That pall of cindery powder made me think of what I had read of the destruction of Pompeii. We got to Hampton Court without misadventure, our minds full of strange and unfamiliar appearances, and at Hampton Court our eyes were relieved to find a patch of green that had escaped the suffocating drift. We went through Bushey Park, with its deer going to and fro under the chestnuts, and some men and women hurrying in the distance towards Hampton, and so we came to Twickenham. These were the first people we saw.

Away across the road the woods beyond Ham and Petersham were still afire. Twickenham was uninjured by either Heat-Ray or Black Smoke, and there were more people about here, though none could give us news. For the most part they were like ourselves, taking advantage of a lull to shift their quarters. I have an impression that many of the houses here were still occupied by scared inhabitants, too frightened even for flight. Here too the evidence of a hasty rout was abundant along the road. I remember most vividly three smashed bicycles in a heap, pounded into the road by the wheels of subsequent carts. We crossed Richmond Bridge about half past eight. We hurried across the exposed bridge, of course, but I noticed floating down the stream a number of red masses, some many feet across. I did not know what these were--there was no time for scrutiny--and I put a more horrible interpretation on them than they deserved. Here again on the Surrey side were black dust that had once been smoke, and dead bodies--a heap near the approach to the station; but we had no glimpse of the Martians until we were some way towards Barnes.

We saw in the blackened distance a group of three people running down a side street towards the river, but otherwise it seemed deserted. Up the hill Richmond town was burning briskly; outside the town of Richmond there was no trace of the Black Smoke.

Then suddenly, as we approached Kew, came a number of people running, and the upperworks of a Martian fighting-machine loomed in sight over the housetops, not a hundred yards away from us. We stood aghast at our danger, and had the Martian looked down we must immediately have perished. We were so terrified that we dared not go on, but turned aside and hid in a shed in a garden. There the curate crouched, weeping silently, and refusing to stir again.

But my fixed idea of reaching Leatherhead would not let me rest, and in the twilight I ventured out again. I went through a shrubbery, and along a passage beside a big house standing in its own grounds, and so emerged upon the road towards Kew. The curate I left in the shed, but he came hurrying after me.

That second start was the most foolhardy thing I ever did. For it was manifest the Martians were about us. No sooner had the curate overtaken me than we saw either the fighting-machine we had seen before or another, far away across the meadows in the direction of Kew Lodge. Four or five little black figures hurried before it across the green-grey of the field, and in a moment it was evident this Martian pursued them. In three strides he was among them, and they ran radiating from his feet in all directions. He used no Heat-Ray to destroy them, but picked them up one by one. Apparently he tossed them into the great metallic carrier which projected behind him, much as a workman's basket hangs over his shoulder.

It was the first time I realised that the Martians might have any other purpose than destruction with defeated humanity. We stood for a moment petrified, then turned and fled through a gate behind us into a walled garden, fell into, rather than found, a fortunate ditch, and lay there, scarce daring to whisper to each other until the stars were out.

I suppose it was nearly eleven o'clock before we gathered courage to start again, no longer venturing into the road, but sneaking along hedgerows and through plantations, and watching keenly through the darkness, he on the right and I on the left, for the Martians, who seemed to be all about us. In one place we blundered upon a scorched and blackened area, now cooling and ashen, and a number of scattered dead bodies of men, burned horribly about the heads and trunks but with their legs and boots mostly intact; and of dead horses, fifty feet, perhaps, behind a line of four ripped guns and smashed gun carriages.

Sheen, it seemed, had escaped destruction, but the place was silent and deserted. Here we happened on no dead, though the night was too dark for us to see into the side roads of the place. In Sheen my companion suddenly complained of faintness and thirst, and we decided to try one of the houses.

The first house we entered, after a little difficulty with the window, was a small semi-detached villa, and I found nothing eatable left in the place but some mouldy cheese. There was, however, water to drink; and I took a hatchet, which promised to be useful in our next housebreaking.

We then crossed to a place where the road turns towards Mortlake. Here there stood a white house within a walled garden, and in the pantry of this domicile we found a store of food--two loaves of bread in a pan, an uncooked steak, and the half of a ham. I give this catalogue so precisely because, as it happened, we were destined to subsist upon this store for the next fortnight. Bottled beer stood under a shelf, and there were two bags of haricot beans and some limp lettuces. This pantry opened into a kind of wash-up kitchen, and in this was firewood; there was also a cupboard, in which we found nearly a dozen of burgundy, tinned soups and salmon, and two tins of biscuits.

We sat in the adjacent kitchen in the dark--for we dared not strike a light--and ate bread and ham, and drank beer out of the same bottle. The curate, who was still timorous and restless, was now, oddly enough, for pushing on, and I was urging him to keep up his strength by eating when the thing happened that was to imprison us.

"It can't be midnight yet," I said, and then came a blinding glare of vivid green light. Everything in the kitchen leaped out, clearly visible in green and black, and vanished again. And then followed such a concussion as I have never heard before or since. So close on the heels of this as to seem instantaneous came a thud behind me, a clash of glass, a crash and rattle of falling masonry all about us, and the plaster of the ceiling came down upon us, smashing into a multitude of fragments upon our heads. I was knocked headlong across the floor against the oven handle and stunned. I was insensible for a long time, the curate told me, and when I came to we were in darkness again, and he, with a face wet, as I found afterwards, with blood from a cut forehead, was dabbing water over me.

For some time I could not recollect what had happened. Then things came to me slowly. A bruise on my temple asserted itself.

"Are you better?" asked the curate in a whisper.

At last I answered him. I sat up.

"Don't move," he said. "The floor is covered with smashed crockery from the dresser. You can't possibly move without making a noise, and I fancy **they** are outside."

We both sat quite silent, so that we could scarcely hear each other breathing. Everything seemed deadly still, but once something near us, some plaster or broken brickwork, slid down with a rumbling sound. Outside and very near was an intermittent, metallic rattle.

"That!" said the curate, when presently it happened again.

"Yes," I said. "But what is it?"

"A Martian!" said the curate.

I listened again.

"It was not like the Heat-Ray," I said, and for a time I was inclined to think one of the great fighting-machines had stumbled against the house, as I had seen one stumble against the tower of Shepperton Church.

Our situation was so strange and incomprehensible that for three or four hours, until the dawn came, we scarcely moved. And then the light filtered in, not through the window, which remained black, but through a triangular aperture between a beam and a heap of broken bricks in the wall behind us. The interior of the kitchen we now saw greyly for the first time.

The window had been burst in by a mass of garden mould, which flowed over the table upon which we had been sitting and lay about our feet. Outside, the soil was banked high against the house. At the top of the window frame we could see an uprooted drainpipe. The floor was littered with smashed hardware; the end of the kitchen towards the house was broken into, and since the daylight shone in there, it was evident the greater part of the house had collapsed. Contrasting vividly with this ruin was the neat dresser, stained in the fashion, pale green, and with a number of copper and tin vessels below it, the wallpaper imitating blue and white tiles, and a couple of coloured supplements fluttering from the walls above the kitchen range.

As the dawn grew clearer, we saw through the gap in the wall the body of a Martian, standing sentinel, I suppose, over the still glowing cylinder. At the sight of that we crawled as circumspectly as possible out of the twilight of the kitchen into the darkness of the scullery.

Abruptly the right interpretation dawned upon my mind.

"The fifth cylinder," I whispered, "the fifth shot from Mars, has struck this house and buried us under the ruins!"

For a time the curate was silent, and then he whispered:

"God have mercy upon us!"

I heard him presently whimpering to himself.

Save for that sound we lay quite still in the scullery; I for my part scarce dared breathe, and sat with my eyes fixed on the faint light of the kitchen door. I could just see the curate's face, a dim, oval shape, and his collar and cuffs. Outside there began a metallic hammering, then a violent hooting, and then again, after a quiet interval, a hissing like the hissing of an engine. These noises, for the most part problematical, continued intermittently, and seemed if anything to increase in number as time wore on. Presently a measured thudding and a vibration that made everything about us quiver and the vessels in the pantry ring and shift, began and continued. Once the light was eclipsed, and the ghostly kitchen doorway became absolutely dark. For many hours we must have crouched there, silent and shivering, until our tired attention failed....

At last I found myself awake and very hungry. I am inclined to believe we must have spent the greater portion of a day before that awakening. My hunger was at a stride so insistent that it moved me to action. I told the curate I was going to seek food, and felt my way towards the pantry. He made me no answer, but so soon as I began eating the faint noise I made stirred him up and I heard him crawling after me.

The Red Weed by Peter Fussey

Chapter Two
What We Saw from the Ruined House

After eating we crept back to the scullery, and there I must have dozed again, for when presently I looked round I was alone. The thudding vibration continued with wearisome persistence. I whispered for the curate several times, and at last felt my way to the door of the kitchen. It was still daylight, and I perceived him across the room, lying against the triangular hole that looked out upon the Martians. His shoulders were hunched, so that his head was hidden from me.

I could hear a number of noises almost like those in an engine shed; and the place rocked with that beating thud. Through the aperture in the wall I could see the top of a tree touched with gold and the warm blue of a tranquil evening sky. For a minute or so I remained watching the curate, and then I advanced, crouching and stepping with extreme care amid the broken crockery that littered the floor.

I touched the curate's leg, and he started so violently that a mass of plaster went sliding down outside and fell with a loud impact. I gripped his arm, fearing he might cry out, and for a long time we crouched motionless. Then I turned to see how much of our rampart remained. The detachment of the plaster had left a vertical slit open in the debris, and by raising myself cautiously across a beam I was able to see out of this gap into what had been overnight a quiet suburban roadway. Vast, indeed, was the change that we beheld.

The fifth cylinder must have fallen right into the midst of the house we had first visited. The building had vanished, completely smashed, pulverised, and dispersed by the blow. The cylinder lay now far beneath the original foundations--deep in a hole, already vastly larger than the pit I had looked into at Woking. The earth all round it had splashed under that tremendous impact--"splashed" is the only word--and lay in heaped piles that hid the masses of the adjacent houses. It had behaved exactly like mud under the violent blow of a hammer. Our house had collapsed backward; the front portion, even on the ground floor, had been destroyed completely; by a chance the kitchen and scullery had escaped, and stood buried now under soil and ruins, closed in by tons of earth on every side save towards the cylinder. Over that aspect we hung now on the very edge of the great circular pit the Martians were engaged in making. The heavy beating sound was evidently just behind us, and ever and again a bright green vapour drove up like a veil across our peephole.

The cylinder was already opened in the centre of the pit, and on the farther edge of the pit, amid the smashed and gravel-heaped shrubbery, one of the great fighting-machines, deserted by its occupant, stood stiff and tall against the evening sky. At first I scarcely noticed the pit and the cylinder, although it has been convenient to describe them first, on account of the extraordinary glittering mechanism I saw busy in the excavation, and on account of the strange creatures that were crawling slowly and painfully across the heaped mould near it.

The mechanism it certainly was that held my attention first. It was one of those complicated fabrics that have since been called handling-machines, and the study of which has already given such an enormous impetus to terrestrial invention. As it dawned upon me first, it presented a sort of metallic spider with five jointed, agile legs, and with an extraordinary number of jointed levers, bars, and reaching and clutching tentacles about its body. Most of its arms were retracted, but with three long tentacles it was fishing out a number of rods, plates, and bars which lined the covering and apparently strengthened the walls of the cylinder. These, as it extracted them, were lifted out and deposited upon a level surface of earth behind it.

Its motion was so swift, complex, and perfect that at first I did not see it as a machine, in spite of its metallic glitter. The fighting-machines were co-ordinated and animated to an extraordinary pitch, but nothing to compare with this. People who have never seen these structures, and have only the ill-imagined efforts of artists or the imperfect descriptions of such eye-witnesses as myself to go upon, scarcely realise that living quality.

I recall particularly the illustration of one of the first pamphlets to give a consecutive account of the war. The artist had evidently made a hasty study of one of the fighting-machines, and there his knowledge ended. He presented them as tilted, stiff tripods, without either flexibility or subtlety, and with an altogether misleading monotony of effect. The pamphlet containing these renderings had a considerable vogue, and I mention them here simply to warn the reader against the impression they may have created. They were no more like the Martians I saw in action than a Dutch doll is like a human being. To my mind, the pamphlet would have been much better without them.

At first, I say, the handling-machine did not impress me as a machine, but as a crablike creature with a glittering integument, the controlling Martian whose delicate tentacles actuated its movements seeming to be simply the equivalent of the crab's cerebral portion. But then I perceived the resemblance of its grey-brown, shiny, leathery integument to that of the other sprawling bodies beyond, and the true nature of this dexterous workman dawned upon me. With that realisation my interest shifted to those other creatures, the real Martians. Already I had had a transient impression of these, and the first nausea no longer obscured my observation. Moreover, I was concealed and motionless, and under no urgency of action.

They were, I now saw, the most unearthly creatures it is possible to conceive. They were huge round bodies--or, rather, heads--about four feet in diameter, each body having in front of it a face. This face had no nostrils--indeed, the Martians do not seem to have had any sense of smell, but it had a pair of very large dark-coloured eyes, and just beneath this a kind of fleshy beak. In the back of this head or body--I scarcely know how to speak of it--was the single tight tympanic surface, since known to be anatomically an ear, though it must have been almost useless in our dense air. In a group round the mouth were sixteen slender, almost whiplike tentacles, arranged in two bunches of eight each. These bunches have since been named rather aptly, by that distinguished anatomist, Professor Howes, the *hands*. Even as I saw these Martians for the first time they seemed to be endeavouring to raise themselves on these hands, but of course, with the increased weight of terrestrial conditions, this was impossible. There is reason to suppose that on Mars they may have progressed upon them with some facility.

The internal anatomy, I may remark here, as dissection has since shown, was almost equally simple. The greater part of the structure was the brain, sending enormous nerves to the eyes, ear, and tactile tentacles. Besides this were the bulky lungs, into which the mouth opened, and the heart and its vessels. The pulmonary distress caused by the denser atmosphere and greater gravitational attraction was only too evident in the convulsive movements of the outer skin.

And this was the sum of the Martian organs. Strange as it may seem to a human being, all the complex apparatus of digestion, which makes up the bulk of our bodies, did not exist in the Martians. They were heads--merely heads. Entrails they had none. They did not eat, much less digest. Instead, they took the fresh, living blood of other creatures, and injected it into their own veins. I have myself seen this being done, as I shall mention in its place. But, squeamish as I may seem, I cannot bring myself to describe what I could not endure even to continue watching. Let it suffice to say, blood obtained from a still living animal, in most cases from a human being, was run directly by means of a little pipette into the recipient canal....

The bare idea of this is no doubt horribly repulsive to us, but at the same time I think that we should remember how repulsive our carnivorous habits would seem to an intelligent rabbit.

The physiological advantages of the practice of injection are undeniable, if one thinks of the tremendous waste of human time and energy occasioned by eating and the digestive process. Our bodies are half made up of glands and tubes and organs, occupied in turning heterogeneous food into blood. The digestive processes and their reaction upon the nervous system sap our strength and colour our minds. Men go happy or miserable as they have healthy or unhealthy livers, or sound gastric glands. But the Martians were lifted above all these organic fluctuations of mood and emotion.

Their undeniable preference for men as their source of nourishment is partly explained by the nature of the remains of the victims they had brought with them as provisions from Mars. These creatures, to judge from the shrivelled remains that have fallen into human hands, were bipeds with flimsy, silicious skeletons (almost like those of the silicious sponges) and feeble musculature, standing about six feet high and having round, erect heads, and large eyes in flinty sockets. Two or three of these seem to have been brought in each cylinder, and all were killed before earth was reached. It was just as well for them, for the mere attempt to stand upright upon our planet would have broken every bone in their bodies.

And while I am engaged in this description, I may add in this place certain further details which, although they were not all evident to us at the time, will enable the reader who is unacquainted with them to form a clearer picture of these offensive creatures.

In three other points their physiology differed strangely from ours. Their organisms did not sleep, any more than the heart of man sleeps. Since they had no extensive muscular mechanism to recuperate, that periodical extinction was unknown to them. They had little or no sense of fatigue, it would seem. On earth they could never have moved without effort, yet even to the last they kept in action. In twenty-four hours they did twenty-four hours of work, as even on earth is perhaps the case with the ants.

In the next place, wonderful as it seems in a sexual world, the Martians were absolutely without sex, and therefore without any of the tumultuous emotions that arise from that difference among men. A young Martian, there can now be no dispute, was really born upon earth during the war, and it was found attached to its parent, partially *budded* off, just as young lilybulbs bud off, or like the young animals in the fresh-water polyp.

In man, in all the higher terrestrial animals, such a method of increase has disappeared; but even on this earth it was certainly the primitive method. Among the lower animals, up even to those first cousins of the vertebrated animals, the Tunicates, the two processes occur side by side, but finally the sexual method superseded its competitor altogether. On Mars, however, just the reverse has apparently been the case.

It is worthy of remark that a certain speculative writer of quasi-scientific repute, writing long before the Martian invasion, did forecast for man a final structure not unlike the actual Martian condition. His prophecy, I remember, appeared in November or December, 1893, in a long-defunct publication, the *Pall Mall Budget*, and I recall a caricature of it in a pre-Martian periodical called *Punch*. He pointed out--writing in a foolish, facetious tone--that the perfection of mechanical appliances must ultimately supersede limbs; the perfection of chemical devices, digestion; that such organs as hair, external nose, teeth, ears, and chin were no longer essential parts of the human being, and that the tendency of natural selection would lie in the direction of their steady diminution through the coming ages. The brain alone remained a cardinal necessity. Only one other part of the body had a strong case for survival, and that was the hand, "teacher and agent of the brain." While the rest of the body dwindled, the hands would grow larger.

There is many a true word written in jest, and here in the Martians we have beyond dispute the actual accomplishment of such a suppression of the animal side of the organism by the intelligence. To me it is quite credible that the Martians may be descended from beings not unlike ourselves, by a gradual development of brain and hands (the latter giving rise to the two bunches of delicate tentacles at last) at the expense of the rest of the body. Without the body the brain would, of course, become a mere selfish intelligence, without any of the emotional substratum of the human being.

The last salient point in which the systems of these creatures differed from ours was in what one might have thought a very trivial particular. Micro-organisms, which cause so much disease and pain on earth, have either never appeared upon Mars or Martian sanitary science eliminated them ages ago. A hundred diseases, all the fevers and contagions of human life, consumption, cancers, tumours and such morbidities, never enter the scheme of their life. And speaking of the differences between the life on Mars and terrestrial life, I may allude here to the curious suggestions of the red weed.

Apparently the vegetable kingdom in Mars, instead of having green for a dominant colour, is of a vivid blood-red tint. At any rate, the seeds which the Martians (intentionally or accidentally) brought with them gave rise in all cases to red-coloured growths. Only that known popularly as the red weed, however, gained any footing in competition with terrestrial forms. The red creeper was quite a transitory growth, and few people have seen it growing. For a time, however, the red weed grew with astonishing vigour and luxuriance. It spread up the sides of the pit by the third or fourth day of our imprisonment, and its cactus-like branches formed a carmine fringe to the edges of our triangular window. And afterwards I found it broadcast throughout the country, and especially wherever there was a stream of water.

The Martians had what appears to have been an auditory organ, a single round drum at the back of the head-body, and eyes with a visual range not very different from ours except that, according to Philips, blue and violet were as black to them. It is commonly supposed that they communicated by sounds and tentacular gesticulations; this is asserted, for instance, in the able but hastily compiled pamphlet (written evidently by someone not an eye-witness of Martian actions) to which I have already alluded, and which, so far, has been the chief source of information concerning them. Now no surviving human being saw so much of the Martians in action as I did. I take no credit to myself for an accident, but the fact is so. And I assert that I watched them closely time after time, and that I have seen four, five, and (once) six of them sluggishly performing the most elaborately complicated operations together without either sound or gesture. Their peculiar hooting invariably preceded feeding; it had no modulation, and was, I believe, in no sense a signal, but merely the expiration of air preparatory to the suctional operation. I have a certain claim to at least an elementary knowledge of psychology, and in this matter I am convinced--as firmly as I am convinced of anything--that the Martians interchanged thoughts without any physical intermediation. And I have been convinced of this in spite of strong preconceptions. Before the Martian invasion, as an occasional reader here or there may remember, I had written with some little vehemence against the telepathic theory.

The Martians wore no clothing. Their conceptions of ornament and decorum were necessarily different from ours; and not only were they evidently much less sensible of changes of temperature than we are, but changes of pressure do not seem to have affected their health at all seriously. Yet though they wore no clothing, it was in the other artificial additions to their bodily resources that their great superiority over man lay. We men, with our bicycles and road-skates, our Lilienthal soaring-machines, our guns and sticks and so forth, are just in the beginning of the evolution that the Martians have worked out. They have become practically mere brains, wearing different bodies according to their needs just as men wear suits of clothes and take a bicycle in a hurry or an umbrella in the wet. And of their appliances, perhaps nothing is more wonderful to a man than the curious fact that what is the dominant feature of almost all human devices in mechanism is absent—the *wheel* is absent; among all the things they brought to earth there is no trace or suggestion of their use of wheels. One would have at least expected it in locomotion. And in this connection it is curious to remark that even on this earth Nature has never hit upon the wheel, or has preferred other expedients to its development. And not only did the Martians either not know of (which is incredible), or abstain from, the wheel, but in their apparatus singularly little use is made of the fixed pivot or relatively fixed pivot, with circular motions thereabout confined to one plane. Almost all the joints of the machinery present a complicated system of sliding parts moving over small but beautifully curved friction bearings. And while upon this matter of detail, it is remarkable that the long leverages of their machines are in most cases actuated by a sort of sham musculature of the disks in an elastic sheath; these disks become polarised and drawn closely and powerfully together when traversed by a current of electricity. In this way the curious parallelism to animal motions, which was so striking and disturbing to the human beholder, was attained. Such quasi-muscles abounded in the crablike handling-machine which, on my first peeping out of the slit, I watched unpacking the cylinder.

It seemed infinitely more alive than the actual Martians lying beyond it in the sunset light, panting, stirring ineffectual tentacles, and moving feebly after their vast journey across space.

While I was still watching their sluggish motions in the sunlight, and noting each strange detail of their form, the curate reminded me of his presence by pulling violently at my arm. I turned to a scowling face, and silent, eloquent lips. He wanted the slit, which permitted only one of us to peep through; and so I had to forego watching them for a time while he enjoyed that privilege.

When I looked again, the busy handling-machine had already put together several of the pieces of apparatus it had taken out of the cylinder into a shape having an unmistakable likeness to its own; and down on the left a busy little digging mechanism had come into view, emitting jets of green vapour and working its way round the pit, excavating and embanking in a methodical and discriminating manner. This it was which had caused the regular beating noise, and the rhythmic shocks that had kept our ruinous refuge quivering. It piped and whistled as it worked. So far as I could see, the thing was without a directing Martian at all.

Chapter Three
The Days of Imprisonment

The arrival of a second fighting-machine drove us from our peephole into the scullery, for we feared that from his elevation the Martian might see down upon us behind our barrier. At a later date we began to feel less in danger of their eyes, for to an eye in the dazzle of the sunlight outside our refuge must have been blank blackness, but at first the slightest suggestion of approach drove us into the scullery in heart-throbbing retreat. Yet terrible as was the danger we incurred, the attraction of peeping was for both of us irresistible. And I recall now with a sort of wonder that, in spite of the infinite danger in which we were between starvation and a still more terrible death, we could yet struggle bitterly for that horrible privilege of sight. We would race across the kitchen in a grotesque way between eagerness and the dread of making a noise, and strike each other, and thrust add kick, within a few inches of exposure.

The fact is that we had absolutely incompatible dispositions and habits of thought and action, and our danger and isolation only accentuated the incompatibility. At Halliford I had already come to hate the curate's trick of helpless exclamation, his stupid rigidity of mind. His endless muttering monologue vitiated every effort I made to think out a line of action, and drove me at times, thus pent up and intensified, almost to the verge of craziness. He was as lacking in restraint as a silly woman. He would weep for hours together, and I verily believe that to the very end this spoiled child of life thought his weak tears in some way efficacious. And I would sit in the darkness unable to keep my mind off him by reason of his importunities. He ate more than I did, and it was in vain I pointed out that our only chance of life was to stop in the house until the Martians had done with their pit, that in that long patience a time might presently come when we should need food. He ate and drank impulsively in heavy meals at long intervals. He slept little.

As the days wore on, his utter carelessness of any consideration so intensified our distress and danger that I had, much as I loathed doing it, to resort to threats, and at last to blows. That brought him to reason for a time. But he was one of those weak creatures, void of pride, timorous, anaemic, hateful souls, full of shifty cunning, who face neither God nor man, who face not even themselves.

It is disagreeable for me to recall and write these things, but I set them down that my story may lack nothing. Those who have escaped the dark and terrible aspects of life will find my brutality, my flash of rage in our final tragedy, easy enough to blame; for they know what is wrong as well as any, but not what is possible to tortured men. But those who have been under the shadow, who have gone down at last to elemental things, will have a wider charity.

And while within we fought out our dark, dim contest of whispers, snatched food and drink, and gripping hands and blows, without, in the pitiless sunlight of that terrible June, was the strange wonder, the unfamiliar routine of the Martians in the pit. Let me return to those first new experiences of mine. After a long time I ventured back to the peephole, to find that the new-comers had been reinforced by the occupants of no fewer than three of the fighting-machines. These last had brought with them certain fresh appliances that stood in an orderly manner about the cylinder. The second handling-machine was now completed, and was busied in serving one of the novel contrivances the big machine had brought. This was a body resembling a milk can in its general form, above which oscillated a pear-shaped receptacle, and from which a stream of white powder flowed into a circular basin below.

The oscillatory motion was imparted to this by one tentacle of the handling-machine. With two spatulate hands the handling-machine was digging out and flinging masses of clay into the pear-shaped receptacle above, while with another arm it periodically opened a door and removed rusty and blackened clinkers from the middle part of the machine. Another steely tentacle directed the powder from the basin along a ribbed channel towards some receiver that was hidden from me by the mound of bluish dust. From this unseen receiver a little thread of green smoke rose vertically into the quiet air. As I looked, the handling-machine, with a faint and musical clinking, extended, telescopic fashion, a tentacle that had been a moment before a mere blunt projection, until its end was hidden behind the mound of clay. In another second it had lifted a bar of white aluminium into sight, untarnished as yet, and shining dazzlingly, and deposited it in a growing stack of bars that stood at the side of the pit. Between sunset and starlight this dexterous machine must have made more than a hundred such bars out of the crude clay, and the mound of bluish dust rose steadily until it topped the side of the pit.

The contrast between the swift and complex movements of these contrivances and the inert panting clumsiness of their masters was acute, and for days I had to tell myself repeatedly that these latter were indeed the living of the two things.

The curate had possession of the slit when the first men were brought to the pit. I was sitting below, huddled up, listening with all my ears. He made a sudden movement backward, and I, fearful that we were observed, crouched in a spasm of terror. He came sliding down the rubbish and crept beside me in the darkness, inarticulate, gesticulating, and for a moment I shared his panic. His gesture suggested a resignation of the slit, and after a little while my curiosity gave me courage, and I rose up, stepped across him, and clambered up to it. At first I could see no reason for his frantic behaviour. The twilight had now come, the stars were little and faint, but the pit was illuminated by the flickering green fire that came from the aluminium-making. The whole picture was a flickering scheme of green gleams and shifting rusty black shadows, strangely trying to the eyes. Over and through it all went the bats, heeding it not at all. The sprawling Martians were no longer to be seen, the mound of blue-green powder had risen to cover them from sight, and a fighting-machine, with its legs contracted, crumpled, and abbreviated, stood across the corner of the pit. And then, amid the clangour of the machinery, came a drifting suspicion of human voices, that I entertained at first only to dismiss.

I crouched, watching this fighting-machine closely, satisfying myself now for the first time that the hood did indeed contain a Martian. As the green flames lifted I could see the oily gleam of his integument and the brightness of his eyes. And suddenly I heard a yell, and saw a long tentacle reaching over the shoulder of the machine to the little cage that hunched upon its back. Then something--something struggling violently--was lifted high against the sky, a black, vague enigma against the starlight; and as this black object came down again, I saw by the green brightness that it was a man. For an instant he was clearly visible. He was a stout, ruddy, middle-aged man, well dressed; three days before, he must have been walking the world, a man of considerable consequence. I could see his staring eyes and gleams of light on his studs and watch chain. He vanished behind the mound, and for a moment there was silence. And then began a shrieking and a sustained and cheerful hooting from the Martians.

I slid down the rubbish, struggled to my feet, clapped my hands over my ears, and bolted into the scullery. The curate, who had been crouching silently with his arms over his head, looked up as I passed, cried out quite loudly at my desertion of him, and came running after me.

That night, as we lurked in the scullery, balanced between our horror and the terrible fascination this peeping had, although I felt an urgent need of action I tried in vain to conceive some plan of escape; but afterwards, during the second day, I was able to consider our position with great clearness. The curate, I found, was quite incapable of discussion; this new and culminating atrocity had robbed him of all vestiges of reason or forethought. Practically he had already sunk to the level of an animal. But as the saying goes, I gripped myself with both hands. It grew upon my mind, once I could face the facts, that terrible as our position was, there was as yet no justification for absolute despair. Our chief chance lay in the possibility of the Martians making the pit nothing more than a temporary encampment. Or even if they kept it permanently, they might not consider it necessary to guard it, and a chance of escape might be afforded us. I also weighed very carefully the possibility of our digging a way out in a direction away from the pit, but the chances of our emerging within sight of some sentinel fighting-machine seemed at first too great. And I should have had to do all the digging myself. The curate would certainly have failed me.

It was on the third day, if my memory serves me right, that I saw the lad killed. It was the only occasion on which I actually saw the Martians feed. After that experience I avoided the hole in the wall for the better part of a day. I went into the scullery, removed the door, and spent some hours digging with my hatchet as silently as possible; but when I had made a hole about a couple of feet deep the loose earth collapsed noisily, and I did not dare continue. I lost heart, and lay down on the scullery floor for a long time, having no spirit even to move. And after that I abandoned altogether the idea of escaping by excavation.

It says much for the impression the Martians had made upon me that at first I entertained little or no hope of our escape being brought about by their overthrow through any human effort. But on the fourth or fifth night I heard a sound like heavy guns.

It was very late in the night, and the moon was shining brightly. The Martians had taken away the excavating-machine, and, save for a fighting-machine that stood in the remoter bank of the pit and a handling-machine that was buried out of my sight in a corner of the pit immediately beneath my peephole, the place was deserted by them. Except for the pale glow from the handling-machine and the bars and patches of white moonlight the pit was in darkness, and, except for the clinking of the handling-machine, quite still. That night was a beautiful serenity; save for one planet, the moon seemed to have the sky to herself. I heard a dog howling, and that familiar sound it was that made me listen. Then I heard quite distinctly a booming exactly like the sound of great guns. Six distinct reports I counted, and after a long interval six again. And that was all.

Chapter Four
The Death of the Curate

It was on the sixth day of our imprisonment that I peeped for the last time, and presently found myself alone. Instead of keeping close to me and trying to oust me from the slit, the curate had gone back into the scullery. I was struck by a sudden thought. I went back quickly and quietly into the scullery. In the darkness I heard the curate drinking. I snatched in the darkness, and my fingers caught a bottle of burgundy.

For a few minutes there was a tussle. The bottle struck the floor and broke, and I desisted and rose. We stood panting and threatening each other. In the end I planted myself between him and the food, and told him of my determination to begin a discipline. I divided the food in the pantry, into rations to last us ten days. I would not let him eat any more that day. In the afternoon he made a feeble effort to get at the food. I had been dozing, but in an instant I was awake. All day and all night we sat face to face, I weary but resolute, and he weeping and complaining of his immediate hunger. It was, I know, a night and a day, but to me it seemed--it seems now--an interminable length of time.

And so our widened incompatibility ended at last in open conflict. For two vast days we struggled in undertones and wrestling contests. There were times when I beat and kicked him madly, times when I cajoled and persuaded him, and once I tried to bribe him with the last bottle of burgundy, for there was a rain-water pump from which I could get water. But neither force nor kindness availed; he was indeed beyond reason. He would neither desist from his attacks on the food nor from his noisy babbling to himself. The rudimentary precautions to keep our imprisonment endurable he would not observe. Slowly I began to realise the complete overthrow of his intelligence, to perceive that my sole companion in this close and sickly darkness was a man insane.

From certain vague memories I am inclined to think my own mind wandered at times. I had strange and hideous dreams whenever I slept. It sounds paradoxical, but I am inclined to think that the weakness and insanity of the curate warned me, braced me, and kept me a sane man.

On the eighth day he began to talk aloud instead of whispering, and nothing I could do would moderate his speech.

"It is just, O God!" he would say, over and over again. "It is just. On me and mine be the punishment laid. We have sinned, we have fallen short. There was poverty, sorrow; the poor were trodden in the dust, and I held my peace. I preached acceptable folly--my God, what folly!--when I should have stood up, though I died for it, and called upon them to repent-repent!... Oppressors of the poor and needy... ! The wine press of God!"

Then he would suddenly revert to the matter of the food I withheld from him, praying, begging, weeping, at last threatening. He began to raise his voice--I prayed him not to. He perceived a hold on me--he threatened he would shout and bring the Martians upon us. For a time that scared me; but any concession would have shortened our chance of escape beyond estimating. I defied him, although I felt no assurance that he might not do this thing. But that day, at any rate, he did not. He talked with his voice rising slowly, through the greater part of the eighth and ninth days--threats, entreaties, mingled with a torrent of half-sane and always frothy repentance for his vacant sham of God's service, such as made me pity him. Then he slept awhile, and began again with renewed strength, so loudly that I must needs make him desist.

"Be still!" I implored.

He rose to his knees, for he had been sitting in the darkness near the copper.

"I have been still too long," he said, in a tone that must have reached the pit, "and now I must bear my witness. Woe unto this unfaithful city! Woe! Woe! Woe! Woe! Woe! To the inhabitants of the earth by reason of the other voices of the trumpet----"

"Shut up!" I said, rising to my feet, and in a terror lest the Martians should hear us. "For God's sake----"

"Nay," shouted the curate, at the top of his voice, standing likewise and extending his arms. "Speak! The word of the Lord is upon me!"

In three strides he was at the door leading into the kitchen.

"I must bear my witness! I go! It has already been too long delayed."

I put out my hand and felt the meat chopper hanging to the wall. In a flash I was after him. I was fierce with fear. Before he was halfway across the kitchen I had overtaken him. With one last touch of humanity I turned the blade back and struck him with the butt. He went headlong forward and lay stretched on the ground. I stumbled over him and stood panting. He lay still.

Suddenly I heard a noise without, the run and smash of slipping plaster, and the triangular aperture in the wall was darkened. I looked up and saw the lower surface of a handling-machine coming slowly across the hole. One of its gripping limbs curled amid the debris; another limb appeared, feeling its way over the fallen beams. I stood petrified, staring. Then I saw through a sort of glass plate near the edge of the body the face, as we may call it, and the large dark eyes of a Martian, peering, and then a long metallic snake of tentacle came feeling slowly through the hole.

I turned by an effort, stumbled over the curate, and stopped at the scullery door. The tentacle was now some way, two yards or more, in the room, and twisting and turning, with queer sudden movements, this way and that. For a while I stood fascinated by that slow, fitful advance. Then, with a faint, hoarse cry, I forced myself across the scullery. I trembled violently; I could scarcely stand upright. I opened the door of the coal cellar, and stood there in the darkness staring at the faintly lit doorway into the kitchen, and listening. Had the Martian seen me? What was it doing now?

Something was moving to and fro there, very quietly; every now and then it tapped against the wall, or started on its movements with a faint metallic ringing, like the movements of keys on a split-ring. Then a heavy body--I knew too well what--was dragged across the floor of the kitchen towards the opening. Irresistibly attracted, I crept to the door and peeped into the kitchen. In the triangle of bright outer sunlight I saw the Martian, in its Briareus of a handling-machine, scrutinizing the curate's head. I thought at once that it would infer my presence from the mark of the blow I had given him.

I crept back to the coal cellar, shut the door, and began to cover myself up as much as I could, and as noiselessly as possible in the darkness, among the firewood and coal therein. Every now and then I paused, rigid, to hear if the Martian had thrust its tentacles through the opening again.

Then the faint metallic jingle returned. I traced it slowly feeling over the kitchen. Presently I heard it nearer--in the scullery, as I judged. I thought that its length might be insufficient to reach me. I prayed copiously. It passed, scraping faintly across the cellar door. An age of almost intolerable suspense intervened; then I heard it fumbling at the latch! It had found the door! The Martians understood doors!

It worried at the catch for a minute, perhaps, and then the door opened.

In the darkness I could just see the thing--like an elephant's trunk more than anything else--waving towards me and touching and examining the wall, coals, wood and ceiling. It was like a black worm swaying its blind head to and fro.

Once, even, it touched the heel of my boot. I was on the verge of screaming; I bit my hand. For a time the tentacle was silent. I could have fancied it had been withdrawn. Presently, with an abrupt click, it gripped something--I thought it had me!--and seemed to go out of the cellar again. For a minute I was not sure. Apparently it had taken a lump of coal to examine.

I seized the opportunity of slightly shifting my position, which had become cramped, and then listened. I whispered passionate prayers for safety.

Then I heard the slow, deliberate sound creeping towards me again. Slowly, slowly it drew near, scratching against the walls and tapping the furniture.

While I was still doubtful, it rapped smartly against the cellar door and closed it. I heard it go into the pantry, and the biscuit-tins rattled and a bottle smashed, and then came a heavy bump against the cellar door. Then silence that passed into an infinity of suspense.

Had it gone?

At last I decided that it had.

It came into the scullery no more; but I lay all the tenth day in the close darkness, buried among coals and firewood, not daring even to crawl out for the drink for which I craved. It was the eleventh day before I ventured so far from my security.

Chapter Five
The Stillness

My first act before I went into the pantry was to fasten the door between the kitchen and the scullery. But the pantry was empty; every scrap of food had gone. Apparently, the Martian had taken it all on the previous day. At that discovery I despaired for the first time. I took no food, or no drink either, on the eleventh or the twelfth day.

At first my mouth and throat were parched, and my strength ebbed sensibly. I sat about in the darkness of the scullery, in a state of despondent wretchedness. My mind ran on eating. I thought I had become deaf, for the noises of movement I had been accustomed to hear from the pit had ceased absolutely. I did not feel strong enough to crawl noiselessly to the peephole, or I would have gone there.

On the twelfth day my throat was so painful that, taking the chance of alarming the Martians, I attacked the creaking rain-water pump that stood by the sink, and got a couple of glassfuls of blackened and tainted rain water. I was greatly refreshed by this, and emboldened by the fact that no enquiring tentacle followed the noise of my pumping.

During these days, in a rambling, inconclusive way, I thought much of the curate and of the manner of his death.

On the thirteenth day I drank some more water, and dozed and thought disjointedly of eating and of vague impossible plans of escape. Whenever I dozed I dreamt of horrible phantasms, of the death of the curate, or of sumptuous dinners; but, asleep or awake, I felt a keen pain that urged me to drink again and again. The light that came into the scullery was no longer grey, but red. To my disordered imagination it seemed the colour of blood.

On the fourteenth day I went into the kitchen, and I was surprised to find that the fronds of the red weed had grown right across the hole in the wall, turning the half-light of the place into a crimson-coloured obscurity.

It was early on the fifteenth day that I heard a curious, familiar sequence of sounds in the kitchen, and, listening, identified it as the snuffing and scratching of a dog. Going into the kitchen, I saw a dog's nose peering in through a break among the ruddy fronds. This greatly surprised me. At the scent of me he barked shortly.

I thought if I could induce him to come into the place quietly I should be able, perhaps, to kill and eat him; and in any case, it would be advisable to kill him, lest his actions attracted the attention of the Martians.

I crept forward, saying "Good dog!" very softly; but he suddenly withdrew his head and disappeared. I listened--I was not deaf--but certainly the pit was still. I heard a sound like the flutter of a bird's wings, and a hoarse croaking, but that was all.

For a long while I lay close to the peephole, but not daring to move aside the red plants that obscured it. Once or twice I heard a faint pitter-patter like the feet of the dog going hither and thither on the sand far below me, and there were more birdlike sounds, but that was all. At length, encouraged by the silence, I looked out.

Except in the corner, where a multitude of crows hopped and fought over the skeletons of the dead the Martians had consumed, there was not a living thing in the pit.

I stared about me, scarcely believing my eyes. All the machinery had gone. Save for the big mound of greyish-blue powder in one corner, certain bars of aluminium in another, the black birds, and the skeletons of the killed, the place was merely an empty circular pit in the sand.

Slowly I thrust myself out through the red weed, and stood upon the mound of rubble. I could see in any direction save behind me, to the north, and neither Martians nor sign of Martians were to be seen. The pit dropped sheerly from my feet, but a little way along the rubbish afforded a practicable slope to the summit of the ruins. My chance of escape had come. I began to tremble.

I hesitated for some time, and then, in a gust of desperate resolution, and with a heart that throbbed violently, I scrambled to the top of the mound in which I had been buried so long.

I looked about again. To the northward, too, no Martian was visible.

When I had last seen this part of Sheen in the daylight it had been a straggling street of comfortable white and red houses, interspersed with abundant shady trees. Now I stood on a mound of smashed brickwork, clay, and gravel, over which spread a multitude of red cactus-shaped plants, knee-high, without a solitary terrestrial growth to dispute their footing. The trees near me were dead and brown, but further a network of red thread scaled the still living stems.

The neighbouring houses had all been wrecked, but none had been burned; their walls stood, sometimes to the second story, with smashed windows and shattered doors. The red weed grew tumultuously in their roofless rooms. Below me was the great pit, with the crows struggling for its refuse. A number of other birds hopped about among the ruins. Far away I saw a gaunt cat slink crouchingly along a wall, but traces of men there were none.

The day seemed, by contrast with my recent confinement, dazzlingly bright, the sky a glowing blue. A gentle breeze kept the red weed that covered every scrap of unoccupied ground gently swaying. And oh! the sweetness of the air!

Chapter Six
The Work of Fifteen Days

For some time I stood tottering on the mound regardless of my safety. Within that noisome den from which I had emerged I had thought with a narrow intensity only of our immediate security. I had not realised what had been happening to the world, had not anticipated this startling vision of unfamiliar things. I had expected to see Sheen in ruins--I found about me the landscape, weird and lurid, of another planet.

For that moment I touched an emotion beyond the common range of men, yet one that the poor brutes we dominate know only too well. I felt as a rabbit might feel returning to his burrow and suddenly confronted by the work of a dozen busy navvies digging the foundations of a house. I felt the first inkling of a thing that presently grew quite clear in my mind, that oppressed me for many days, a sense of dethronement, a persuasion that I was no longer a master, but an animal among the animals, under the Martian heel. With us it would be as with them, to lurk and watch, to run and hide; the fear and empire of man had passed away.

But so soon as this strangeness had been realised it passed, and my dominant motive became the hunger of my long and dismal fast. In the direction away from the pit I saw, beyond a red-covered wall, a patch of garden ground unburied. This gave me a hint, and I went knee-deep, and sometimes neck-deep, in the red weed. The density of the weed gave me a reassuring sense of hiding. The wall was some six feet high, and when I attempted to clamber it I found I could not lift my feet to the crest. So I went along by the side of it, and came to a corner and a rockwork that enabled me to get to the top, and tumble into the garden I coveted. Here I found some young onions, a couple of gladiolus bulbs, and a quantity of immature carrots, all of which I secured, and, scrambling over a ruined wall, went on my way through scarlet and crimson trees towards Kew--it was like walking through an avenue of gigantic blood drops--possessed with two ideas: to get more food, and to limp, as soon and as far as my strength permitted, out of this accursed unearthly region of the pit.

Some way farther, in a grassy place, was a group of mushrooms which also I devoured, and then I came upon a brown sheet of flowing shallow water, where meadows used to be. These fragments of nourishment served only to whet my hunger. At first I was surprised at this flood in a hot, dry summer, but afterwards I discovered that it was caused by the tropical exuberance of the red weed. Directly this extraordinary growth encountered water it straightway became gigantic and of unparalleled fecundity. Its seeds were simply poured down into the water of the Wey and Thames, and its swiftly growing and Titanic water fronds speedily choked both those rivers.

At Putney, as I afterwards saw, the bridge was almost lost in a tangle of this weed, and at Richmond, too, the Thames water poured in a broad and shallow stream across the meadows of Hampton and Twickenham. As the water spread the weed followed them, until the ruined villas of the Thames valley were for a time lost in this red swamp, whose margin I explored, and much of the desolation the Martians had caused was concealed.

In the end the red weed succumbed almost as quickly as it had spread. A cankering disease, due, it is believed, to the action of certain bacteria, presently seized upon it. Now by the action of natural selection, all terrestrial plants have acquired a resisting power against bacterial diseases--they never succumb without a severe struggle, but the red weed rotted like a thing already dead. The fronds became bleached, and then shrivelled and brittle. They broke off at the least touch, and the waters that had stimulated their early growth carried their last vestiges out to sea.

My first act on coming to this water was, of course, to slake my thirst. I drank a great deal of it and, moved by an impulse, gnawed some fronds of red weed; but they were watery, and had a sickly, metallic taste. I found the water was sufficiently shallow for me to wade securely, although the red weed impeded my feet a little; but the flood evidently got deeper towards the river, and I turned back to Mortlake. I managed to make out the road by means of occasional ruins of its villas and fences and lamps, and so presently I got out of this spate and made my way to the hill going up towards Roehampton and came out on Putney Common.

Here the scenery changed from the strange and unfamiliar to the wreckage of the familiar: patches of ground exhibited the devastation of a cyclone, and in a few score yards I would come upon perfectly undisturbed spaces, houses with their blinds trimly drawn and doors closed, as if they had been left for a day by the owners, or as if their inhabitants slept within. The red weed was less abundant; the tall trees along the lane were free from the red creeper. I hunted for food among the trees, finding nothing, and I also raided a couple of silent houses, but they had already been broken into and ransacked. I rested for the remainder of the daylight in a shrubbery, being, in my enfeebled condition, too fatigued to push on.

All this time I saw no human beings, and no signs of the Martians. I encountered a couple of hungry-looking dogs, but both hurried circuitously away from the advances I made them. Near Roehampton I had seen two human skeletons--not bodies, but skeletons, picked clean--and in the wood by me I found the crushed and scattered bones of several cats and rabbits and the skull of a sheep. But though I gnawed parts of these in my mouth, there was nothing to be got from them.

After sunset I struggled on along the road towards Putney, where I think the Heat-Ray must have been used for some reason. And in the garden beyond Roehampton I got a quantity of immature potatoes, sufficient to stay my hunger. From this garden one looked down upon Putney and the river. The aspect of the place in the dusk was singularly desolate: blackened trees, blackened, desolate ruins, and down the hill the sheets of the flooded river, red-tinged with the weed. And over all--silence. It filled me with indescribable terror to think how swiftly that desolating change had come.

For a time I believed that mankind had been swept out of existence, and that I stood there alone, the last man left alive. Hard by the top of Putney Hill I came upon another skeleton, with the arms dislocated and removed several yards from the rest of the body. As I proceeded I became more and more convinced that the extermination of mankind was, save for such stragglers as myself, already accomplished in this part of the world. The Martians, I thought, had gone on and left the country desolated, seeking food elsewhere. Perhaps even now they were destroying Berlin or Paris, or it might be they had gone northward.

Chapter Seven
The Man on Putney Hill

I spent that night in the inn that stands at the top of Putney Hill, sleeping in a made bed for the first time since my flight to Leatherhead. I will not tell the needless trouble I had breaking into that house--afterwards I found the front door was on the latch--nor how I ransacked every room for food, until just on the verge of despair, in what seemed to me to be a servant's bedroom, I found a rat-gnawed crust and two tins of pineapple. The place had been already searched and emptied. In the bar I afterwards found some biscuits and sandwiches that had been overlooked. The latter I could not eat, they were too rotten, but the former not only stayed my hunger, but filled my pockets. I lit no lamps, fearing some Martian might come beating that part of London for food in the night. Before I went to bed I had an interval of restlessness, and prowled from window to window, peering out for some sign of these monsters. I slept little. As I lay in bed I found myself thinking consecutively--a thing I do not remember to have done since my last argument with the curate. During all the intervening time my mental condition had been a hurrying succession of vague emotional states or a sort of stupid receptivity. But in the night my brain, reinforced, I suppose, by the food I had eaten, grew clear again, and I thought.

Three things struggled for possession of my mind: the killing of the curate, the whereabouts of the Martians, and the possible fate of my wife. The former gave me no sensation of horror or remorse to recall; I saw it simply as a thing done, a memory infinitely disagreeable but quite without the quality of remorse. I saw myself then as I see myself now, driven step by step towards that hasty blow, the creature of a sequence of accidents leading inevitably to that. I felt no condemnation; yet the memory, static, unprogressive, haunted me. In the silence of the night, with that sense of the nearness of God that sometimes comes into the stillness and the darkness, I stood my trial, my only trial, for that moment of wrath and fear. I retraced every step of our conversation from the moment when I had found him crouching beside me, heedless of my thirst, and pointing to the fire and smoke that streamed up from the ruins of Weybridge. We had been incapable of co-operation--grim chance had taken no heed of that. Had I foreseen, I should have left him at Halliford. But I did not foresee; and crime is to foresee and do. And I set this down as I have set all this story down, as it was. There were no witnesses--all these things I might have concealed. But I set it down, and the reader must form his judgment as he will.

And when, by an effort, I had set aside that picture of a prostrate body, I faced the problem of the Martians and the fate of my wife. For the former I had no data; I could imagine a hundred things, and so, unhappily, I could for the latter. And suddenly that night became terrible. I found myself sitting up in bed, staring at the dark. I found myself praying that the Heat-Ray might have suddenly and painlessly struck her out of being. Since the night of my return from Leatherhead I had not prayed. I had uttered prayers, fetish prayers, had prayed as heathens mutter charms when I was in extremity; but now I prayed indeed, pleading steadfastly and sanely, face to face with the darkness of God. Strange night! Strangest in this, that so soon as dawn had come, I, who had talked with God, crept out of the house like a rat leaving its hiding place--a creature scarcely larger, an inferior animal, a thing that for any passing whim of our masters might be hunted and killed. Perhaps they also prayed confidently to God. Surely, if we have learned nothing else, this war has taught us pity--pity for those witless souls that suffer our dominion.

The morning was bright and fine, and the eastern sky glowed pink, and was fretted with little golden clouds. In the road that runs from the top of Putney Hill to Wimbledon was a number of poor vestiges of the panic torrent that must have poured Londonward on the Sunday night after the fighting began. There was a little two-wheeled cart inscribed with the name of Thomas Lobb, Greengrocer, New Malden, with a smashed wheel and an abandoned tin trunk; there was a straw hat trampled into the now hardened mud, and at the top of West Hill a lot of blood-stained glass about the overturned water trough. My movements were languid, my plans of the vaguest. I had an idea of going to Leatherhead, though I knew that there I had the poorest chance of finding my wife. Certainly, unless death had overtaken them suddenly, my cousins and she would have fled thence; but it seemed to me I might find or learn there whither the Surrey people had fled. I knew I wanted to find my wife, that my heart ached for her and the world of men, but I had no clear idea how the finding might be done. I was also sharply aware now of my intense loneliness. From the corner I went, under cover of a thicket of trees and bushes, to the edge of Wimbledon Common, stretching wide and far.

That dark expanse was lit in patches by yellow gorse and broom; there was no red weed to be seen, and as I prowled, hesitating, on the verge of the open, the sun rose, flooding it all with light and vitality. I came upon a busy swarm of little frogs in a swampy place among the trees. I stopped to look at them, drawing a lesson from their stout resolve to live. And presently, turning suddenly, with an odd feeling of being watched, I beheld something crouching amid a clump of bushes. I stood regarding this. I made a step towards it, and it rose up and became a man armed with a cutlass. I approached him slowly. He stood silent and motionless, regarding me.

As I drew nearer I perceived he was dressed in clothes as dusty and filthy as my own; he looked, indeed, as though he had been dragged through a culvert. Nearer, I distinguished the green slime of ditches mixing with the pale drab of dried clay and shiny, coaly patches. His black hair fell over his eyes, and his face was dark and dirty and sunken, so that at first I did not recognise him. There was a red cut across the lower part of his face.

"Stop!" he cried, when I was within ten yards of him, and I stopped. His voice was hoarse. "Where do you come from?" he said.

I thought, surveying him.

"I come from Mortlake," I said. "I was buried near the pit the Martians made about their cylinder. I have worked my way out and escaped."

"There is no food about here," he said. "This is my country. All this hill down to the river, and back to Clapham, and up to the edge of the common. There is only food for one. Which way are you going?"

I answered slowly.

"I don't know," I said. "I have been buried in the ruins of a house thirteen or fourteen days. I don't know what has happened."

He looked at me doubtfully, then started, and looked with a changed expression.

"I've no wish to stop about here," said I. "I think I shall go to Leatherhead, for my wife was there."

He shot out a pointing finger.

"It is you," said he; "the man from Woking. And you weren't killed at Weybridge?"

I recognised him at the same moment.

"You are the artilleryman who came into my garden."

"Good luck!" he said. "We are lucky ones! Fancy **you**!" He put out a hand, and I took it. "I crawled up a drain," he said. "But they didn't kill everyone. And after they went away I got off towards Walton across the fields. But---- It's not sixteen days altogether--and your hair is grey." He looked over his shoulder suddenly. "Only a rook," he said. "One gets to know that birds have shadows these days. This is a bit open. Let us crawl under those bushes and talk."

"Have you seen any Martians?" I said. "Since I crawled out----"

"They've gone away across London," he said. "I guess they've got a bigger camp there. Of a night, all over there, Hampstead way, the sky is alive with their lights. It's like a great city, and in the glare you can just see them moving. By daylight you can't. But nearer--I haven't seen them--" (he counted on his fingers) "five days. Then I saw a couple across Hammersmith way carrying something big. And the night before last"--he stopped and spoke impressively--"it was just a matter of lights, but it was something up in the air. I believe they've built a flying-machine, and are learning to fly."

I stopped, on hands and knees, for we had come to the bushes.

"Fly!"

"Yes," he said, "fly."

I went on into a little bower, and sat down.

"It is all over with humanity," I said. "If they can do that they will simply go round the world."

He nodded.

"They will. But---- It will relieve things over here a bit. And besides----" He looked at me. "Aren't you satisfied it **is** up with humanity? I am. We're down; we're beat."

I stared. Strange as it may seem, I had not arrived at this fact--a fact perfectly obvious so soon as he spoke. I had still held a vague hope; rather, I had kept a lifelong habit of mind. He repeated his words, "We're beat." They carried absolute conviction.

"It's all over," he said. "They've lost *one*--just *one.* And they've made their footing good and crippled the greatest power in the world. They've walked over us. The death of that one at Weybridge was an accident. And these are only pioneers. They kept on coming. These green stars--I've seen none these five or six days, but I've no doubt they're falling somewhere every night. Nothing's to be done. We're under! We're beat!"

I made him no answer. I sat staring before me, trying in vain to devise some countervailing thought.

"This isn't a war," said the artilleryman. "It never was a war, any more than there's war between man and ants."

Suddenly I recalled the night in the observatory.

"After the tenth shot they fired no more--at least, until the first cylinder came."

"How do you know?" said the artilleryman. I explained. He thought. "Something wrong with the gun," he said. "But what if there is? They'll get it right again. And even if there's a delay, how can it alter the end? It's just men and ants. There's the ants builds their cities, live their lives, have wars, revolutions, until the men want them out of the way, and then they go out of the way. That's what we are now--just ants. Only----"

"Yes," I said.

"We're eatable ants."

We sat looking at each other.

"And what will they do with us?" I said.

"That's what I've been thinking," he said; "that's what I've been thinking. After Weybridge I went south--thinking. I saw what was up. Most of the people were hard at it squealing and exciting themselves. But I'm not so fond of squealing. I've been in sight of death once or twice; I'm not an ornamental soldier, and at the best and worst, death--it's just death. And it's the man that keeps on thinking comes through. I saw everyone tracking away south. Says I, "Food won't last this way," and I turned right back. I went for the Martians like a sparrow goes for man. All round"--he waved a hand to the horizon--"they're starving in heaps, bolting, treading on each other...."

He saw my face, and halted awkwardly.

"No doubt lots who had money have gone away to France," he said. He seemed to hesitate whether to apologise, met my eyes, and went on: "There's food all about here. Canned things in shops; wines, spirits, mineral waters; and the water mains and drains are empty. Well, I was telling you what I was thinking. "Here's intelligent things," I said, "and it seems they want us for food. First, they'll smash us up--ships, machines, guns, cities, all the order and organisation. All that will go. If we were the size of ants we might pull through. But we're not. It's all too bulky to stop. That's the first certainty." Eh?"

I assented.

"It is; I've thought it out. Very well, then--next; at present we're caught as we're wanted. A Martian has only to go a few miles to get a crowd on the run. And I saw one, one day, out by Wandsworth, picking houses to pieces and routing among the wreckage. But they won't keep on doing that. So soon as they've settled all our guns and ships, and smashed our railways, and done all the things they are doing over there, they will begin catching us systematic, picking the best and storing us in cages and things. That's what they will start doing in a bit. Lord! They haven't begun on us yet. Don't you see that?"

"Not begun!" I exclaimed.

"Not begun. All that's happened so far is through our not having the sense to keep quiet--worrying them with guns and such foolery. And losing our heads, and rushing off in crowds to where there wasn't any more safety than where we were. They don't want to bother us yet. They're making their things--making all the things they couldn't bring with them, getting things ready for the rest of their people. Very likely that's why the cylinders have stopped for a bit, for fear of hitting those who are here. And instead of our rushing about blind, on the howl, or getting dynamite on the chance of busting them up, we've got to fix ourselves up according to the new state of affairs. That's how I figure it out. It isn't quite according to what a man wants for his species, but it's about what the facts point to. And that's the principle I acted upon. Cities, nations, civilisation, progress--it's all over. That game's up. We're beat."

"But if that is so, what is there to live for?"

The artilleryman looked at me for a moment.

"There won't be any more blessed concerts for a million years or so; there won't be any Royal Academy of Arts, and no nice little feeds at restaurants. If it's amusement you're after, I reckon the game is up. If you've got any drawing-room manners or a dislike to eating peas with a knife or dropping aitches, you'd better chuck 'em away. They ain't no further use."

"You mean----"

"I mean that men like me are going on living--for the sake of the breed. I tell you, I'm grim set on living. And if I'm not mistaken, you'll show what insides **you've** got, too, before long. We aren't going to be exterminated. And I don't mean to be caught either, and tamed and fattened and bred like a thundering ox. Ugh! Fancy those brown creepers!"

"You don't mean to say----"

"I do. I'm going on, under their feet. I've got it planned; I've thought it out. We men are beat. We don't know enough. We've got to learn before we've got a chance. And we've got to live and keep independent while we learn. See! That's what has to be done."

I stared, astonished, and stirred profoundly by the man's resolution.

"Great God!," cried I. "But you are a man indeed!" And suddenly I gripped his hand.

"Eh!" he said, with his eyes shining. "I've thought it out, eh?"

"Go on," I said.

"Well, those who mean to escape their catching must get ready. I'm getting ready. Mind you, it isn't all of us that are made for wild beasts; and that's what it's got to be. That's why I watched you. I had my doubts. You're slender. I didn't know that it was you, you see, or just how you'd been buried. All these--the sort of people that lived in these houses, and all those damn little clerks that used to live down that way--they'd be no good. They haven't any spirit in them--no proud dreams and no proud lusts; and a man who hasn't one or the other--Lord! What is he but funk and precautions? They just used to skedaddle off to work--I've seen hundreds of 'em, bit of breakfast in hand, running wild and shining to catch their little season-ticket train, for fear they'd get dismissed if they didn't; working at businesses they were afraid to take the trouble to understand; skedaddling back for fear they wouldn't be in time for dinner; keeping indoors after dinner for fear of the back streets, and sleeping with the wives they married, not because they wanted them, but because they had a bit of money that would make for safety in their one little miserable skedaddle through the world. Lives insured and a bit invested for fear of accidents. And on Sundays--fear of the hereafter. As if hell was built for rabbits! Well, the Martians will just be a godsend to these. Nice roomy cages, fattening food, careful breeding, no worry. After a week or so chasing about the fields and lands on empty stomachs, they'll come and be caught cheerful. They'll be quite glad after a bit. They'll wonder what people did before there were Martians to take care of them. And the bar loafers, and mashers, and singers--I can imagine them. I can imagine them," he said, with a sort of sombre gratification. "There'll be any amount of sentiment and religion loose among them. There's hundreds of things I saw with my eyes that I've only begun to see clearly these last few days. There's lots will take things as they are--fat and stupid; and lots will be worried by a sort of feeling that it's all wrong, and that they ought to be doing something. Now whenever things are so that a lot of people feel they ought to be doing something, the weak, and those who go weak with a lot of complicated thinking, always make for a sort of do-nothing religion, very pious and superior, and submit to persecution and the will of the Lord. Very likely you've seen the same thing. It's energy in a gale of funk, and turned clean inside out. These cages will be full of psalms and hymns and piety. And those of a less simple sort will work in a bit of--what is it?--eroticism."

He paused.

"Very likely these Martians will make pets of some of them; train them to do tricks--who knows?--get sentimental over the pet boy who grew up and had to be killed. And some, maybe, they will train to hunt us."

"No," I cried, "that's impossible! No human being----"

"What's the good of going on with such lies?" said the artilleryman. "There's men who'd do it cheerful. What nonsense to pretend there isn't!"

And I succumbed to his conviction.

"If they come after me," he said; "Lord, if they come after me!" and subsided into a grim meditation.

I sat contemplating these things. I could find nothing to bring against this man's reasoning. In the days before the invasion no one would have questioned my intellectual superiority to his--I, a professed and recognised writer on philosophical themes, and he, a common soldier; and yet he had already formulated a situation that I had scarcely realised.

"What are you doing?" I said presently. "What plans have you made?"

He hesitated.

"Well, it's like this," he said. "What have we to do? We have to invent a sort of life where men can live and breed, and be sufficiently secure to bring the children up. Yes--wait a bit, and I'll make it clearer what I think ought to be done. The tame ones will go like all tame beasts; in a few generations they'll be big, beautiful, rich-blooded, stupid--rubbish! The risk is that we who keep wild will go savage--degenerate into a sort of big, savage rat.... You see, how I mean to live is underground. I've been thinking about the drains. Of course those who don't know drains think horrible things; but under this London are miles and miles--hundreds of miles--and a few days' rain and London empty will leave them sweet and clean. The main drains are big enough and airy enough for anyone. Then there's cellars, vaults, stores, from which bolting passages may be made to the drains. And the railway tunnels and subways. Eh? You begin to see? And we form a band--able-bodied, clean-minded men. We're not going to pick up any rubbish that drifts in. Weaklings go out again."

"As you meant me to go?"

"Well--I parleyed, didn't I?"

"We won't quarrel about that. Go on."

"Those who stop obey orders. Able-bodied, clean-minded women we want also--mothers and teachers. No lackadaisical ladies--no blasted rolling eyes. We can't have any weak or silly. Life is real again, and the useless and cumbersome and mischievous have to die. They ought to die. They ought to be willing to die. It's a sort of disloyalty, after all, to live and taint the race. And they can't be happy. Moreover, dying's none so dreadful; it's the funking makes it bad. And in all those places we shall gather. Our district will be London. And we may even be able to keep a watch, and run about in the open when the Martians keep away. Play cricket, perhaps. That's how we shall save the race. Eh? It's a possible thing? But saving the race is nothing in itself. As I say, that's only being rats. It's saving our knowledge and adding to it is the thing. There men like you come in. There's books, there's models. We must make great safe places down deep, and get all the books we can; not novels and poetry swipes, but ideas, science books. That's where men like you come in. We must go to the British Museum and pick all those books through. Especially we must keep up our science--learn more. We must watch these Martians. Some of us must go as spies. When it's all working, perhaps I will. Get caught, I mean. And the great thing is, we must leave the Martians alone. We mustn't even steal. If we get in their way, we clear out. We must show them we mean no harm. Yes, I know. But they're intelligent things, and they won't hunt us down if they have all they want, and think we're just harmless vermin."

The artilleryman paused and laid a brown hand upon my arm.

"After all, it may not be so much we may have to learn before-- Just imagine this: four or five of their fighting machines suddenly starting off--Heat-Rays right and left, and not a Martian in 'em. Not a Martian in 'em, but men--men who have learned the way how. It may be in my time, even--those men. Fancy having one of them lovely things, with its Heat-Ray wide and free! Fancy having it in control! What would it matter if you smashed to smithereens at the end of the run, after a bust like that? I reckon the Martians'll open their beautiful eyes! Can't you see them, man? Can't you see them hurrying, hurrying--puffing and blowing and hooting to their other mechanical affairs? Something out of gear in every case. And swish, bang, rattle, swish! Just as they are fumbling over it, **swish** comes the Heat-Ray, and, behold! man has come back to his own."

For a while the imaginative daring of the artilleryman, and the tone of assurance and courage he assumed, completely dominated my mind. I believed unhesitatingly both in his forecast of human destiny and in the practicability of his astonishing scheme, and the reader who thinks me susceptible and foolish must contrast his position, reading steadily with all his thoughts about his subject, and mine, crouching fearfully in the bushes and listening, distracted by apprehension. We talked in this manner through the early morning time, and later crept out of the bushes, and, after scanning the sky for Martians, hurried precipitately to the house on Putney Hill where he had made his lair. It was the coal cellar of the place, and when I saw the work he had spent a week upon--it was a burrow scarcely ten yards long, which he designed to reach to the main drain on Putney Hill--I had my first inkling of the gulf between his dreams and his powers. Such a hole I could have dug in a day. But I believed in him sufficiently to work with him all that morning until past midday at his digging. We had a garden barrow and shot the earth we removed against the kitchen range. We refreshed ourselves with a tin of mock-turtle soup and wine from the neighbouring pantry. I found a curious relief from the aching strangeness of the world in this steady labour. As we worked, I turned his project over in my mind, and presently objections and doubts began to arise; but I worked there all the morning, so glad was I to find myself with a purpose again. After working an hour I began to speculate on the distance one had to go before the cloaca was reached, the chances we had of missing it altogether. My immediate trouble was why we should dig this long tunnel, when it was possible to get into the drain at once down one of the manholes, and work back to the house. It seemed to me, too, that the house was inconveniently chosen, and required a needless length of tunnel. And just as I was beginning to face these things, the artilleryman stopped digging, and looked at me.

"We're working well," he said. He put down his spade. "Let us knock off a bit" he said. "I think it's time we reconnoitred from the roof of the house."

I was for going on, and after a little hesitation he resumed his spade; and then suddenly I was struck by a thought. I stopped, and so did he at once.

"Why were you walking about the common," I said, "instead of being here?"

"Taking the air," he said. "I was coming back. It's safer by night."

"But the work?"

"Oh, one can't always work," he said, and in a flash I saw the man plain. He hesitated, holding his spade. "We ought to reconnoitre now," he said, "because if any come near they may hear the spades and drop upon us unawares."

I was no longer disposed to object. We went together to the roof and stood on a ladder peeping out of the roof door. No Martians were to be seen, and we ventured out on the tiles, and slipped down under shelter of the parapet.

From this position a shrubbery hid the greater portion of Putney, but we could see the river below, a bubbly mass of red weed, and the low parts of Lambeth flooded and red. The red creeper swarmed up the trees about the old palace, and their branches stretched gaunt and dead, and set with shrivelled leaves, from amid its clusters. It was strange how entirely dependent both these things were upon flowing water for their propagation. About us neither had gained a footing; laburnums, pink mays, snowballs, and trees of arbor-vitæ, rose out of laurels and hydrangeas, green and brilliant into the sunlight. Beyond Kensington dense smoke was rising, and that and a blue haze hid the northward hills.

The artilleryman began to tell me of the sort of people who still remained in London.

"One night last week," he said, "some fools got the electric light in order, and there was all Regent Street and the Circus ablaze, crowded with painted and ragged drunkards, men and women, dancing and shouting till dawn. A man who was there told me. And as the day came they became aware of a fighting-machine standing near by the Langham and looking down at them. Heaven knows how long he had been there. It must have given some of them a nasty turn. He came down the road towards them, and picked up nearly a hundred too drunk or frightened to run away."

Grotesque gleam of a time no history will ever fully describe!

From that, in answer to my questions, he came round to his grandiose plans again. He grew enthusiastic. He talked so eloquently of the possibility of capturing a fighting-machine that I more than half believed in him again. But now that I was beginning to understand something of his quality, I could divine the stress he laid on doing nothing precipitately. And I noted that now there was no question that he personally was to capture and fight the great machine.

After a time we went down to the cellar. Neither of us seemed disposed to resume digging, and when he suggested a meal, I was nothing loath. He became suddenly very generous, and when we had eaten he went away and returned with some excellent cigars. We lit these, and his optimism glowed. He was inclined to regard my coming as a great occasion.

"There's some champagne in the cellar," he said.

"We can dig better on this Thames-side burgundy," said I.

"No," said he; "I am host today. Champagne! Great God! We've a heavy enough task before us! Let us take a rest and gather strength while we may. Look at these blistered hands!"

And pursuant to this idea of a holiday, he insisted upon playing cards after we had eaten. He taught me euchre, and after dividing London between us, I taking the northern side and he the southern, we played for parish points. Grotesque and foolish as this will seem to the sober reader, it is absolutely true, and what is more remarkable, I found the card game and several others we played extremely interesting.

Strange mind of man! that, with our species upon the edge of extermination or appalling degradation, with no clear prospect before us but the chance of a horrible death, we could sit following the chance of this painted pasteboard, and playing the "joker" with vivid delight. Afterwards he taught me poker, and I beat him at three tough chess games. When dark came we decided to take the risk, and lit a lamp.

After an interminable string of games, we supped, and the artilleryman finished the champagne. We went on smoking the cigars. He was no longer the energetic regenerator of his species I had encountered in the morning. He was still optimistic, but it was a less kinetic, a more thoughtful optimism. I remember he wound up with my health, proposed in a speech of small variety and considerable intermittence. I took a cigar, and went upstairs to look at the lights of which he had spoken that blazed so greenly along the Highgate hills.

At first I stared unintelligently across the London valley. The northern hills were shrouded in darkness; the fires near Kensington glowed redly, and now and then an orange-red tongue of flame flashed up and vanished in the deep blue night. All the rest of London was black. Then, nearer, I perceived a strange light, a pale, violet-purple fluorescent glow, quivering under the night breeze. For a space I could not understand it, and then I knew that it must be the red weed from which this faint irradiation proceeded. With that realisation my dormant sense of wonder, my sense of the proportion of things, awoke again. I glanced from that to Mars, red and clear, glowing high in the west, and then gazed long and earnestly at the darkness of Hampstead and Highgate.

I remained a very long time upon the roof, wondering at the grotesque changes of the day. I recalled my mental states from the midnight prayer to the foolish card-playing. I had a violent revulsion of feeling. I remember I flung away the cigar with a certain wasteful symbolism. My folly came to me with glaring exaggeration. I seemed a traitor to my wife and to my kind; I was filled with remorse. I resolved to leave this strange undisciplined dreamer of great things to his drink and gluttony, and to go on into London. There, it seemed to me, I had the best chance of learning what the Martians and my fellowmen were doing. I was still upon the roof when the late moon rose.

Chapter Eight
Dead London

After I had parted from the artilleryman, I went down the hill, and by the High Street across the bridge to Fulham. The red weed was tumultuous at that time, and nearly choked the bridge roadway; but its fronds were already whitened in patches by the spreading disease that presently removed it so swiftly.

At the corner of the lane that runs to Putney Bridge station I found a man lying. He was as black as a sweep with the black dust, alive, but helplessly and speechlessly drunk. I could get nothing from him but curses and furious lunges at my head. I think I should have stayed by him but for the brutal expression of his face.

There was black dust along the roadway from the bridge onwards, and it grew thicker in Fulham. The streets were horribly quiet. I got food--sour, hard, and mouldy, but quite eatable--in a baker's shop here. Some way towards Walham Green the streets became clear of powder, and I passed a white terrace of houses on fire; the noise of the burning was an absolute relief. Going on towards Brompton, the streets were quiet again.

Here I came once more upon the black powder in the streets and upon dead bodies. I saw altogether about a dozen in the length of the Fulham Road. They had been dead many days, so that I hurried quickly past them. The black powder covered them over, and softened their outlines. One or two had been disturbed by dogs.

Where there was no black powder, it was curiously like a Sunday in the City, with the closed shops, the houses locked up and the blinds drawn, the desertion, and the stillness. In some places plunderers had been at work, but rarely at other than the provision and wine shops. A jeweller's window had been broken open in one place, but apparently the thief had been disturbed, and a number of gold chains and a watch lay scattered on the pavement. I did not trouble to touch them. Farther on was a tattered woman in a heap on a doorstep; the hand that hung over her knee was gashed and bled down her rusty brown dress, and a smashed magnum of champagne formed a pool across the pavement. She seemed asleep, but she was dead.

The farther I penetrated into London, the profounder grew the stillness. But it was not so much the stillness of death--it was the stillness of suspense, of expectation. At any time the destruction that had already singed the northwestern borders of the metropolis, and had annihilated Ealing and Kilburn, might strike among these houses and leave them smoking ruins. It was a city condemned and derelict....

In South Kensington the streets were clear of dead and of black powder. It was near South Kensington that I first heard the howling. It crept almost imperceptibly upon my senses. It was a sobbing alternation of two notes, "Ulla, ulla, ulla, ulla," keeping on perpetually. When I passed streets that ran northward it grew in volume, and houses and buildings seemed to deaden and cut it off again. It came in a full tide down Exhibition Road. I stopped, staring towards Kensington Gardens, wondering at this strange, remote wailing. It was as if that mighty desert of houses had found a voice for its fear and solitude.

"Ulla, ulla, ulla, ulla," wailed that superhuman note--great waves of sound sweeping down the broad, sunlit roadway, between the tall buildings on each side. I turned northwards, marvelling, towards the iron gates of Hyde Park. I had half a mind to break into the Natural History Museum and find my way up to the summits of the towers, in order to see across the park. But I decided to keep to the ground, where quick hiding was possible, and so went on up the Exhibition Road. All the large mansions on each side of the road were empty and still, and my footsteps echoed against the sides of the houses. At the top, near the park gate, I came upon a strange sight--a bus overturned, and the skeleton of a horse picked clean. I puzzled over this for a time, and then went on to the bridge over the Serpentine. The voice grew stronger and stronger, though I could see nothing above the housetops on the north side of the park, save a haze of smoke to the northwest.

"Ulla, ulla, ulla, ulla," cried the voice, coming, as it seemed to me, from the district about Regent's Park. The desolating cry worked upon my mind. The mood that had sustained me passed.

The wailing took possession of me. I found I was intensely weary, footsore, and now again hungry and thirsty.

It was already past noon. Why was I wandering alone in this city of the dead? Why was I alone when all London was lying in state, and in its black shroud? I felt intolerably lonely. My mind ran on old friends that I had forgotten for years. I thought of the poisons in the chemists' shops, of the liquors the wine merchants stored; I recalled the two sodden creatures of despair, who so far as I knew, shared the city with myself....

I came into Oxford Street by the Marble Arch, and here again were black powder and several bodies, and an evil, ominous smell from the gratings of the cellars of some of the houses. I grew very thirsty after the heat of my long walk. With infinite trouble I managed to break into a public-house and get food and drink. I was weary after eating, and went into the parlour behind the bar, and slept on a black horsehair sofa I found there.

I awoke to find that dismal howling still in my ears, "Ulla, ulla, ulla, ulla." It was now dusk, and after I had routed out some biscuits and a cheese in the bar--there was a meat safe, but it contained nothing but maggots--I wandered on through the silent residential squares to Baker Street--Portman Square is the only one I can name--and so came out at last upon Regent's Park. And as I emerged from the top of Baker Street, I saw far away over the trees in the clearness of the sunset the hood of the Martian giant from which this howling proceeded. I was not terrified. I came upon him as if it were a matter of course. I watched him for some time, but he did not move. He appeared to be standing and yelling, for no reason that I could discover.

I tried to formulate a plan of action. That perpetual sound of "Ulla, ulla, ulla, ulla," confused my mind. Perhaps I was too tired to be very fearful. Certainly I was more curious to know the reason of this monotonous crying than afraid. I turned back away from the park and struck into Park Road, intending to skirt the park, went along under the shelter of the terraces, and got a view of this stationary, howling Martian from the direction of St. John's Wood. A couple of hundred yards out of Baker Street I heard a yelping chorus, and saw, first a dog with a piece of putrescent red meat in his jaws coming headlong towards me, and then a pack of starving mongrels in pursuit of him. He made a wide curve to avoid me, as though he feared I might prove a fresh competitor. As the yelping died away down the silent road, the wailing sound of "Ulla, ulla, ulla, ulla," reasserted itself.

I came upon the wrecked handling-machine halfway to St. John's Wood station. At first I thought a house had fallen across the road. It was only as I clambered among the ruins that I saw, with a start, this mechanical Samson lying, with its tentacles bent and smashed and twisted, among the ruins it had made. The forepart was shattered. It seemed as if it had driven blindly straight at the house, and had been overwhelmed in its overthrow. It seemed to me then that this might have happened by a handling-machine escaping from the guidance of its Martian. I could not clamber among the ruins to see it, and the twilight was now so far advanced that the blood with which its seat was smeared, and the gnawed gristle of the Martian that the dogs had left, were invisible to me.

Wondering still more at all that I had seen, I pushed on towards Primrose Hill. Far away, through a gap in the trees, I saw a second Martian, as motionless as the first, standing in the park towards the Zoological Gardens, and silent. A little beyond the ruins about the smashed handling-machine I came upon the red weed again, and found the Regent's Canal, a spongy mass of dark-red vegetation.

As I crossed the bridge, the sound of "Ulla, ulla, ulla, ulla," ceased. It was, as it were, cut off. The silence came like a thunderclap.

The dusky houses about me stood faint and tall and dim; the trees towards the park were growing black. All about me the red weed clambered among the ruins, writhing to get above me in the dimness. Night, the mother of fear and mystery, was coming upon me. But while that voice sounded the solitude, the desolation, had been endurable; by virtue of it London had still seemed alive, and the sense of life about me had upheld me. Then suddenly a change, the passing of something--I knew not what--and then a stillness that could be felt. Nothing but this gaunt quiet.

London about me gazed at me spectrally. The windows in the white houses were like the eye sockets of skulls. About me my imagination found a thousand noiseless enemies moving. Terror seized me, a horror of my temerity. In front of me the road became pitchy black as though it was tarred, and I saw a contorted shape lying across the pathway. I could not bring myself to go on. I turned down St. John's Wood Road, and ran headlong from this unendurable stillness towards Kilburn. I hid from the night and the silence, until long after midnight, in a cabmen's shelter in Harrow Road. But before the dawn my courage returned, and while the stars were still in the sky I turned once more towards Regent's Park. I missed my way among the streets, and presently saw down a long avenue, in the half-light of the early dawn, the curve of Primrose Hill. On the summit, towering up to the fading stars, was a third Martian, erect and motionless like the others.

An insane resolve possessed me. I would die and end it. And I would save myself even the trouble of killing myself. I marched on recklessly towards this Titan, and then, as I drew nearer and the light grew, I saw that a multitude of black birds was circling and clustering about the hood. At that my heart gave a bound, and I began running along the road.

I hurried through the red weed that choked St. Edmund's Terrace (I waded breast-high across a torrent of water that was rushing down from the waterworks towards the Albert Road), and emerged upon the grass before the rising of the sun. Great mounds had been heaped about the crest of the hill, making a huge redoubt of it--it was the final and largest place the Martians had made--and from behind these heaps there rose a thin smoke against the sky. Against the sky line an eager dog ran and disappeared. The thought that had flashed into my mind grew real, grew credible. I felt no fear, only a wild, trembling exultation, as I ran up the hill towards the motionless monster. Out of the hood hung lank shreds of brown, at which the hungry birds pecked and tore.

In another moment I had scrambled up the earthen rampart and stood upon its crest, and the interior of the redoubt was below me. A mighty space it was, with gigantic machines here and there within it, huge mounds of material and strange shelter places. And scattered about it, some in their overturned war-machines, some in the now rigid handling-machines, and a dozen of them stark and silent and laid in a row, were the Martians--*dead!*--slain by the putrefactive and disease bacteria against which their systems were unprepared; slain as the red weed was being slain; slain, after all man's devices had failed, by the humblest things that God, in his wisdom, has put upon this earth.

For so it had come about, as indeed I and many men might have foreseen had not terror and disaster blinded our minds. These germs of disease have taken toll of humanity since the beginning of things--taken toll of our prehuman ancestors since life began here. But by virtue of this natural selection of our kind we have developed resisting power; to no germs do we succumb without a struggle, and to many--those that cause putrefaction in dead matter, for instance--our living frames are altogether immune. But there are no bacteria in Mars, and directly these invaders arrived, directly they drank and fed, our microscopic allies began to work their overthrow. Already when I watched them they were irrevocably doomed, dying and rotting even as they went to and fro. It was inevitable. By the toll of a billion deaths man has bought his birthright of the earth, and it is his against all comers; it would still be his were the Martians ten times as mighty as they are. For neither do men live nor die in vain.

Here and there they were scattered, nearly fifty altogether, in that great gulf they had made, overtaken by a death that must have seemed to them as incomprehensible as any death could be. To me also at that time this death was incomprehensible. All I knew was that these things that had been alive and so terrible to men were dead. For a moment I believed that the destruction of Sennacherib had been repeated, that God had repented, that the Angel of Death had slain them in the night.

I stood staring into the pit, and my heart lightened gloriously, even as the rising sun struck the world to fire about me with his rays. The pit was still in darkness; the mighty engines, so great and wonderful in their power and complexity, so unearthly in their tortuous forms, rose weird and vague and strange out of the shadows towards the light. A multitude of dogs, I could hear, fought over the bodies that lay darkly in the depth of the pit, far below me. Across the pit on its farther lip, flat and vast and strange, lay the great flying-machine with which they had been experimenting upon our denser atmosphere when decay and death arrested them. Death had come not a day too soon. At the sound of a cawing overhead I looked up at the huge fighting-machine that would fight no more for ever, at the tattered red shreds of flesh that dripped down upon the overturned seats on the summit of Primrose Hill.

I turned and looked down the slope of the hill to where, enhaloed now in birds, stood those other two Martians that I had seen overnight, just as death had overtaken them. The one had died, even as it had been crying to its companions; perhaps it was the last to die, and its voice had gone on perpetually until the force of its machinery was exhausted. They glittered now, harmless tripod towers of shining metal, in the brightness of the rising sun.

All about the pit, and saved as by a miracle from everlasting destruction, stretched the great Mother of Cities. Those who have only seen London veiled in her sombre robes of smoke can scarcely imagine the naked clearness and beauty of the silent wilderness of houses.

Eastward, over the blackened ruins of the Albert Terrace and the splintered spire of the church, the sun blazed dazzling in a clear sky, and here and there some facet in the great wilderness of roofs caught the light and glared with a white intensity.

Northward were Kilburn and Hampsted, blue and crowded with houses; westward the great city was dimmed; and southward, beyond the Martians, the green waves of Regent's Park, the Langham Hotel, the dome of the Albert Hall, the Imperial Institute, and the giant mansions of the Brompton Road came out clear and little in the sunrise, the jagged ruins of Westminster rising hazily beyond. Far away and blue were the Surrey hills, and the towers of the Crystal Palace glittered like two silver rods. The dome of St. Paul's was dark against the sunrise, and injured, I saw for the first time, by a huge gaping cavity on its western side.

And as I looked at this wide expanse of houses and factories and churches, silent and abandoned; as I thought of the multitudinous hopes and efforts, the innumerable hosts of lives that had gone to build this human reef, and of the swift and ruthless destruction that had hung over it all; when I realised that the shadow had been rolled back, and that men might still live in the streets, and this dear vast dead city of mine be once more alive and powerful, I felt a wave of emotion that was near akin to tears.

The torment was over. Even that day the healing would begin. The survivors of the people scattered over the country--leaderless, lawless, foodless, like sheep without a shepherd--the thousands who had fled by sea, would begin to return; the pulse of life, growing stronger and stronger, would beat again in the empty streets and pour across the vacant squares. Whatever destruction was done, the hand of the destroyer was stayed. All the gaunt wrecks, the blackened skeletons of houses that stared so dismally at the sunlit grass of the hill, would presently be echoing with the hammers of the restorers and ringing with the tapping of their trowels. At the thought I extended my hands towards the sky and began thanking God. In a year, thought I--in a year...

With overwhelming force came the thought of myself, of my wife, and the old life of hope and tender helpfulness that had ceased for ever.

The Pit and Primrose Hill by Peter Fussey

Chapter Nine
Wreckage

And now comes the strangest thing in my story. Yet, perhaps, it is not altogether strange. I remember, clearly and coldly and vividly, all that I did that day until the time that I stood weeping and praising God upon the summit of Primrose Hill. And then I forget.

Of the next three days I know nothing. I have learned since that, so far from my being the first discoverer of the Martian overthrow, several such wanderers as myself had already discovered this on the previous night. One man--the first--had gone to St. Martin's-le-Grand, and, while I sheltered in the cabmen's hut, had contrived to telegraph to Paris. Thence the joyful news had flashed all over the world; a thousand cities, chilled by ghastly apprehensions, suddenly flashed into frantic illuminations; they knew of it in Dublin, Edinburgh, Manchester, Birmingham, at the time when I stood upon the verge of the pit. Already men, weeping with joy, as I have heard, shouting and staying their work to shake hands and shout, were making up trains, even as near as Crewe, to descend upon London. The church bells that had ceased a fortnight since suddenly caught the news, until all England was bell-ringing. Men on cycles, lean-faced, unkempt, scorched along every country lane shouting of unhoped deliverance, shouting to gaunt, staring figures of despair. And for the food! Across the Channel, across the Irish Sea, across the Atlantic, corn, bread, and meat were tearing to our relief. All the shipping in the world seemed going Londonward in those days. But of all this I have no memory. I drifted--a demented man. I found myself in a house of kindly people, who had found me on the third day wandering, weeping, and raving through the streets of St. John's Wood. They have told me since that I was singing some insane doggerel about "The Last Man Left Alive! Hurrah! The Last Man Left Alive!" Troubled as they were with their own affairs, these people, whose name, much as I would like to express my gratitude to them, I may not even give here, nevertheless cumbered themselves with me, sheltered me, and protected me from myself. Apparently they had learned something of my story from me during the days of my lapse.

Very gently, when my mind was assured again, did they break to me what they had learned of the fate of Leatherhead. Two days after I was imprisoned it had been destroyed, with every soul in it, by a Martian. He had swept it out of existence, as it seemed, without any provocation, as a boy might crush an ant hill, in the mere wantonness of power.

I was a lonely man, and they were very kind to me. I was a lonely man and a sad one, and they bore with me. I remained with them four days after my recovery. All that time I felt a vague, a growing craving to look once more on whatever remained of the little life that seemed so happy and bright in my past. It was a mere hopeless desire to feast upon my misery. They dissuaded me. They did all they could to divert me from this morbidity. But at last I could resist the impulse no longer, and, promising faithfully to return to them, and parting, as I will confess, from these four-day friends with tears, I went out again into the streets that had lately been so dark and strange and empty.

Already they were busy with returning people; in places even there were shops open, and I saw a drinking fountain running water.

I remember how mockingly bright the day seemed as I went back on my melancholy pilgrimage to the little house at Woking, how busy the streets and vivid the moving life about me. So many people were abroad everywhere, busied in a thousand activities, that it seemed incredible that any great proportion of the population could have been slain. But then I noticed how yellow were the skins of the people I met, how shaggy the hair of the men, how large and bright their eyes, and that every other man still wore his dirty rags. Their faces seemed all with one of two expressions--a leaping exultation and energy or a grim resolution. Save for the expression of the faces, London seemed a city of tramps. The vestries were indiscriminately distributing bread sent us by the French government. The ribs of the few horses showed dismally. Haggard special constables with white badges stood at the corners of every street. I saw little of the mischief wrought by the Martians until I reached Wellington Street, and there I saw the red weed clambering over the buttresses of Waterloo Bridge.

At the corner of the bridge, too, I saw one of the common contrasts of that grotesque time--a sheet of paper flaunting against a thicket of the red weed, transfixed by a stick that kept it in place. It was the placard of the first newspaper to resume publication--the *Daily Mail*. I bought a copy for a blackened shilling I found in my pocket. Most of it was in blank, but the solitary compositor who did the thing had amused himself by making a grotesque scheme of advertisement stereo on the back page. The matter he printed was emotional; the news organisation had not as yet found its way back. I learned nothing fresh except that already in one week the examination of the Martian mechanisms had yielded astonishing results. Among other things, the article assured me what I did not believe at the time, that the "Secret of Flying," was discovered. At Waterloo I found the free trains that were taking people to their homes. The first rush was already over. There were few people in the train, and I was in no mood for casual conversation. I got a compartment to myself, and sat with folded arms, looking greyly at the sunlit devastation that flowed past the windows. And just outside the terminus the train jolted over temporary rails, and on either side of the railway the houses were blackened ruins. To Clapham Junction the face of London was grimy with powder of the Black Smoke, in spite of two days of thunderstorms and rain, and at Clapham Junction the line had been wrecked again; there were hundreds of out-of-work clerks and shopmen working side by side with the customary navvies, and we were jolted over a hasty relaying.

All down the line from there the aspect of the country was gaunt and unfamiliar; Wimbledon particularly had suffered. Walton, by virtue of its unburned pine woods, seemed the least hurt of any place along the line. The Wandle, the Mole, every little stream, was a heaped mass of red weed, in appearance between butcher's meat and pickled cabbage. The Surrey pine woods were too dry, however, for the festoons of the red climber. Beyond Wimbledon, within sight of the line, in certain nursery grounds, were the heaped masses of earth about the sixth cylinder. A number of people were standing about it, and some sappers were busy in the midst of it. Over it flaunted a Union Jack, flapping cheerfully in the morning breeze. The nursery grounds were everywhere crimson with the weed, a wide expanse of livid colour cut with purple shadows, and very painful to the eye. One's gaze went with infinite relief from the scorched greys and sullen reds of the foreground to the blue-green softness of the eastward hills.

The line on the London side of Woking station was still undergoing repair, so I descended at Byfleet station and took the road to Maybury, past the place where I and the artilleryman had talked to the hussars, and on by the spot where the Martian had appeared to me in the thunderstorm. Here, moved by curiosity, I turned aside to find, among a tangle of red fronds, the warped and broken dog cart with the whitened bones of the horse scattered and gnawed. For a time I stood regarding these vestiges....

Then I returned through the pine wood, neck-high with red weed here and there, to find the landlord of the Spotted Dog had already found burial, and so came home past the College Arms. A man standing at an open cottage door greeted me by name as I passed.

I looked at my house with a quick flash of hope that faded immediately. The door had been forced; it was unfast and was opening slowly as I approached.

It slammed again. The curtains of my study fluttered out of the open window from which I and the artilleryman had watched the dawn. No one had closed it since. The smashed bushes were just as I had left them nearly four weeks ago. I stumbled into the hall, and the house felt empty. The stair carpet was ruffled and discoloured where I had crouched, soaked to the skin from the thunderstorm the night of the catastrophe. Our muddy footsteps I saw still went up the stairs.

I followed them to my study, and found lying on my writing-table still, with the selenite paper weight upon it, the sheet of work I had left on the afternoon of the opening of the cylinder. For a space I stood reading over my abandoned arguments. It was a paper on the probable development of Moral Ideas with the development of the civilising process; and the last sentence was the opening of a prophecy: "In about two hundred years," I had written, "we may expect----" The sentence ended abruptly. I remembered my inability to fix my mind that morning, scarcely a month gone by, and how I had broken off to get my *Daily Chronicle* from the newsboy. I remembered how I went down to the garden gate as he came along, and how I had listened to his odd story of "Men from Mars."

I came down and went into the dining room. There were the mutton and the bread, both far gone now in decay, and a beer bottle overturned, just as I and the artilleryman had left them. My home was desolate. I perceived the folly of the faint hope I had cherished so long. And then a strange thing occurred. "It is no use," said a voice. "The house is deserted. No one has been here these ten days. Do not stay here to torment yourself. No one escaped but you."

I was startled. Had I spoken my thought aloud? I turned, and the French window was open behind me. I made a step to it, and stood looking out.

And there, amazed and afraid, even as I stood amazed and afraid, were my cousin and my wife--my wife white and tearless. She gave a faint cry.

"I came," she said. "I knew--knew----"

She put her hand to her throat--swayed. I made a step forward, and caught her in my arms.

Chapter Ten
The Epilogue

I cannot but regret, now that I am concluding my story, how little I am able to contribute to the discussion of the many debatable questions which are still unsettled. In one respect I shall certainly provoke criticism. My particular province is speculative philosophy. My knowledge of comparative physiology is confined to a book or two, but it seems to me that Carver's suggestions as to the reason of the rapid death of the Martians is so probable as to be regarded almost as a proven conclusion. I have assumed that in the body of my narrative.

At any rate, in all the bodies of the Martians that were examined after the war, no bacteria except those already known as terrestrial species were found. That they did not bury any of their dead, and the reckless slaughter they perpetrated, point also to an entire ignorance of the putrefactive process. But probable as this seems, it is by no means a proven conclusion.

Neither is the composition of the Black Smoke known, which the Martians used with such deadly effect, and the generator of the Heat-Rays remains a puzzle. The terrible disasters at the Ealing and South Kensington laboratories have disinclined analysts for further investigations upon the latter. Spectrum analysis of the black powder points unmistakably to the presence of an unknown element with a brilliant group of three lines in the green, and it is possible that it combines with argon to form a compound which acts at once with deadly effect upon some constituent in the blood. But such unproven speculations will scarcely be of interest to the general reader, to whom this story is addressed. None of the brown scum that drifted down the Thames after the destruction of Shepperton was examined at the time, and now none is forthcoming.

The results of an anatomical examination of the Martians, so far as the prowling dogs had left such an examination possible, I have already given. But everyone is familiar with the magnificent and almost complete specimen in spirits at the Natural History Museum, and the countless drawings that have been made from it; and beyond that the interest of their physiology and structure is purely scientific.

A question of graver and universal interest is the possibility of another attack from the Martians. I do not think that nearly enough attention is being given to this aspect of the matter. At present the planet Mars is in conjunction, but with every return to opposition I, for one, anticipate a renewal of their adventure. In any case, we should be prepared. It seems to me that it should be possible to define the position of the gun from which the shots are discharged, to keep a sustained watch upon this part of the planet, and to anticipate the arrival of the next attack.

In that case the cylinder might be destroyed with dynamite or artillery before it was sufficiently cool for the Martians to emerge, or they might be butchered by means of guns so soon as the screw opened. It seems to me that they have lost a vast advantage in the failure of their first surprise. Possibly they see it in the same light.

Lessing has advanced excellent reasons for supposing that the Martians have actually succeeded in effecting a landing on the planet Venus. Seven months ago now, Venus and Mars were in alignment with the sun; that is to say, Mars was in opposition from the point of view of an observer on Venus. Subsequently a peculiar luminous and sinuous marking appeared on the unillumined half of the inner planet, and almost simultaneously a faint dark mark of a similar sinuous character was detected upon a photograph of the Martian disk. One needs to see the drawings of these appearances in order to appreciate fully their remarkable resemblance in character.

At any rate, whether we expect another invasion or not, our views of the human future must be greatly modified by these events. We have learned now that we cannot regard this planet as being fenced in and a secure abiding place for Man; we can never anticipate the unseen good or evil that may come upon us suddenly out of space. It may be that in the larger design of the universe this invasion from Mars is not without its ultimate benefit for men; it has robbed us of that serene confidence in the future which is the most fruitful source of decadence, the gifts to human science it has brought are enormous, and it has done much to promote the conception of the commonweal of mankind. It may be that across the immensity of space the Martians have watched the fate of these pioneers of theirs and learned their lesson, and that on the planet Venus they have found a securer settlement. Be that as it may, for many years yet there will certainly be no relaxation of the eager scrutiny of the Martian disk, and those fiery darts of the sky, the shooting stars, will bring with them as they fall an unavoidable apprehension to all the sons of men.

The broadening of men's views that has resulted can scarcely be exaggerated. Before the cylinder fell there was a general persuasion that through all the deep of space no life existed beyond the petty surface of our minute sphere. Now we see further. If the Martians can reach Venus, there is no reason to suppose that the thing is impossible for men, and when the slow cooling of the sun makes this earth uninhabitable, as at last it must do, it may be that the thread of life that has begun here will have streamed out and caught our sister planet within its toils.

Dim and wonderful is the vision I have conjured up in my mind of life spreading slowly from this little seed bed of the solar system throughout the inanimate vastness of sidereal space. But that is a remote dream. It may be, on the other hand, that the destruction of the Martians is only a reprieve. To them, and not to us, perhaps, is the future ordained.

I must confess the stress and danger of the time have left an abiding sense of doubt and insecurity in my mind. I sit in my study writing by lamplight, and suddenly I see again the healing valley below set with writhing flames, and feel the house behind and about me empty and desolate. I go out into the Byfleet Road, and vehicles pass me, a butcher boy in a cart, a cabful of visitors, a workman on a bicycle, children going to school, and suddenly they become vague and unreal, and I hurry again with the artilleryman through the hot, brooding silence. Of a night I see the black powder darkening the silent streets, and the contorted bodies shrouded in that layer; they rise upon me tattered and dog-bitten. They gibber and grow fiercer, paler, uglier, mad distortions of humanity at last, and I wake, cold and wretched, in the darkness of the night.

I go to London and see the busy multitudes in Fleet Street and the Strand, and it comes across my mind that they are but the ghosts of the past, haunting the streets that I have seen silent and wretched, going to and fro, phantasms in a dead city, the mockery of life in a galvanised body. And strange, too, it is to stand on Primrose Hill, as I did but a day before writing this last chapter, to see the great province of houses, dim and blue through the haze of the smoke and mist, vanishing at last into the vague lower sky, to see the people walking to and fro among the flower beds on the hill, to see the sight-seers about the Martian machine that stands there still, to hear the tumult of playing children, and to recall the time when I saw it all bright and clear-cut, hard and silent, under the dawn of that last great day....

And strangest of all is it to hold my wife's hand again, and to think that I have counted her, and that she has counted me, among the dead.

A Strange Document

By Tony Wright

FROM A LETTER TO A WELL KNOWN INVESTIGATIVE JOURNALIST FROM A SOURCE AT THE MINISTRY OF DEFENCE.
File Ref – MOD/WOW3/PO24a/HGW/JW

London 18th September 2004

Jeff,

Was just searching through the files we were discussing the other day and I came across this manuscript. I remembered you were researching THAT war and thought you might be interested in this. Perhaps I should draw your attention to Chapter 7, as it directly relates to your current interest. In case you were wondering, the chap responsible for the files at that time slapped an order on it after being tipped off by the publisher. Policy at the time forbade discussion of the subject in any form once things had calmed down, as you will know. So, unfortunately, the poor old bugger never did get his memoirs published. Not the definitive proof you were after alone, maybe, but interesting in the light of recent rumours I referred to in that excellent restaurant the other night. Put it together with the other stuff I gave you and make your own mind up.

I don't need to tell you that I know nothing of this,
Cheers!

H.

NEPTUNE'S WARRIOR
by Capt. J.C.B.Smythe (Retd.)

Chapter 7: The Demise of a Brave Ship by One Proud to Serve on Her.

Attentive readers will be aware that, by the turn of the century, I was already familiar with the peculiar things that can happen in the service of this great nation's Navy.

As a young, fresh officer in 1891, and aforementioned in this humble collection of reminiscences, I had served aboard the HMS Scorpion on her voyage to Noble's Isle. There I had seen sights to chill the blood, but, as I have touched upon this subject earlier, I shall say no more.

Nothing, however, could prepare me for the events that occurred a few years into the new reign of His Majesty King Edward. Shortly after these events I saw, in a popular news sheet of the time by the name of 'The Pall Mall Budget' or some such, an account of the war which mentioned in passing the brave stand made by HMS Thunder Child. I then vowed to put forth my own account of this struggle, having been 'in the thick of it' as the popular saying goes. Now I can fulfil that solemn vow.

By the time of my transfer to *Thunder Child*, I had made the rank of 1st Lieutenant and had some considerable experience with men and ships. *Thunder Child* was a queer type of vessel, cigar shaped and low-lying, but her crew were of the most robust and hardy type that I ever had the honour of serving with.

Built in Chatham in 1879, *Thunder Child* was one of only two in the Polyphemus Class designed by the late Admiral of the Fleet Sartorius. Her sister ship, the *Polyphemus,* was the other. Both were Ironclad Torpedo Ram ships of 2,640 tons each, thrust through the water by twin screws at a top speed of 18 knots. They were both initially armed with five torpedo tubes, six Hotchkiss machine guns and, of course, a formidable ram. In 1882 they were both commissioned and served for long stretches in the Mediterranean.

It was shortly before the coming of the Martians that they separated. *Thunder Child* was returned to Chatham for refitting where I joined her, whilst *Polyphemus* remained on active duty for refitting at a later date. *Thunder Child* was fitted with 12 pounder guns, fore and aft, as it was hoped to make her more flexible in battle.

I had been in my new position for a few months when news of the spreading chaos in the South East of England reached us. Rumours were rife as to what was the nature of this new threat. Several times I had to 'calm the fever', as it were. The lack of news and that human malady they call 'curiosity' caused tongues to wag among the lower ranks.

The general feeling in those early days though was that we would crush this new terror like we would crush any other insurrection within the British Empire; swiftly and cleanly, with the minimum of fuss.

After the Surrey defeats and the Martian advance, we hurriedly put to sea to join a small Channel Defence Fleet. There were three other Ironclads that I distinctly remember in this fleet, namely *Miskatonic*, *Carrie* and *Cavor*. I later served aboard *Cavor* as my first command. My extraordinary experiences with the experimental metal cladding the 'boffins' gave her will be laid down in another chapter.

Thunder Child, at any rate, soon lay off the Essex Coast amongst the most extraordinary flotilla of assorted ships and boats which were gathered to carry a seemingly unending stream of humanity across to the continent and safety.

I remember well, as if I could forget that dreadful time, standing on the quarterdeck at the side of the Captain, as the great man muttered darkly under his breath at the seemingly suicidal manoeuvrings of this strange collection of vessels. We watched with baited breath as this fishing smack narrowly avoided that yacht, as people crammed into small boats struggled against the waves, with varying success.

That night, at dinner, we discussed the latest turn of events.

'Apparently, the Army are taking heavy casualties in Surrey,' said the ship's Doctor quietly.

'London will be next, I'll wager,' intoned the Commander toying a wineglass.

There was silence for a moment.

'Dash it all … I'd much rather be at the front line giving those … those … things a taste of British steel. In a matter of days we have been reduced to scurrying rabbits while those bastards stalk about the country on their metal legs … murdering!' exclaimed the Doctor, his unseemly outburst suddenly breaking the hushed atmosphere of the dining room.

The Captain spoke up. 'Our place is here. They have not, so far, made it to the coast. We may yet be the last line of defence, Gentlemen.' He paused to look about the room, savings a special glance for the Doctor.

'I will not hear any more of this, especially in front of the men. We are all chomping at the bit, I am sure, but I am also of the mind that our time will come.' The Captain spoke quietly, that is, as quietly as a bear-like man with a booming voice can speak. He spoke in a calming manner, though, and presently the conversation turned to other things.

I glanced at the Doctor and his thin, red face grinned sheepishly at me, his anger at his perceived inaction abated. Dinner resumed as usual.

I did not join in the forced, but otherwise light, banter. My thoughts were with my wife and daughter at home. Were they safe? I tried to calm my fears in the knowledge that my wife's brother (a dependable fellow if ever there was one) would likely ensure their safety and, soon, I felt a little better. In my bunk later, though, I gazed at their pictures and I am not ashamed to say that I prayed to the Almighty that he would keep them safe from the clutches of evil.

The next day I awoke at dawn to the thump of faraway guns.

Hurriedly, I dressed and headed to the quarterdeck. The Captain was already there. Indeed, despite his usual upright bearing, his huge bearded face gave away the fact that he must have been up all night.

'What's happening, Sir?' I asked.

He turned his great, owl-like visage towards me. 'Looks like our friends are heading this way. Gunfire coming from the coastal gun batteries.' He nodded landwards then returned his gaze to a distant point on the horizon.

Above the land, plumes of smoke rose lazily into the air. At intervals there came distant thumping as the Army guns bravely fought this unseen menace. The chaos in the water around us continued. Foam churned as a myriad of floating transport carried frantic, crying figures over the channel. How long the continent would be safe I did not know. How long before green flashes would be seen above the skies of France, Spain or Germany? Would those in the New World or our Antipodean cousins, perhaps, soon gaze with dread at those ghostly streaks of light tearing up the black blanket of night? Why should the Martians stop here unless we stopped them? I wondered how many other minds had pondered this.

A steward brought in hot black coffee and we sipped it silently as we watched the billowing smoke and tried to imagine the terrible struggle that was taking place on land. It seemed to me that the guns thumped with the regularity of a great beast's heart. The heart of England … an England fighting for its very life. I'm sure that, like me, every soul on board *Thunder Child* willed that great heart to beat stronger and stronger, to give our England the strength to shake of this dreadful virus that had invaded its body. More than one silent prayer was, I could tell by the rapt faces around me, said in those quiet moments.

It was my practice to take a turn around the ship a few times a day, to 'grease the wheels'. After I had finished my coffee, I made my excuses and did so, shrugging off the melancholy and thinking businesslike thoughts.

In the lower quarters, I noticed a small knot of men standing around talking in low tones.

'Lacking something to do, Gentlemen?' I asked sharply, causing a jolt in one or two of them. Most of them drifted away into the bowels of the ship on some most likely urgent errand. One Able Seaman, however, remained behind.

'What is it, Jenkins?' I peered at him with the beadiest eye I could muster. It was a trick I had seen a Master-At-Arms use early in my career and, after much practice, I found that it always worked most admirably in putting off complainers and malingerers.

The boy, painfully slight and looking barely of age to be in the Service, approached me slowly.

'Well, spit it out, lad,' I said eyeing him again.

The boy stood for a moment wringing his hands as if searching for the right words.

'Sir,' he took a deep breath. 'Sir, me an' the lads was a-wonderin' … wha' with the Marshuns an' all … Well, Sir … wha' chance do we 'ave? We've 'erd terrible things about them … murderin' an' killin' … Big machines we've 'erd about … an' 'orrible guns of fire …'

The boy was obviously terribly afraid and my heart went out to him. Of course, I could not pander to him, that would not have done at all.

'Jenkins, what did you join His Majesty's Navy for?' I asked him sternly.

The boy thought for a moment, then answered. 'Sir, I joined up 'cause I wanted to see the world an' have adventures like my Father an' his Father before 'im.' He looked at me hopefully, wondering if this was what I wanted to hear.

'And adventures you shall have, Jenkins,' I answered. 'Out there no more than a few miles away is adventure. Just think what stories you will be able to tell your children, and your grandchildren. You can tell them that you served on the triumphant *Thunder Child* when she helped drive the Martian invaders clean back to where they came from. You can tell them that you saw those machines fall one by one as we showed them what real British grit can do. You can tell them that you helped to preserve the great British Empire for them and their children.' I waited and watched him.

Presently, a small smile flickered across his boyish face. 'Right you are, Sir! I'll be sure to do jus' that!' Jenkins exclaimed and, flicking a quick salute in my direction scampered off, his oversized uniform flapping on his thin frame.

Smiling, despite myself, I returned the salute to his scrawny back. At that, I returned to my duties.

It seems that perhaps my talk with Jenkins must have had a better effect than I could have hoped, as no more word of dissent or unease reached my ears. Indeed, morale seems to have risen, along with the healthy tension that goes with a wish to get 'stuck in' before a battle.

The ship's company waited with baited breath but, for a time, no sign of the Martian invasion showed, barring the ever increasing palls of smoke and the thump of the guns away to the distance. We had more news; London had fallen and part of His Majesty's Government had retreated to the Midlands to direct operations. The Martians did indeed have huge machines in which they stalked the land, although we had yet to see one. We did not have long to wait.

The morning was taken trying to instil some semblance of order into the general rout that was taking place in our stretch of water. Boat hit boat, we would intervene in the ensuing chaos and get jabbered at for our pains in English, Danish, French or whatever language the Captains of these motley vessels spoke. As the day drew on, the smoke from the coast grew thicker and the thump of the guns more intermittent. I did not think this was a good sign.

Soon after 2 o'clock in the afternoon we saw the first of them. The bright sun glinted at first on a small metallic object on the horizon and, suddenly, the alert rang out.

Coming swiftly down the coast was a Martian Tripod. Even at that distance we could only gape at the immense size of it.

On the quarterdeck, the Captain swore into his beard. At the enemy's approach, some guns to the South began a quick thumping. The game was afoot!

As we watched, two more Martians appeared, single file, as rapidly as the first.

With the slick ease of a greased wheel, *Thunder Child* sprang to life, the Captain barking orders that were obeyed with astonishing speed and precision. Beside him, my heart thudded in my chest as adrenaline surged through my system. My God, nothing we had heard had prepared us for the sight of those monstrous machines that filed towards our strange armada along the coast.

My esteemed reader will doubtless have read descriptions of these diabolical things but I shall attempt my own as descriptions seem to differ to varying degrees.

Each machine was something in the area of 100 feet high. Like a great shining ovoid that perched, somewhat precariously it seemed to me, on three delicate looking legs. For their speed, theirs was not a graceful motion, rather rolling gait, strange to behold and hard to describe. A writer once described it as 'like a milking stool walking' or some such. It was a little like that but also not so. The spindly legs of the machines crawled, spider like, as they propelled the contraptions and little puffs of some kind of green steam or smoke sprayed from the joints as they bent.

The machines had a kind of cabin projecting from the forward part of the ovoid which swayed about, gracefully, on a stalk not unlike a swan's neck. I understand, from information since received, that this 'head' or 'cabin' was where the Martian drivers lurked. From under the 'head' dangled a small forest of metal cables or tentacles that waved about expressively as the thing moved. These loathsome giants periodically emitted an uncanny, wailing howl that I took to be their method of communication. I have since learned that this may not, in fact, be the case, although I do not profess to comprehend the details given later by the scientists.

The first of these machines waded out to sea toward us and our little charges that, with renewed vigour at the sight of these invaders, frantically battled their way toward safety.

The Captain barked more orders and *Thunder Child* headed at full power towards the behemoth that staggered towards the panicking vessels so near to freedom. The twin smoke stacks belched sparks and billowing black clouds as we rushed headlong towards our quarry. The Captain, ashen-faced, but with a clear, calm voice spoke. 'We are not to fire until I give the order.'

'Sir?' I asked, not a little confused.

'We will charge the closest machine first. Wait for my signal.' That said, he turned and stared resolutely at the enemy ahead.

We steamed on. The distance between our ship and the machine closed rapidly. The Martian in his craft was directing a strange beam at some of the small vessels, those that it touched turned to fire instantly or exploded in a fearful fashion. Great clouds of steam and smoke probed the already soot-streaked sky. I fancied that the little white waves that broke against the monster's spindly legs glowed with some unearthly light.

It must have tired quickly of this game, because it swung its 'head' round swiftly as if looking for more worthy prey. Soon enough it alighted on a large steamer that was painfully pulling out to sea behind us, crammed full with people. As it headed towards the overloaded vessel, it suddenly seemed to spot us as we sped towards it. The machine stopped dead and seemed to look with some surprise at the low slung, grey shape that approached it.

'Damn it! On my order!' bellowed the Captain, as if to stay any gunner's itchy fingers. 'Go and keep an eye on those gunners, Smythe.'

'Sir!' I said and rushed out on deck.

Men were there, staring transfixed at the looming shape above us.

'Why doesn't it attack, Sir?' asked a familiar reedy voice. I turned and saw Jenkins at my side, his face a mask of horror at the apparition before us.

'We've got it surprised, Jenkins,' I said, wondering the very same thing.

As I spoke, the Martian raised its head, seemed to look directly into my eyes and fired some form of projectile from a gun it unhitched from its body. The canister glanced harmlessly off the armoured sides of our great ship and span off into the sea, discharging as it went a dense, black smoke. The other Martians approached us now as our nearest adversary raised a large metallic box in one of its repulsive tentacles. As the Martians' terrible Flame Ray pierced the side of *Thunder Child*, throwing great clouds of steam and showers of white hot metal in all directions, the Captain bellowed 'FIRE!' and our forward guns boomed.

The ship lurched alarmingly like a wounded animal but the Gunner's aim was true. The first Martian machine seemed to wheel about on one leg, then crash with a great spray of water into the depths. A whoop of joy issued from the men assembled on the deck and, turning towards the steamer, I could see distant figures jumping on her deck and waving their arms.

Dense black fog and intense heat radiated from the side of our plucky ship but still she sped on, turning a little to confront the second form looming nearby.

'See, Jenkins, your grandchildren will thrill to this yarn!' I said, excited as the rest at our success.

'Reckon as they will, Sir,' breathed the boy.

As she went, her guns spoke again and again. Shells splashed into the water, some even hit other human vessels, but we were oblivious to this, concentrating as we were on the second Martian that was heading toward us at an alarming rate.

A few shells ineffectually burst around the Martian's 'head' as it swung its awful weapon around wildly, trying to strike a bead on us.

Then, that deadly flame leapt out at us and I suddenly found myself thrown, like a child's doll, far up into the air and out to sea. Even as I flew, though, I saw the deck explode into shards of metal and splinters of wood as if at a quarter speed. The blast obliterated the giant spindly tower as *Thunder Child* played her last card. She, outraged, took a terrible revenge against her attacker and scattered it to the four winds. Through the hissing of the superheated water around the shattered ship, I fancied I heard poor, young Jenkins scream as he was torn from his body and sent to the place where all brave sailors go to their final rest.

Of that awful day, there is not much more to relate. As the valiant Ironclad Torpedo Ram *Thunder Child* breathed her last, she had indeed taken with her the one that had melted her brave heart. With her supreme sacrifice and that of her crew, she facilitated the escape of many thousands of terrified, helpless people. For a few brief moments, she showed humankind that there could still be hope, even against the greatest adversity.

As I floated, vulnerable but strangely tranquil, in the seething water, I could swear that I saw a giant flat, metallic shape, not unlike a tea saucer and bigger than the largest dirigible, float slowly overhead. This vision was quickly lost to my burning eyes as it suddenly accelerated towards land.

I was rescued, bleeding, severely burned and half drowned a short time later. My war was over. I recovered eventually, as will be seen, and resumed my career. To this day, though, I often wake in the still of night, soaked with sweat and sobbing. My ears still sometimes ring with the remembrance of the last, agonised scream of the *Thunder Child's* passing.

Of *Thunder Child's* entire crew I, alone, survived to mourn her.

Thunder Child by George Jones

The Martian and the Raven
By Bayne MacGregor

Based on the poem "The Raven" by Edgar Allen Poe

Invading London dreary, my weight growing, great and weary,
Fighting gravity so much stronger than I'd ever felt before,
While my lungs struggled, near collapsing, suddenly there came a tapping,
As of something come loose and rapping, rapping on my hoods hatch door,
"'Tis some cable" I muttered, "flapping against my hoods hatch door –
Only this, and nothing more."

So distinctly I remember those humans we did dismember,
And each separate dying member fought its death upon the floor.
Eagerly I wished the morrow – vainly I had sought to follow
From my dissections end of sorrow – from my lungs so rent and sore –
From the painful gross infection that left my lungs so rent and sore –
Coughing sputum phlegm and more.

And the twitching and uncertain flailing of my tentacles trailing,
Writhing – filled with painful tremors never felt before;
So that now to keep the beating of my heart I thought repeating
"'Tis some cable needing repairs come loose at my hoods hatch door –
Some frayed cable needing repairs come loose at my hoods hatch door –
That it is and nothing more."

Presently my flesh grew stronger, hesitating then no longer,
Heaving up my bulk and crawling, crawling over the cold floor,
Taking up my tools and mapping, of the wires and the cladding,

I crawled towards the constant tapping, tapping at my hoods
hatch door,
Pulling levers, switches, catches – here I opened up the door –
Darkness there and nothing more.

Deep into that darkness peering, long I sat there wondering,
fearing,
Doubting, thinking thoughts no immortal Martian ever thought
before;
But the silence was unbroken, and the darkness gave no token,
And the only word there spoken came from my throat burning
and sore
This I shouted, in my panic, cried "Ullaa" till my vocal cords near
tore
Of response there was no more.

Back into the chamber turning, all my nerves within me burning,
Soon I heard again a tapping somewhat louder than before.
"Surely," thought I, "surely that is something caught on my view-
port lattice;
Let me see, then, what thereat is, and this mystery explore –
Let my heart be still a moment and this mystery explore –
'Tis the wind and nothing more!"

Open here I flung the shutter, when, with many a flit and flutter,
In there stepped a strange winged creature like the great Martians
of lore;
Not the least obeisance made he; not an instant stopped or
stayed he;
But, with a flapping of his wings he perched above my hoods
hatch door –
Perched before the map of Paris just above my hoods hatch door
–
Perched and sat, and nothing more.

Then this ebony bird distracting the ache of my lungs wracking,
By the strange evolutionary structure that it bore,

Through Telepathy I'd undertaken to communicate and make ken,
The need for some sort of haven to tend my illness sick and sore –
To tell me what his species name is on this heavy planets shore.
Quoth the Raven "Eaten raw."

Much I marvelled this ungainly fowl to hear discourse so plainly,
Though it's answer little meaning – little relevancy bore;
For we cannot help agreeing that no living Martian being
Ever yet was blessed with seeing bird above his hoods hatch door –
Bird or beast before that orbital map above his hoods hatch door,
With such name as "Eaten raw"

But the black bird, sitting lonely fore the blurry map, spoke only
That one word, as if his mind in that one word he did outpour.
Nothing farther then he uttered – not a feather then he fluttered –
While my brachioles were ruptured through coughing worse than that before –
I spake "This haemorrhaging will leave me so much worse than was before."
Then the bird said "Eaten raw"

Startled at the stillness broken by reply so oddly spoken,
"Doubtless," said I, "What it utters is its only stock and store
Misidentified as smarter, this bird surely was not the master
But a slave freed by disaster learned by rote that which it swore
So the hope that had in me sprung turned to misery once more
Of my lungs bleeding and sore.

But the creature still beguiling some distraction from my dying,
Straight I pulled my command seat in front of bird and hood hatch door,
Then upon the cushion climbing, I betook myself to striving
Logic piled on logic considering this strange black bird I saw

What this ugly terrestrial bird with its sharp beak and wicked claw
Meant in croaking "Eaten raw."

This I sat engaged in guessing, but not one brainwave expressing,
To the fowl whose strange black eyes a deep dark expression wore;
This and more I sat divining as my tendrils lolled reclining
On the aluminium shining by the light of fires score
All of London burning from the Martian heat-rays score
Still I cough with lungs so sore.

Then methought the air grew denser, fraught with some bacterial danger
From this wretched life-form perched above my hoods hatch door.
"Wretch", I cried, "Thy world is conquered by our forces that invaded
and we shall not be defeated by your microscopic war;
Our science implemented will end your futile tiny war!"
Quoth the Raven, "Eaten raw."

Swiftly the black bird upstarting took to its wing and darting
Darting down and biting – my left front tentacle it tore,
Once again it then alighted on its perch so much contented –
While I was quite far from delighted with this brand new pain I bore –
From the torn and bleeding tentacle which pain I now did bore.
Quoth the Raven, "Eaten raw."

The blood it was a-spurting from the ragged wound so hurting
I writhed and flailed asserting, "That was my tentacle you tore,
Is this the response given to my communicative striving?
A more undiplomatic gesture there never was before!
Acknowledge me your Master and desist your futile petty war!"
Quoth the Raven, "Eaten raw."

"Be that our word of parting, bird or fiend!" I shrieked, upstarting
tumbling from my cushion flailing for a weapon to make war.
"This doom shall not overtake me", I blurted as I raised the –
device of vengeance, pain and death in my rent tentacle so sore,
The gun did slip though, dropping from my tendril febrile and sore.
Quoth the Raven, "Eaten raw."

And the raven never flitting, still is sitting, still is sitting
Perched before the map of Paris just above my hoods hatch door;
my weakness ever growing, my doom it is approaching,
Carried on these black wings beating, pecking my tendrils on the floor.
Torn to shreds as I lie dying, dying on this ice cold floor
Torn to shreds and – eaten raw!

The Crystal Egg
By H.G. Wells

There was, until a year ago, a little and very grimy-looking shop near Seven Dials, over which, in weather-worn yellow lettering, the name of "C. Cave, Naturalist and Dealer in Antiquities," was inscribed. The contents of its window were curiously variegated. They comprised some elephant tusks and an imperfect set of chessmen, beads and weapons, a box of eyes, two skulls of tigers and one human, several moth-eaten stuffed monkeys (one holding a lamp), an old-fashioned cabinet, a fly-blown ostrich egg or so, some fishing-tackle, and an extraordinarily dirty, empty glass fish-tank. There was also, at the moment the story begins, a mass of crystal, worked into the shape of an egg and brilliantly polished. And at that two people who stood outside the window were looking, one of them a tall, thin clergyman, the other a black-bearded young man of dusky complexion and unobtrusive costume. The dusky young man spoke with eager gesticulation, and seemed anxious for his companion to purchase the article.

While they were there, Mr. Cave came into his shop, his beard still wagging with the bread and butter of his tea. When he saw these men and the object of their regard, his countenance fell. He glanced guiltily over his shoulder, and softly shut the door. He was a little old man, with pale face and peculiar watery blue eyes; his hair was a dirty grey, and he wore a shabby blue frock-coat, an ancient silk hat, and carpet slippers very much down at heel. He remained watching the two men as they talked. The clergyman went deep into his trouser pocket, examined a handful of money, and showed his teeth in an agreeable smile. Mr. Cave seemed still more depressed when they came into the shop.

The clergyman, without any ceremony, asked the price of the crystal egg. Mr. Cave glanced nervously towards the door leading into the parlour, and said five pounds. The clergyman protested that the price was high, to his companion as well as to Mr. Cave--it was, indeed, very much more than Mr. Cave had intended to ask when he had stocked the article--and an attempt at bargaining ensued. Mr. Cave stepped to the shop door, and held it open. "Five pounds is my price," he said, as though he wished to save himself the trouble of unprofitable discussion. As he did so, the upper portion of a woman's face appeared above the blind in the glass upper panel of the door leading into the parlour, and stared curiously at the two customers. "Five pounds is my price," said Mr. Cave, with a quiver in his voice.

The swarthy young man had so far remained a spectator, watching Cave keenly. Now he spoke. "Give him five pounds," he said. The clergyman glanced at him to see if he were in earnest, and when he looked at Mr. Cave again, he saw that the latter's face was white. "It's a lot of money," said the clergyman, and, diving into his pocket, began counting his resources. He had little more than thirty shillings, and he appealed to his companion, with whom he seemed to be on terms of considerable intimacy. This gave Mr. Cave an opportunity of collecting his thoughts, and he began to explain in an agitated manner that the crystal was not, as a matter of fact, entirely free for sale. His two customers were naturally surprised at this, and inquired why he had not thought of that before he began to bargain. Mr. Cave became confused, but he stuck to his story, that the crystal was not in the market that afternoon, that a probable purchaser of it had already appeared. The two, treating this as an attempt to raise the price still further, made as if they would leave the shop. But at this point the parlour door opened, and the owner of the dark fringe and the little eyes appeared.

She was a coarse-featured, corpulent woman, younger and very much larger than Mr. Cave; she walked heavily, and her face was flushed. "That crystal is for sale," she said. "And five pounds is a good enough price for it. I can't think what you're about, Cave, not to take the gentleman's offer!"

Mr. Cave, greatly perturbed by the irruption, looked angrily at her over the rims of his spectacles, and, without excessive assurance, asserted his right to manage his business in his own way. An altercation began. The two customers watched the scene with interest and some amusement, occasionally assisting Mrs. Cave with suggestions. Mr. Cave, hard driven, persisted in a confused and impossible story of an inquiry for the crystal that morning, and his agitation became painful. But he stuck to his point with extraordinary persistence. It was the young Oriental who ended this curious controversy. He proposed that they should call again in the course of two days--so as to give the alleged inquirer a fair chance. "And then we must insist," said the clergyman. "Five pounds." Mrs. Cave took it on herself to apologise for her husband, explaining that he was sometimes "a little odd," and as the two customers left, the couple prepared for a free discussion of the incident in all its bearings.

Mrs. Cave talked to her husband with singular directness. The poor little man, quivering with emotion, muddled himself between his stories, maintaining on the one hand that he had another customer in view, and on the other asserting that the crystal was honestly worth ten guineas. "Why did you ask five pounds?" said his wife. "Do let me manage my business my own way!" said Mr. Cave.

Mr. Cave had living with him a step-daughter and a step-son, and at supper that night the transaction was re-discussed. None of them had a high opinion of Mr. Cave's business methods, and this action seemed a culminating folly.

"It's my opinion he's refused that crystal before," said the step-son, a loose-limbed lout of eighteen.

"But Five Pounds!" said the step-daughter, an argumentative young woman of six-and-twenty.

Mr. Cave's answers were wretched; he could only mumble weak assertions that he knew his own business best. They drove him from his half-eaten supper into the shop, to close it for the night, his ears aflame and tears of vexation behind his spectacles. Why had he left the crystal in the window so long? The folly of it! That was the trouble closest in his mind. For a time he could see no way of evading sale.

After supper his step-daughter and step-son smartened themselves up and went out and his wife retired upstairs to reflect upon the business aspects of the crystal, over a little sugar and lemon and so forth in hot water. Mr. Cave went into the shop, and stayed there until late, ostensibly to make ornamental rockeries for gold-fish cases, but really for a private purpose that will be better explained later. The next day Mrs. Cave found that the crystal had been removed from the window, and was lying behind some second-hand books on angling. She replaced it in a conspicuous position. But she did not argue further about it, as a nervous headache disinclined her from debate. Mr. Cave was always disinclined. The day passed disagreeably. Mr. Cave was, if anything, more absent-minded than usual, and uncommonly irritable withal. In the afternoon, when his wife was taking her customary sleep, he removed the crystal from the window again.

The next day Mr. Cave had to deliver a consignment of dog-fish at one of the hospital schools, where they were needed for dissection. In his absence Mrs. Cave's mind reverted to the topic of the crystal, and the methods of expenditure suitable to a windfall of five pounds. She had already devised some very agreeable expedients, among others a dress of green silk for herself and a trip to Richmond, when a jangling of the front door bell summoned her into the shop. The customer was an examination coach who came to complain of the non-delivery of certain frogs asked for the previous day. Mrs. Cave did not approve of this particular branch of Mr. Cave's business, and the gentleman, who had called in a somewhat aggressive mood, retired after a brief exchange of words--entirely civil, so far as he was concerned. Mrs. Cave's eye then naturally turned to the window; for the sight of the crystal was an assurance of the five pounds and of her dreams. What was her surprise to find it gone!

She went to the place behind the locker on the counter, where she had discovered it the day before. It was not there; and she immediately began an eager search about the shop.

When Mr. Cave returned from his business with the dogfish, about a quarter to two in the afternoon, he found the shop in some confusion, and his wife, extremely exasperated and on her knees behind the counter, routing among his taxidermic material. Her face came up hot and angry over the counter, as the jangling bell announced his return, and she forthwith accused him of "hiding it."

"Hid what?" asked Mr. Cave.

"The crystal!"

At that Mr. Cave, apparently much surprised, rushed to the window. "Isn't it here?" he said. "Great Heavens! what has become of it?"

Just then Mr. Cave's step-son re-entered the shop from, the inner room--he had come home a minute or so before Mr. Cave--and he was blaspheming freely. He was apprenticed to a second-hand furniture dealer down the road, but he had his meals at home, and he was naturally annoyed to find no dinner ready.

But when he heard of the loss of the crystal, he forgot his meal, and his anger was diverted from his mother to his step-father. Their first idea, of course, was that he had hidden it. But Mr. Cave stoutly denied all knowledge of its fate, freely offering his bedabbled affidavit in the matter--and at last was worked up to the point of accusing, first, his wife and then his stepson of having taken it with a view to a private sale. So began an exceedingly acrimonious and emotional discussion, which ended for Mrs. Cave in a peculiar nervous condition midway between hysterics and amuck, and caused the step-son to be half-an-hour late at the furniture establishment in the afternoon. Mr. Cave took refuge from his wife's emotions in the shop.

In the evening the matter was resumed, with less passion and in a judicial spirit, under the presidency of the step-daughter. The supper passed unhappily and culminated in a painful scene. Mr. Cave gave way at last to extreme exasperation, and went out banging the front door violently. The rest of the family, having discussed him with the freedom his absence warranted, hunted the house from garret to cellar, hoping to light upon the crystal.

The next day the two customers called again. They were received by Mrs. Cave almost in tears. It transpired that no one could imagine all that she had stood from Cave at various times in her married pilgrimage. ... She also gave a garbled account of the disappearance. The clergyman and the Oriental laughed silently at one another, and said it was very extraordinary. As Mrs. Cave seemed disposed to give them the complete history of her life they made to leave the shop. Thereupon Mrs. Cave, still clinging to hope, asked for the clergyman's address, so that, if she could get anything out of Cave, she might communicate it. The address was duly given, but apparently was afterwards mislaid. Mrs. Cave can remember nothing about it.

In the evening of that day the Caves seem to have exhausted their emotions, and Mr. Cave, who had been out in the afternoon, supped in a gloomy isolation that contrasted pleasantly with the impassioned controversy of the previous days. For some time matters were very badly strained in the Cave household, but neither crystal nor customer reappeared.

Now, without mincing the matter, we must admit that Mr. Cave was a liar. He knew perfectly well where the crystal was. It was in the rooms of Mr. Jacoby Wace, Assistant Demonstrator at St. Catherine's Hospital, Westbourne Street. It stood on the sideboard partially covered by a black velvet cloth, and beside a decanter of American whisky. It is from Mr. Wace, indeed, that the particulars upon which this narrative is based were derived. Cave had taken off the thing to the hospital hidden in the dog-fish sack, and there had pressed the young investigator to keep it for him. Mr. Wace was a little dubious at first. His relationship to Cave was peculiar. He had a taste for singular characters, and he had more than once invited the old man to smoke and drink in his rooms, and to unfold his rather amusing views of life in general and of his wife in particular. Mr. Wace had encountered Mrs. Cave, too, on occasions when Mr. Cave was not at home to attend to him. He knew the constant interference to which Cave was subjected, and having weighed the story judicially, he decided to give the crystal a refuge. Mr. Cave promised to explain the reasons for his remarkable affection for the crystal more fully on a later occasion, but he spoke distinctly of seeing visions therein. He called on Mr. Wace the same evening.

He told a complicated story. The crystal he said had come into his possession with other oddments at the forced sale of another curiosity dealer's effects, and not knowing what its value might be, he had ticketed it at ten shillings. It had hung upon his hands at that price for some months, and he was thinking of "reducing the figure," when he made a singular discovery.

At that time his health was very bad--and it must be borne in mind that, throughout all this experience, his physical condition was one of ebb--and he was in considerable distress by reason of the negligence, the positive ill-treatment even, he received from his wife and step-children. His wife was vain, extravagant, unfeeling, and had a growing taste for private drinking; his step-daughter was mean and over-reaching; and his step-son had conceived a violent dislike for him, and lost no chance of showing it. The requirements of his business pressed heavily upon him, and Mr. Wace does not think that he was altogether free from occasional intemperance. He had begun life in a comfortable position, he was a man of fair education, and he suffered, for weeks at a stretch, from melancholia and insomnia. Afraid to disturb his family, he would slip quietly from his wife's side, when his thoughts became intolerable, and wander about the house. And about three o'clock one morning, late in August, chance directed him into the shop.

The dirty little place was impenetrably black except in one spot, where he perceived an unusual glow of light. Approaching this, he discovered it to be the crystal egg, which was standing on the corner of the counter towards the window. A thin ray smote through a crack in the shutters, impinged upon the object, and seemed as it were to fill its entire interior.

It occurred to Mr. Cave that this was not in accordance with the laws of optics as he had known them in his younger days. He could understand the rays being refracted by the crystal and coming to a focus in its interior, but this diffusion jarred with his physical conceptions. He approached the crystal nearly, peering into it and round it, with a transient revival of the scientific curiosity that in his youth had determined his choice of a calling. He was surprised to find the light not steady, but writhing within the substance of the egg, as though that object was a hollow sphere of some luminous vapour. In moving about to get different points of view, he suddenly found that he had come between it and the ray, and that the crystal none the less remained luminous. Greatly astonished, he lifted it out of the light ray and carried it to the darkest part of the shop. It remained bright for some four or five minutes, when it slowly faded and went out. He placed it in the thin streak of daylight, and its luminousness was almost immediately restored.

So far, at least, Mr. Wace was able to verify the remarkable story of Mr. Cave. He has himself repeatedly held this crystal in a ray of light (which had to be of a less diameter than one millimetre). And in a perfect darkness, such as could be produced by velvet wrapping, the crystal did undoubtedly appear very faintly phosphorescent. It would seem, however, that the luminousness was of some exceptional sort, and not equally visible to all eyes; for Mr. Harbinger--whose name will be familiar to the scientific reader in connection with the Pasteur Institute--was quite unable to see any light whatever. And Mr. Wace's own capacity for its appreciation was out of comparison inferior to that of Mr. Cave's. Even with Mr. Cave the power varied very considerably: his vision was most vivid during states of extreme weakness and fatigue.

Now, from the outset, this light in the crystal exercised a curious fascination upon Mr. Cave. And it says more for his loneliness of soul than a volume of pathetic writing could do, that he told no human being of his curious observations. He seems to have been living in such an atmosphere of petty spite that to admit the existence of a pleasure would have been to risk the loss of it. He found that as the dawn advanced, and the amount of diffused light increased, the crystal became to all appearance non-luminous. And for some time he was unable to see anything in it, except at night-time, in dark corners of the shop.

But the use of an old velvet cloth, which he used as a background for a collection of minerals, occurred to him, and by doubling this, and putting it over his head and hands, he was able to get a sight of the luminous movement within the crystal even in the day-time. He was very cautious lest he should be thus discovered by his wife, and he practised this occupation only in the afternoons, while she was asleep upstairs, and then circumspectly in a hollow under the counter. And one day, turning the crystal about in his hands, he saw something. It came and went like a flash, but it gave him the impression that the object had for a moment opened to him the view of a wide and spacious and strange country; and turning it about, he did, just as the light faded, see the same vision again.

Now it would be tedious and unnecessary to state all the phases of Mr. Cave's discovery from this point. Suffice that the effect was this: the crystal, being peered into at an angle of about 137 degrees from the direction of the illuminating ray, gave a clear and consistent picture of a wide and peculiar country-side. It was not dream-like at all: it produced a definite impression of reality, and the better the light the more real and solid it seemed. It was a moving picture: that is to say, certain objects moved in it, but slowly in an orderly manner like real things, and, according as the direction of the lighting and vision changed, the picture changed also. It must, indeed, have been like looking through an oval glass at a view, and turning the glass about to get at different aspects.

Mr. Cave's statements, Mr. Wace assures me, were extremely circumstantial, and entirely free from any of that emotional quality that taints hallucinatory impressions. But it must be remembered that all the efforts of Mr. Wace to see any similar clarity in the faint opalescence of the crystal were wholly unsuccessful, try as he would. The difference in intensity of the impressions received by the two men was very great, and it is quite conceivable that what was a view to Mr. Cave was a mere blurred nebulosity to Mr. Wace.

The view, as Mr. Cave described it, was invariably of an extensive plain, and he seemed always to be looking at it from a considerable height, as if from a tower or a mast. To the east and to the west the plain was bounded at a remote distance by vast reddish cliffs, which reminded him of those he had seen in some picture; but what the picture was Mr. Wace was unable to ascertain. These cliffs passed north and south--he could tell the points of the compass by the stars that were visible of a night--receding in an almost illimitable perspective and fading into the mists of the distance before they met. He was nearer the eastern set of cliffs; on the occasion of his first vision the sun was rising over them, and black against the sunlight and pale against their shadow appeared a multitude of soaring forms that Mr. Cave regarded as birds. A vast range of buildings spread below him; he seemed to be looking down upon them; and as they approached the blurred and refracted edge of the picture they became indistinct. There were also trees curious in shape, and in colouring a deep mossy green and an exquisite grey, beside a wide and shining canal. And something great and brilliantly coloured flew across the picture. But the first time Mr. Cave saw these pictures he saw only in flashes, his hands shook, his head moved, the vision came and went, and grew foggy and indistinct. And at first he had the greatest difficulty in finding the picture again once the direction of it was lost.

His next clear vision, which came about a week after the first, the interval having yielded nothing but tantalising glimpses and some useful experience, showed him the view down the length of the valley. The view was different, but he had a curious persuasion, which his subsequent observations abundantly confirmed, that he was regarding the strange world from exactly the same spot, although he was looking in a different direction. The long faÃ§ade of the great building, whose roof he had looked down upon before, was now receding in perspective. He recognised the roof. In the front of the faÃ§ade was a terrace of massive proportions and extraordinary length, and down the middle of the terrace, at certain intervals, stood huge but very graceful masts, bearing small shiny objects which reflected the setting sun. The import of these small objects did not occur to Mr. Cave until some time after, as he was describing the scene to Mr. Wace. The terrace overhung a thicket of the most luxuriant and graceful vegetation, and beyond this was a wide grassy lawn on which certain broad creatures, in form like beetles but enormously larger, reposed. Beyond this again was a richly decorated causeway of pinkish stone; and beyond that, and lined with dense red weeds, and passing up the valley exactly parallel with the distant cliffs, was a broad and mirror-like expanse of water. The air seemed full of squadrons of great birds, manoeuvring in stately curves; and across the river was a multitude of splendid buildings, richly coloured and glittering with metallic tracery and facets, among a forest of moss-like and lichenous trees. And suddenly something flapped repeatedly across the vision, like the fluttering of a jewelled fan or the beating of a wing, and a face, or rather the upper part of a face with very large eyes, came as it were close to his own and as if on the other side of the crystal. Mr. Cave was so startled and so impressed by the absolute reality of these eyes that he drew his head back from the crystal to look behind it. He had become so absorbed in watching that he was quite surprised to find himself in the cool darkness of his little shop, with its familiar odour of methyl, mustiness, and decay. And as he blinked about him, the glowing crystal faded and went out.

Such were the first general impressions of Mr. Cave. The story is curiously direct and circumstantial. From the outset, when the valley first flashed momentarily on his senses, his imagination was strangely affected, and as he began to appreciate the details of the scene he saw, his wonder rose to the point of a passion. He went about his business listless and distraught, thinking only of the time when he should be able to return to his watching. And then a few weeks after his first sight of the valley came the two customers, the stress and excitement of their offer, and the narrow escape of the crystal from sale, as I have already told.

Now, while the thing was Mr. Cave's secret, it remained a mere wonder, a thing to creep to covertly and peep at, as a child might peep upon a forbidden garden. But Mr. Wace has, for a young scientific investigator, a particularly lucid and consecutive habit of mind. Directly the crystal and its story came to him, and he had satisfied himself, by seeing the phosphorescence with his own eyes, that there really was a certain evidence for Mr. Cave's statements, he proceeded to develop the matter systematically. Mr. Cave was only too eager to come and feast his eyes on this wonderland he saw, and he came every night from half-past eight until half-past ten, and sometimes, in Mr. Wace's absence, during the day. On Sunday afternoons, also, he came. From the outset Mr. Wace made copious notes, and it was due to his scientific method that the relation between the direction from which the initiating ray entered the crystal and the orientation of the picture were proved. And, by covering the crystal in a box perforated only with a small aperture to admit the exciting ray, and by substituting black holland for his buff blinds, he greatly improved the conditions of the observations; so that in a little while they were able to survey the valley in any direction they desired.

So having cleared the way, we may give a brief account of this visionary world within the crystal. The things were in all cases seen by Mr. Cave, and the method of working was invariably for him to watch the crystal and report what he saw, while Mr. Wace (who as a science student had learnt the trick of writing in the dark) wrote a brief note of his report. When the crystal faded, it was put into its box in the proper position and the electric light turned on. Mr. Wace asked questions, and suggested observations to clear up difficult points. Nothing, indeed, could have been less visionary and more matter-of-fact.

The attention of Mr. Cave had been speedily directed to the bird-like creatures he had seen so abundantly present in each of his earlier visions. His first impression was soon corrected, and he considered for a time that they might represent a diurnal species of bat. Then he thought, grotesquely enough, that they might be cherubs. Their heads were round and curiously human, and it was the eyes of one of them that had so startled him on his second observation. They had broad, silvery wings, not feathered, but glistening almost as brilliantly as new-killed fish and with the same subtle play of colour, and these wings were not built on the plan of bird-wing or bat, Mr. Wace learned, but supported by curved ribs radiating from the body. (A sort of butterfly wing with curved ribs seems best to express their appearance.) The body was small, but fitted with two bunches of prehensile organs, like long tentacles, immediately under the mouth. Incredible as it appeared to Mr. Wace, the persuasion at last became irresistible that it was these creatures which owned the great quasi-human buildings and the magnificent garden that made the broad valley so splendid. And Mr. Cave perceived that the buildings, with other peculiarities, had no doors, but that the great circular windows, which opened freely, gave the creatures egress and entrance. They would alight upon their tentacles, fold their wings to a smallness almost rod-like, and hop into the interior. But among them was a multitude of smaller-winged creatures, like great dragon-flies and moths and flying beetles, and across the greensward brilliantly-coloured gigantic ground-beetles crawled lazily to and fro. Moreover, on the causeways and terraces, large-headed creatures similar to the greater winged flies, but wingless, were visible, hopping busily upon their hand-like tangle of tentacles.

Allusion has already been made to the glittering objects upon masts that stood upon the terrace of the nearer building. It dawned upon Mr. Cave, after regarding one of these masts very fixedly on one particularly vivid day that the glittering object there was a crystal exactly like that into which he peered. And a still more careful scrutiny convinced him that each one in a vista of nearly twenty carried a similar object.

Occasionally one of the large flying creatures would flutter up to one, and folding its wings and coiling a number of its tentacles about the mast, would regard the crystal fixedly for a space,--sometimes for as long as fifteen minutes. And a series of observations, made at the suggestion of Mr. Wace, convinced both watchers that, so far as this visionary world was concerned, the crystal into which they peered actually stood at the summit of the end-most mast on the terrace, and that on one occasion at least one of these inhabitants of this other world had looked into Mr. Cave's face while he was making these observations.

So much for the essential facts of this very singular story. Unless we dismiss it all as the ingenious fabrication of Mr. Wace, we have to believe one of two things: either that Mr. Cave's crystal was in two worlds at once, and that while it was carried about in one, it remained stationary in the other, which seems altogether absurd; or else that it had some peculiar relation of sympathy with another and exactly similar crystal in this other world, so that what was seen in the interior of the one in this world was, under suitable conditions, visible to an observer in the corresponding crystal in the other world; and vice versa. At present, indeed, we do not know of any way in which two crystals could so come en rapport, but nowadays we know enough to understand that the thing is not altogether impossible. This view of the crystals as en rapport was the supposition that occurred to Mr. Wace, and to me at least it seems extremely plausible...

And where was this other world? On this, also, the alert intelligence of Mr. Wace speedily threw light. After sunset, the sky darkened rapidly-- there was a very brief twilight interval indeed--and the stars shone out. They were recognisably the same as those we see, arranged in the same constellations. Mr. Cave recognised the Bear, the Pleiades, Aldebaran, and Sirius; so that the other world must be somewhere in the solar system, 7 and, at the utmost, only a few hundreds of millions of miles from our own. Following up this clue, Mr. Wace learned that the midnight sky was a darker blue even than our midwinter sky, and that the sun seemed a little smaller. And there were two small moons! "like our moon but smaller, and quite differently marked," one of which moved so rapidly that its motion was clearly visible as one regarded it. These moons were never high in the sky, but vanished as they rose: that is, every time they revolved they were eclipsed because they were so near their primary planet. And all this answers quite completely, although Mr. Cave did not know it, to what must be the condition of things on Mars.

Indeed, it seems an exceedingly plausible conclusion that peering into this crystal Mr. Cave did actually see the planet Mars and its inhabitants. And if that be the case, then the evening star that shone so brilliantly in the sky of that distant vision was neither more nor less than our own familiar earth.

For a time the Martians--if they were Martians--do not seem to have known of Mr. Cave's inspection. Once or twice one would come to peer, and go away very shortly to some other mast, as though the vision was unsatisfactory. During this time Mr. Cave was able to watch the proceedings of these winged people without being disturbed by their attentions, and although his report is necessarily vague and fragmentary, it is nevertheless very suggestive. Imagine the impression of humanity a Martian observer would get who, after a difficult process of preparation and with considerable fatigue to the eyes, was able to peer at London from the steeple of St. Martin's Church for stretches, at longest, of four minutes at a time. Mr. Cave was unable to ascertain if the winged Martians were the same as the Martians who hopped about the causeways and terraces, and if the latter could put on wings at will. He several times saw certain clumsy bipeds, dimly suggestive of apes, white and partially translucent, feeding among certain of the lichenous trees, and once some of these fled before one of the hopping, round-headed Martians. The latter caught one in its tentacles, and then the picture faded suddenly and left Mr. Cave most tantalisingly in the dark. On another occasion a vast thing, that Mr. Cave thought at first was some gigantic insect, appeared advancing along the causeway beside the canal with extraordinary rapidity. As this drew nearer Mr. Cave perceived that it was a mechanism of shining metals and of extraordinary complexity. And then, when he looked again, it had passed out of sight.

After a time Mr. Wace aspired to attract the attention of the Martians, and the next time that the strange eyes of one of them appeared close to the crystal Mr. Cave cried out and sprang away, and they immediately turned on the light and began to gesticulate in a manner suggestive of signalling. But when at last Mr. Cave examined the crystal again the Martian had departed.

Thus far these observations had progressed in early November, and then Mr. Cave, feeling that the suspicions of his family about the crystal were allayed, began to take it to and fro with him in order that, as occasion arose in the daytime or night, he might comfort himself with what was fast becoming the most real thing in his existence.

In December Mr. Wace's work in connection with a forthcoming examination became heavy, the sittings were reluctantly suspended for a week, and for ten or eleven days--he is not quite sure which--he saw nothing of Cave. He then grew anxious to resume these investigations, and, the stress of his seasonal labours being abated, he went down to Seven Dials. At the corner he noticed a shutter before a bird fancier's window, and then another at a cobbler's. Mr. Cave's shop was closed.

He rapped and the door was opened by the step-son in black. He at once called Mrs. Cave, who was, Mr. Wace could not but observe, in cheap but ample widow's weeds of the most imposing pattern. Without any very great surprise Mr. Wace learnt that Cave was dead and already buried. She was in tears, and her voice was a little thick. She had just returned from Highgate. Her mind seemed occupied with her own prospects and the honourable details of the obsequies, but Mr. Wace was at last able to learn the particulars of Cave's death. He had been found dead in his shop in the early morning, the day after his last visit to Mr. Wace, and the crystal had been clasped in his stone-cold hands. His face was smiling, said Mrs. Cave, and the velvet cloth from the minerals lay on the floor at his feet. He must have been dead five or six hours when he was found.

This came as a great shock to Wace, and he began to reproach himself bitterly for having neglected the plain symptoms of the old man's ill-health. But his chief thought was of the crystal. He approached that topic in a gingerly manner, because he knew Mrs. Cave's peculiarities. He was dumfounded to learn that it was sold.

Mrs. Cave's first impulse, directly Cave's body had been taken upstairs, had been to write to the mad clergyman who had offered five pounds for the crystal, informing him of its recovery; but after a violent hunt, in which her daughter joined her, they were convinced of the loss of his address. As they were without the means required to mourn and bury Cave in the elaborate style the dignity of an old Seven Dials inhabitant demands, they had appealed to a friendly fellow-tradesman in Great Portland Street. He had very kindly taken over a portion of the stock at a valuation. The valuation was his own, and the crystal egg was included in one of the lots. Mr. Wace, after a few suitable condolences, a little off-handedly proffered perhaps, hurried at once to Great Portland Street. But there he learned that the crystal egg had already been sold to a tall, dark man in grey. And there the material facts in this curious, and to me at least very suggestive, story come abruptly to an end. The Great Portland Street dealer did not know who the tall dark man in grey was, nor had he observed him with sufficient attention to describe him minutely. He did not even know which way this person had gone after leaving the shop. For a time Mr. Wace remained in the shop, trying the dealer's patience with hopeless questions, venting his own exasperation. And at last, realising abruptly that the whole thing had passed out of his hands, had vanished like a vision of the night, he returned to his own rooms, a little astonished to find the notes he had made still tangible and visible upon, his untidy table.

His annoyance and disappointment were naturally very great. He made a second call (equally ineffectual) upon the Great Portland Street dealer, and he resorted to advertisements in such periodicals as were lively to come into the hands of a bric-a-brac collector. He also wrote letters to The Daily Chronicle and Nature, but both those periodicals, suspecting a hoax, asked him to reconsider his action before they printed, and he was advised that such a strange story, unfortunately so bare of supporting evidence, might imperil his reputation as an investigator. Moreover, the calls of his proper work were urgent. So that after a month or so, save for an occasional reminder to certain dealers, he had reluctantly to abandon the quest for the crystal egg, and from that day to this it remains undiscovered. Occasionally, however, he tells me, and I can quite believe him, he has bursts of zeal, in which he abandons his more urgent occupation and resumes the search.

Whether or not it will remain lost for ever, with the material and origin of it, are things equally speculative at the present time. If the present purchaser is a collector, one would have expected the enquiries of Mr. Wace to have reached him through the dealers. He has been able to discover Mr. Cave's clergyman and "Oriental"--no other than the Rev. James Parker and the young Prince of Bosso-Kuni in Java. I am obliged to them for certain particulars. The object of the Prince was simply curiosity--and extravagance. He was so eager to buy because Cave was so oddly reluctant to sell. It is just as possible that the buyer in the second instance was simply a casual purchaser and not a collector at all, and the crystal egg, for all I know, may at the present moment be within a mile of me, decorating a drawing-room or serving as a paper-weight--its remarkable functions all unknown. Indeed, it is partly with the idea of such a possibility that I have thrown this narrative into a form that will give it a chance of being read by the ordinary consumer of fiction.

My own ideas in the matter are practically identical with those of Mr. Wace. I believe the crystal on the mast in Mars and the crystal egg of Mr. Cave's to be in some physical, but at present quite inexplicable, way en rapport, and we both believe further that the terrestrial crystal must have been--possibly at some remote date--sent hither from that planet, in order to give the Martians a near view of our affairs. Possibly the fellows to the crystals on the other masts are also on our globe. No theory of hallucination suffices for the facts.

Crystal Egg by Peter Fussey

The War of the Worlds: Aftermath

By Tony Wright

Based on characters created by Herbert George Wells

PROLOGUE

Mr Wells had been most insistent so, as the reader can surely see, I relented.

The story of my adventures has been very well received around the world, and it is due in no small part, to my mind, to Mr Wells' embellishment in his, admittedly highly readable, accounts. It is true that my experiences during that dark time were harrowing but I still fail to see why he chose my reminiscences over those of someone in His Majesty's Government or perhaps a soldier of his armies. In his reedy voice, Wells once told me that the common man would, in some future in which we shall be no part of, be able to feel the horror more than if told from the point of view of some warhorse of a General. What he didn't say was that the military, whilst they fought as bravely as any man in service could, were shown as ineffectual against the monsters within a very short time. So be it.

Wells approached me again, shortly after his work began to create interest.

'A sequel!' he cried as he poured us drinks at his house, 'You have to tell the world the rest of the story.'

'Why?' I asked bluntly.

'Why not?' Wells replied simply. He handed me a glass. 'Look. I know that there is much more to tell. When news of my story about you came out, you were approached to document the subsequent investigations on my recommendation, were you not?'

'I was,' I admitted.

'So,' he said. 'I understand you being reluctant to publish your experiences personally last time. God knows we all experienced the horror of what happened. But I feel that you should set down what happened afterwards for posterity. From what you have told me, it certainly fills in some of the details that people will want to know.'

'I don't know,' I said. 'Much of it was beyond me.'

'Then just give what you do know. Mankind needs to know.'

I sighed. 'Very well, I will give it some thought.'

And so I did.

Later, in the dark of night, with my beloved wife breathing softly beside me, I thought of how I would document such a thing. I was reluctant, still, but the idea had gripped me.

The story of my involvement with the Government is perhaps stranger than that of the war itself, as my esteemed reader will soon see. I also thought of the confidentially agreement I had signed. Could I expect not to feel the full force of the law in telling what I know?

This document, dear reader, is the result of these thoughts. If it is published, I hope it helps to supplement what has been told before.

Note: Whilst my fame, stemming from those who have worked out who I am, is most gratifying, it has somewhat invaded upon my privacy and that of my family of late. Therefore, for that reason, and to facilitate more ease in setting down my tale, I shall here assume the penname of John Smith.

Whilst my readers will doubtless have had their own experiences of the war, before I begin my narrative, I feel it may be prudent to say a little about my own in order to put the following tale into context. The following synopsis briefly covers only my own tribulations. For a more in-depth history of the war, there are other, far more learned, accounts available of events that interested parties can consult.

During the opposition of Mars that occurred in the latter days of the old Queen's reign, observers saw, through their telescopes, strange sights on the red Planet Mars.

First came odd green illuminations, marks on the surface and finally a spurt of green gas ejected into space. Following the last, more jets of gas were seen to erupt from Mars at 24 hourly intervals. The puzzled astronomers had little idea what these strange omens signified. Had they known, much hardship may have been avoided and many lives saved.

My friend, the noted astronomer Ogilvy, showed me a Martian eruption at his observatory one clear night and stated categorically that nothing could live on that barren desert of a world. How wrong he was.

As life went on, as always, on Earth, huge objects sped toward us at tremendous speed through the deep black void of space.

The first cylinder struck, many days later, at Midnight on Horsell Common in Surrey, not far from my home.

Ogilvy was at the site early and by mid morning a large crowd of curious onlookers had gathered. In the afternoon Ogilvy, the Journalist Henderson and Stent, the Astronomer Royal, began to direct men in the task of excavating the cylinder. At Sunset, the cylinder suddenly opened and the crowds moved back, alarmed. Inside the cylinder the gathered people could see the occupants of this vast conveyance; huge grotesque creatures with writhing tentacles and leathery skin.

After much discussion on how to proceed, it was decided to send a deputation to meet these travellers and offer them the hand of friendship. Waving a white flag, Ogilvy, Stent, Henderson and some other hardy souls advanced on the cylinder.

A loud drone emanated from the craft and suddenly, the Deputation were turned to flaming torches by a ray of heat fired by the invaders. The crowd panicked and scattered at this outrage, I was amongst them.

Soldiers arrived and threw a cordon around the Common, whilst, periodically, the Heat-ray pierced the darkness of the night.

Another cylinder fell the next day at Byfleet and the Army moved into place to meet it. That same day, the first of the Martians' Fighting Machines; great metal tripods, one hundred feet tall and carrying the dreaded Heat-rays, destroyed the Artillery at Horsell Common. This diabolical machine marched on and attacked Woking.

I saw my first machines in a storm on the road back to Maybury Hill from Leatherhead, where I had taken my wife to stay with her cousins. The dog-cart I had hired from the Landlord of The Spotted Dog had overturned as the horse reared at sight of the first machine and broke its neck. I watched in awe as the machines stalked away. At home in my study, I saw flames rise in the distance and machines busy at unknown tasks.

An Artilleryman came to my house and told me how his unit had been wiped out and of the destruction that the machines had wrought on the Common.

We decided, at dawn the next day to leave the house; the Artilleryman to report to his unit in London, whilst I would go back to Leatherhead to rejoin my wife.

At Shepperton Lock, more machines appeared and let loose their terrible weapons. One machine fell after a hit from a cannon shell, but the others had their terrible revenge. The Artilleryman and I were separated in the confusion; I barely escaped with my life after jumping into the water to escape the Heat-ray.

Heavy fighting took place South of London and the Martians machines continued their inexorable march towards London, emitting deafening howls – 'Ulla!'

As I carried on my journey, a Curate came across me. He was of the mind that these creatures that had set upon us were doing the Lord's work. Perhaps some terrible holy revenge for all Man's transgressions.

Together, we headed northwards.

Whilst moving on, we saw that the Martians unleashed yet another terrible weapon: the Black Smoke. This was fired from tubes on the machines and loosed toxic gases at anyone, or anything, in its path. When this weapon had done its foul work, the Martians sprayed jets of steam that turned the gas into an inert dust.

My brother, a medical student in London, had joined the exodus from the City after the reports of the carnage the Martians had begun reached the capital's citizens. With the train drivers refusing to return to London, and with the Martians fast approaching, my brother set off on foot. At High Barnet, he came upon two ladies in a pony-chaise. They were Mrs Elphinstone and Miss Elphinstone, her sister-in-law, and, after my brother had helped them to fight off some roughs out to steal their transport, he joined them on their journey to find a boat out of England.

At the Essex coast, they witnessed the well-reported battle between The Ironclad Ram *Thunder Child* and some of the Martian machines that appeared to threaten the fleeing shipping. With many other onlookers, he experienced the exultation of the initial success of this plucky ship in bringing down a metal monster, then the crashing despair as she was sent to her doom beneath the waves by a counter attack from the machine's companions, taking another of the machines with her as she expired.

As the smoke of battle cleared, my brother saw a great black shape soar overhead. This was the Martian's Flying Machine.

The Curate and I had now sheltered in an abandoned building. Suddenly, a cylinder landed on the house burying us in the cellar.

We stayed there for many days, hungry and thirsty with the Curate's rantings become more and more desperate and incomprehensible.

On seeing Martians feeding in the pit – feasting on the warm blood of living human beings – the Curate's fragile mind had snapped and he invited death by screaming out his anguish and horror. I, in desperation, knocked him out and he, to my abject horror, was pulled out right before my eyes by a claw a curious Martian had probed the cellar with.

I spent many more days in that pit until I could stand it no longer and I left my prison when signs of Martian activity seemed to cease.

I continued my weary journey toward London where, at Putney Hill, I again met up with the Artilleryman.

The soldier had taken refuge in a house there and had decided that Mankind's best hope was to take to the sewers and to begin anew down there. He felt that we could perhaps capture a Fighting Machine one day and even learn how to make them ourselves. He had begun digging a tunnel, which he showed me. At seeing how little he had done and how wide was the gulf between his dreams and his powers, I resolved to leave him and continue on my way.

London was deathly quiet. In a moment of extreme loneliness and anguish, I decided to end it all. I would throw myself at the mercy of the Martians! I approached one of the machines that stood stock-still and silent. I was not sent to my maker by this thing; the Martians were dying!

In a strange twist of fate, bacteria had attacked the creatures as soon as they had landed amongst us. Defenceless against these insignificant organisms due to their eradication on their home planet, the Martians had literally rotted from the inside.

As they fed on our blood, their fate had been sealed.

The invasion was over!

Now you are apprised of the facts of my experiences so far, dear reader, I will continue with my tale.

CHAPTER 1
The Approach

Perhaps a month had passed since the great disillusionment. I trust my esteemed reader will perhaps forgive me using one of Wells' phrases for that terrible war that cost so much, but I always found it most apt.

Plumes of smoke still rolled lazily over some parts of London and the South East. Great metal machines stood silent and unmoving here and there, glittering in the sun, like huge chess pieces carelessly dropped by the gods. Weeds, of a green and entirely earthly nature, already grew around the parts that touched the ground.

In the capital, bridges engineered by some of Mankind's most brilliant minds lay broken, their once proud arches snapped and torn, scattered like piles of toy bricks kicked by some petulant child in a nursery. The top of the Clock Tower had been sliced off cleanly, as though by a surgeon's knife, by a Heat-ray and stood, oddly intact and upright, a short way away as if the tower itself had sunk into the ground. Clumps of brown sludge still floated serenely down the river along with other debris. From time to time, the authorities, grim faced and muttering in hushed tones, patrolled in police launches fishing pale and bloated bodies from the murky water of the Thames.

My house in Surrey, unlike so many others, had escaped most of the destruction, barring a few displaced roof tiles and a smashed garden wall, and was quite habitable. The only real sign that something was amiss was a faint but omnipresent smell of burning inside that we could not disperse, no matter what we tried.

The noise and bustle of humanity was at full pace as I sat staring from the window of my study. Across the road I saw men swarming over houses, rebuilding. People rushed to and fro with carts containing building materials and furniture. A mangy, flea-bitten dog scurried nervously past. The so recently dead and black wreathed streets were alive with activity as man once again stamped his mark on the landscape that had seemed so surely lost. I imagined this was happening everywhere. The newspapers were often found calling the public to arms in the fight against decay and disease and despite the heavy death toll of the war, thousands had returned from their flight and were, sometimes unwillingly, being tasked with the rebuilding of the damaged areas. Grubby children chased each other noisily amongst the ruined houses and clambered over the fallen Martian machines as primates in the jungle whoop and jump amongst the trees.

The door to my study opened to reveal my wife's sweet face, disturbing my reverie.

'John? There are some men here to see you.'

'Who are they, my dear?' I asked, puzzled.

'Well, that's the odd thing. They say they represent the Government.'

'Very well,' I said. 'I will be in presently.'

Opening the sitting room door, I saw two men, to whom my wife, ever the gracious hostess, was handing steaming cups of tea. As usual when we had visitors, she had taken out the best china and the gleaming silver service and was offering sugar from a small bowl when I entered. A warm fire burned in the grate and the Grandfather clock ticked solidly in the corner.

My first visitor was an important looking fellow of around sixty years. A great handlebar moustache was draped over his lip and chops like a snowy white banner. His portly frame barely fit into the chair he was perched on and his small watery eyes regarded me as I entered.

'Ah! Here's our man,' he said in a gruff, but friendly, voice.

The other man looked up from stirring his tea. He was around thirty with dark wavy hair and a goatee. He was slight in frame and dressed impeccably in black.

'Indeed,' he said quietly. His eyes showed no emotion at all.

'Sir,' said the portly man, standing with some difficulty. 'Allow me to introduce myself. I am Sir George Cavendish and my assistant is James Horton. We are representatives of His Majesty's Government.' The man offered me a pudgy hand, which I shook. His grip was firm but his palms clammy.

The younger man nodded slightly, his blank eyes never leaving mine. His hands stayed firmly, I noticed, behind his back.

'Pleased to meet you, gentlemen. May I ask, to what do I owe this honour?' I found a chair and my wife handed me some tea, gave me a small nervous smile and then quietly left the room.

The portly man sat on the chair again and was answered with a small wooden creak of protest.

'Yes, of course. Well, you know Mr Wells, do you not?'

'Herbert? Why, yes I do,' I replied.

'He is an acquaintance of mine, also, and I have heard that he plans to publish your memories of our recent troubles.'

'Yes, he was most insistent. I think he wished to put forth the 'ordinary man's' view of events.'

'Quite so,' said Cavendish, his eyes fixed steadily on me. 'Most admirable.'

'Although, why his own memories are not enough is beyond me,' I continued. 'He is not forthcoming on the matter.'

'Well,' Cavendish explained. 'We have seen the drafts that you wrote for him and we were most impressed. On Wells' recommendation, we would like you to join us and document our further investigations.'

'I hardly think I am qualified,' I began.

'Please, let me finish. We very much need the 'man of the street's' view of things. We are not short of scientists, nor of military men. They will write their own reports. Whilst we expect that we cannot make much of what we may find public, we need a representative of the people, who will write in a way that they will understand and you would seem to fit the bill admirably. Your original draft shows a remarkable grasp of things. It's a pity we have had to ask Mr Wells to excise some of the finer details in the work he is undertaking based on your experiences.'

'You have?' I was shocked. Perhaps I should not have been, on reflection, but it came as a surprise at the time.

'Indeed. It would not do for some of the more … technical … aspects to be known.'

Horton, who had been silent until this point, spoke.

'It is for the good of the country, Mr Smith. Surely you must understand that.'

‘Of course. What do you have in mind?’

‘We will need you to pack some things …enough for a week or so, initially. You must not tell anyone where you are going, which is why I will say no more for now. Can we rely on you?’ Cavendish asked, setting down his cup.

I thought for a moment. The trauma of my experiences during the war was still very much with me. I awoke sweating and screaming every night as I remembered what had happened to my friend Ogilvy, and what the terrible consequences of my actions with the Curate had been. Not to mention the horrible fate that befell so many of my fellow men and women. Without my wife’s succour, I would surely be in some institution, like so many other poor wretches who had been found wandering the countryside, aimless and without hope or reason, after the carnage had ended.

Would this help exorcise those demons that lurked in the darkest reaches of the night, waiting to trouble me?

‘Would I be free to leave at any time?’

Cavendish nodded his great shaggy head. ‘We should like you to submit to a confidentiality agreement. You can only publish that which is cleared by either myself or Horton. Other than that, there are no restrictions.’

Curiosity had ridden rough shod over my doubts now. If only I had known what was to come.

‘Yes, then.’

‘Splendid!’ Cavendish beamed and both men stood. ‘You will be collected at 8 o’clock sharp tomorrow. Until then.’

With that, my strange guests said curt goodbyes and left, leaving me alone with my thoughts.

CHAPTER 2
An Old Companion

I slept little, and such sleep as came to me was, as usual, haunted by huge, glowing saucer eyes and the bloodcurdling screams of the dying.

Somewhat bleary eyed and deep in thought, I was sat before an untouched plate of kedgeree in my dining room when the cab arrived to take me to London at eight sharp. I took a swig of cooling tea and made my way to the front of the house to collect my bags.

My wife sobbed quietly as I left. She held me as passionately as she had when we found each other again on my return to the house weeks before and she trembled a little as I gently stroked her hair and muttered comforting words in her ear. We had lost each other once before and she was reluctant to let me go again. I whispered to her that I would be perfectly safe and that I would be back within a week. Both, as it turned out, were false.

Outside, a black cab sat waiting, the horse, steaming in the cool morning air, pawing impatiently at the ground with a hoof. The driver jumped down from his perch atop the cab and shambled toward me.

The cabbie, a rough-looking, red faced fellow of the city, unceremoniously threw my luggage, and me for that matter, into the transport and, with a sharp 'Hyah!' roused the horse into a trot towards London.

In normal circumstances, a train would have been the best mode of transport, but engineering works were still underway to clear debris and repair the tracks in many areas, making rail travel impractical. Resigned, I settled back into the cracked leather of the cab's interior, amid the smell of stale sweat and tobacco, and tried to make myself as comfortable as I could against the chill.

So on we went, but I remember little of the first part of the journey. As the cab clattered through the Surrey countryside, the driver swigged every so on from a flask. My tiredness and the rocking motion of our conveyance finally overcame me and I drifted off into sleep.

Primal dread and darkness surrounded me. A wet shuffling sound quickly turned my head. I peered fearfully into thick impenetrable gloom, trying to see what approached me.

I found myself powerless to move as the Martian lurched toward me. The huge eyes glowed like burning embers and the thing's lipless mouth was coated with a viscous drool. Thick cable-like tentacles rippled and powerful muscles under its glistening, grey-brown hide bunched as it came. Very close now, I felt the monstrosity's foul, stinking breath on my face and I could see every pore in the tough leathery skin.

The creature regarded me balefully for a moment and then it flourished a horrifyingly familiar instrument in one tentacle. I had seen this thing in a pit under a ruined house what seemed like years ago … and in my dreams ever since. The monster hooted softly as it pushed the spiked end of the apparatus closer and closer to me. I could only watch, paralysed, as my flesh was finally and inevitably pierced by the cold, sharp metal. As my blood began to flow, I cried out from the icy pain and I heard in the distance that dreadful howl.

'Ulla!'

With a start, I awoke again. A hulking shape loomed over me and I started. It was no foul beast from the stars regarding me but the cab driver. He stared at me curiously for a moment then shrugged.

''Alf hour,' he drawled and shambled away, muttering under his breath.

I unfolded myself from the cab, body aching from the rough journey, and stretched, taking a moment to absorb in my surroundings and shake off the disorientation that the nightmare had left.

We had stopped, I found, by Shepperton Lock under a cloudy sky, and immediately memories of the battle I had seen here before swamped me. I remembered vividly my flight into the water and the horror as I had waited for the Heat-ray to strike me. A light drizzle fell from the heavens as if in memory of that terrible day.

The church tower was still ruined, but scaffolding had been erected and piles of stone and other materials were ready for the rebuilding. Looking around, I saw the Inn was nearly unscathed and open for business, so I headed toward it, my mouth suddenly dry.

The Inn was busy but I managed to find a table and sat down. A young, rosy-cheeked woman came and cheerily took my order … a stiff drink. I suddenly missed my wife terribly. In the Inn, hushed whispering was punctuated occasionally by loud laughter or gruff exclamations. A thick haze of tobacco smoke hung in the alcohol-soaked air like fog.

As my drink arrived, raucous laughter from the corner of the room drew my attention. A loud, somehow familiar, voice was raised.

'We beat the blighters! Oh yes, my boys! They came and they couldn't take the pressure! They thought they had us, but they were no match for the human race!'

A small, drunken cheer came from the orator's companions.

The landlord glared from behind the bar at them.

'Landlord! More drinks, if you please! We wish to toast the human race!'

I tried to place the toastmaster's voice. Where had I heard it before?

I caught a glimpse of the man's back as he lurched to his feet and staggered to the bar.

The Landlord whispered harshly to him and the man dug into the pockets of his army uniform and, dragging out a heap of change, slammed it onto the wet bar. The Landlord shook his head despairingly, but took the coins and began pouring more drinks.

That was it. The man was wearing a very familiar uniform. Surely not?

As he turned round, I realised that it was indeed the Artilleryman. The very same man I had met twice before as calamity threatened the Earth. At the moment of that realisation, his eyes met mine and he started.

'You!' he mouthed silently. The startled look on his face changed slowly as a great grin broke onto his handsome face.

I found myself smiling.

His motley band of companions in the corner temporarily forgotten, he wandered over to me.

'It's you, my friend from Maybury Hill!' he exclaimed. 'Good lord!' Reaching me, he pumped my hand eagerly.

'Hullo!' I said simply. I could think of nothing else better as surprise was still on me. I had met this man twice before, during the war, but I had not expected to see him again after our last meeting.

'Landlord! A drink for my friend here! Champagne!' he called as he sat next to me. 'Just like old times, eh?' He winked conspiratorially.

Two glasses arrived with a bottle and the Artilleryman poured for us. Taking up a glass, he proposed a toast.

'To us, survivors!'

I waved my glass vaguely at him and sipped the drink. I remembered my old disgust at our last encounter and gave the bubbling drink a bitter aftertaste.

'So, how have you been?' the Artilleryman asked. He swigged his drink down and wiped his mouth on his sleeve.

'Very well,' I replied. I was increasingly aware that the gulf between this man and I was wider than ever.

'I thought you lost once again,' he said. 'You had that wild-eyed look I saw much during the war. Those others with it generally ended up as Martian fodder, I found.'

I smiled, I was only too aware, unconvincingly. 'Well, I am all right, as you can see. I went home and found my wife. All is well.' I did not mention that I had thought, like others it seems in that dark time, to sacrifice myself to the Fighting Machines and their hideous controllers.

'Good for you,' the soldier beamed. 'I continued with my plan. You remember?'

'I do,' I said grimly.

'It was going well too. But the monsters died and that was that. I had such great plans for getting back at them.' He suddenly looked unhappy.

'I remember. What are you doing now?'

'Well,' he said, smiling again. 'Soon after those things started to die off, a unit of soldiers came through mopping them up. Finishing them off. I joined up with them.'

'Finishing them off?'

'Yes. Helping them on their way,' he grinned. 'We showed them what English steel tastes like as they breathed their last.' He mimed stabbing at something on the ground and the gleam in his eyes disturbed me, somehow.

For some reason, despite all the Martians had done and what fate they had in store for us, I found the whole idea distasteful. It must have showed on my face.

'What?' His visage darkened visibly. 'You think we should have shown them mercy? They were as good as dead anyway. In a way, we did them a kindness. Stopped their suffering. More than they did for us, eh?'

Somehow, I doubted that kindness was in his heart as he skewered the creatures as they lay dying.

I was confused by these new feelings and changed the subject.

'I cannot stay long; I am again heading for London and my transport leaves soon.'

'Really?' The Artilleryman brightened again. 'Business?'

'Yes, something like that.'

He raised his glass which he had filled, again.

'To business!' I had the idea that this man would toast anything.

I sipped again from my glass and stood up.

'Well,' I said, extending my hand. 'It was very good seeing you again.'

He grasped my hand and shook it. 'And you too. Look me up if you are in this area again. I believe we are to be stationed here for some while yet.'

'That I will.'

Turning as I left the Inn, I saw the Artilleryman wander back to his friends and I wondered vaguely if fate would bring us together again in the future.

CHAPTER 3
A Brave New World

The final stage of the journey was fairly uneventful. The only incident came when a motor-car careered, screaming like a banshee, around a blind corner and made our horse rear. The cabbie snarled curses at it as he fought to control the frightened horse and he was answered by the shrill parping of the contraption's horn, which did nothing to lighten the man's mood.

We travelled on through countryside scorched and black in places. Through towns busy with activity and ringing with the laughs and good humour of the saved. Here and there, birds perched on the remnants of the great titans that had so threatened to destroy all.

We arrived, after some time, at our destination.

So unlike the dead, silent wasteland I had wandered in the last days of the war, wishing only for death myself, London was breathing strong and sure once again. Like a living creature, it had fought against the invading alien organisms and was healing once more. Through busy streets we weaved for a time, the cabbie expertly steering us amidst the throng and bustle, the calls of street vendors and newspaper boys following us.

To my surprise, we eventually stopped, not at some Government building, but at South Kensington Underground Station. People and vehicles passed us, rushing to and fro, as the cab halted. I stared at the ornate frontage of the station for a moment uncertainly.

'Is this the right place?' I leaned out of the window and asked the driver finally.

'We are to wait here,' he replied simply and sank into his cloak until only his hat showed.

Soon, I spied Cavendish and Horton emerging from the Station. Horton's face was as impassive as it had been the day before, but Cavendish was radiating warmth like a small sun.

'My dear fellow!' he cried shaking my hand as I stepped out of the cab. 'A pleasant trip?'

'Pleasant enough' I replied, rather grumpily. 'The train would have been quicker.'

'Yes,' Cavendish said, non-committally, and motioned me towards the station. 'Don't worry about your things, I'll have them sent on.'

'Where are we going?' I asked, curious now.

'Underground,' Cavendish winked and marched off into the station building. I followed and Horton fell in behind.

I was extremely puzzled now. Underground? What could he mean?

A small grizzled man, dressed in a dark uniform with no visible markings, appeared and whisked us through the concourse and we found ourselves on a platform. It was quite deserted. I felt, rightly as it turned out, that this was not a platform for the public use. The small man left us.

Cavendish made small talk while we waited and presently a train arrived. It had only one carriage and we boarded and sank into plush seats.

'Don't get too comfortable,' Cavendish said. 'It's not far.'

The train screeched along a dark tunnel for a short while then began to slow. We stopped at another station. This one gleamed as if quite new and was kept in very good order indeed. A couple of men in dark uniforms stood to attention on either side a short distance away. Hobbs Lane was the name of the station, a sign informed me.

'Hobbs Lane?' I said. 'I've never heard of this station.'

A small smile touched Horton's lips.

'That, Mr Smith, is because it is not a public station. It is for His Majesty's Government use only. Simply put, it doesn't exist.'

'I see,' I said, but I didn't.

We alighted from the carriage and walked across the platform. The men on the platform looked straight ahead as if we were not there. A gate opened and an officious looking man in yet another plain black uniform cast suspicious eyes over us.

'Ah. You are expected, Sir George,' he said and held the gate open for us.

At the end of a short brightly lit corridor was a gate. This opened to reveal an ornate gilt lift. The lift operator tipped his hat in our direction and shut the gate behind us. He pressed a small red button and the lift lurched down the shaft.

My curiosity was running rampant now.

'What on –?'

'Please have patience, my dear fellow. All will be revealed soon,' Cavendish said.

The lift gate was opened once more and we entered into a small lobby. Two great steel doors were before us. As we approached, a small slot in the right hand door slid aside to reveal two grey eyes that regarded us carefully for a moment. The slot slid back again with a snap and there was silence. Then, a minute or so later, a rumbling whine and the sound of great pistons started up and the doors slowly parted.

'Hydraulic,' said Cavendish, as if it explained everything.

Another man in black was waiting behind the doors and we were ushered respectfully into an unexpectedly cavernous space. Looking around, I could see, far in the distance above, small pin-pricks that could only be electric lights. They looked, to me, like the aloof stars in the night sky. What was the purpose of such an enormous space beneath the feet of the unsuspecting public, I wondered, awe struck. We walked upon a smooth, dry surface and the air was pleasantly warm and I could not help but marvel at what a feat of engineering the excavation of this place must have been. A low hum and whir of distant machinery hit my ears from all around.

Here and there in the huge space were things covered with scaffolding. Huge shapes, some smooth, some more angular had enormous tarpaulins draped over them. I instinctively had the impression of machinery of some sort. White coated men were looking at charts and swarming over the scaffolding, busily writing notes on clipboards and chatting animatedly amongst themselves.

Men in army uniforms brandishing rifles watched the scientists intently, for that is what the men in white obviously were.

Cavendish gently steered me toward a great glinting shape. I approached but jumped back as I saw a small puff of green smoke.

My mind racing, I stared harder at the thing. I saw a great bulk of metallic body with something protruding from it. Disbelievingly, I watched as the protuberance moved.

'Here we are, Smith,' beamed Cavendish proudly and gestured grandly at the thing. His look of satisfaction quickly changed to alarm at my reaction.

As the hood of the Fighting Machine swung round to regard me with what seemed like huge, dead eyes, I screamed.

Human Fighting Machine Schematics by Michael Grote

CHAPTER 4
Explanations

As light pierced the darkness and my consciousness returned, I caught muffled voices which slowly became clearer.

'… should not have brought him!' a voice hissed.

'Now, now, Horton, I am entirely at fault. I should have explained to him beforehand what we are doing here. The man has had a long day and was quite unprepared for what he saw.' As my vision cleared, I saw the second voice belonged to Cavendish.

I caught the vague reek of smelling salts and saw a white – coated man standing over me.

'Gentlemen!' the man said.

Cavendish marched over to my side and his concerned face peered at me.

'How are you, my dear chap?' he boomed. 'You gave us quite a fright.'

Panic gripped me as I remembered what I had seen before I had, evidently, fainted. I sat up on the couch I had been laid on.

'The machine!' I breathed. 'What-?'

'Calm yourself,' Cavendish said gently. 'I will explain presently, when you feel a little better. I can assure you that you are in no danger here.'

Despite Cavendish's promise, I felt alarm bells ringing frantically within my head again. Nevertheless, I sank back into the couch.

Horton appeared next to his colleague. His face was as impassive as ever as he studied me, but I thought that, for a second, I saw something flash across his eyes.

The white-coated man handed me a small glass of brandy, which I sank with one gulp. The liquid instantly spread warmth through my body.

'A fine way to treat my exquisite Napoleon brandy,' Cavendish chortled. 'How do you feel?'

'A little better, but, I must confess, perplexed,' I said. 'A Martian machine is loose in this …place and you appear not the least bit concerned.'

'Not loose. Everything is entirely under human control.' Cavendish flashed the same proud smile that I had seen before. Yellow teeth glinted in the dimly lit room. Looking around I caught glimpses of ornate brass fittings and acres of leather upholstery. A large wooden desk stood before a large bookshelf stuffed with books and papers. The couch in which I lay creaked gently when I shifted.

'You mean to say that you can control those things?' I was amazed.

'Some of the finer details elude us for the moment, but we are making great strides on that front daily.'

'But how did you get them in here?'

'Magic!' he said, grinning like a schoolboy again. 'Seriously, it was not easy, but there are more ways into this laboratory than the way we entered.'

'I see,' I said nodding, but I did not see at all.

Horton stepped forward. 'Mr Smith must be very tired and hungry.'

Cavendish glared at him, suddenly quite at odds with the jovial figure he had thus far portrayed to me. It was if this man greatly objected to having his boasts interrupted. Then, as if remembering himself, he turned back to me, the ever-present grin back on his chubby face.

'Of course. You must go and refresh yourself. I think we shall have dinner soon.'

An orderly was summoned and I was ushered out of the room down a long corridor of whitewashed stone. My guide turned a corner and opened a door for me.

I found my luggage already in the extravagantly decorated room and, still puzzled, I took in my surroundings. The bed was covered with thick blankets and the plush carpet was thick and springy underfoot. Polished brass lamps stood on small tables and a chestnut writing table stood to one side laden with clean, watermarked sheets of paper and writing implements standing ready for use. A large richly upholstered wing chair stood in a corner. Pictures of sea and land battle scenes from history covered the walls here and there; Nelson sailed at Trafalgar and Wellington spurred his troops on at Waterloo in vivid colours.

I was slightly baffled to find that there were curtains hanging on one wall of the room but I did not know why. Closer inspection revealed the reason for my puzzlement. There were no windows behind them. Of course windows deep underground would have been superfluous to say the least and I momentarily found the whole situation vaguely ridiculous. I was surprised to hear a guffaw and it took a few seconds to realise that it came from me, not some interloper. Suddenly deflated, I lay down on the huge comfortable bed and tried to clear my mind.

Dinner was excellent. It appeared that the Government spared no expense in making its workers and guests comfortable in this facility. We dined on the finest beef I have ever tasted, washed down by expensive red wine in a spacious, yet cosy, dining room. I ate my meal in the company of Horton and Cavendish but was vaguely surprised not to see others there. I supposed that the workers ate elsewhere.

After the huge and satisfying dinner, eaten with gold cutlery off finest bone china, we all retired to a panelled library and sank into comfortable leather armchairs. We each clutched a glass of port and huge cigars.

'So, Smith,' Cavendish said at length. 'It's time I filled you in on a few details, what?'

I nodded silently, contemplating the dark liquid in my glass.

Cavendish puffed on his cigar briefly as if deciding where to start.

'You know all about the war, of course and how it ended. Without our allies, the bacteria, we would have been finished.'

'Quite,' I said. 'A lucky escape.'

'Exactly!' Cavendish pointed his cigar at me. 'You are quite right. The Martian fiends were bent on destruction and slavery. They planned to use their machinery to take what is rightfully ours and feed off us like so many cattle. We had no chance; our soldiers fought bravely, but many who resisted were wiped out like ants by the Heat-ray and the sheer power of the Fighting Machines.'

'Yes,' I said. 'But they failed.'

'Of course! But it was by accident, not design. We cannot assume they will not try again.'

This made me sit up in my chair sharply, my mind racing as I considered this. The port sloshed around my glass like a miniature tidal wave.

'Good God!' I exclaimed. 'Do you really think that's possible?'

'They made a mistake,' Cavendish said gravely. 'They will surely learn from it.'

There was silence as that sobering thought hung in the air. I sank back into the chair.

'So,' Cavendish continued after a moment. 'His Majesty's Government wishes to be ready for such an eventuality.'

'You mean to learn how to use the machines?' I asked.

'We do. We have made great progress, even in this short time, but we still have much to discover. The operation of the machines is not as complex as we first thought but HOW they work is still very much a mystery. Many of the machines left behind are wrecked or partially inoperable. We have to discover how to build them ourselves.'

It made sense to me. If the Martians concocted some form of antidote to their weakness, we would have to be ready to fight. I sipped at my drink distractedly.

'We are watching Mars closely, obviously. Telescopes worldwide are trained on Mars, looking for activity. We are lucky also to have other means.'

'Other means?' I was again curious.

Cavendish grinned. 'Yes. Finish your Port, I have something I'd like you to see.'

CHAPTER 5
Observations

Cavendish rummaged in his pocket for a moment and pulled out a set of keys.

'Ah, here we are,' he said, advancing on a huge walk-in safe at the corner of his office.

Horton took folded himself into a wing chair in the corner of this plush, yet functional, room and sat quietly watching, his fingers steepled under his long chin.

Inserting the keys, Cavendish dextrously twisted the number dial this way and that, stood back and yanked the handle. With a solid sounding clank, the door was pulled open.

Cavendish's large frame disappeared into the darkness within for a moment, then re-emerged holding a large, ornately carved wooden box.

Placing it carefully and reverently on his massive oaken desk amidst a jumble of inkwells, blotters and writing implements and papers, as if it contained a relic of the Lord himself, he spoke.

'This box, my friend, contains one of our most important finds. This device could give us the warning we need in the event our erstwhile conquerors resume their plans.' He took a small key on his key ring, inserted it into a small golden lock in the box and slowly lifted the lid.

Inside the box, on a cushion of blue-black velvet, was an ovoid shape covered in a cloth. Cavendish pulled this last away to reveal an egg-like object.

'Beautiful, is it not?' Sir George breathed. Horton, as usual, remained quite silent.

'It is not a Faberge,' I said with authority. I had an acquaintance who had shown me one of the Imperial Eggs.

Cavendish regarded me for a moment with his watery eyes. 'Indeed it is not. Those trinkets cannot touch this in terms of beauty, nor rarity.'

The Crystal Egg was beautiful. But somehow it seemed to me beautiful in the way Nature at her most cruel can be. The thing was eerie to behold.

It was like a giant cut diamond. Not a flaw could I see within its fabric. Its facets shone in the electric lights of the study. I looked closer. Within, as I watched, small flecks of light appeared to play. The lights almost instantly held a slight mesmerizing sway over me. If Cavendish and Horton had left me, I may well have stared into that strange device forever.

'You see them, eh? Not everyone can.' Cavendish grinned proudly at me as if I were a promising pupil. My trance was broken by his voice.

'What is it?' I asked tearing my eyes away. 'Who made this?'

'Who made it is unclear,' he admitted. 'But we have every reason to believe it is of Martian origin.'

'Martian?' I was surprised.

'Horton came upon it quite by chance. It had sat for some time in a little antique shop run by a queer little fellow by the name of Cave and Horton learned about it from a friend of his at St Catherine's Hospital. When Mr Cave died recently, Horton 'acquired' it. Blind luck we found it at all, really.'

I glanced at Horton, briefly, but he merely returned my gaze with those unreadable eyes of his and said nothing.

'If it is Martian, how did it get here? Did they bring it with them?' I asked.

Cavendish shook his head. 'It was here before they landed.'

I was more baffled than ever. 'How can that be?'

'I wish we knew,' the man seemed uncomfortable with his lack of knowledge. 'What is important is what it can do for us.'

'What is that?' I asked.

'Sit in this chair before the egg.'

I moved to the chair that Cavendish indicated and sat down with, I admit, a little apprehension.

'That's it,' Cavendish continued in hushed tones. 'Now look into the Egg. No, move your head up a little. There, that should be about the right angle.'

I, shifted my weight on the chair a little and, feeling as comfortable as I could be, stared into the Egg once again. The lights danced before my eyes once more then seemed to home in on each other. There was now one soft light that slowly grew brighter. I began to see pictures.

I saw odd-looking buildings, domes and spinnerets; buildings that reminded me of the mosques of the East. They stood next to canals in which murky water flowed sluggishly, choked, seemingly, by a familiar plant. I saw this vegetation everywhere. Red Vegetation.

'My God!' I breathed.

Bulky, grey-brown shapes bounced and leaped on thick tentacles around this surreal city. A five-legged, crab-like machine stalked by, the sun glinting off its metallic surface. Pale biped figures sat passively in a great basket on its back. More bipeds were being led, like docile cows, across a vast city square by other brown shapes.

Other machines stalked by as I watched, familiar and yet different, their uses unfathomable.

The scene changed, suddenly, to a large, desert-like area. I could see buildings in the distance so I assumed that this was outside of the city. I saw a huge black bulk lift ponderously off the arid ground, blowing up huge clouds of red dust. A crowd of the brown shapes beneath the machine danced around excitedly at this.

I tore my disbelieving eyes away from the somehow nightmarish sight.

'Is this Mars?' I asked finally.

'It can be nowhere else,' Cavendish replied simply.

'Well,' I said after a moment. 'Now I see what you meant by other ways of observing. Incredible!'

Cavendish nodded. 'We can observe much of what happens on the planet. Any undue activity and we shall spot it.'

A thought sped into my mind. 'Can they not see us through this thing?'

'We don't know,' Cavendish answered. 'They seem to peer into it from time to time. It is most disconcerting to look into it and see the eyes of a Martian seemingly look straight back at you, I can assure you. We have guessed that they have similar devices on Mars but they show no sign of actually seeing us looking at them. The view in the Egg changes periodically, but we have no idea why and how.'

I could think of nothing else to say. This thing was truly one of the strangest devices I had seen yet.

Cavendish stood. 'I think that's enough wonders for one day, Smith. It is late and we have a full day ahead of us tomorrow. We should all get some rest.'

Back in my room, it took me some time to quiet my thoughts and to try to make sense of all I had seen so far. I wrote a rough account of this first most amazing day in my journal. When I had finished, still confused and utterly exhausted, I went to bed.

I was asleep the moment my head touched the pillow.

CHAPTER 6
The Tour

I awoke at around ten the next morning much refreshed. I had not dreamt of the Martians or their machines for the first time, perhaps, since the war had ended.

Perhaps, I think, the massive sensory overload of the previous day had prompted my weary mind to protect me from further depravations. Whatever the reason, I felt much better and ready to face whatever new amazements the day might hold.

As I was washing, an orderly in black trousers and a white jerkin rapped on my door and, opening it, peered into the room.

'Breakfast, Sir?' he said and, when he had seen I was awake, disappeared the way he had come.

When I had dressed, the orderly, who had waited for me outside my door, escorted me to the dining room where I found Cavendish and Horton waiting for me. They had evidently eaten long before and sat nursing steaming cups of coffee.

'Did you sleep well, old man?' Cavendish asked, placing his cup on its bone china saucer.

'Like a top,' I answered. 'I'm ravenous. What's for breakfast?'

The orderly appeared again, as if by some unspoken command, and placed before me a plate of freshly caught Scottish kippers, accompanied by scrambled egg and a pile of hot buttered toast. The smell instantly made my mouth water and I jumped into a chair and set to the repast with gusto, washing it down with good, strong coffee.

As I devoured the meal, Horton watched me silently whilst Cavendish made small talk.

'When you are ready, Smith,' the older man said at length, 'we shall take you on a tour of our facility. To write properly of our work you will need to see it for yourself.'

Pushing my empty plate away and finishing the last of my coffee, I stood satisfied.

'Then there is no time like the present.'

We walked together down another long, sloping corridor, Cavendish chatting animatedly, as was his way, and Horton bringing up the rear like some silent shadow. I found myself feeling disoriented as there were no signs and one corridor looked much alike another. Unlike the extravagantly decorated rooms I had seen so far, the walls were rough, bare stone and the smooth floor was painted a dull, battleship grey.

Electric lights were fixed to the walls at intervals and we cast strange distorted shadows around us.

I had the idea that, as the slope of the corridor got slightly steeper, I thought I knew how Verne's Professor Hardwigg and his party must have felt as they started on their journey into the bowels of the Earth. Unlike those intrepid explorers, though, we had no runes to guide us.

Soon, we came to a dog-leg in the corridor and Cavendish pulled and held open some large wooden double doors.

I went ahead and found myself in another cavernous chamber. In this one, my ears caught a dull throbbing sound and in front of me, a large metal stand held something bulky. It was a large, matt black, rectangular box with a tube protruding from one end of it. I realised quickly that the sound was emanating from this thing.

'Do you recognise that?' Cavendish asked from over my shoulder.

'Dear God! It's a Heat-ray, isn't it?'

'It is,' Cavendish confirmed, grinning. 'Soon, we hope to be able to fire it and perhaps even make our own.'

I was astounded. 'You mean to fire it? It's too dangerous man! I've seen what those things can do!'

I glanced at Horton and caught him gazing at me once more. I thought I saw a glimpse of a look of curiosity pass his eyes, but it was gone as soon as quickly as it had appeared.

'I'm assured it will be quite safe under the right conditions,' Cavendish said dismissively. 'It is apparently quite undamaged and we will take every precaution possible.'

'Do you know how it works?' I asked. 'The papers said that its workings were unfathomable.'

'Putting it extremely simply, we are coming to the conclusion that it works using energy created at an atomic level. We cannot be sure how this happens, though, and we continue to investigate.'

'You understand it so little and yet you think to fire it?' It struck me as madness.

'We will,' Cavendish answered determinedly, 'when the time is right. These devices could be our best defence. Imagine being able to use the Martian's own weapons to defeat them! We must continue our research'

I said no more but I thought of the Artilleryman, who had made a similar plea in a different and more turbulent time.

There was no more to be said on the subject, it seemed and our group fell silent. I turned to see a small group of scientists, that were gathered around the Heat-ray tube, watching us, but they glanced busily at papers and clipboards when they saw me observe them.

We continued the tour.

The next area I was shown contained another Martian machine, or part of one anyway. It was a Fighting Machine, without doubt, but the legs had been severed, whether by design or accident I could not say, about ten feet from where they joined the body of the machine. The body of the machine had dark, rusty-red splashes on it, which, I realised with some dismay as we grew closer, appeared to be blood. Elsewhere, a large scratch and scuff-marks covered the side of the device, as if this machine had fallen heavily as its occupant perished. A large dent in the metal toward the rear seemed to confirm this.

As I watched, a young man in a one-piece suit clambered up a ladder into the hood and disappeared from view.

'The controls, as I suggested before, are quite simple,' Cavendish explained. 'There are a system of levers in the hood which move the thing around. The machines are, essentially, driven by way of a sort of artificial muscle. It really is quite something. You will, of course, have seen the green smoke that emanates from the machines as they walk and we are analysing this substance to see if it can be replicated. At the moment, we can only drive machines that have been left operational, but we hope to be able to create our own if we can unlock their secrets.'

Fascinated, I watched as the hood of the machine swayed from side to side, then up and down. Suddenly, the machine lurched forward uncertainly as the driver struggled with the controls, the truncated legs making sharp clanks as they impacted with the stone floor. It was a disturbing sight, even if the being at the controls was human.

I glanced at my companions. Horton looked as impassive and unimpressed as ever, Cavendish was making small clapping motions with his hands. He reminded me of an oversized schoolboy spying his first steam engine.

The Fighting Machine jerked forward a little more and then stopped. Suddenly, there was a whine and one of the legs swung violently and unexpectedly out to the side. Nearby scientists scattered. The whole machine wobbled slightly and the hood flailed around like the head of a wounded snake. Then the device slowly toppled over onto its belly with a resounding crash that echoed like the report of a cannon around the huge space. White-coated scientists rushed into the resulting cloud of dust to help the stunned driver out, whilst others, with dismayed faces, inspected the machine. A scientist walked quickly over to us and whispered something into Cavendish's ear. Cavendish whispered harshly back and the man disappeared again.

'Problems?' I asked. To my surprise, I imagined I saw a smirk, ever so briefly, flicker across Horton's face.

'Teething troubles,' Cavendish grumbled. 'It's to be expected. Come, Smith, I think it's time you saw our biggest secret.' As we left, the driver of the Fighting Machine, shaking his head as if in a daze but seemingly otherwise uninjured, was led away, supported by two soldiers.

After traversing more corridors, as blank and featureless as before, we wandered through a kind of airlock fronted by a huge steel door, not unlike one you would see in a bank vault, into another room. This place was smaller than some of the other spaces I had thus seen and was dimly lit. My nose was assailed by a sickly sweet smell that I knew but could not place, as I entered, and the air felt thick and oppressive. It was very warm in this room.

At one end I saw a great steel door with several locks on it. Huge rivets dotted its surface and it gleamed as if highly polished … or new.

An army sergeant with cropped salt and pepper hair and a neatly trimmed moustache, stood up quickly from behind his desk near the door, his chair squealing on the floor, and hurriedly dropped a copy of Pearson's Magazine to the, otherwise empty, wooden surface.

'Stand easy, Sergeant,' Cavendish said, amiably. 'How is our guest?' Who was he talking about? I was puzzled.

'Restless, Suh!' barked the soldier, evidently, from the drawl, a Scotsman. 'Made a helluva din earlier. I don't think he likes the food, Suh!' He winked, almost imperceptibly, at Cavendish and neither seemed aware that I had seen it.

'Well, he'll have to make do won't he?' Cavendish said. 'Come, Smith, meet our friend.'

I walked forward, uncertain. The Sergeant, with great care I noted, unlocked a slot in the door and Cavendish waved me forward, a slight smile on his ruddy face. I glanced at Horton. He nodded almost imperceptibly but, for a second, I thought I caught a look of concern cross his face. A slight hissing and the sound of something heavy shifting suddenly emanated, it seemed, from whatever lay in the room beyond.

Taking a deep breath and steeling myself, although I knew not why, I put my eyes to the slot.

Hooting softly, the Martian stared steadily and menacingly back at me.

Human Fighting Machine by Brendan Perkins

CHAPTER 7
Exorcising Demons

Physiologically speaking, the Martians are far more complex and hard to fathom than my friend Wells ever imagined. This fact was proved by the presence of that thing before my disbelieving eyes.

'Surprised?' Cavendish smiled. This smile had none of the usual warmth and I suddenly felt that cruelty, not unlike the cruelty of the schoolboy who delights in pulling the legs asunder from a helpless daddy-long-legs, lurked within this man.

'I … how?' I could say no more.

'You're quite safe. It cannot escape.' Cavendish's small eyes gleamed with barely concealed excitement.

I turned to face the man and felt the Martian's eyes bore into my back. I fancied I was bathed in the stare of that loathsome creature, as if bombarded by the rays of some malignant sun. I felt very uncomfortable but endeavoured to ignore the feeling and satiate my curiosity.

I gathered myself together a little. 'How is it alive? Did they not all die?'

'We found it within the pit in Horsell Common. The first landing site, as you will no doubt know. I believe you were there upon the opening of the cylinder, were you not? Terrible business, I am told. Anyway, our friend here was in the cylinder surrounded by its dead comrades. Barely alive then, but it appears to be doing well at the moment. '

'Yes, but why is it alive at all?' I felt the question was being avoided.

Cavendish was not smiling now and he sighed. 'We think that some, certainly this specimen you have just seen at any rate, were immune. Not many are thought to have survived but that is not the last of it. We think they were working to combat their demise.'

My God. This latest news caused a flutter of panic. I flopped into a chair next to the guard's desk.

The guard appeared by my side with a glass of water so quickly that I had the idea that he had seen the reactions to the imprisoned monstrosity before, but I ignored the glass he offered me and simply stared at Cavendish. The guard placed the water carefully on the desk next to me and melted back into the shadows.

'How?' I continued. 'An antidote? But that means–'

'Yes. Which is why our work here is so important. It is almost certain that they will return.'

'The people must be warned!' I demanded. 'Not only could they return, but there could be more survivors out there.'

Cavendish shook his head slowly. 'This is not possible. No, no. Would you see another panic? Civilisation was taken to the brink of destruction, could our society survive if mankind took flight again? I think not. We must find out more before we act further. We have troops searching high and low for any other surviving Martians. They cannot stay hidden for long.'

'This really is too much, man!' I stood again, my cheeks burning with anger. 'We cannot keep this from the people! We must prepare them for the worst.'

'No, we must NOT!' The Knight of the Realm fought for control of his temper, his already red face a crimson storm. 'You must understand. We do not know if and when they will try again and news of this will certainly create a panic, perhaps needlessly. We are watching Mars using both our telescopes and the Egg device. We must prepare unimpeded and we WILL be ready!'

I sat slowly down into the chair again and thought for a moment. Horton leaning on the wall on the other side of the room, watched throughout this exchange, his brow furrowed.

'How much time do we have?' I asked quietly.

'Weeks, months – perhaps even years. We cannot say,' Cavendish had won his battle with his anger and he even tried to offer a comforting smile. 'We are working around the clock. We will find the answers.'

My mind went back to the monstrosity in the cell and a thought occurred to me.

'That thing,' I said quietly pointing toward the cell. 'What do you feed it?'

'Would you like to see?' Cavendish asked and glanced at his pocket watch. 'It's about that time'

I don't know why I nodded. I suppose now that my curiosity had to be satisfied. Perhaps I felt that observing the thing would help me face my fears. It seems strange now, this morbid curiosity, but I had seen so much and I just had to know everything.

We went through a small door and I found myself in a room next to the cell. In the wall a large window had been cut.

'The glass is very thick,' Cavendish explained. 'We use this room to observe it.'

'Does it not know?' I asked.

'Oh yes. But it seems not to care. It does little, except at meal times.'

As we watched a steel panel at the back of the cell moved aside by some unknown means. I could just see a soldier, bearing arms, standing beyond.

The Martian turned lazily and glared at the opening as a cow was pushed, none too gently, into the cell.

'Not their favourite food,' Cavendish muttered, his eyes fixed on what was unfolding.

The panel at the end of the cell slid closed and the Martian slithered, slowly like a beast of the Serengeti stalking its prey, up to the hapless animal. As if from nowhere, it quickly flourished a long tube with a spiked end, I had seen this before.

The Martian regarded the cow for a moment and then with a dextrous leap, thrust the pipette into the cow's neck, its other tentacles wrapping themselves tightly around the poor animals body. As the startled cow lowed pitifully and struggled to shake the creature off it's back, the Martian inserted the other end of the tube somewhere out of sight on it's own body and drank its fill.

As the bloody spectacle of the circus must have transfixed the Romans, the sight now before me held a horrid fascination. Horrified as I was, I could not look away. The Martian drank and the animal's lowing became weaker.

I finally managed to tear my eyes away, glancing first at Cavendish and then Horton. Cavendish was staring thoughtfully at the scene, a strange smile twisting his features. Horton, to my surprise, looked as shocked as I. Evidently this was his first view of the prisoner's eating habits, as well.

The Martian had finished. It withdrew the pipette and turned slowly toward the window in the wall, its eyes burned like coals. As quick as a flash, it grasped the head of the now prone cow and, with a quick flick of a tentacle, tore it clean off. Hooting happily, it flourished its prize then, flicking the tentacle again, threw the head at the window.

We jumped back as one as a red stain covered the viewing window and the cow's head fell with a thump to the cell floor.

'Not their favourite food,' Cavendish repeated grimly.

Exorcising Demons by Peter Fussey

CHAPTER 8
Alone

When the orderly called me at nine the next morning, I had, much to my surprise, enjoyed another night of deep, dreamless sleep. I felt sure, as I had laid my head on the pillow the night before, that my dreams would be haunted by Martian terrors once more after the terrible things I had witnessed.

After the incident at the Martian holding area, Cavendish and Horton had been called away on some unknown business and had not returned. As I was still unsure of the way around the facility, I was escorted to my room and deposited there unceremoniously, but ever so politely, like so much left luggage. Meals were brought to me in my room by the orderly, whom I discovered went by the name of Johnson, but he was my sole human contact for the next few days. I tried to strike up conversation with him on a number of occasions but, though he was always polite, he pointedly avoided all but the most necessary of intercourse. Whether this was down to orders or a lack of social skills I could not say.

On the third day, the Johnson appeared again at nine thirty with a laden breakfast tray. The man informed me that my hosts were away still and asked if I would like to see the library. Needing to occupy my mind, I agreed.

The library was not too far from my room. Like much of the living area of the facility, it was as if it had been lifted from some country pile, all panelled wood and elaborately woven Persian rugs.

I spent some hours perusing the books on offer: rare works by the great philosophers, scientific texts and contemporary fiction all rubbed shoulders on the many shelves. I was astonished to see works by Dee, 'The Discoverie of Witches', the 'Malleus Malificarum' and other obscure and rare books there. The library even boasted a copy of the mad Arab Al Hazred's 'Necronomicon' in a glass case, a rare tome indeed. Many of the books were priceless and my mind boggled at the sheer weight of knowledge in this room and I marvelled at how Cavendish had managed to pull all of these rare works together into one place.

I chose a work by Verne – the Frenchman possessed an imagination I much admired – and sat in a wing chair beside the fire that roared in the grate on one wall.

The book did not hold my attention, though, and my mind drifted back to the Martian that would, at that moment, be sitting seething, and perhaps plotting, in its cell.

Intellectually speaking, it is obvious that these creatures are as far apart at least from us as we are from the apes. Yet, I had seen this creature, consisting mainly of brain and, seemingly, part of a remarkably ordered and sophisticated society, petulantly play with its food and throw a tantrum not unlike a human child in the nursery.

They seem to us a war-like race, bent only on destruction and conquest, but I wondered then if perhaps we are too ready to impose human qualities onto them and this is why we find their behaviour difficult to fathom.

It seemed to me, I concluded, that the Martian psyche was as complex as their machinery and I found myself eager to know more about them.

I was given dinner, slices of beef that melted in my mouth and fresh vegetables, after being led to the dining room this time, and Cavendish and Horton joined me as I began to tuck into my meal.

'Sorry we left you alone, old chap,' Cavendish said sitting down and eyeing his food greedily. 'We had pressing business with the PM,'

'Quite alright,' I replied, around a mouthful of delicious beef. 'I made use of your excellent library.'

'Ah yes. I chose all the works there myself. Had the devil of a job finding some of them. It's a bit of a hobby of mine, not that I really have time for such things now.'

Horton spoke, then. 'We would appreciate it if you don't wander alone too far in the complex, Smith. As you can imagine there are some areas that could be highly dangerous if you don't know where you are going.'

'Of course, I fully understand.'

Horton simply nodded.

'Anyway, tomorrow we have to go on a recovery party,' Cavendish said. 'We would be pleased if you would come with us. It should be an interesting trip.'

'Recovery?' I asked, curious. 'Recovering what?'

'Martian artefacts, machinery, anything we can find. Our friends can still teach us much.'

'Why yes, I should be glad to come along.' A chance to get out of this sumptuous, yet stuffy, place and into the fresh air appealed to me very much.

'Good man. Warm clothes will be the order of the day, we will provide you with rain gear. The weather is atrocious today and will apparently be no better tomorrow.'

'May I ask where we are going?'

'Tomorrow,' Cavendish paused dramatically for a moment and then continued, 'we shall be investigating a Martian cylinder.'

I was just about to drift into slumber when there was a soft knock at the door.

Momentarily disorientated, I assumed it would be the orderly calling me to breakfast.

'Come,' I mumbled and sat up in bed rubbing my eyes.

The door opened and a dark figure slipped into the room.

'I cannot stay long here,' Horton said, his voice almost a whisper.

'What? What is it?' I fumbled for my spectacles on the dresser, but putting them on allowed me no better sight of the room.

'Smith, I have to warn you. You are in grave danger, we all are. There is more going on here than you know. I hope you never find out.' I peered at him, to try to catch his expression, but the gloom in my windowless quarters was too impenetrable and I could only vaguely make out his dark outline facing me.

'What do you mean?' I demanded.

'You must leave. You are free to go, if you wish, whilst you know so little. Use that freedom. Leave.' Unease gripped me now. Why was this man who had barely spoken to me before, but was part of my recruitment in this endeavour, suddenly trying to warn me off?

'Horton, what are you babbling on about? There is so much–'

'If you value your life, just go!' Horton hissed.

I went to speak again but the door closed quietly and Horton was gone, leaving me alone in the dark to puzzle over this strange and unexpected behaviour.

CHAPTER 9
An Explanation

The next day, my curiosity of the Martians and all their works was still in me, but I also had a strange heavy feeling in my stomach. Horton's words of the previous night echoed around my head and, at breakfast, I caught him looking at me surreptitiously from time to time.

As I sat, deep in thought and chewing toast in the dining room, Cavendish exhibited his usual schoolboy enthusiasm for all that he expected of the day.

'It's going to be an exciting day, what?' he said through a mouthful of scrambled egg. 'We have done some preliminary investigations on the cylinders but we hope to have some more wonders to bring back with us before the day is out.'

"Wonders", I had learned, was how Cavendish referred, in a rather childish way, I thought, to the Martian technology he had ordered, salvaged and utilised.

'I am surprised that the people have not taken souvenirs,' I said, feigning a little more enthusiasm than I now felt, due to the strange warning the night before. Still, I had decided that it would not do to arouse Cavendish's suspicion and I would sit tight, for now, and see what emerged. I was now on my guard and I hoped that that would be enough to alert me to any trouble, should it arise.

'Ah,' Cavendish continued. 'Well, we have guards posted at most of the major landing sites against just that eventuality. We did not waste any time on that front. The wonders therein are too precious and we are sure that not just the ordinary man on the street would like to get their hands on such treasures.'

'What do you mean?'

'Spies, man!' Cavendish exclaimed. 'We have word that at least one foreign government have people on our soil sniffing around. They have asked for information through diplomatic channels, of course, but we are reluctant to share whilst we know so little.'

'Would we share at all?' I asked. I was beginning to see how having such advances in our possession would mean a great advantage in many ways.

'Of course,' said Cavendish. 'When the time is right.' But I felt that he was not telling the whole truth and he would say no more on the subject.

Later, wrapped up in warm, waterproof clothing and boasting stout walking boots on our feet, we were ushered into the lift back to the surface. A short trip on the private underground train took us to an overland train waiting at Kings Cross.

It seemed that the problems with the rail services had been overcome, enough, at least, for us to be able to travel to Woking in the comfort of a plush carriage: myself, Cavendish, the ever-present Horton, who pointedly avoided my attempts to catch his eye and three other men whom I had not met before.

So, we were headed for Horsell Common! A slight feeling of dread lurked in the pit of my stomach, not just because of Horton's words, but also because I was to revisit the place where I had stood with my late friend Ogilvy and observed at the cylinder that was to cause so much strife to humanity, in a time that seemed so long ago.

Shortly into the trip, Cavendish fell asleep, snoring loudly and with his chubby hands crossed over his considerable girth. Horton engrossed himself in some papers he had taken out from a valise and periodically scribbled notes on them with a pencil.

The weather that day was indeed as miserable as Cavendish had predicted. The rain poured from leaden skies and clattered noisily against the roof and windows of the carriage as I regarded the newcomers to our excursion.

As I have intimated, as well as Cavendish, Horton and myself, our party consisted of three others. The men who shared our carriage, I learned after one, Peters, struck up a conversation with me, were scientists at the apex of their fields. Baxter, a small, grey, bearded man, was involved in Biology. He sat nervously twitching his fingers and muttering under his breath.

Peters favoured physics and was a tall black haired man. He chatted amiably to all and spoke a little of some of his work so far. His talk was, of course, mostly beyond my understanding. Carter, a young Engineer with a swept-back mop of blonde hair and long, bushy sideburns, stared quietly, through the rain dashed window, at the countryside as it passed.

We were not travelling unguarded. In the next carriage travelled ten troops, armed to the teeth and led by a grizzled Welsh Sergeant by the name of Jones. Even from the next carriage, the Sergeant's barked orders reached my ears from time to time. Quite what trouble was expected on this trip was unclear, but I felt better for the presence of these men.

At Woking, a town like many others, still showing scars from the war but with re-building well underway, carriages and a few motor vehicles waited. Some were full of bulky looking equipment under tarpaulins, some obviously meant for our transportation. We climbed aboard one of the latter and travelled on still pitted and rutted roads to Horsell Common.

The inclement weather reminded me of the first night I saw a Martian machine, as I stood terrified next to my overturned dogcart. In my mind, the machine's ghostly howl reverberated once again.

As our vehicles rattled up to the Common, my feelings of unease evidently became more apparent. Horton looked concerned at me.

'Don't worry,' he said quietly, 'you're safe for now.' This man was quite an enigma to me.

The bushes and trees around the common still stood blackened and charred, pointing at the dark sky like the accusing fingers of the dead. Great swathes of the area showed the scars of what had occurred when the cylinder had opened. Mounds of churned up earth lay here and there along with the wreckage of guns and other equipment. The horrible memories of those early battles were again fresh in my mind.

Here now was the cylinder, glistening in the wet and like some great misshapen metal cathedral. An edifice dedicated entirely to the engineering of our destruction, once ringing with the howling prayers of our persecutors, now silent and deserted. A Fighting Machine loomed, like some giant unholy priest, on guard close by.

As we approached, I noticed that there was a small encampment near to the entrance of the cylinder. Soldiers milled around, smoking and talking in low voices. I saw none of the usual soldierly bravado and humour here. The gaping maw of the Cylinder entrance exuded some sobering influence. I felt it only too strongly as I stood nearby.

We were shown to a large marquee, which was crowded with wet soldiers and smelled accordingly. As the wagons containing the equipment were unloaded we were given battered mugs containing hot, sweet tea. Cavendish wrinkled his nose a little at the lowly appearance of the drinking vessel he was handed, but the rest of us gratefully supped the warming drink as if we drank from the best bone china.

Cavendish called for quiet and the chatter in the tent lessened.

'Today gentlemen,' he boomed, 'we will be looking for more equipment to take back with us. I know our scientists are anxious to learn more about the workings of the cylinder and we have only scratched the surface here. Please be careful. There is still much we do not know and we can't afford to lose any more of you because of some silly mishap. After all, there are none of our Martian friends here to cause the trouble, are there?'

This off-colour comment was met with a little nervous laughter from some. I thought the joke, if it were one, in very poor taste indeed. One or two evidently agreed as one or two men near the back scowled and muttered to one another.

'Anyway,' Cavendish continued, 'please ask if you have any concerns or questions. Are we ready, gentlemen?' He led the way out of the tent as the chatter from the people inside began again, Horton, as always, shadowing him.

I set down my, now empty, mug, fastened my coat close about my neck and followed.

Once outside, we scrambled down the walls of the pit and approached the cylinder opening. At the entrance, planking had been laid in an effort to cut down on the amount of mud created by the comings and goings of the soldiers and scientists. The group assembled for exploration of the Cylinder consisted Cavendish, Horton, the three scientists from the train carriage and myself. For a moment, we glanced nervously at one another; the cylinder aperture was exuding that malign influence once more. A group of four soldiers, including the Sergeant, Jones, joined us and we entered.

CHAPTER 10
In the Belly of the Beast

It was warm inside the cylinder. Much to my surprise, it was also not as dark as I expected. No earthly light source illuminated our progress, but the metal walls themselves glowed with an eerie, blue-green luminescence. Once my eyes had accustomed themselves, I could see quite clearly.

Nothing could prepare me for the smell, though.

'My God, what is that smell?' Carter asked covering his nose, evidently noticing it as I did.

'Putrescence,' answered Baxter grimly. 'Death, call it what you will. Sir George, have the bodies been cleared from here?'

'We have penetrated little into the cylinder's mysteries,' Cavendish said. 'We have, until now, not ventured much farther than the openings. Some soldiers have been further looking for survivors but that is about all. I am as new to much of this as you.'

'You don't know what is in here?' I asked, incredulous. Some of the others looked vaguely queasy and not a little concerned.

'We have the stories of the soldiers, of course. Many other things have occupied our time. Guards were posted at the opening until we could spare the time to investigate properly.'

'What did the soldiers find?' asked Baxter, twitching nervously, his hands fluttering with his obvious agitation.

'Well, we shall soon find out if the gossip is correct, eh?' Cavendish said and strode off.

The space inside the cylinder was cavernous, but oddly without echoes. It was if this vast space greedily swallowed our quietly spoken words and our soft footsteps almost as soon as they sounded. Walking through, it seemed impossible that such a huge thing could fly through space at many thousands of miles an hour, as this must have done. It seemed to me like finding that an Ironclad could soar up into the sky as lightly as a bird.

But here it was, as if to prove just how little our civilisation knew about the mysterious laws of the Universe.

The floor of the cylinder was a sort of metallic mesh that our feet sank into slightly. As our feet rose again, the surface reshaped itself and was as flat as before. Carter, the Engineer, found this especially interesting and jumped up and down experimentally.

'This is astounding,' he enthused. 'I must test some of this substance. Fascinating!'

The walls of the cylinder had been bare near the entrance, but as we walked, on either side, dim shapes became gradually apparent. We moved in our group towards one of the shapes.

A partially built Fighting Machine squatted there, or at least the hood. Leg sections, which must have constituted parts of the same Machine, were stacked neatly and securely against the gently curving wall, along with what looked like some kind of engines and other parts, the use of which I could not fathom.

Further we went, past more of these partly built machines. The smell of death grew stronger as another shadowy shape loomed.

As we drew closer we saw that it was an enormous basket. A surge of horror from deep within me reminded me that I had seen such things before. The Handling Machines had carried such baskets on their backs and had stored human beings in there for their diabolical needs.

Inside this cage were bodies. Twisted human bodies. Men, women and children, in death, acting out grotesque tableaux of terror and fear.

Perhaps these poor souls had seen their captors start to die and thought that they were saved. But fate, or more properly the Martians, had dealt them a cruel hand.

'Poor devils!' breathed Jones.

'How did they die?' I asked.

'See the black powder scattered around?' asked Baxter pointing. Small drifts of the dreaded substance were indeed all over the floor.

'Bastards!' breathed a young soldier, horrified. 'They gassed 'em! They were helpless and they killed 'em like insecks!'

'Steady, lad,' said Jones resting a calming hand on the boy's shoulder.

It appeared that the Martians in the cylinder had, in a last act of defiance, unleashed their most horrific weapon, the Black Smoke, on their defenceless captives when they had started to die themselves. Was this an act of sheer spite? It appeared we would never know.

Cavendish led us away from the carnage and further into the depths of the cylinder. Along the way, we saw the putrefying bodies of Martians here and there. Even in the cold depths of this unearthly machine, a place where no earthly laws seemed to hold sway, nature was taking her course and flies buzzed around the stinking remains. The young soldier kicked at one of the prone creatures as we passed.

'Please, don't do that!' Cavendish said, eyes wide. 'We may need the bodies for testing later and we cannot have them damaged any more than they already are.'

'That's enough, lad,' Jones said quietly to the boy, but his face spoke of the possession of as much anger boiling inside him as the boy was venting.

The boy glared at Cavendish as he continued on.

Soon, we came upon a large area of wall with a sliding door, which was open. This led into another smaller space.

'The control cabin?' asked Peters glancing around.

'So it would appear,' said Carter. 'Those look like controls to me.'

The engineer was referring to a panel on which were many levers and switches. A set of three portholes sat in the centre of the panel, each with a switch next to it. The portholes were blank and they appeared to be closed.

Carter reached towards one of the switches.

'No don't!' Cavendish said. It was too late though, and the switch had been pushed.

To our surprise, the porthole next to the switch lit up and we could see a rainy landscape.

'Look! That's outside!' exclaimed Peters.

It was indeed outside. The scene was of the encampment at the cylinder opening.

We could see soldiers standing around shivering, capes slick with the driving rain.

Carter pushed the other two switches, this time Cavendish did not try to stop him.

The other portholes lit up and more scenes appeared. On one was what I took to be the other side of the cylinder and I could see a wooded area and the wreckage of a fallen Martian Digging Mechanism. The other showed stars. Only stars. Was this outer space? The open mouthed expressions of the others told me that they had similar ideas.

'Incredible!' breathed Peters, rather unnecessarily.

We turned our attention to the rest of the cabin. On the other wall we saw a row of large tanks, not unlike large upended metal horse troughs fronted with glass. A complicated array of tubes and wires left each tank and entered into a large console.

'What are these?' I asked.

Baxter answered. 'I have an idea about these. They may actually go someway to explain how the Martians managed to survive the journey here at such terrific speed.'

'Go on,' I said, intrigued.

'Well,' Baxter continued. 'In the terms of the Layman, I think perhaps the Martians were suspended in some kind of liquid in these tanks. Somehow it kept them being crushed by the forces that the speed of this conveyance must have put them under.'

It was a mystery to me as to how he reached such conclusions, but it seemed feasible to at least some of the party, so I asked no further questions. I had a feeling that more answers might muddy the water for me somewhat, anyway.

There were more panels around the walls with dials and switches on them. The scientist agreed that it must have needed a crew of three or four to pilot this vehicle. Would this vessel have had a Captain directing operations, like our own, seagoing, ships?

It has been supposed by some that this first cylinder was the 'flagship' of the fleet, as it were. Perhaps this is just because it landed first. It certainly appeared to have given directions to the cylinders that landed elsewhere, but was this just a case of imposing human qualities on an unknown race once more?

There were no indications, to me, that this was a special vessel. No insignia, no writing of any kind, just those glowing metal walls.

We left the cabin for now and went deeper into the cylinder. Another room opened up before us and we, to a man, almost gagged at the smell. Handkerchiefs were quickly raised to mouths and noses at this latest violation on our senses.

Inside the room were more bodies scattered carelessly around. I thought at first that these were more of our unfortunate fellow humans, but further investigation proved otherwise. My eyes watering from the rancid, cloying air in the room, I saw that these were biped figures, but they were very pale, almost white. The creatures had protruding foreheads and prominent jaws and they looked, even to my untrained eye, like some strange hybrid of human and ape. Their arms were long and their naked bodies were almost completely hairless.

I realised that these were the food that the Martians had brought with them, possibly denizens of the Martian's home world, bred, like we breed livestock, for our own needs. Or perhaps, it suddenly occurred to me, they were harvested from some other world that we knew nothing about: a world that had also felt the fiery touch of the Martian Heat-ray. I had, along with many of my fellow man I assumed, never before considered that the Martians might have visited other worlds apart from ours, before finally setting their sights on Earth. It was a thought that I pondered on, but kept to myself. After all, as I have stated before, I am no scientist.

A glance around this foul-smelling room told me that this was some kind of feeding area. Complicated looking machines sprouted from the walls and from these came spiked tubes, ending in instruments that looked like the pipettes the Martians used to drink the blood of other creatures. Everywhere, the smell of corruption mixed with the coppery reek of putrefying blood pounded at our senses and I felt oppressed and claustrophobic. Several of the party were looking increasingly shaken and unwell and it was decided that we should not stay in that room for long.

CHAPTER 11
Deeper

On we went into the depths of the cylinder, the eerie light within the walls showing us the way.

We passed more compartments, all containing more machinery and unfathomable instruments. Cavendish was like a child in a toyshop and did not try to hide his glee at each new discovery.

'Such wonders!' he would exclaim periodically. He and the scientists would coo over each new thing like a flock of pigeons over crumbs.

Horton stayed silent as usual but still cast glances at me now and then, the look in his eyes spoke volumes. What danger did he foresee for me? Was I not safe with our armed guards? Once I went to question him, but I saw that Cavendish was looking over curiously and Horton waved me away with a small flick of his hand.

Finally, we appeared to come to the end. A great wall faced us with another of the sliding doors set into it. This too was half open.

We entered into a final cavernous space. A dull thrumming sound came from the black machinery that took up a great part of the room. The vibrations and enormous power evident in this strange machinery literally shook my body. I felt strangely weightless, as if I would float away, should I push myself up from the floor. Some of the others looked around themselves curiously, almost as if they felt the same thing. Small green puffs of smoke hissed from joints in the black metal, as the machine worked at some unknown purpose.

'The engine room!' Carter said reverently, casting quick, excited glances around him.

'Magnificent!' exclaimed Cavendish. 'Can you imagine the power? I'll warrant one of these could produce enough energy to power all of London!'

'At least,' said Carter.

We stared at the engine for a short while; the dull thrumming had an almost hypnotic quality.

'We must discover how this works,' Cavendish said finally. 'Can you do it, Carter?'

'I couldn't say,' the engineer answered. 'To even try, I will need a team of men under my direction and access to funding.'

'You shall have it,' Cavendish said. 'As we discussed before, anything you need, you shall have. We must discover the secrets!'

'Very well,' Carter nodded his agreement.

Cavendish turned to address the whole group.

'Gentlemen, we have many discoveries here to be made. I would suggest we move back outside and plan the extraction of these items. Obviously, the engine will have to stay in situ for the present; it is obviously far too unwieldy to move. Carter, you and your team will set up a workshop here at the back of the cylinder.'

Carter looked decidedly nervous by this prospect, but nodded once more.

This decided, our group shuffled out of the engine room and began the arduous trek back to the outside. I, for one, was not looking forward to passing some of the horrors we had seen on the inward trip again.

The journey back was without incident. The soldiers seemed nervous, but I could not blame them for that. I wondered how many of them had seen friends in the service scattered to the four winds by the Martian Heat-ray, or choked by the black smoke. I actually felt better that they were wary; as it seemed to me that they would be on guard and ready to face any eventuality.

One of the soldiers, Perkins, began to chat cheerily with his comrades as we walked. Perhaps he was attempting to raise their spirits in this sinister place but eventually Jones, the sergeant, hissed at him to be quiet.

I turned my eyes away as we passed the charnel houses of the feeding room and the baskets. I had no wish to see those poor wretches within again.

From time to time as we travelled through this strange monument to destruction, the soldiers muttered, but Jones silenced them with harshly whispered words. The scientists, for the most part, whispered excitedly amongst themselves, while Cavendish strode ahead like the proud, strutting Drum Major of a military band.

At length we saw the fading light of the sky in the opening. Had we been inside that long? It didn't seem possible. I realised that we hadn't even stopped to eat all day. It was probably just as well.

As we left the cylinder, I felt like a great weight had been lifted from me. I took a great lungful of chill evening air and let the slight breeze gently blow the foul odours that had clouded my senses away.

The rain had stopped and clouds scudded like ships across a rising moon. As darkness fell, we retired to the mess tent for refreshment. Despite my lack of food for the day, I did not feel like eating.

That night, I lay in a folding bunk within a tent that had been provided for me. It appeared we would be staying on the Common for at least another day whilst Cavendish directed operations.

I could not sleep, at first, so I lay and tried not to think of the horrors I had seen. I thought of my wife and better times. Times before the Martians came.

Occasionally, the low murmurs of our guards and the pop and crackle of their campfire drifted to me.

Finally, sleep began to take me and my eyelids grew heavy. I drifted away.

A scream woke me almost, it seemed, as soon as I had fallen asleep. I jumped like lightning from my bunk and fumbled for my clothes. What was happening?

Angry shouts now, then a clanging of an alarm bell.

I left my tent to be confronted with a scene of utter confusion.

CHAPTER 12
Sabotage

Soldiers rushed here and there whilst Jones stood, dressed only in his under garments and uniform trousers, in the middle of it all barking short, sharp orders and pointing quickly in all directions. The pungent smell of smoke assailed my nostrils and, looking around, I saw that a couple of the tents were aflame. A man throwing water at the tent got too close and his coat caught fire. A soldier wrestled him to the ground and rolled him before the flames could take proper hold.

The action stopped at the sound of a single gunshot. Buckets full of water were held in still hands as all eyes turned to the far edge of the camp, where a soldier, Perkins I saw, was standing looking down the sights of his rifle. Another shot pierced the, suddenly deathly quiet, night.

The ruckus resumed as the other soldiers dropped buckets and other fire-fighting materials and ran to grab their weapons. Weapons raised, these men made their way cautiously to where Perkins stood.

'What are you shooting at lad?' the Sergeant bellowed at the top of his lungs as he ran to join his men.

Perkins did not look round, nor lower his weapon. He merely carried on firing at something we could not see.

The other soldiers got to within a few yards of Perkins, when they fell back suddenly. It was as if something invisible had swept past and knocked them over like skittles.

With horror, I realised what it was. A Heat-ray!

Perkins stood stock still for a moment then, silhouetted against the flames that now surrounded him, arched his back and screamed. Although I could not see clearly, I knew that his skin would now be peeling, blackening and cracking. His eyeballs would be turned to liquid in their sockets and his hair would have been ablaze. A small pop sounded as, I assume, his ammunition ignited. Mercifully, the torment would not have lasted long for him.

In a moment, his still burning remains fell to the ground.

A shocked silence fell on the camp. Then, the chaos resumed as people ran towards the remaining soldiers.

A few, who had nearly reached the young warrior, were quite badly burned but would live. The others were winded but otherwise unharmed. Jones picked himself of the ground and looked around with a practised eye to see where the ray had come from. Bushes and patches of ground in the area that had been touched by the Heat-ray smouldered, just like poor Perkins. The trees where the ray seemed to have come from hissed accusations at one another in a rising breeze but no further attack came and there was no sign of any assailant.

Jones swore mightily and assembled a small group of unhurt soldiers to make a thorough search.

As the soldiers left to scout the surrounding area, the rest of us set to putting out the fires and bringing back some semblance of order to the camp.

We gathered in the mess tent an hour or so later.

Cavendish looked around the assemblage grimly but said nothing until the search party returned.

'Nothing, Sir! We could find no sign of anyone … or anything,' Jones said, breathlessly entering the tent.

Baxter spoke next. 'Sir George, who do you think attacked us? Martians?'

Cavendish thought for a moment. 'Perhaps. We cannot say for sure that there aren't roving bands of Martian survivors somewhere out there. Of course, this information is not to leave this camp.'

'Well who else could it have been?' I asked. 'They had a Heat-ray!'

'Anarchists, foreign governments – we cannot rule out anything. Many people want to get their hands on the machines we are discovering. This was some kind of sabotage, but who instigated it, I could not say.'

'The Martians will want their playthings back, too,' observed Peters stroking his chin thoughtfully. 'Their numbers may be severely depleted but they can still cause us a lot of bother, I am sure. Keep us busy until their comrades arrive, perhaps. If they arrive.'

'Is anything missing? Any of the captured weaponry?' Carter asked.

Cavendish shook his head. 'We don't think so. We have checked the lists and all appears in order.'

'So where did whoever it was get the Heat-ray from?'

'This was a Heat-ray, alright,' Cavendish answered, 'but a portable one. Did you notice that the effect was much more localised than usual and only claimed one victim.'

I saw Jones kick the ground and grit his teeth a little at the casual manner in which the death of one of his soldiers was described.

'Something new?' Carter wondered.

'No. We have found Heat-ray rifles before. We think they were putting the finishing touches to them when they met their demise. They were experimenting with many things.' This last reminded me of the Flying Machine my brother and his companions had seen. I made a mental note to ask Cavendish about that later.

'So I suppose they have raided some other cylinder or some such to get weaponry, whoever they may turn out to be,' Peters said.

'It's not impossible,' Cavendish conceded. 'But we have had no word from the other camps that this is the case.'

There was little else to be said for the moment and, with that, we retired to our tents to snatch what little sleep we could.

CHAPTER 13
A Warning

A few hours later, I was awoken, un-refreshed, from a restless slumber by the sound of activity in the camp. I made use of the washing facilities provided and then wandered over to the mess tent.

The weather had taken a decided turn for the better and the sky was a bright blue. Small, fluffy clouds meandered across this airy landscape like lazily grazing sheep. A bright sun gently warmed and dried the earth and was reflected dazzlingly off the cylinder and the sentinel tripod that stood nearby.

The three scientists were poring over some artefacts that had been placed on trestle tables near the mess tent. I heard disjointed snatches of conversation coming from their little huddle.

'… powered by some kind of atomic power …'

'… possible applications in the Empire …'

'… our own machines!'

I stood a little way off trying to catch more but Carter saw me and muttered something to the others. They took to talking more quietly after that. It appeared that I was not to be included in all that occurred in these investigations.

In the mess tent, some soldiers sat soberly sipping tea. One had a bandage on his hand and his hair was singed. I nodded to him. I understood his pain for the loss of his brave comrade Perkins. If it wasn't for that man's thoughtless actions, we could all have fallen prey to the same horrible burning death as befell him. We owed him an un-repayable debt of gratitude.

Cavendish was talking animatedly to Horton as I took a seat near them. He looked up.

'Smith, that was a terrible business last night. We must get the artefacts back to the laboratory. We have much more control over security there.'

I felt exposed here out on the Common, despite our guards, and could not disagree.

'We hope to leave by noon. Carter will, of course, be staying here to work on the engine of the cylinder and we have more soldiers on the way to subsidise the forces already here. I have business outside now; I will leave you in Horton's capable hands for the moment.' With that, he shuffled out of the tent.

Horton regarded me for a moment with his black eyes and then he stood.

'Shall we take a walk?'

We left the tent and walked silently for a while. I found myself superstitiously avoiding burnt patches of ground as if they were cursed. It occurred to me that perhaps, with the Martians still a possible threat, the whole of our Planet Earth was cursed.

When we were out of immediate earshot of the main camp Horton spoke. 'Smith, I know you are suspicious of my motives, but I assure you I mean you no harm. On the contrary, I wish only to save you any more trials. I ask you again to leave as soon as you can.'

'I have too many questions. I must know what is going on,' I replied.

'I can understand that.' Horton stopped and faced me. 'However, you have seen the danger that lies around our work. For Heaven's sake, man! We were all nearly killed in our beds last night. Whoever it was that attacked us meant to sabotage our operations. If it hadn't been for that soldier, we might not be speaking now.'

'What do you know of the sabotage attempt last night?' I asked, suddenly suspicious.

Something flashed behind Horton's eyes but was gone as quickly as I noticed it.

'Nothing I can divulge with any certainty,' he said. I could detect no untruth in his voice or manner, but something still felt wrong. Horton continued.

'All I can say is that I have information that this will not be an isolated case. Last week a strange turn of events began.' He paused for a moment, as if wondering how much to tell me. 'Scientists who have recently worked on various projects for the Government started to disappear. A few days ago one reappeared but he had been killed. In fact, he was horribly burned and mutilated. We were only able to identify the man through personal effects that were with the body.'

'Why?' I asked. 'Is there some conspiracy afoot?'

'Yes, I believe so. I am working hard to find out what this is about and who is responsible but I fear that the danger will deepen. That is why I wish you to leave.'

I regarded the man for a moment. I could see no reason why he would wish me ill. I was not even a pawn in this game. I was here only to report on the investigation and offer explanations to the public, was I not?

My mind was now made up.

'Horton, I thank you for your concern but I cannot leave now. I have seen too much and I was asked to do a job. I will follow it through.'

'I think you are a fool,' Horton sighed. 'I cannot guarantee your safety and you stay with this project at your own risk.'

I nodded. 'Understood.'

'Your misplaced sense of duty and adventure could well get you killed, Smith. I hope you don't have cause to remember my words.' Shaking his head, he led us back to camp.

Work continued apace and wagons were being loaded with Martian weaponry and machinery whilst some soldiers watched curiously. Other military men stood on guard at the edges of the camp, much more wary than before.

Cavendish directed all this activity like a true maestro conducting an orchestra.

The man looked up as Horton and I approached.

'Ah. We are nearly ready for the off. Gather your things.'

We finally left the camp in our convoy of wagons and carriages at one p.m. Soldiers and orderlies ushered us on our way us like fussy nannies and the journey back to the laboratory went by uneventfully.

CHAPTER 14
I, Spy

Cavendish, my steward informed me the next morning, had to leave again on urgent business. I assumed Horton would have gone with him and was resigned to another day of boredom, so I was surprised when there was a sharp knock at the door, a little after ten, and Horton entered.

'Good morning,' he said and strode over to where I sat at my desk writing notes in my journal.

'And to you,' I replied. I still had in mind the Government man's previous visit a few nights before and I readied myself for more warnings.

'May I?' he asked, indicating my notes with a raised eyebrow.

'Of course.' I settle back in my chair and watched.

He picked up my sheaf of papers with a well-manicured hand and sat lightly on the arm of an easy chair. There was silence for some minutes as he thumbed his way through my notes. He gave little sign of what he thought of my work, barring a frown or a slight nod from time to time, until he had finished.

'Does my work meet your satisfaction?' I asked finally.

'Splendid!' he said and placed the sheaf of papers carefully back on the desk.

He regarded me for a moment from his perch on the chair like some great black bird and I fancied I could see that he was thinking hard about something. His hooded eyes gave away nothing but I felt a question coming.

He slapped his knee after a moment as he obviously came to a decision.

'Have you anything planned today?' he asked.

I fought back ironic laughter at this. Without my hosts around I was shepherded around like a spring lamb and, I sometimes felt, penned up like one.

'Well no,' I said, a little too straight faced.

'The missing scientists trail seems to be paying off. I have to go topside to do some sniffing around.'

'Really?' I asked, but said no more.

'Indeed,' Horton took on that look of intense thought yet again for a few moments, then spoke again. 'How would you like to accompany me?'

Now that was more like it! A trip outside into the real world, away from strange machinery and stranger people.

'Of course I would!' I exclaimed.

'Make no mistake, Smith, this could be dangerous. I have no idea what we shall find.'

'I think I have seen enough danger in my life to be able to take care of myself,' I answered.

'Very well, we leave at five,' Horton said, getting up and smoothing down his trouser creases. 'Warm clothing, Smith.' The Government man left the room.

As we left the facility, at five sharp, Horton dug into the pocket of his coat.

'Here,' he said handing me a metal object. A revolver. 'Do you know how to use one of these?'

'Point and shoot?' I said with a grin.

Horton glared at me for a moment as if disapproving then a small smile turned up the corners of his mouth.

'Yes,' he said. 'Something like that.'

I stashed the weapon away in the deep pocket of my overcoat.

'Come along, the train leaves in two minutes,' Horton said, his smile fading as quickly as it had come, and stalked away. I followed quickly.

The journey was monotonous, once over-ground, a cab was waiting for us. I saw the driver was the same man who had brought me to London. He cast a surly nod at me and gee'd his long-suffering horse along.

The weather was cold and foggy. Great dark clouds loomed over the city like a damp blanket and the streetlamps were burning brightly.

The hooves of our horse and the wheels of the cab disturbed patches of mist that lay here and there on the road as we rushed through the busy city streets.

I sank a little further into my coat trying to gain what warmth I could.

'Where are we going?' I asked Horton.

'Whitechapel,' Horton replied. 'I had a tip that someone may be being held in a house there.'

'A scientist?' I breathed.

'A local saw the man being bundled roughly into an abandoned property and he seems to have fitted our man's description.'

'I see. Do you mean to try to free him? If it is your man, that is?'

Horton eyes peered at me from the dark shadows beneath his hat brim. 'If the opportunity arises. You, my friend, will likely not be part of any such action, though. We will see how the land lies, in any case.'

As we made our way, now silent, I pictured all kinds of secret agent derring-do taking place before my eyes. This appealed greatly to the schoolboy within me. But, as a man, I was less full of bravado.

Presently, the cab stopped.

'Thank you, Nichols,' Horton said to the cabman as we left the comparatively warm interior of the cab to feel the force of a cold breeze. 'We shall be walking from here.'

Whitechapel was a ruin, although not due to Martian intervention. In fact, the invading forces had hardly touched this area. No, this place was purely the victim of the East End nemesis – neglect.

The Commercial Road was bustling, but the lost souls scurrying here and there had a look of desperation that was not brought on by the hardships of war. Their plight was poverty.

Surly looking men in threadbare clothes eyed us as we walked the murky streets avoiding piles of refuse heaped and rotting here and there. Hard-faced, drunken women lurked here and there on corners and in doorways and shouted out lewd comments and offered promises as we passed.

Horton and I waded through this tide of sad humanity like dogged rats swimming through a sewer.

The street lamps grew less and less frequent as we progressed and the streets quieter and darker. Nerves set in as the fog grew thicker and looming shapes of passers-by came and went.

'Keep your wits about you,' Horton muttered. 'At the first sign of trouble run back the way we came.'

At Dorset Street we passed the bright windows of a public house. Loud singing and raucous laughter floated in the damp air from the run down building. A man careered out of the door as if thrown, narrowly missing me as I passed, and fell with a thump to the floor. A loud cheer came from the pub as if this man being thrown out was universally approved of and the door slammed shut again. I went to the man but he lay still muttering and dead drunk. A little blood oozed from his mouth where teeth had broken on the hard stone of the pavement.

'Leave him,' Horton said sharply and marched off again.

A little further up the street, I saw a youth leaning against a lamppost whistling. As we made to pass, he spoke.

'Pardon me, gents, but where do you fink you is goin'?'

The youth must still be in his teens but he was, I now saw, holding a nasty looking club. He tossed it up and down meaningfully.

'Get out of our way, or you shall regret it' Horton hissed, his hand in his pocket.

'Shall I now, your 'ighness?' the lad said. 'Boys!'

Suddenly, we were surrounded.

At least eight more youths appeared, all dressed in the same scruffy way as their leader and armed with blunt weapons, standing around us.

'Y'know,' the leader said. 'We don't see many of your sort round here, these days. Not so long back, there was thrill seekers as would come dahn from the West End and look round where old Saucy Jack did the Devil's work. Used to make a pretty penny, showing 'em around, I did. Very good business!'

‘F’rinstance,’ he continued, gesturing grandly further up the road, ‘over yonder a little ways is Millers Court where pretty Mary Kelly got a necklace and some rouge wot finished her. She wasn’t so pretty then, I can tell yer. Saw it meself. ’Orrible! Then the Marshuns came along and put a stop to my ’onest little trade.’ The lad stared at his club for a moment.

‘So,’ he continued, doffing his dirty cap mockingly. ‘If you fine gents would be so kind as to part with your valuables, we can all be on our way.’

CHAPTER 15
The Irregulars

Horton glared at the young faces before him.

'I say again,' he said quietly. 'You don't understand. It would be in your best interests to get out of our way this minute.'

'No,' the leader said, prodding Horton's chest with his club. 'You don't understand, M'lord! Hand over the loot and I'll let yer go. If not, you'll know how poor Mary felt as that Devil made his mark on her.'

The boy, despite his outward bravado, began to look a little nervous now. Perhaps he was used to being obeyed immediately in the face of such odds. This worried me more. A frightened criminal can be like a cornered tiger when provoked.

I saw Horton begin to draw his hand slowly out of his pocket. His eyes were like ice as he glared at the youth. I began to feel for my weapon. If it was all going to start, I had best be prepared.

Suddenly, there was the sound of someone clearing their throat.

The leader of the gang of ruffians looked around sharply, peering into the foggy air.

'Wiggins, has it really come to this?' a cultured voice said. 'I had such high hopes for you.' The voice had a note of genuine sadness in it.

The youth dropped his club immediately as if it wasn't his and motioned for the others to do the same.

'Sir?' he said incredulously to the shape approaching out of the murk. 'Is that you?'

'Indeed it is. I am very disappointed in you.' A match was struck and the flare lit aquiline, refined features. The face was somehow familiar. There was a moment's silence, barring a sucking noise, as the newcomer used the match to light a large pipe. Presently, smoke drifted away to join the fog in the air.

'Sir, I–' the lad began.

'Sir, nothing, Wiggins,' the man said. 'I should think the least you owe these gentlemen is an apology.' This man obviously held some kind of power over these young men.

Wiggins hung his head and muttered something unintelligible.

'Not a moment too soon,' Horton said marching up to the man. Then, I suddenly recognised him.

Not so long before the war, a consulting detective had been the toast of the world. Solving puzzling cases for Royalty and the masses alike, his fame always preceded him. News of his exploits sold papers by the ton, all written by his accomplice, a Doctor. I had read several of these exploits and thought them acceptable if taken as fiction, but a little too much to take as fact. I often told my wife that I thought his adventures were probably embellished beyond all recognition for the benefit of sensationalism. To the Detective's credit, I had heard that he was supposedly uncomfortable with the way that some of these stories were told, but indulged his old friend who had written them.

So, here he was. The slicked back hair had a touch of salt and pepper that had not been present in the likenesses I had seen of him and deep lines cut across his strong features, but the icy eyes were as sharp and piercing as those in the images.

'Smith, this is–' Horton began.

'Yes, I know,' I said stepping forward and taking the great man's cool hand in mine. 'It's a pleasure.'

'It's all mine, I assure you. I have heard much about you, Mr. Smith. How is Wells?' the Detective asked.

'He is well,' I answered. So this man knew Wells, too! Wells, whom I thought to be an intimate friend, was turning out to have hidden depths.

'Capital!' the Detective said around his pipe. 'Now, Horton, I think we should be off. The Inspector should be around here somewhere in this soup with a few of the Force's finest.'

'Was the tip correct?' asked Horton, all business now.

'Ah, that is what we are about to find out,' the Detective said. 'We have cabs on the way to take us on.'

'Will the Doctor not be joining us?' I asked.

A look of genuine sadness flickered across the Detectives face at this.

'I fear not. My friend was killed during the invasion.'

'I'm sorry, I didn't know.'

'Why should you?' the Detective asked with a small sad smile and said no more on the subject.

'Now, Wiggins,' the Detective said, turning to the young ruffian. 'I have a job for you and your scoundrels should you wish to begin to travel the right road once more.'

'Of course, Sir!' Wiggins said, his dirty face a picture of genuine gratitude and adoration.

The Detective nodded, placed an arm around the youth's shoulders and walked away a little with him, muttering instructions. A few moments later, the conference was over.

'Very good, Sir! Come on, lads!' Wiggins shouted excitedly. A cab, at that moment, clattered up. The boys clambered, like a small group of monkeys, onto and into it. The overloaded cab careered crazily off again, the horse whinnying in protest.

The Detective watched them go, another small smile on his face. When the cab had disappeared into the fog he turned back toward us.

'Are we ready? Let's see if we can find your man, Horton. Ah, Inspector, how kind of you to join us.'

A man, flanked by two uniformed men had arrived in another cab and was just disembarking. The Inspector, a short, rotund man with a moustache and a balding pate jumped heavily to the pavement and looked wearily at the Detective.

'Well back in your cab, man!' the Detective said. 'We must be off!'

The Inspector, without saying a word, shot off an annoyed look and climbed back into the conveyance.

CHAPTER 16
On the Trail

We did not have far to travel. Our cabs pulled up outside a dark, crumbling building a few streets away. The windows facing the street were quite dark.

'Ready, gentlemen?' the Detective asked, pulling out a revolver from within his overcoat.

'Smith, you wait outside until I deem it safe for you to enter,' Horton mumbled to me.

I nodded and, as I exited the cab, I put a hand on the revolver in my pocket. The metal weight of the weapon gave me some small comfort.

The Detective, the Inspector, the two uniformed officers and Horton carefully approached the building carrying lamps turned low. A figure was waiting in the doorway.

One of the Bobbies braced himself and began, at a signal from the Detective, to put his shoulder to the door. At the third heave, the door gave way with a loud crack and the policeman nearly fell to the floor. The group quickly entered the building with the unknown figure following hesitantly. I could see the jogging lights of the lamps flitting across the walls as the men made their way through the building. I glanced nervously around my surroundings, but there was not a soul about.

My grip on the revolver in my pocket tightened a little.

After what seemed like many long minutes, Horton appeared at the door and nodded his head toward the inside.

'It's safe,' he said, his manner somewhat dejected.

I followed him into the place and a strange, sickly smell that almost made me gag, instantly intruded upon my senses. At one end of the hall, a rotten staircase ascended into impenetrable blackness. Somewhere in the house, I heard the squeak of rats.

The walls, I could see from the dim lamps now placed here and there, were covered with huge patches of black and silver mould and the wallpaper was peeling off on great swathes. Heaps of plaster lay here and there on the damply carpeted floor and, looking up, I could see that the ceiling had collapsed in places. In one area I could see right through to the night sky and, although I may have imagined it, amongst the few stars I could see through the clouds, was the red eye of Mars mockingly winking at me.

The sickly smell became stronger as I followed Horton through the rotting house.

In a room towards the back, with great black curtains draped across the window, I assumed, to keep out curious eyes, the Detective was bent over a shape on the floor. A poor looking old woman, probably a local, was quietly sobbing in the corner. She must have been the figure waiting outside the house as we arrived, and the original informant.

'It was like I said, Sir!' the woman gasped at the Detective between sobs. 'I saw some grim lookin' fellows bundle this poor man into this 'ouse. I didn't get a good look at 'em seeing as 'ow they was all wearing big cloaks. Just shapes really, Sir. I lives next door an' this place 'as been empty for a few years now.'

'Thank you, Madam,' the Detective said distractedly, without looking up. 'I don't think we need detain you any longer.'

The woman shuffled away, wiping her face with a filthy handkerchief.

I went to where the men were gathered around to see what interested them so.

The shape was a man, or the remains of one, and the smell was more intense than ever in his immediate area. I pulled out my handkerchief and held it over my nose and mouth, my eyes watering a little. I noticed that one of the young Bobbies was hunched over in a corner, quietly retching.

As I took in more detail, the horror of the man's situation hit me. He was quite dead, for in his grim state he could have been nothing else. One of his legs was missing from the knee down. The place where the severance had occurred was literally melted. Half of his face was black and his chest had a great hole burned in it through which I could see charred and shrivelled internal organs and the blackened bones of his ribcage. A pair of twisted spectacles hung off his one intact ear, the lenses darkened and cracked. One arm was twisted around unnaturally over his head. Above him, on the ceiling, was a large patch of soot and a large smear of yellow, sickly looking grease stained the wall upon which his motionless body leaned.

'Spontaneous combustion,' the Inspector said sagely, a grimace of disgust on his face. 'I've seen it before, twenty years back–'

'Nonsense!' the Detective snapped, springing to his feet. 'This was no supernatural event!'

'Why, many scientists think it is worthy of investigation,' the Inspector retorted stiffly. 'Sir Arthur Conan-Doyle himself says that some things like this are proven fact.'

'Quite so,' the Detective replied. 'The great, but gullible, Sir Arthur also believes, I have it on good authority, that children talk to fairies!' The Inspector looked at him sulkily but said no more.

The Detective turned to Horton.

'Is this unfortunate fellow your man?'

Horton nodded slowly, his eyes still fixed on the stinking corpse.

'Then, alas, we were too late. But we may still catch the culprits! My unruly troops should return presently and I think that we have not long missed those responsible.'

The grim faced men left the building and I followed.

We set foot on the damp street just in time for the return of Wiggins and his clamorous mob. Their cab clattered to a halt outside, the horse panting and steaming in the cold air, and they spilled, en mass, out of the vehicle like a swarm of rats.

Wiggins presented himself immediately to the Detective.

'We found them all right, Sir! Seems you was correct as you always are,' the lad beamed. They is holed up down Limehouse way. The old warehouse next to the opium den, if you knows which one I means.' A strange look passed between the boy and the Detective.

'Good man,' the Detective said, after a moment, tossing him some coins casually. 'Get yourselves some lodging for the night, you have done well. And stay out of trouble!'

'Thank you very much indeed, Sir,' Wiggins said and made to be off.

'Oh, Wiggins,' the Detective said. ' I may have more work for you soon so I will be in touch. It appears my retirement will have to wait.'

'Very good, Sir!' the youth said and the rabble disappeared into the night.

'Well gentlemen,' the Detective addressed us. 'If we mean to catch these villains we should be off. The cabs are waiting.'

CHAPTER 17
Peril in Limehouse

Our cabs clattered noisily through the London streets once more as we attempted to capture those responsible for the terrible death of the scientist.

As we went, thoughts flashed through my mind. Who were these mysterious assailants? Terrorists perhaps? Foreign spies trying to get at the British secrets so far discovered with regard to the Martian machinery? Or worse, were these shadowy figures Martians who had survived the destruction of their brethren, just like the creature I had seen held in the underground facility? If they were Martians, why had they holed up within the city?

Certainly all of these entities might have reason to mean harm to Government people. The description given by the old woman helped little. Strange figures wreathed in cloaks. That did not sound like a typical Martian trick to me, but perhaps in their desperation they were now going forth into the human world. Perhaps they had decided to hide in plain sight. The death of the scientist seemed to fit a hurried Martian attempt at silencing an enemy and the apparatus used to burn the man must have generated incredible heat. The knowledge, that it was now all the more likely that there were Martians skulking around using Heat-rays on British citizens once more, worried me greatly.

Horton looked at me with a look on his face that mirrored the one I felt I had. Perhaps he had come to similar conclusions.

The cabs soon slowed and the Detective peered through the window into the fog.

'We have arrived,' he declared. 'Mr Smith, I should be grateful if you would wait outside should assistance need to be called.'

'Very well,' I said, in no mood to argue.

The huge building we were now halted outside was a rundown warehouse. A large painted sign, illegible due to the battering of the elements was fixed above the doors. On the other side of the dock I could just see, through thick drifting fog, black, inky water. The sound of small waves lapping the dock sounded, in this darkness, menacing.

To the right of the building was another smaller edifice. Dim lamps burned in its few windows and there were a few men slumped, in a stupor, by the door. This must be the opium den.

The party of police and Government sponsored people carefully approached the warehouse. The two uniformed officers, at a gesture from the Inspector, skirted the building and headed towards the back, the others heading for the huge front doors.

As I watched from the comparative safety of a few yards away, my hand again in my pocket on my revolver, the deep, wounded animal bellow of a foghorn from some distant vessel sounded across the dark water. I thought instantly of one of the Martians' huge machines and started, my heart racing. I, with no small effort, pulled myself together and tried to concentrate on what was happening before me.

Horton and his companions reached the doors and the Detective gingerly pulled at a smaller door inset into one of the larger ones. It swung open with a loud squeak. The party of men raced inside, revolvers at the ready. The small door swung shut behind them.

There was no further sign of any life then and deathly quiet set in, making me feel more nervous.

Then, after a few moments, shouts from the building became audible then a shrill human scream pierced the night.

Three shots were fired then there was more shouting. I shuffled a little closer to the doors. There was silence once more. I strained my ears trying to hear any other sign of what was happening.

Suddenly one of the large doors exploded outwards in a shower of wood splinters. I put up my arms instinctively to shield my face and fell to the floor.

A large, black shape burst at incredible speed from the hole in the door and rushed, it seemed, headlong at me. I cried out and cowered on the cold floor, fearing this thing would be upon me. More shots followed the dark shape and one appeared to bounce off it with a metallic clang.

I saw a brief glint of what seemed to be metal and the thing, just before it reached me, launched itself into the air right over my head. This was followed a loud splash as the thing hit the water beyond the dock and sank quickly out of sight.

My companions ran out of the warehouse at full pelt.

Nichols, the cabman, was standing on the dock next to his cab, scratching his head.

'What in the Devil was that?' he breathed.

'Can you still see it?' Horton shouted as he ran up.

I shook my head shakily. No words would come.

The Detective went to the edge of the water and peered out.

'No sign. It has made good its escape,' he said, a note of anger in his voice.

'By God it was fast!' the Inspector exclaimed unnecessarily as he puffed up behind the rest. One of the Bobbies, I noticed, was missing and I knew then it was from he whom that awful scream had come from.

'The other policeman?' I asked. Horton shook his head slowly.

'It ran him down. He had no time to react.'

'Did you see what it was?' I asked. 'It nearly ran me down too, I could not see it, it moved so fast.'

'It was too dark,' the Detective said.

'I could swear it was – no,' I began.

'Go on,' Horton prompted.

'Well, I am sure I saw metal on it. A shot hit it and bounced off, I am also sure of that.'

The Detective looked thoughtful.

'I fear Smith may be right,' he said.

'A metal man?' the Inspector scoffed, then instantly regretted it after the look the Detective gave him.

'Inspector, where have you been this past year or so? We have seen metal machines a plenty on our fair land of late. Indeed they were almost our undoing, or had you forgotten?'

'Yes, but the Martians is all dead,' the Inspector said defensively, great droplets of sweat standing out on his brow.

'Are they now?' the Detective said. 'However, as far as the public are concerned this is definitely the case. Perhaps for the time being at least, you should leave such flights of fancy out of your report?' He glared at the bristling Policeman meaningfully. The man did not reply.

'This does not bode well at all,' the Detective muttered, absently filling his pipe.

Horton gave me a glance that spoke volumes.

More police soon arrived and the dead officer, who would leave a young widow and two little ones, was carefully placed into an ambulance carriage. The sheet that covered his remains was stained red with blood. The other constables muttered darkly amongst themselves and swore to catch the killer of their comrade.

We did not dare, nor wish to, intrude upon their grief and point out the unlikelihood of that occurrence.

The Detective spent a few minutes talking quietly to the Inspector and Horton. Presently he came over to me.

'Well Smith, it was good to meet you. I believe you and Horton are now to head back to Hobbs Lane.'

I shook his hand.

'We will, no doubt, meet again,' he said. 'Meanwhile, there is much to do. Farewell.'

'Are you ready, Smith?' Horton said coming over, a troubled look on his face.

'Yes,' I said simply. In truth, tiredness had hit me suddenly and I wished for nothing more than a comfortable bed. Nichols was atop his cab and, as soon as we were in, we were carried off into the fog.

CHAPTER 18
The Flying Machine

The next few days I passed in compiling notes and pondering my experiences. I often thought of my wife and whether she worried about me. I wrote a letter to her, that I was promised by my Steward would be delivered, which I filled with calming phrases and implications of a fictional banality of my situation so that she would not fret. I think that had she known what had already happened to me since my arrival in the underground laboratories, she would have set out to find me and take me back home herself. I, for myself, was still full of curiosity as to how this whole affair would play out and wished to see it through, despite my gut feeling that I had not yet seen all of the hardships I would face before I could return to my old life.

Cavendish was gone on one of his missions in the City and Horton was mostly absent, I assumed in his further investigations on the sabotage attempt and the disappearances of the scientists. Horton did not ask me to accompany him on any subsequent expeditions.

Horton did, on the third day after the adventure in the East End, conduct for me a tour of other areas of the facility, mostly huge laboratories where white-coated men worked at studying some of the artefacts we had brought back with us. Horton warned me of my perilous situation no more. Indeed he acted as if nothing had happened and we had never spoken of the danger that my presence here posed to me. Even when he was not there, though, I had the strangest feeling that he was watching me. Was he a sort of guardian angel or was he keeping his enemy close? Time would tell, I thought.

On that day, for some reason I do not understand, I asked if I could see the live Martian again. Horton seemed reluctant to allow it but finally he relented. Why I wished to go back and see that monstrosity again, I could not say, but I felt that I had to.

So, Horton and I stood at the observation window. The Martian was squatting faced the other way at first, swaying like it were in some reverie. Perhaps it was dreaming of its home world or scheming as to how to escape. But after a short while, it wriggled around on its tentacles and faced us. Slowly, it slithered across the floor of the cell until it was almost at the window. The great glowing eyes locked onto mine and it stared.

'Careful, Smith,' Horton muttered. I ignored him.

All I could see were the great glowing eyes like twin burning suns. They burned into my mind and, my mind began to wander. Suddenly, I saw images in my head.

I saw Mars with many of these creatures moving around the streets, just like I had seen in the Crystal Egg. I saw a scene inside a cylinder, the Martian crew in the tanks full of liquid we had seen in the cylinder. I saw Martians pouncing on pale bipeds and feeding. I saw a group of these creatures sitting in some kind of council chamber hooting excitedly at each other.

I felt something probing at my mind. It was reading my thoughts!

I heard a voice, far away: 'Smith! Smith!'

These strange mind pictures were stopped abruptly when a sharp pain on my cheek was the result of a slap from Horton. I stared uncomprehendingly at the man for a moment.

'What happened?' Horton asked. 'Are you all right?'

'It was talking to me. Showing me things,' I answered distractedly.

'Hmm. It has tried that with a very few. We order the guards not to look at it at all. Perhaps some people are more susceptible. Come, we must go'

I was starting to wonder how long I was to be at the facility. When I had agreed to document events there, I had not envisioned the length of my stay as being so long as it had so far. I did not seem to be performing any function at this time and I intended to ask Cavendish, when he returned, if I could visit my wife. The Knight returned two days later, his usual ebullient self.

'Ready for a trip then, Smith?'

'Where to?' I asked rather grumpily. I felt I knew how a neglected and forgotten child might feel.

'How would you like to see the Flying Machine tested?' Cavendish had a glint in his eye.

'The Flying Machine? You have it? Of course I should like to see it!' I said brightening. I remembered my brother's account of having seen the machine that had, as he put it, rained darkness upon the land.

'We leave in an hour,' Cavendish went to leave but turned back to me at the door.

'Oh, I should appreciate if you did not visit our Martian friend any more. You have had, I gather, a taste of the powers that those beasts possess. Until we understand more, please stay away.'

We went via overland train to the Essex coast, I am not entirely sure exactly of our destination. I asked, during the journey, how they had secured the Flying Machine. Cavendish answered simply that they had found it abandoned in a field near a cylinder. The station that our train stopped at appeared to have no signs and I neglected to ask my hosts of the name of the place. Perhaps this was yet another unmarked station for use only by my Government hosts.

We were conveyed from the station by carriage and travelled a short way on windswept and pitted roads to a rural area with no sign of habitation around. In a large field, a tall fence had been erected and I could not see what lay beyond. The fence stretched for a goodly number of yards either way.

Our carriages pulled up at some great wooden gates in the fence and two soldiers, after checking our identities, let us through.

Beyond were more soldiers, all armed, and the machine.

It sat in the middle of the fenced area like a huge, squat black bird. It was a matt black, not shiny and it appeared to absorb light rather than reflect it. If this thing was metal, I had not seen it's like before.

The machine was shaped like a massive 'V' and had little in the way of surface features. I could see a small window at the pointed front end and a pale green light could be seen within.

A little knot of men stood chatting animatedly nearby and we headed in their direction.

Cavendish shook hands enthusiastically with a tall uniformed army man and made introductions.

'Smith, this is Frederick Roberts, Commander-in-Chief of His Majesty's Forces. He has come from London, like us, to watch this event.'

The man nodded curtly and introduced the various men he was with. They were all minor dignitaries, there to represent their various governmental and forces departments.

A scientist went to Cavendish and muttered something. Cavendish seemed pleased. He jabbered something to Horton, then addressed the assembly.

'Gentlemen, we are ready to start. Now we are all aware of the advances that the Wright brothers in America, and others, are making in the field of manned flight. If this test is successful, we will push those advances far ahead and will re-write history. Shall we begin?' He nodded at the scientist.

There must have been a man in the machine already for the scientist waved a finger and there was a coughing report from the huge contraption then a deep throbbing noise. Small green puffs of smoke hissed from vents in the wings and the noise gradually became higher in pitch.

After a pause, the whole thing began to lift, slowly, straight up in the air.

I saw that the air under the thing was rippling and it reminded me of the heat haze on hot pavement. As the thing rose into the air, a small ripple of applause came from the gathered dignitaries and the guarding soldiers craned their necks to watch, open mouthed. The machine had gone up, perhaps twenty feet or so when there was a commotion at the gate. Shouting floated toward us, just audible over the hum of the machine's engines. Heads swung round, en masse, from the majestic sight before us to see what the trouble was.

Soldiers ran this way and that then there was a tremendous explosion. The gates had imploded scattering splinters and chunks of wood every which way. Then, all that could be heard was the machine. Everyone stopped dead as if time had been frozen.

'NO!' Cavendish exclaimed suddenly. 'Not again!'

Roberts started marching towards the gates barking orders. Soldiers rushed to obey.

Through the smoke at the gate came four glittering metallic figures. They made strange whining, whirring noises as they walked and I was struck with the odd appearance of them. Thinking back, the closest approximation I can come up with is of two-legged dogs. Six feet tall two legged dogs, to be precise. The legs both looked much like a dog's rear legs and they sprouted from odd, rounded bodies topped by a small head thrust forward on long necks.

They marched steadily through the ruined gates and onwards towards us.

'What devilry is this?' someone gasped. No one answered.

Roberts barked again and the soldiers again moved quickly. Raising their rifles, they fired off volleys at the strange intruders. Bullets bounced off the shining metal bodies and on the things marched.

'What are they doing?' Cavendish asked, then realising where the machines were headed, his face took on a look of horror.

'Stop them!' he screamed at the top of his lungs, his face a livid red.

Then, with an escalating sense of dread, I spotted the small funnels that protruded from the heads of the machines. The first soldier that was hit by a miniature Heat-ray did not know what hit him. Others dropped their weapons and ran only to be picked off by this vile death regardless. The dignitaries and I ran blindly away as the machines came close to where the Flying Machine was hovering. They stood stock still for a moment, then loosed their rays, as if by some unspoken command, on one of the wings of the floating giant.

The Flying Machine wobbled slightly from the impact of these blasts then, as more rays were unleashed, tipped over onto one side. A wingtip churned the grass as the machine performed a slow, graceful pirouette then crashed the ground.

Green smoke poured out of the machine then there were muffled explosions deep within its belly. Bits of black metal flew through the air and I ran faster, terror filling my mind. I was now a being of pure instinct, survival was all I could think of.

Horton, who was running beside me, shouted a sharp warning. I looked around but Horton suddenly pushed me hard to the floor. I looked up to see his face turn pale, then there was a whistling sound through the air and he toppled over, a large piece of metal wreckage sticking out of his body. I momentarily forgot the danger and went over to the prone man. He looked at me with pain filled eyes, opened and closed his mouth a few times as if trying to say something to say something.

'Don't try to speak, Horton,' I said. Another explosion rent the air. 'We have to get you some help.'

Horton coughed wetly and black blood issued, in a gout, from his mouth. His eyes glazed over and he was suddenly still.

Filled suddenly with rage at this new waste of life, I went to stand up.

Something hit my head and there was blackness.

Martian Flying Machine by Richard Daborn

Remote Walkers by Peter Fussey

CHAPTER 19
To Hell and Back

It is hard, in many ways, for me to describe how the next year of my life passed.

Anyone who has suffered the deep darkness and despair of madness may understand, for those who have not it may be more to comprehend. I shall endeavour to piece together events as coherently as I am able.

In that field when the strange machines had attacked the captured Flying Machine, as I stood over the body of poor Horton, I had myself been hit on the head by a piece of flying metal. The wound was not serious, but I had been knocked for six for a moment or two.

I next remember standing with blood trickling down the side of my face, quite dazed and disorientated.

The mighty Flying Machine was a useless, smoking pile of metal scrap in the middle of the field and the cries of the wounded drifted on the wind. Here and there, blackened piles of bones and ash marked the last stands of the brave soldiers who had tried to defend us.

A whirring sound made me turn my head slightly. To one side, one of the strange new machines was regarding me curiously.

Again I felt something like fingers probing my mind. I saw more images.

Water, a huge stretch of water. White capped waves. Dark, rainy skies.

More Martians at work at some machinery I did not recognise. Dextrous tentacles flourishing tools. A huge dark insect-like shape I could not see clearly.

My head began to throb. Green flashes tore across my mind.

I saw more Martians grouped around a metal table. A struggling shape strapped down.

I could now see clearly what was happening. A terrified man was being dissected by those vile creatures. Alive!

As the Martians hooted triumphantly, a human scream started and grew louder and louder.

I realise now that it was not the man at the table screaming. The keening wail was coming from my own throat.

The last thing I remember in that field is hearing an odd, stifled version of that nightmarish howl, 'Ulla!', coming from the odd machines as they stalked away.

This final assault on my mind had torn at the already silk thin threads that held my mind together. Weakened by all I had experienced over those months, my mind had no defence left and gave. Those last threads snapped under the strain, and that is all that I remember fully for a long time.

Time had no meaning from then on. I spent many days beneath crisp white sheets, being tended by white-coated doctors and brisk nurses.

From time to time, I would be wheeled out in a bath chair to some fragrant gardens and I would sit staring, without seeing, out at the distance.

My wife came to visit me often, but in the early days, I do not think I even recognised her.

A jolly looking man with big, white side-whiskers would also appear before me and say things to me that I cannot remember. I am told I would think him an orderly or doctor and open my mouth, like a hungry chick in the nest, for food or medicine. This man would shake his head sadly, pat me on the shoulder and go away.

The days and months passed in this sorry state. I lived as if in an impenetrable fog. My days passed in a world which I was not part of and the nights, I am told, I spent, screaming and sweating, tortured by memories and dreams of all the terrible things I have witnessed.

Gradually, though, my tortured soul began to heal, and with the diligent care of the Doctors, the fog that clouded my mind slowly lifted.

I began to speak coherently to my wife. I could enjoy the fresh air in the garden, the bright colours of the flowerbeds and the feel the warmth of the sun on my face.

Nearly a full year after I had lost myself, I was declared fit to leave the institution and I went home to my beloved wife. We spent a few happy weeks rebuilding our life together.

Until the day that Cavendish reappeared.

Cavendish perched on the edge of a chair in my sitting room, a cup of tea lost in his big hand.

'We were very worried about you, Smith,' he said with a concerned expression. 'I trust you feel better.'

'Much,' I said. 'I gather I have you to thank for the care I received.'

'Least we could do, old man. Only the best for those who work for us, you were in very safe hands.'

'Quite. Alas, I can remember little of my time there. One thing I do remember, with hindsight, was your visits. I fear I did not recognise you at the time.'

'Bah!' Cavendish said with a wave of his hand. 'Think nothing of it. I quite understand. One thing I must ask though.'

'Yes?' I asked warily.

Cavendish stared me straight in the eye. 'They spoke to you again, did they not? Those machines.'

'Yes,' I said slowly. 'It was quite horrible. Cavendish, those things … were they Martians?'

My visitor nodded.

'But they are so much smaller than any machine we have seen so far,' I said baffled.

'When I say that they were Martians, I mean that they were of Martian origin. Horton had been looking into reports of such things being seen. Your adventure with him in Limehouse: it is possible that you saw those things then.'

Horton. A wave of sadness washed over me as I remembered how he had sacrificed himself to save me.

'Horton was a good man,' I said.

'Yes he was,' Cavendish agreed. 'He is sorely missed.'

There was silence for a moment.

'Smith,' Cavendish said finally, 'Those machines were unmanned Martian machines. We think they could be controlled remotely to create havoc without causing any loss of Martian life. We call them Remote Walkers.'

'Where do they come from?'

'That's the thing. We believe we have found out their origin. A Martian base that we never knew existed. We are going to try and find them and when we do, we will destroy them all.'

'Where do they come from?' I repeated.

'I cannot tell you as a civilian. To announce this would cause panic. Smith, I want you to join us again.'

I was afraid of something like this as soon as Cavendish had reappeared. 'Why me?'

'I cannot think of anyone better suited to observe this endeavour,' Cavendish said. 'You have seen much of our work and have proved yourself trustworthy. Not only that, but you seem to have some sort of a link with the enemy that is rare to find. Of course, should you wish to decline, I will respect your wishes. I do not want to put you through any more hardships unless you feel up to it'

He paused and absent-mindedly stirred his tea with his spoon.

'But,' he continued, 'It would be a good opportunity for you to see those things eradicated, once and for all.'

My mind whirled again. I had been through so much and yet I had an idea that seeing the Martians destroyed could be the best medicine I could have. I thought for a moment.

'I will come with you. I wish to see this ended.'

Cavendish nodded but said nothing.

'So now, tell me,' I said. 'Where are we going?'

Cavendish looked at me evenly, 'The North Sea,' he replied.

CHAPTER 20
Returning to the Fold

Much had changed in England whilst I had been held, captive and despairing, in my cage of starched cotton sheets and wicker.

Many buildings damaged in the war had been rebuilt along with the lives of those who returned to reside in them. People again worked, slept and ate, going about their little human affairs as if nothing had happened.

Industry once more filled the sky with smoke and the trains again shunted and grumbled, ferrying the swarm of humanity about its business.

Not all was well, though.

As we travelled, on comfortable seats in a Pullman, back to the underground laboratories, Cavendish explained events so far.

'The terror attacks have continued,' he said, puffing on a great wooden pipe. Oddly, I couldn't remember him having had that habit before.

'And the perpetrators, I assume you mean Martians,' I put in.

'Yes, that is correct. The Remote Walkers have been spotted all over the country, seemingly trying to cause as much disruption as possible. They appear, as if out of nowhere, destroy targets and disappear again just as easily. Upwards of forty targets – mostly industrial and Government related – have been hit.'

'Are they trying to soften us up? For another invasion perhaps?' I wondered.

'It could be, although there appear, at the moment, to be no signs of activity on Mars. We have been watching the Egg very closely.'

'Have you traced the exact origin of the machines?' I asked.

'We have a fairly good idea of where they come from,' Cavendish said from behind a cloud of fragrant pipe smoke. 'We engaged the consulting detective, whom I believe you have met, and he was of great assistance to us. Helped to collate reports of sightings of the machines and we were able to gain an approximate location. Alas, we could not persuade him to accompany us on our mission; he would have been a valuable asset.'

'So you really think they come from the North Sea, as you said before?' I asked.

'Yes. Extraordinary, I grant you, and we would never have guessed that our friends would actually think to land a cylinder under water. But it seems to be so.'

I shook my head in wonder. 'Indeed. So what is the plan?'

'We go and destroy their base. Stop this nonsense once and for all. We have to give their comrades on Mars reason to think again about coming here for another visit.'

'That I have to see,' I said. 'But how can we touch them underwater? Some new weapon?'

Cavendish grinned, 'Exactly so. We have some new toys to play with.'

The laboratories were, as before, a hive of activity.

'We have made great strides in our work on the machines,' Cavendish said as we walked through the cavernous testing areas. I soon found out that he was not exaggerating.

I was amazed to see a new Fighting Machine being put through its paces in one area. A prototype of a human machine!

I gathered, from what I understood of Cavendish's excited chatter, that the makeup of the Martian metals was still causing some problems for our scientists and the prototype Fighting Machine was heavily armoured with steel, like an Ironclad, and its dull battleship-grey surface was dotted with rivets. The legs were thicker than those on their Martian counterparts, to take the extra weight I assumed, and they ended with sprung gripped feet. The engines were based on those of the Martian machinery, but, apparently, so far, much less efficient. Cavendish informed me that they were working flat out to remedy these problems.

So, a year after I had last been here, I saw our own human Fighting Machine clatter and thud jerkily across the rock floor, steam hissing noisily from the joints of its legs.

'Marvellous, is it not?' Cavendish beamed. 'Soon we will be able to take on the Martians on their own terms. Who knows, perhaps even on their own world!'

'We could go to Mars?' I asked shocked.

'Why ever not?' Cavendish said. 'We have been experimenting with various things, not least that marvel Cavorite'

'The metal from Wells' book?' I said. What he was talking about was pure fiction.

'The very same. Well, the real metal, anyway,' Cavendish affirmed, chuckling. 'Our friend Wells knows more than he might perhaps let on.'

I could get little more from him about that.

'You still haven't told me how you mean for us to travel to the Martian base in the North Sea,' I reminded Cavendish. 'Do you have some new kind of Ironclad?'

'We have something much better,' the Knight said, winking. 'A submersible.'

That night I had lucid dreams of machines floating gracefully across the sky, land Ironclads clanking around the Earth and great ships that could cross the black gulf of space and carry men to other planets.

CHAPTER 21
What Really Happened at Kensington

Preparations had begun for the expedition to the North Sea in earnest. Weaponry and other equipment was already on the way to our sea base, although I knew not where it was apart from the fact that it was somewhere on the West coast of Scotland.

The consulting Detective, visited me one day and, much to my surprise, greeted me warmly. I had heard that his reputation was that of a bit of a 'cold fish' but I was treated like a long lost friend.

He walked now, with the aid of a cane. He had sustained some injury during his investigations and this was why he would not accompany us on our mission.

Apparently, the Detective was here only to impart final intelligence and to wish us 'Bon Voyage'. Cavendish seemed very disappointed that this man would not be with us for the duration, as was I.

I asked Cavendish, over dinner that night, what had become of the Martian in the holding cell.

'Martians,' he said grimly.

'What ever do you mean?' I asked.

'It's the strangest thing,' Cavendish said. 'The thing reproduced! More of the blighters popped off it like peas out of a pod! The scientists call it 'budding'. Apparently, the young ones just grow out of the parent. An extraordinary sight!'

'How many?' I asked incredulous.

'We now have 5 of them in there. Quite a handful they are. We have had to put them in separate cells as they were causing our guards a lot of trouble. They grow very quickly.'

'I can imagine,' I shivered, not entirely comfortable with the thought of having that many of the creatures in close proximity.

It later appeared that I was right to be worried.

Two days later, I was with Cavendish watching the last of the supplies being loaded ready for transport.

A soldier ran up to us.

'Sir, we have to leave,' the man said, trying to catch his breath.

'Why? What is it?' Cavendish asked, visibly confused.

'They have found us.'

Cavendish's ruddy face paled as a horn began to bellow out a hoarse warning.

'I was afraid of this,' he said. He hurried to his office with me in tow and began to gather up papers and documents.

'Cavendish,' I shouted, as the rumbling of an explosion sounded. 'Leave those!'

The man looked at me blankly for a moment, dropped the papers and grabbed the box that contained the Crystal Egg.

'We cannot leave this!' he exclaimed. I grabbed his sleeve and dragged him away clutching his precious cargo.

We were hurried out in a small group, just in time to see five of the Remote Walkers stalk into the testing area, Heat-rays blasting everything, and everyone, in sight. Small fires raged in areas of the room.

'Get out of here!' someone shouted, somewhat needlessly.

The machines steadily progressed through the base leaving wreckage in their wake. We came upon a dirt-streaked and bleeding soldier as we entered the lift to the surface and he informed us that the walkers had freed the captive Martians.

'Cavendish,' I said, dismayed, as the lift rose to the surface. 'How did they find us?'

'I do not know,' Cavendish replied. 'I suppose it was a matter of time. Luckily, we have moved much of our machinery to other laboratories and to the sea base. They cannot do much harm here.'

A terrifying thought occurred to me. 'Do you think they are following me?'

It suddenly seemed to make sense. How many times had disaster and carnage happened when I was present?

'I do not think so,' Cavendish brushed some dust off the shoulder of his jacket. 'Make no mistake, they do seem to be able to communicate with you in some way but you are not alone. Take heart from that fact. If I thought you were a danger to our mission, I should never have asked you along.'

Still, I was unsure and the thought echoed around my head.

We reached the underground train just in time to see the machines stalk quickly out into the tunnel. Explosions boomed deep in the bowels of the Earth and smoke poured out of rents in the walls. The liberated Martians clung on to the machines with their tentacles like nightmarishly deformed new world cowboys. The glittering machines, seemingly unencumbered by their joyously hooting riders, gathered speed and we soon lost them from sight.

As we left the train at the station there was another tremendous explosion and a huge fireball came at us at a tremendous pace down the dark tunnel.

'Run!' I shouted.

As we made the street, just in time, the glass blew out the windows of the station showering passers-by outside. There were more deep booms and the ground heaved. The station building and some of those around it began to crumble and dust clouds flew into the air. Rubble flew this way and that knocking running pedestrians off their feet.

Pedestrians screamed and ran as there was one last terrific report, a rippling of the pavement and some of the buildings finally, slowly toppled over.

As the dust cleared, we stood dazed in the sunlight, staring at the great pile of rubble that had been caused by the end of the underground laboratory at Kensington.

CHAPTER 22
Jealousy Abroad

We did not linger long in Kensington. We found a large group of soldiers had been waiting for us, very much on edge, outside the station. It turned out they were barracked in one of the buildings nearby as a precautionary measure in case of just such an attack as befell the laboratory. They had not seen the Remote Walkers enter, a captain told us, but the machines had been spotted racing away toward the Thames as the soldiers arrived to investigate the explosions coming from the Station area. Some of the men had apparently given chase but despondently joined us a short while later, having finally lost the attackers somewhere along the embankment.

When a roll call had been taken of people who had escaped the attack, we found that somewhere around thirty souls has been lost. Cavendish took comfort in the fact that the toll could have been larger, had not operations already been largely transferred elsewhere, but I was appalled and was eager for retribution. Any basic thoughts of empathy with these creatures I may once have had were draining away at each new outrage. Where once I had pondered over our right to exterminate them, I now wished only for their eradication.

The injured were taken away to hospital and our group, in a motley convoy of carriages and motorcars, made our way to the railway station. We only had a short wait until the train arrived.

The train that clunked into the station was quite unlike any I had seen before. It was armoured like an ironclad and was bristling with turrets. The wheels were covered in great metal guards and a large scoop, like the American 'cowcatchers', was fixed to the front. It looked like some great metal fortress that moved.

'Are those Heat-rays?' I asked Cavendish, pointing at the turrets.

'Of a sort,' he replied. 'I admit that they are not quite as effective as the Martian Heat-ray, yet, but much more so than conventional weaponry. We have all sorts of toys we have developed. Quite extraordinary in such a short space of time, would you agree?'

This man's pride in the minor successes with this wholly alien technology was quite unflappable. I would believe how well these things worked when I saw it for myself.

'Just think of the applications for atomic power,' Cavendish continued. 'We have made great leaps in that field thanks to the Martians. We have a lot to thank them for in actuality. They have unwittingly given us the means to not only fight them, but also to improve ourselves.'

I had my doubts. Would the usage of this new technology drive us forward to enlightenment or would it change us in an altogether more unpleasant fashion?

'Other governments still wish to get their hands on this stuff, you know,' Cavendish said. 'We have managed to keep them from infiltrating so far through strict border controls and the like. We will not share until we are ready. You have heard that there have been warlike rumblings on the continent, of course.'

I had. It seemed that some of our European neighbours were getting impatient and their jealousy was getting the better of them. France and Germany, in particular, were openly demanding in public that Britain share the findings in regard to the technology we were discovering. There were public demonstrations in these countries, which were spreading to others, and some of our less reputable newspapers had already taken to using jingoistic rhetoric in their defence of our Government's stand. I wondered how much worse matters would be if it were generally known how far Cavendish and his scientists had advanced. It was only a matter of time before we would find out.

Despite the fearsome outward appearance of the train, it was quite comfortable inside and we settled into our seats for the long journey to Scotland. I doubted a Pullman car could have been fitted out less extravagantly. We had a carriage to ourselves but the whole thing was spoiled somewhat by the fact that there were only slits for windows. The air soon became warm and, with Cavendish puffing on his pipe, somewhat smoky. I tried to engross myself in a newspaper but the reports of unrest abroad began to depress me and I tried to stare out at what countryside I could see through the narrow window.

Soon, it became dark and even this diversion became impossible.

I retired to the sleeper car and tried to sleep.

At some unearthly time before dawn, with the moon riding high in the clear, cloudless sky, the train screeched to a halt. A great tree trunk had fallen across the track and men got out to move it.

As this task was being completed, a shout went up and the men ran back to the train. I gathered, from the excited chatter of others on board, that Remote Walkers had been spotted moving across a clearing in a nearby wood and I strained to see, without success, what was happening. I did think I may have seen the glint of metal, momentarily, in amongst the trees, but I cannot be sure. There was a thrumming and a whoosh from above my head as a Heat-ray turret spoke and some of the trees in the wood burst into flame. I think I might then have heard that odd, strangled 'Ulla' cry of a walker, but it could just have been wind rushing through the branches of the trees.

The train moved off without further incident.

CHAPTER 23
Holy Loch

The base at Holy Loch had its own railway station not too far away. The armoured train was unloaded quickly and efficiently and we soon found ourselves at the gates of the sea base complex.

The defences here were quite impressive. Huge metal gates topped with spikes and barbed wire. The fences themselves were electrified and any interloper would, if they passed these, have to cross a mined no-man's land only to face tall, smooth walls of plastered brick, topped with broken glass. At intervals along the fence and either side of the gates, stood tall towers with Heat-rays mounted on them.

The base itself was full of uniformed men dashing this way and that at various tasks. In the compound I saw some human Fighting Machines standing in a row like grotesque metal soldiers on parade. Technicians in one piece coveralls swarmed over one machine that had smoke pouring out of its hood, another machine was twitching fitfully like a sleeping dog and I wondered if Cavendish's faith that these clumsy-looking machines would be an effective defence, or indeed offence, against the Martians was entirely misplaced.

We were shown to our quarters and left to unpack. My room was small but very comfortable. Gleaming brass trim framed everything and I felt as if I were in the first class cabin of a steamer. Another example, I'm sure Cavendish would have stated, of the taxpayers money well spent.

There was a knock on the door and Cavendish appeared.

'Would you like to see our transport for the mission, old man? She's just coming back from testing at sea.'

'Very much,' I said throwing some clothes in a drawer. 'I'm ready.'

I found myself, a short while later, in a cavernous building. This was an enormous boatshed and there was a large docking area in the middle. I looked carefully over the edge of the decking into the water and it seemed very deep. My undulating reflection looked back curiously at me from the dark, cold water.

'Ah, this must be her,' Cavendish said and I looked up.

A klaxon sounded and an amplified voice boomed out from speakers that I could not see.

'All land crews prepare for docking.'

The water in the huge bay was churning now as bubbles rose to the surface. Then the water suddenly parted as a tall black tower began to rise up and out. More and more of the black shape became visible and I began to get an idea of the sheer size of this thing. Now, the deck cast off water and rose up. A minute later, I could see the whole thing. It was easily wider than any vessel I had ever seen before and was certainly longer. The smooth black surface contained no visible joins and few features, much like the Flying Machine. The design was so obviously of the same origin I gasped. I realised that this thing could not be human!

'Smith,' said Cavendish grandly. 'Meet Nautilus!'

Cavendish cut into my stunned thoughts and confirmed what I thought about this new machine.

'Yes, she is a Martian vessel,' he said. 'We found her adrift off the South coast, all her crew dead. We took her and adapted her for our needs. It was decided that she was, by nature, so fantastic that she should have a name to suit.'

'Most fitting,' I agreed. Verne, I felt, would have approved.

'She possesses enormous power, Smith. I believe that we can defeat the Martians utterly with this machine and the weapons we have developed. She is a submarine like no other!'

I knew that the submarine vessel was not a new concept … many nations were already deploying these stealthy and dangerous machines. But, although I had never seen a human one 'in the flesh', I could clearly see that this vessel before me was something else entirely.

'I hope you are right,' I said, 'When do we go aboard?'

'Later, old chap, first, I think I shall introduce you to the people we will be sailing with.'

The barracks were not quite as opulent as my cabin, but seemed clean and functional.

Five men lay around on bunks reading or chatting amongst themselves. They stopped talking and looked up as Cavendish and I entered. Before Cavendish could say anything, another door opened and another man entered.

'Squad, shun!' one of the men said. The other men stood to attention.

'Ah, Lieutenant Churchill,' Cavendish said to the newcomer. 'This is Smith, would you be so kind as to introduce the men?'

The Lieutenant nodded.

'Of course, Sir. This is Corporals Jameson and Glenn, and these gentlemen are Thomas, Dawson and Wayne.' The soldiers tipped their heads as they were introduced.

'Is this it? I asked disbelievingly. The men by the bunks looked at me curiously.

'No,' said Cavendish. 'These men are the best His Majesty's Forces have to offer, specially trained to do a particular job. There will be another one hundred men going with us.'

'I apologise,' I said sheepishly to the men. 'I meant no slight to anyone.'

'Don't worry about it, old man,' Cavendish said. 'Churchill, could you outline the plan for Smith?'

Churchill, a gruff looking man somewhere in his thirties, looked at me doubtfully.

'Smith is along for the mission as my guest,' Cavendish prompted. 'He can be trusted completely.'

Churchill nodded and told me what they had planned.

Special Regiment by Peter Fussey

CHAPTER 24
How it Would be Done

Churchill, I later discovered, had been an MP before the war. He had become disillusioned with his party and was on the verge of changing allegiance when the Martians had landed.

He had immediately decided to spring to his country's defence and had taken up arms. As a war correspondent during the Boer War before his career in politics began, he had seen battle before and slipped into the military life with comparative ease.

He stood now, puffing on a cigar and speaking of the plan for the assault on the Martians undersea lair. I did not wonder at his previous vocation, as his voice was steady, clear and confident. This was a man well used to oration.

'Our plan is to use the larger force as a diversion. When we locate it precisely, these men will attack the cylinder from several sides whilst our little force of commandos here slip in quietly and enter the base separately. Of course, we know little of what we will be facing and much will need to be decided on the field. At any rate, our smaller force will, if possible, set charges within the Martian base and slip away again. With luck and the grace of God, we will blow the blighters to kingdom come!'

I thought this plan a little vague and said so.

'But there are so many unknown factors, are there not? The Martians are not to be underestimated.'

'Indeed,' said Churchill looking me squarely in the eye. 'But the basis of the plan is sound and the rest will come as we discover more. The truth is, we do not know just what we will face down there and we must be prepared to improvise.'

'What weapons do we have?' I asked.

Cavendish stepped in.

'All in good time, Smith! For now we are keeping our cards closely to our chests. Needless to say, we will not be embarking on this endeavour half cocked. We feel sure we can defeat these creatures and win the day.'

This show of confidence brought murmurs of approval from the men. I sincerely hoped that this bravado was not misplaced and wondered what poor Horton would have thought of this plan.

'So this small group of men will destroy the cylinder?' I said. 'Again I mean no offence, but it still strikes me as suicide! Why there are only six of them.'

'Seven, actually,' said a familiar voice from the doorway.

Many times, incidents in my life have taken me by surprise. In times of war, perhaps, this is not so unusual. Events in war themselves are far more unusual than in peacetime. However, since the war began, my life had been composed of an unending succession of bad luck, horror and coincidence. It is little wonder, perhaps that I fancied, at times, that some bored god was using me as some kind of plaything.

The man standing at the door was another reason for my mind to reel once more with the pure strangeness of it all.

'Ah, Sergeant!' Cavendish said. 'Come in.'

'Good Lord!' I spluttered finally as the man sauntered into the room. 'The Artilleryman!'

'Sergeant, actually,' said the man grinning and pointing at the stripes on his uniform. 'Done well for myself haven't I?'

The man came over to me and pumped my hand just as he had so long before.

'Don't look so shocked, my friend,' he said. 'I find the fact that we keep meeting, and in one piece, to be a good sign.'

'Yes, of course,' I said, simply. I was not so sure that I agreed with his thoughts but I saw his point. We had both lived through much and continued to survive to meet again.

'So what do you think of this motley bunch?' he asked sweeping a hand grandly at the men seat around the room. 'A finer lot I couldn't wish to see. We'll show the Martians a thing or two, eh?'

The men around the room gave a small cheer and I was reminded of when I had last seen this man in the public house.

'Thank you, Sergeant,' Churchill rumbled. 'We were just informing our guest of our plan.'

'Ah,' said the Sergeant. 'I take it you are coming with us?'

'I am,' I said.

'Excellent. It will be like old times, eh? This man, Lieutenant, is a survivor. Just the sort we need with us.'

'He will not be fighting. Sergeant,' Churchill said levelly. 'Smith is here purely to observe.'

'It doesn't matter. It's good to see him nonetheless. He can be our lucky mascot!'

This exchange seems to have quietened the men's suspicion of me and, from then on, they looked at me in a much more friendly fashion. It seemed that the Sergeant vouching for me meant that I was all right by them.

CHAPTER 25
Waiting for the Off

The next week was spent in preparing for the voyage. I was escorted around the base and saw the men training. A few times the men went outside of the compound. Many vehicles took them, large wagons, which travelled more quickly than any motor vehicle I had seen before. I gathered these were derived from the machinery that the Martians had left behind and some contained men and the backs of others were covered with tarpaulins. Cavendish told me vaguely that they were going for training that could not be done at the base.

One day, I was allowed to go on one of these expeditions and watching the men running at stuffed target with fixed bayonets and practicing for various eventualities was, I had to admit quite a stirring sight.

I counted ten human Fighting Machines staggering about the compound, as I wandered around the complex, in clouds of steam and noticed that they had odd boiler shaped tanks fitted to their backs.

They also had tubes on either side that looked like some kind of weapons but not like the Heat-ray cannons.

After much questioning from me, Cavendish finally admitted that these human machines had been refitted for use underwater and would be carried on *Nautilus* as part of the assault. He also intimated that there were more 'wonders', as he put it, yet to be seen but would say no more.

I saw Heat-rays being tested on vehicles and other sorts of weaponry being fired.

Seeing the whole force on parade in the middle of the base towards the end of the wait for our mission was a most impressive sight and, despite my misgivings, I felt my spirits lift. I had been assured that these men had all been handpicked from the cream of His Majesty's forces and they certainly looked an army to be reckoned with. They all wore specially made, dark blue, uniforms for this mission. Embroidered patches were carried proudly on sleeves that proclaimed them to be part of the 'King's Expeditionary Force'.

I just hoped that the Martians would be as easy to defeat as everyone seemed to believe.

The Sergeant came and visited me in my cabin, after dinner one night, and we played cards. He regaled me with tales of his exploits since I had last seen him and I, in turn, told him of the things I had seen since I had last seen him.

'Sounds like you have had quite the time of it, mate!' he exclaimed as I finished my tale. 'You are a lucky man indeed to escape so often. Seems like someone is watching over you, eh?'

I was not so convinced.

I, rather tactlessly, reminded him of his dreams of an underground Utopia but he changed the subject. I think he found his behaviour then a little shameful and wished not to talk about it. I, in light of my own hardships since the war, thought I understood him better now than I had before.

Whilst preparations carried on, reports came in of harassment of shipping in the North Sea. Cavendish told me that ships had been attacked and sunk and strange machines had been sighted speeding away in those waters. There had also been a further two Remote Walker attacks on land; one successful, the other repelled using the Human Heat-ray. The Martians were evidently still trying to disrupt things as much as possible.

I did not escape the training. Even though I was only an observer, I had to be taught how to use the underwater suits that had been developed, from existing and new technology, for this mission. Apparently, even Cavendish had learned this new skill and the thought had amused me greatly.

These strange suits would allow members of the force to be underwater for an extended length of time. I was a very good swimmer but, for my own safety, it was decided that I had to learn how to use them in case of emergency. I was assured that I would be aboard *Nautilus* throughout the mission but was submitted to the training anyway. Just in case, as Cavendish said with a small smile.

The base had a large water tank that was used for training and testing and a soldier was assigned to help me into the suit and show me how to use it.

The suits were lighter versions of the suits that I knew deep-sea divers use and seeing them reminded me of Verne again. The helmet was fashioned out of brass with little portholes around it and there was a large tank, for air, to be worn on the back. I spent some hours learning to control my breathing in the helmet and how to walk in the great heavy boots that were made to allow the wearer to walk on the sea floor. I hoped, sincerely, that all of this was a waste of time.

Soon came time for the voyage to begin. Cavendish woke me at eight one morning and told me we would be off at dawn the next day.

Butterflies fluttered in my stomach that day. I had seen and experienced much but the fear of the unknown still had an effect on me.

I had little appetite for food and I tried to busy myself in bringing my notes up to date.

The rest of the base, too, seemed affected. The men were quiet throughout the day and there was none of the usual joking and raucousness that could be expected in a great gathering of fighting men.

Final tests were carried out on the machines and I heard explosions coming from the far side of the base. I gathered that the weaponry was being taken through last minute tests as well.

The day passed very slowly and I retired early but slept only fitfully.

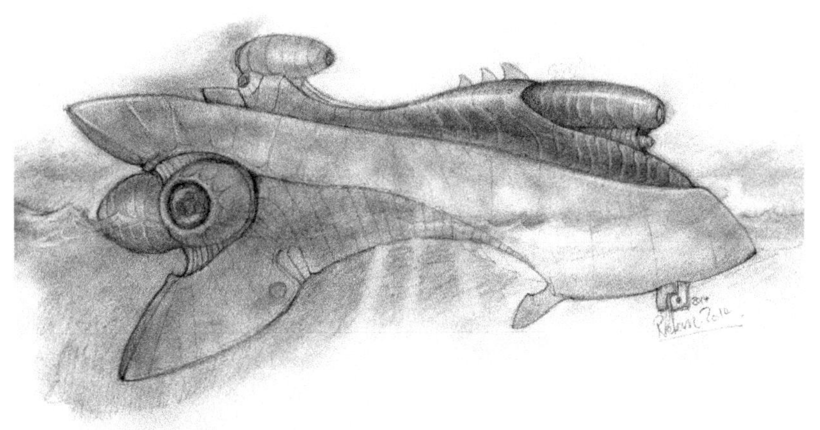

Nautilus by Richard Daborn

CHAPTER 26
Bon Voyage!

The next morning, I stood nervously in the docking bay watching the final pieces of equipment being loaded onto *Nautilus*.

There was much light-hearted chatter from the men of the commando squad and the Sergeant turn occasionally to wink or grin at me as if to allay my, evidently obvious, fears.

Churchill stood alone silently watching operations and puffing on his ever-present cigar, but seemed to me like a coiled spring, as ready to get going as his men.

The main body of troops were next stowed away deep in the belly of the huge submersible, through huge doors at her nose, and it soon became our time to board.

The front of the machine was open, like the jaws of some massive undersea beast, and I entered with trepidation. I felt some primal fear that this enormous thing would swallow me whole and I would never be seen again.

Inside, it was not unlike being within the cylinder on Horsell Common. That same sickly glow emanated from the metal walls and no man-made lighting was either needed or in evidence. As Cavendish and I crossed the threshold, the 'jaws' started to slowly close with a high-pitched whine. As we walked inside, our footsteps clattered on the grated floor.

The human Fighting Machines were secured against the walls of the vessel as we passed and there were other bulky shapes covered in tarpaulins. Soldiers and the vessel's crew, who were also dressed in dark blue uniforms but with jaunty sailor's caps on their heads, went busily around the area carrying weapons and equipment here and there.

We were eventually ushered, past a bewildering array of unknown machinery and controls, to our cabins and I saw that the human touch had, unexpectedly, been added. My quarters were almost as opulent as those I occupied in the underground laboratories in Kensington, all wooden panelling, brass fittings and superfluous curtains. This amalgamation of human decor and Martian superstructure struck me as vaguely unsettling.

After a short time of trying to acclimatise to these odd surroundings, Cavendish came to me and asked if I wished to stand on the bridge of the vessel whilst we put out to sea. To get there, we had to negotiate many corridors and staircases which, I was told, had been adapted for human use, as had much of the inside of this alien craft. It appeared she had been virtually gutted, save the machines for her control, of course, and adapted as required for this mission.

The bridge was yet another large space lined with lit up instrumentation. Around twenty sailors stooped over dials or manipulated levers on these instruments. I was, I admit, impressed by how the use of such strange technology had been adapted, seemingly so easily, by man. Cavendish said some things about these controls and such, but much of it, I confess, went over my head.

Cavendish steered me towards a tall greying man who stood barking orders before a large viewing window. I wasn't sure if this window was real or was, perhaps, a projected image like those 'portholes' I had seen in the cylinder. I could see the entrance to the docking bay through it.

'Smith,' Cavendish said motioning towards the man. 'This is the Captain of Nautilus.'

'Smith,' grunted the Captain and brusquely shook my hand. 'I have heard much about you. Welcome aboard.'

'Thank you, Captain,' I replied. 'This is a most impressive vessel.'

'Indeed she is,' the Captain said, simply.

Cavendish steered me away from the Captain and we stood a little away as he returned to his duties.

'I have to tell you,' Cavendish said in a low voice. 'The Captain had a special reason for requesting this mission. His brother was also a naval man and commanded a ship you may have heard of.'

'Really?' I said. 'Which vessel is that? I confess to not knowing much about these things.'

'Nevertheless, this one will mean something to you. The vessel the Captain's brother commanded was HMS Thunder Child.'

Again, the odd synchronicity of this struck me. This man was the brother of the man whose ship had battled valiantly to defend shipping during the war, and my own brother had seen that brave vessel sink, with all hands, in that defence.

That so many things could be tied together in such ways seemed impossible to be mere chance.

A dull rumbling deep within *Nautilus* signalled the start of our journey. Through the viewing window, we could see the docking bay slip away to either side and soon we were heading to open sea. Land crews waved and cheered as we passed. I saw that we were being escorted by heavily armed Ironclads, four in all, and they were all seemingly carrying newly added Heat-ray funnels. I hoped that we would not hit trouble this early in the voyage.

If it hadn't been for the distant rumble and whine of the engines and the view through the window, I would have been hard pressed to know if were actually moving at all. I have never before, nor since, travelled in such a smooth fashion. I had expected the vague feeling of nausea or disorientation that had accompanied all my previous sea journeys but there was nothing of that sort on board this vessel. I marvelled at how something so huge could slip through the water like a hot knife through butter.

So now, for better or worse, we were on our way.

CHAPTER 27
Out to Sea

Cavendish never ceased to amaze me with his encyclopaedic knowledge of how all the machinery adapted from Martian technology worked. Although he himself never told me much about his life, in fact he seemed to make a point of not doing so, I do know that he had a background in engineering and other similar sciences. Apparently, he was an advisor in the sciences to the Government, although in what exact capacity I never found out. Our American cousins might have called Cavendish a 'trouble-shooter', although I felt that he would have disapproved of that term.

Whatever his exact origins, he was obviously much in demand in those post-war years.

I was surprised to hear, from overhearing some idle gossip amongst the men, that there was a Mrs Cavendish. Somehow, he had the air of the eternal bachelor about him and he did not seem the married type at all. Thinking about that, and wondering quite how this woman stood his continued absence, brought to mind my own sweet wife who must, I thought, feel a kinship with her. I felt ashamed that I had neglected my wife so, of late, especially as I had already put her through so much, and I made up my mind to return home to her as soon as our task was completed. If I survived.

Nautilus was fitted with an array of the latest developments in technology as I have intimated before, and it seemed that much of this equipment was enhanced by items the Martians had left behind.

Rows and rows of consoles lined the control rooms and the bridge and little lights winked and flashed, like tiny stars amidst the firmament, though to what purpose I could not even begin to comprehend. Young and fresh-faced sailors, some barely out of their teens I guessed, hovered around these banks of equipment. These young men were overseen by a grizzled and bearded Mate who perched, an old, unlit pipe clenched between his yellow teeth, on a raised chair, overlooking all this activity. The Mate reminded me, rather absurdly, of some strange tennis umpire keenly watching a game.

Cavendish proudly showed me the vessel's radio system, again staffed by a boy who I warranted could barely grow a beard had he tried, and I watched as the Captain contacted Holy Loch with details of our course on it. The scratchy, clipped tones of the voice that came from the contraption in answer gave me an idea and I asked if I could talk to my wife on the machine. Cavendish frowned a little at this. Apparently, this equipment was for official use only but he said he would see what he could do. From his manner, I assumed that this request would be conveniently forgotten and I felt a flash of annoyance.

I watched as a crewmember tested out the 'sonar' equipment. The man had his eyes locked to some form of appliance attached to yet another console. The appliance reminded me of the binoculars I had once seen my late friend Ogilvy using. A light from within bathed the attendant's face in a sickly green glow. This 'sonar' was apparently something that was on board when *Nautilus* was found and its usage had been learned since by trial and error. I gathered that it worked by projecting sound waves outward from the vessel, which then bounced back from any objects that these waves hit and the results showed on a display within these 'binoculars'. It was then possible, I gathered, to ascertain what lay ahead of the vessel from quite some distance. Cavendish explained that this would be our most likely method of finding the location of the Martian lair.

In the afternoon, I joined some men up on the huge, flat deck of the submersible. I took in the bracing, spray-filled air and the cries of the seagulls that circled and whirled in the air above us. Our Ironclad escorts steamed along beside us, dwarfed by this great hulk we stood upon. The whoops of the ships' horns sounded periodically and the sailors on board lined the rails and waved enthusiastically at us. I saw the little flags on the masts, buffeted by the light breeze, and heard the cheers of the men on these ships and momentarily felt a celebratory atmosphere. It was like a street party and the men on deck with me seemed thoroughly caught up in it. They waved and cheered at their comrades over the sea, filled with pride at having been chosen to staff this extraordinary vessel. These high spirits were soon dissipated for me, however, when the thought of the unknown that yet faced us elbowed its way roughly into my mind. Cavendish, through all this, stood alone further up the deck, gazing unflinchingly out into the horizon. I wondered at the thoughts that must be crossing his mind.

The weather took a sudden turn for the worse, as it often does in those waters, and we were all ushered back into the bowels of the vessel, as dark, ominous clouds quickly blew in and a sudden heavy rain lashed the deck.

The first sign of trouble came early the next morning.

A loud klaxon sounded and I stumbled wearily from my bed to see what caused this noise. I quickly dressed and made my way, through men rushing too and fro around the corridors, to the bridge and found Cavendish already there. I wondered then if he ever slept.

'What is it?' I asked him, now fully awake and not a little concerned.

'An attack,' he replied evenly. 'One of our escorts has been holed by some sort of small machine that came from the water. I gather she is sinking fast.'

'They do not waste any time,' I said. 'Do they wish to take Nautilus back?'

'They will take her over my dead body,' Cavendish asserted, rather oddly I thought, as if he were the only person who could guard this vessel. 'Captain, I think it is time we submerged.'

The Captain turned and stared at him.

'What about the other ships?' I said. 'Surely we cannot just leave them?'

'We can do exactly that. This vessel is the only machine we have that can help us complete our mission successfully. We have to preserve her for what is to come and cannot take the chance that there is a whole fleet of those things waiting for us at this stage.'

I thought of those sailors that I had seen waving so happily the afternoon before now fighting selflessly to defend us. Through the viewing windows an explosion, some distance away, lit up the darkness outside.

'Captain,' Cavendish said grimly. 'If you please.'

Something flashed across the Captain's eyes then. I wondered if these orders went against his wishes as much as mine. The Captain turned after a moment and shouted orders and sailors pushed levers and flicked switches.

There was a slight lurch, and as another explosion flashed through the viewing window, *Nautilus* began to sink into the cold, black water.

CHAPTER 28
Submerged

The mood onboard *Nautilus* was much subdued. Some men looked grim, and some a little frightened, but applied themselves, with every ounce of professionalism they possessed, to their various tasks. Cavendish stood, hands behind his back, looking as self-important and defiant as ever. From time to time, I caught various crewmembers surreptitiously casting sharp glances at him. The Knight either pretended not to notice or was too wrapped up in his own thoughts. Rather than a penny, if I could, I would have given the Royal Mint for them.

There was little to see through the viewing window but gloom until the Captain gave an order and powerful lamps lit up the sea ahead. Startled shoals of fish glinted as they hurried this way and that in a frantic effort to make way for this huge invader of their territory.

Away from the battle on the surface we travelled, I could not guess at the speed but there was no feeling of movement. I could only gather that we were travelling very fast indeed.

'Captain, small object coming at us ahead!' a sailor cried. He was hunched over the sonar binoculars and the green glow made his eyes appear wider than they perhaps were.

'Evasive action!' the Captain growled. A crewman whirled a great wheel around and there was a slight change in the pitch of the distant engine sound, but that was the only sign I could detect of any change of pace or direction.

'Ready the sonic weapon,' the Captain said.

Ahead, through the window, I could now see a small shape keeping pace with us. As we had changed course, it had raced to follow. This new machine looked like a much smaller version of *Nautilus*, a black shadow in the murk, punctuated with green lights that shone along its length. It was getting closer and it seemed to me that if neither vessel changed course or slowed, there would be a collision.

'Fire!' the Captain shouted.

A sailor pressed a lever and there was a high-pitched whine. From the front and side of *Nautilus* the water seemed to ripple.

The Martian craft chasing us turned and quickly fired off some sort of missile. This small black missile came rapidly toward us but narrowly missed, shooting straight past us at incredible speed. A young crewman near me breathed an audible sigh of relief and I saw that sweat beaded his brow.

'Fire!' the Captain repeated. Again, the water rippled ahead of us and the nose of the other craft jerked to one side as if it had been roughly pushed by some giant's hand. Our pursuer tried to return to its intercepting course but the water rippled once more and the craft was suddenly enveloped in bubbles as it disintegrated. The torn pieces of the machine began to sink slowly to the sea floor as we sped past.

The bridge erupted in cheers and sailors jumped up and down with glee.

'The sonic weapon works perfectly,' Cavendish beamed at the Captain, who did not seem inclined to join in the celebration. The Captain nodded.

'That is just as well,' he muttered.

The sailor on the sonar instrument confirmed that that there were no more enemy craft in the vicinity so the Captain barked orders for us to resume our original course. Our search for the Martian base began in earnest.

I retired to my cabin after this conflict and tried to concentrate in writing notes for my account. I soon gave this up, however, and lay on my bed to mull over things. Despite my tiredness, my mind was again racing and sleep was impossible.

I felt I could understand, if not agree, with Cavendish's reasons for his orders for us to flee the scene of the Martian attack on the Ironclads, but that understanding did not make me feel any better. It seemed obvious to me that many of the crew, and perhaps the Captain, were wracked by similar doubts. We had left brave men to die and I could not come to terms with that. I wondered if the crew felt as cowardly as I, even if there was nothing I personally could have done and it may have, as Cavendish insisted, ended in the failure of this crucial mission.

I was not left to my thoughts for long, though, as the Sergeant appeared at my door and asked if I would like to join him and the commandos in their mess.

As a distraction from my thoughts was most welcome at this point, I followed him through the vessel to a smoky mess room where the men lolled about laughing and joking. I wondered if they were even aware of the drama that had played out in the sea so recently.

At first, this frivolity in our situation grated on me slightly but it soon became infectious. I allowed my thoughts of guilt slip away and I laughed at times as the Sergeant and his colleagues told risqué stories and sat absorbed as they took turns in telling exciting stories of their army exploits. At a request from Glenn, a stocky red-haired fellow, the Sergeant prodded me into telling of my own experiences and of our previous meetings. The others took up this cry and I stood to address them. Gratified by their rapt attention, I related what had happened to me in the war and the assemblage gasped, cheered and booed, like an enthusiastic music hall audience, at appropriate parts of the story. When I had finished, they clapped and cheered then insisted on toasting me with some rather palatable wine. They even proposed a toast to my wife so many miles away.

Dawson and Glenn were the real wags of this bunch and had us laughing mightily with their tales and horseplay. The camaraderie of this little band of commandos affected me greatly and, for the first time that I could remember since leaving my home to go to the underground laboratories with Cavendish and Horton, I felt myself truly relax in that jolly atmosphere.

We talked long into the small hours until, one by one, the men drifted off, for the most part slightly the worse for wear, to their bunks. The Sergeant and I talked a short while longer and then I myself had to retire or I should have slept were I sat. I went to my cabin, staggering a little in the warm embrace of a cloud of wine, but full of good cheer.

That night came the first nightmare I had had for many months. It was not the usual one of the Martians feeding upon me, this time our mighty vessel cracked and broke open by some unknown means. As I watched myself sink, eyes wide and limbs flailing ineffectually, to the ocean floor.

CHAPTER 29
The Search

The next day, when I awoke with a headache, *Nautilus* had already begun her search of the seabed. The Captain had the vessel steered up and down in a wide grid pattern whilst the sonar swept the sea floor. The sonar device was so sophisticated, Cavendish told me, that it could detect a single ha'penny from miles away if properly tuned. As the Martian base we were looking for was obviously expected to be bigger than this coin of the realm, however, detection this precise was unnecessary. In fact it may have confused the issue. Too sensitively tuned, the device would have picked up every piece of wreckage and any other sea rubbish that had accumulated over many hundreds of years of shipping.

I found the viewing screen fascinating during this time and watched as fish and other creatures of the sea regarded this immense intruder curiously.

The sonar picked up several large targets as we searched, but they turned out to be shipwrecks many years old. One wreck, however, appeared to be of a much more recent origin and had a huge gash in its side. One of her funnels was tilted forlornly to one side and flags and insignia still fluttered, eerily, in the current. Some of the contents of the ship were scattered about her and I somehow knew that this ship had been a victim of our quarry. Cavendish considered sending a search party on board to investigate but, after a moment's thought, decided that it would serve no purpose. He ordered curtly that we resume the search.

There was no further incident until later that afternoon when more, smaller targets were picked up by the sonar device. These objects seemed to be observing us as they came no closer and kept pace with *Nautilus* for a while. They were five in number and appeared to be moving at great speed as the little dots that represented them danced, around and about each other, at the top of the sickly green screen where the sonar returns were displayed. They carried on this strange display for something like ten minutes and then disappeared as soon as they had come.

Cavendish took this development as a bad sign and recommended that extra watchfulness be exercised.

I asked again that day about the possibility of talking to my wife on the radio set but Cavendish told me that radio silence was now being observed.

He evidently felt that the Martians, if nearby, may be able to monitor any such transmissions and would get more warning than we could comfortably allow.

I felt sure that, although the reason for this certainty was unknown to me, they already knew we were on their trail but realised the futility of arguing the point. Cavendish barely acknowledged my presence during the search, he merely stared distantly out through the viewing window.

The search continued on and periodically we saw the strange objects come into view on the screen and perform their eerie display. Nothing else of any size was spotted that day, though and, weary of the silent tension on the bridge, I went and joined the commandos in their mess.

The Sergeant was sitting smoking in a chair with his feet up on the table as young Jameson led the men in singing some bawdy music-hall standards. Private Wayne skilfully accompanied this gleeful troupe on an accordion.

I had at first wondered why the commandos did not mix with the other men who were quartered elsewhere in the submersible. As I grew to know them, I felt that perhaps their group's whole foundation was built upon an unshakeable bedrock of trust and experience and, whilst they did not shun fellow servicemen, they were as close as a family and spent their time together accordingly.

The jolly mood in the mess, as before, lifted my spirits and, after a glass or two, I joined in the singing and laughing with great gusto. How different and refreshing was my time in this simple mess in contrast with the staid quiet of being in the company of Cavendish. These times were made further unbearable as the Captain seemed to despise Cavendish, although whether this was purely because of the orders Cavendish had given or there was something else, I did not know. Cavendish, for his part, was as aloof and untouchable as always.

I allowed myself, again to immerse myself in the company of my new friends and I found that my glass was never empty.

An orderly came to find me later and asked if I would be joining Sir George for dinner. I, rather the worse for wine by this stage, told him that I wished him to tell my host that food was for scoundrels and women and I would drink more wine instead. The poor orderly left with the rough laughter of my companions ringing in his ears.

Later that night, alone in my room, I realised I may have gone too far and, with my head pounding and with the room gently spinning, made a mental note that I would apologise to Cavendish in the morning. As it turned out, I had no need to worry, as the orderly had evidently, with the good judgement and discretion typical of such men, told him that I was 'feeling unwell'. I later thanked him.

CHAPTER 30
The Flagship

Two long days later, the search of the seabed bore fruit at last.

There was no chatter on the *Nautilus* bridge save from the Captain muttering new headings and a sailor calling out small targets caught on the sonar screen. The men flitted around like ghosts, pressing this switch or pulling that lever, making course adjustments and checking gauges. The humming and chirping of various instruments working acted as the musical backing to this quiet ballet of activity.

Mid morning, there came a shrill cry from the young seaman with his eyes glued to the sonar console.

'Captain, a target dead ahead! We're coming up fast on it and it's not moving.'

The Captain turned quickly, the excitement in the boy's voice making him instantly attentive.

'A ship?'

'If it is, Sir, it's a big'un! This is like nothing I've seen before on the screen!'

'Any other targets?' the Captain asked.

'No, Sir, not a one.'

As one, the gathered ensemble turned to look through the viewing screen. There was nothing to see there but the usual darkness dashed with small fish that glittered like tiny stars in the night sky. I wondered briefly if I would see a similar view from a ship in the depths of space.

'Ahead slow, ready weapons!' the Captain snapped.

Cavendish breathlessly appeared behind me. A sailor, under some previous order, had fetched him from his room at this latest development.

'What is it, Smith?' he puffed.

'Looks like we may have arrived,' I replied.

'Keep a sharp eye out,' the Captain told the sailor at the sonar. 'Anything else comes along, sing out, sharp and clear!'

'Aye, Sir.'

The darkness in the viewing screen held our attention as we approached this object. Presently, a dim shape appeared in the murky distance and grew larger.

'The cylinder!' Cavendish uttered. 'That's it! We were correct!'

'But where are the Martians?' I wondered aloud, a sense of impending doom growing as we neared this awful thing.

'Inside, perhaps?' Cavendish said. 'Captain! I think we should stop and ready the troops.'

The cylinder was now visible on the screen. It was a glinting black and looked much larger than even the cylinder on Horsell Common. A line of dim green lights went from the nose to tail of it and it sat on the seabed like some nightmarish sleeping sea monster. It was rested with its back to a large hill with what appeared to be a sharp drop behind it.

'It's enormous!' said an awestruck sailor, rather obviously.

'The flagship!' Cavendish said excitedly. 'It has to be!'

Churchill appeared at the door of the bridge now, grimly chewing on his cigar.

'Churchill, the troops?' Cavendish asked him.

'They are on standby; do you wish me to ready them?'

'No time like the present, eh?'

Churchill now sat at his own small console on the bridge. On it he could monitor events as they unfolded.

After a brief conference, it was decided that the original plan for the assault would be adhered to. The main body of troops would approach, en masse, the cylinder from the front, hopefully diverting the Martians attention from the Commandos who would try to enter the cylinder elsewhere and destroy it. The submersibles weapons could have been brought to bear and we could have tried to destroy the cylinder from the vessel without the need for loss of human life, I thought, but Cavendish wanted, he said, to try to take the cylinder intact. This new revelation disturbed me and did not seem to please the Captain either. On hearing this, he cast another malevolent glance at Cavendish before turning back to his duties. Churchill, for his part, looked more grim than usual for a moment but gave no other indication of his feelings away.

I imagined men rushing to and fro, machinery being readied and weapons checked as the tension built on the bridge. The cylinder was still the only target to be seen on the sonar.

I wondered why the Martians did not attack as they surely must have known this huge vessel was so close to them. The feeling of unease in my stomach grew.

There was a radio link up to the Sergeant's men that had been built into their suits. That this technology existed was quite astounding and brought home to me again that, since the war, we were advancing rapidly in our knowledge.

Churchill now called to the Sergeant on this device and I heard my new friend's voice scratchily make a brief reply.

'We are ready,' said Churchill turning in his seat.

'Very well, let's begin,' Cavendish answered.

CHAPTER 31
Spider to the Flies

A high-pitched whine signalled the start of the campaign. The great doors at *Nautilus'* front opened and the main body of troops disembarked. A sailor, at a barked command from the Captain, flicked a switch and the viewing window suddenly showed two different views; one from within the front of the vessel looking out, as before, and another from just outside at the level of the seabed. I assumed that the latter view was generated by some additional device somewhere on the outer hull.

I watched as the human Fighting Machines jerkily stepped out onto the seabed and, bubbles rising from their joints, began to make their way toward the cylinder.

I could just see one of the men in the hood of one of these machines looking nervously around as he drove his vehicle past the device showing this view. He did not seem, to me, to have much faith in the ability of his machine to keep the water out. I could not say I would have blamed him. I had seen the 'teething troubles' that these machines had had.

Accompanying these lumbering machines were the be-suited troops, one hundred in number, walking as if in slow motion and obviously fighting the friction of the water that surrounded them. All carried weaponry of some sort or other and big square packs sat like the shells of crabs on their backs. Little trails of bubbles emanated from the bulky helmets they wore and rose slowly toward the surface so far above.

In the corner of the viewing window another display flickered into life showing what I assumed to be the sonar console. Green concentric circles emanated from a single point at the centre and a paler green 'hand', like that of a clock, swept speedily around the display. Here we could see these soldiers and machines start as a green mass of pale blobs, which then gradually became small individual dots as they slowly spread out.

Churchill sat stiffly at his console muttering orders into the radio set, occasionally scratchy voices answered.

'The main body of troops is underway,' Churchill said, looking in Cavendish's direction.

'Very good,' Cavendish answered. 'Send the Commandos on their way.'

Churchill muttered something into his radio and he turned to watch the sonar.

On the screen, a small green dot appeared at the front of the vessel and headed off to the side of the rest of the men and away.

'Commandos despatched,' the Lieutenant snapped.

'Excellent,' Sir George answered.

The tension was rising on the bridge but I noticed that a small smile played around Cavendish's lips.

The sailor on the sonar screen seemed coiled like a spring, ready to shout out should any foreign targets appear. None did.

'Why don't they come?' I asked finally. 'Cavendish, something is wrong about all this.'

Cavendish regarded me for a moment.

'Calm yourself, man. I expect they are in the cylinder wondering what to do about us. Soon we will have them surrounded and they will not have a hope. I expect a full surrender from them at any moment.'

'Surrender?' I said, incredulously. 'The Martians do not surrender! Have you taken leave of your senses?'

'Certainly not,' Cavendish retorted. 'Have you? These creatures, aggressive as they may be, will surely see that they have no option but to give up. We are holding all of the cards now, Smith, mankind need not fear them anymore.'

I shook my head but said nothing more. The Captain cast a quick glance at me and I again wondered what this man was thinking. Did he think me, or Cavendish, to be the fool?

We watched on as the troops grew nearer to the cylinder. One of the Fighting Machines ground to a halt, barely staying upright. I could imagine the driver in a state of panic, as I would surely have been. There were a few excited conversations on the radio as some men came to the aid of the driver. After a few moments of activity around the stricken machine, it began moving again.

I saw from the sonar screen that the Commandos were now well away from the main group and were rounding on the cylinder from the side. I tried to imagine what it would be like to be one of these men, in a hostile environment and sweating in a bulky suit with the adrenaline pulsing through their bodies. The sheer physical effort of making headway through the freezing water, let alone the feelings of claustrophobia, must have put an enormous strain on these frail human bodies and I did not envy them.

Again, I began to wonder why the Martians did not attack when there was a panicked cry from the sonar operator.

'Sir! Multiple targets approaching!'

Cavendish hurried to the boy's side and I peered at the viewing screen.

'Where?' Cavendish asked excitedly.

'Sir, they're everywhere, all around!'

I looked closer, my heart beating rapidly, at the screen. I could see our soldiers clustered near to the cylinder, which showed as a large pale bulk. Around the rim of the ghostly image appeared many small dots encircling all within the centre. Horrified, I realised that the men were suddenly and completely surrounded.

'My God, Cavendish! They've walked into a trap!' I shouted. 'Get them out of there!'

Cavendish stood frozen to the spot, a look of utter disbelief on his face, as this deadly net slowly and inexorably closed in on our forces.

CHAPTER 32
Disquiet in the Ranks

I grabbed Cavendish's shoulders and shook him. His limp body gave as much resistance as would some overstuffed rag doll.

'Come on, man!' I shouted straight into his now pale face. 'We have to do something!'

'But what can we do?' Cavendish eventually replied in a small voice. His watery eyes met mine like an admonished puppy. I pushed him away from me in disgust.

'Churchill?' I pleaded, turning to the Lieutenant who sat grim faced at his console.

Churchill looked at me steadily for a moment then he flicked a switch on the panel before him.

'Mother Hen to Chicks, Mother Hen to Chicks,' he barked urgently into his radio device. 'Return to nest immediately. Repeat; return to nest immediately. Targets closing in all around you, over.'

A harsh whine emanated from the speaker and then a far away sounding voice answered.

'Chicks to Mother Hen; no visual on targets. I repeat; no visual. Are you sure, Mother Hen?'

'Positive returns on targets. You are ordered to withdraw immediately,' Churchill shouted into the device.

'Returning to nest, Mother Hen,' the distorted voice answered. Despite the scratchiness of the reply, a new note of uncertainty had crept into the voice.

Cavendish seemed to return to himself a little at this exchange. He shook his shaggy head and moved forward a little.

'No!' he spluttered. 'They must fight!'

'What?' I asked incredulously. 'Cavendish, those men are surrounded by God alone knows how many of the Martians. They must get back here or they will all die! Churchill, can we not just destroy the cylinder with the weapons on this vessel?

Without a base of operations, surely it would be just a matter of tracking down any surviving Martians then?'

Churchill nodded soberly. 'Perhaps that could work.'

Cavendish shook his head again emphatically. 'Order them to fight, Churchill or I will have you Court-martialled.'

The Captain, who had been silent up until now, stepped forward. His whole frame shook with barely concealed anger and his hands clenched and unclenched by his sides.

'Now look here, Cavendish. I am Captain of this vessel and am responsible for the safety of all aboard her. I will not stand here and watch those men massacred because you wish to save a few more of those Martian trinkets.'

Cavendish eyed the Captain coldly and spat a reply. 'I am in overall charge of this mission and I will not have my orders questioned. Get back to your post, Captain, or I will have you relieved of duty immediately.'

On the sonar screen, the small dots closed in on the mass of men who were now visibly heading back toward the safety of *Nautilus*.

The radio hissed suddenly and a frantic voice could be heard.

'Mother Hen, Mother Hen! Targets sighted. They are Martians all right! I think we are going to have to fight our way through them, they are coming at us too quickly.'

Those of us on the bridge turned our gazes to the viewing window. I could see the men returning, walking as quickly as they could in their bulky suits. I could not see the Martians yet. A Fighting Machine came into view amongst the men and headed jerkily backwards toward the submersible, covering the retreat. Some seaweed was caught in one of its legs and flapped behind it like pennants in a strong breeze.

Then the men and machines suddenly stopped dead and all appeared to be looking frantically around them, weapons ready. I soon saw what gave them pause.

Out of the murky gloom to the right and left came Martians. There must have been at least a hundred, perhaps more. They wore strange bronze coloured helmets and skipped along the seabed on their tentacles with an amazing turn of speed. Accompanying them were numerous Remote Walkers, small hoods swaying to and fro as they came.

'My God!' Churchill breathed.

The Martians slowed as they neared our force and brandished strange looking weapons. Some of our men knelt and took aim. Then nothing happened for a moment.

For what seemed like hours, but must have only have been seconds, this standoff continued. Man facing Martian in a hostile wasteland.

The conflict between us on the bridge was momentarily forgotten as we all stood breathlessly transfixed.

The radio hissed to life again. Somebody yelled one word.

'Fire at will!'

With the utterance of this one small word, there was no turning back and chaos ensued.

CHAPTER 33
A Fight for Survival

It has never been never discovered who started the battle with that fateful cry. The military analysts who have studied the more technical aspects of the carnage are, to a man, of the mind that it little mattered. Conflict was unavoidable and one single creature, be it Man or Martian, was all it took to begin the fight.

As it was, our forces were first to begin firing from their position in the middle of a closing circle of enemy creatures and deadly projectiles headed with lightning speed towards their targets.

The weapons used were of the harpoon type, small, wickedly barbed metal arrows fired, by pressurised air, from a specially adapted type of rifle.

Some of these projectiles bounced harmlessly off the Martians helmets, doing little more than knocking the recipients back a little. Others, however, found their mark and the creature hit would thrash about wildly as their lifeblood billowed out into the water around them like dark smoke.

Almost as one, the Martians raised their own weapons and, with the twitch of their tentacles, fired. The enemy had their own harpoon weapons and groups of our men fell back screaming and bleeding as the enemy harpoons pierced their suits.

The human Fighting Machines hurriedly took position surround, as far as possible, the panicked soldiers and brought their own weapons to bear. They too were armed with harpoon weapons and soon the water was filled with deadly metal death.

Churchill screamed into his radio.

'Fall back in groups! Those not moving lay down suppressing fire!' Despite his best efforts to regain control of events, panic and the instinct of self-preservation had set in too deeply with the retreating troops and they continued firing wildly around themselves.

The carnage continued.

The Remote Walkers came forward from the Martian ranks and began to target the Fighting Machines. Trails of bubbles marked the progress of the projectiles these machines released.

I saw, as the view on the screen panned around the battle, the horrified driver of a Fighting Machine frantically pulling levers in the hood of his machine as he tried to get out of the way of this onslaught. He had no time to scream as a black missile ruptured the glass in front of him letting in the freezing water under enormous pressure.

The machine staggered around drunkenly for a moment then its legs splayed out in three different directions. As its body hit the floor, it suddenly exploded in a huge cloud of bubbles, almost knocking another nearby machine over and ripping a small group of unlucky soldiers around it asunder. A man staggered away from the explosion with air billowing out of his ruptured helmet. He made it a few steps toward us, then fell slowly to the seabed.

Another human machine targeted the walker and fired a hail of harpoons at it. Most of these missiles were easily deflected by the hard metal, making the machine stagger a little but not penetrating its armour. One missile, though, tore right through its thin neck, decapitating it. It ran crazily away like a headless chicken, knocking the Martians in its path this way and that. Clouds of blood bloomed in the murky water.

Another soldier ran as a nearby Martian stared at him with greedy eyes. The creature skipped quickly toward him and pounced on his back. It wrestled the struggling man to the ground and grasped hold of his helmet and tugged hard. The locking mechanisms on the helmet failed and, with a rush of bubbles, the helmet was ripped away. The man's eyes told of his terror as blood tinged water rushed into his mouth and on to his lungs. He feebly pounded at the Martian that straddled his chest with his fists until, after a moment, he moved no more. Then a crack appeared in the visor of the Martian's helmet as a nearby soldier took aim and fired at it. The stricken creature let go of its prey and span off, tentacles waving frantically, into the murk.

Hand to hand struggles ensued everywhere as the distance between the opposing forces lessened. Tentacles effortlessly pulled off flailing limbs and human blades stabbed at thick Martian skin. More blood made the murky water darker still.

There were many losses on both sides now as the struggle continued. Bodies of man and Martian alike drifted, limbs waving slowly, in the current.

The Martians, despite heavy losses, had the sheer force of numbers on their side. It was amazing to me that so many of them had survived the death that had overcome so many on land, even allowing for their curious method of reproduction. It was becoming plainly obvious to all the spectators of this vicious struggle that, unless something was done, the Martians would be triumphant and the whole mission would have been in vain.

On the bridge of *Nautilus*, another, quite different, struggle had begun.

'Cavendish,' I shouted pointing and accusing finger. 'Did you know there would be this many of them?'

'How could I?' the rotund man replied. 'I can assure you I had no idea this would happen.'

'Either way, you have shown no regard for the life of your fellow man. All you wish for is the Martian machines to use for your own ends. You would happily let those men out there die for that.'

'For the good of the country, Smith,' Cavendish said soothingly. 'How much better a world will we have with what we can learn from them?'

'All the Martian machines have brought is misery and death. We must help those men out there and if we have to destroy the cylinder to do it, so be it!'

'I rather think it is too late for them,' Cavendish answered coldly.

The battle raged on and the Martians slowly pushed the remnant of our force closer together. Soon only a fraction of our men were left and they were, it was revealed in their frantic radio calls, running dangerously low on ammunition.

Churchill, frustrated and purple with anger, slammed a hand down on his console. His battle experience, planning and sense of discipline had come to nought in this unexpected battle and he drew from the last dregs of soldierly professionalism he possessed.

'Fall back!' he screamed uselessly into the radio. 'For God's sake get back to the ship! Can anyone hear me?'

The only answer was the scratchy and eerily disjointed screams of the panicked and dying.

Suddenly deflated and powerless, Churchill sank back into his chair and fell into a shocked silence. I could see him mentally willing those out on the battlefield to make their way back to us. To safety.

Outside, all that remained now of the force that had seemed so impressive before, was a small knot of men huddled together, perhaps thirty in number, their weapons swinging wildly around at the multiple creatures that edged toward them.

All they could do now was fire the occasional shot to keep the circling Martians at bay.

The human machines were all standing still or destroyed, bodies of men littered the sea floor and floated in the current.

Many Martians had also paid with their lives or lay twitching in the sand. Of the Remote Walkers, only a few remained and they stood watching silently, their heads cocked curiously, as the Martians slowly advanced.

Finally, the human weapons were useless as the ammunition ran out. The weapons were discarded and, somewhat hopefully knowing the brutal disregard of human life that the Martians had shown time and time again, the men all raised their hands in surrender. The Martians moved in and led them away.

On the bridge, the Captain stepped forward.

'This has gone far enough. I will end this once and for all.'

We turned to see him picking up a device and his voice was projected around the vessel.

'Now hear this. This is your Captain speaking. Abandon ship. I repeat, abandon ship.'

'What are you d-?' Cavendish began to ask turning to face him, but was silenced by the sight of the revolver that the Captain now held in an unwavering hand. It was aimed squarely between Cavendish's eyes.

CHAPTER 34
Desperation

Cavendish stared at the Captain, his face pale. His mouth flapped like that of a fish drowning in the air.

I stepped forward carefully and spoke as soothingly as my ragged nerves would allow. 'Captain, what is this? We can still destroy the cylinder even if the men are lost.'

'Look through the window, Smith,' the Captain replied quietly. 'See them come.'

There were Martian machines, accompanied by yet more scores of the Martians in their helmets, cautiously approaching the Submersible.

'It's time to end this and end it now,' the Captain said.

'But–' Cavendish began, eyes never wavering from the barrel of the gun levelled at him.

'You will all leave this vessel now,' the Captain said finally. A strange calm passed over his face and I knew that he was quite insane.

Cavendish and I started to back away but suddenly Churchill darted forward and grabbed at the Captain. A struggle ensued and the two men wrestled for the control of the revolver. A shot rang out and a bullet embedded itself in the sonar console, sparks and smoke emitting from the damaged device. I started forward but the Captain gave a great roar and threw Churchill away from him and to the floor. Churchill made to get up but was stopped by the sight of the revolver being pointed directly at him.

'No, Lieutenant,' the Captain said breathing heavily. 'If you wish to take your chance with the others, you may do so. But try to stop me again and I will shoot you like a dog.'

'What do you plan to do?' I asked.

'Finish the task my brother failed to complete. Now go. All of you.' The Captain said no more but just waved us away with the revolver.

Grabbing Cavendish by the arm I backed away toward the bridge door. As we reached it, I saw that the Martians were getting bolder and moved closer by the second.

It seemed that the sailors had done immediately as they were ordered and *Nautilus* was almost deserted. Just a few panicked sailors rushed here and there.

'What do we do?' I asked Churchill.

'We leave the vessel,' the Lieutenant answered. 'Quickly, I think. I have an idea what the Captain has planned.'

We hurried through corridors and eventually reached a large room that was lined with many cabinets. Churchill opened one and I saw that it contained an underwater suit. I groaned.

I had to open a few cabinets before I found a suit, it seemed many had already been taken. As I started to put the heavy suit on, I saw Cavendish move as if in a trance to another Cabinet in the corner and open it with a small key on a ring he held.

The suit inside was more suited to Cavendish's girth and had obviously been tailored for him. He picked the suit up then dropped it suddenly. He hurried out of the room.

'Cavendish! Where are you going?' I shouted. I made to follow him but a thought occurred to me and I instead resolved to let Cavendish chase his errands if he must. I had remembered his callous lack of regard for human life and was finished with him.

Churchill and I helped each other into our suits as quickly as we were able and I was fastening Churchill's brass helmet when Cavendish reappeared clutching a box. It was the box that contained the Crystal Egg.

Cavendish smiled nervously. 'We can't go without this now, can we?'

Despite the revulsion for Cavendish that Churchill and I shared, we helped him squeeze into his suit and we were soon all ready.

Suddenly, there was a muffled bang and the vessel shook a little. With renewed urgency, we hurried through another door to be faced with a wall. There was a sign that had been placed there, by human hands I assumed, that said simply 'Air Lock'.

Churchill pushed at a sunken switch and a door that I could not see before appeared and started to slide back with a slight hissing sound.

Churchill clicked a switch on his suit and motioned for me to do the same. The Lieutenants gruff voice rang around my helmet. 'Are you ready?'

I took a deep breath then answered. 'Yes. At least as ready as I will ever be.'

Churchill nodded slightly behind his visor. 'Then let's go.'

We stepped through the door into a small chamber with another door at the other side. Cavendish followed meekly behind clutching his box like a child clutches its favourite toy.

The door slid behind us and there was a loud hissing. The hissing died down and then I heard a whine and the chamber began to fill with water.

There was another muffled bang and the rising water rippled violently.

As the water rose to neck level, it took a supreme effort for me not to panic. Breathing as evenly as I could, I attempted to imagine that being underwater was perfectly natural. Each time I took a breath, a deep hiss sounded in my ears and despite my thick suit, the water felt very cold. The air that the breathing apparatus provided for me smelled vaguely of rubber.

When the chamber was full of water, the door in the hull opened and the three of us shuffled out into the darkness.

CHAPTER 35
The Captain's War

My eyes, spoilt by the eerie light inside *Nautilus*, took a short while to acclimatise to the darkness.

As I stood squinting in the gloom, a shape with a bright light attached to the end appeared before me.

I couldn't, at first, make out what it was but I then realised with horror than it was a human arm. The hand, still clenched, held a portable electric lamp. It floated gracefully toward my face, then a current caught it and it swirled crazily away again like some grotesque Catherine Wheel.

Panic set in and I started to take quick, panting breaths. Churchill grabbed my arm and steadied me.

'Easy, Smith,' his tinny voice echoed around my head. 'We must move on.'

We started to move cautiously away from the huge vessel. Cavendish stood and stared straight ahead as if in a trance until Churchill grabbed his arm and shook him roughly. The man blinked then followed close behind us. I saw the last of the sailors from *Nautilus* stride off to either side.

Then, there was a disturbance in the water behind us and a cloud of bubbles pushed at me, I turned to look and I saw that *Nautilus* was now lifting herself slowly and gracefully from the seabed. I tapped Churchill's shoulder and he swivelled around to look with me. Cavendish walked along unsteadily a short way then, noticing we were not with him, turned and staggered back.

'What is he going to do?' I wondered aloud.

'I have an idea,' said Churchill, but said no more.

By now the Martians and their machines were at the vessel and some of the creatures sprang lightly at the hull, clamping on to the metal like limpets. One or two of the Remote Walkers fired off missiles that exploded at the behemoth's skin. There appeared to be little, if any, damage.

A few Martians grasped and hung on to the ship as it lifted then began to move toward the cylinder.

One of the things groped with its tentacles at an airlock door but a sailor turned from behind me and loosed off a harpoon. The Martians tentacles splayed out around its body as if in surprise as it was hit. It pirouetted away as it was caught and buffeted by the submersible's gathering wake.

Nautilus slowly turned her great head straight toward the cylinder and the water ahead of her rippled. The Captain must have used the sound weapon.

'Take that!' I heard in my ears. The Captain must have left the radio channel open!

'Captain!' I shouted. 'If you can hear me, please, stop this madness! I know we must destroy the cylinder but you need us! We can help you!'

There was silence for a moment apart from the hissing of my breathing apparatus.

'This is something I must do alone,' the Captain said finally.

I turned to look at Cavendish. His small eyes were red and his mouth flapped with frustration.

So, the sound weapon had been unleashed. Yet, the cylinder still stood.

Nautilus fired off more weapons, great missiles that resembled enormous black sharks. They exited tubes at the nose of our former home and travelled at an amazing speed toward the Martian cylinder.

As they approached, the Remote Walkers fired at them but all missed.

We watched with baited breath for the explosions. When they came, I let out a small whoop of delight. Perhaps now, our task had been completed and we could go home. A huge bubble obscured the view for a moment then I saw, to my dismay, that the base had barely been scratched. The Martians gathered nearby it that hadn't been obliterated in the explosions, danced crazily around on the tips of their tentacles.

'Blast it!' the Captain's angry voice rang around my head.

'You have to come back and pick us up,' I said into my device. 'We can regroup and–'

'No!' the Captain howled. 'It ends now! They want their damn vessel back, they shall have it!'

Cavendish's eyes widened at this and Churchill looked grimmer than ever before as her engines were pushed into full power.

Nautilus hung for a moment in the dark water then there was another cloud of furious bubbles from behind her.

'We have to get as far away as we can!' Churchill shouted. I caught his meaning now and knew what the Captain intended to do. We began to run as fast as we could against the water.

Nautilus sped forward. Martians and wreckage alike in her path were knocked spinning out of the way. Nearer and nearer to the cylinder she went, faster and faster.

I saw Martians near the huge Martian machine scatter, panicking, as they understood what was happening. Again, a few Remote Walkers fired their weapons uselessly at the vessel.

We reached a rocky part of the seabed and crouched down behind it. I peered over the top just as the huge speeding bulk of *Nautilus* rammed the cylinder squarely on its side. A short, mad laugh from the Captain rang around the inside of my helmet but was abruptly cut off as *Nautilus* exploded.

CHAPTER 36
Fish Out of Water

Nautilus' death throes turned our world upside down.

She was travelling at such a tremendous speed at impact that her collision with the cylinder must have crumpled her hull like paper. Again much of what happened next was obscured from our view from a great cloud of bubbles but I assume that something within her gave and exploded because there was a bright light and the water was agitated into a frenzy of bubbles and debris.

A great force moved outward from the impact area and we were knocked completely off our feet. On our backs, we were buffeted around, involuntarily waving our limbs as if in imitation of so many upturned crabs. Some sailors nearer to the site of the explosion were blown clear away from it, helpless in the raging water. The cries of the disorientated men rang around my helmet.

I tried to right myself as other, smaller, explosions rocked the great vessel all along its length. Pieces of metal flew in all directions as *Nautilus* tore herself apart.

Gradually, the explosions stopped and grew lesser in vehemence and what was left of the wounded submersible sank slowly to the seabed. I struggled to see what had occurred at the impact point but, for a while, my view was obscured by tumbling wreckage and air bubbles. I stood up, with some effort, and found that Churchill had made his way to my side.

'My God,' I said breathlessly. 'Why did he do that?'

'I cannot say,' the Lieutenant replied. 'Let us hope it was not in vain.'

The water near the cylinder finally cleared and I could see the result of the Captain's sacrifice. A great rent had appeared in the side of the cylinder and air poured out of it in many places. I could see a few stunned Martians staggering around nearby and a Remote Walker stalked jerkily around, headless.

'Look!' I exclaimed. 'I do believe it worked!'

'Indeed,' Churchill nodded grimly.

A quiet sobbing sounded in my ears and I looked around for the source. Nearby, Cavendish sat rocking slowly. On getting closer to him, I saw that tears streaked his chubby cheeks. On our approach, he looked up like a sad puppy.

'Nautilus is gone,' he quietly uttered.

'But the cylinder is damaged badly,' I answered offering the man a hand. He grabbed at it and pulled himself up.

'We can build another, can't we?' Cavendish said hopefully, like a child that has had its favourite toy broken by some mishap. 'Another Nautilus?'

'Yes. Yes we can,' I said in as comforting manner as I could, although I still felt less than charitable to him. What concerned me was that we make good our escape in case there were further Martians lurking somewhere and, if we had to take this man with us, it should be sooner rather than later.

Churchill spoke up.

'We must leave here. There are Martians around and they are still dangerous.'

'Yes,' I agreed. 'Can you walk, Cavendish?'

'I can,' the Knight asserted, brightening a little. With some obvious effort, he made to put on his old demeanour and he soon appeared to be as the old Cavendish we knew. A slight twitch in his eye gave away the fact that all was still not well with this man. Then he gasped, remembering something, and looked quickly around.

'The egg!' he shouted. 'Where is the egg?'

The box in which the egg rested was nearby, laying on its side on a rock. We walked forward to fetch it.

Cavendish picked up his prize and beamed happily. I made to join him but was brought up short by a sudden, intense pain in my head.

My head felt as if it was being ripped open and I let out an involuntary whimper. I felt probing in my head again, just like I had several times before and pictures came to me. I saw the scene inside the cylinder, water flooding in, dead Martians lay around here and there and smoke was pouring from damaged machinery. Then, another scene came. Martians were taking up weapons in another area that appeared not to be damaged. Human beings stood cowed in some sort of holding area. Where was this? Was it an undamaged part of the cylinder, perhaps? The probing abruptly stopped.

Churchill was staring at me with concern.

'What is it?' he asked.

'The Martians were–' I did not finished the sentence as my eyes had now cleared and I saw the scene before me.

Cavendish stood near the rock, oblivious and clutching his box. Behind him stood a small troop of Martians, weapons raised.

'Cavendish, behind you!' I shouted.

The Knight spun around in panic and groaned.

'Don't make any sudden moves,' Churchill warned in a low voice.

Cavendish dropped his box and raised his hands. Churchill and I slowly raised our hands too. I wondered vaguely if the Martians would understand, or even acknowledge, this human sign of surrender.

The Martians moved forward menacingly.

CHAPTER 37
Out of the Frying Pan …

Having come so far and seen so much, it seemed to me a measure of the way fate had twisted and turned since the war that we were now prisoners of the very creatures we had set out, with such determination and hope, to destroy once and for all.

Behind us, the wreckage of the great and immensely powerful *Nautilus* lay wreathed in a dark cloud of bubbles and her innards lay scattered around her. Beyond that huge, dead bulk sat the ruptured cylinder, its life-blood also pouring out of it and rising swiftly to the surface far above us.

The fact that the Martian base of operations had seemingly been damaged beyond repair appeared not to deter our captors in the slightest. They made it plain, by pointing with their tentacles, that we were to go with them, to where I did not know.

We did not move for a moment. Cavendish stood, his mouth flapping in that way he adopted when things were beyond him and Churchill threw grim glances my way.

Again I felt a probing in my head. There were no pictures this time, just a sort of vague pulling at my mind. The pulling grew stronger and stronger and my head was suddenly pierced by red agony. Through near blinded eyes, I dimly saw the Martians regarding me curiously.

The pain stopped again, as rapidly as it had started, and one of the creatures emphatically resumed its pointing.

'They wish us to follow,' I said, gasping, to Churchill.

'That much I had gathered,' the Lieutenant answered dryly. 'Perhaps we are lucky they do not shoot us where we stand.'

'Perhaps not,' I said, knowing full well what fate met prisoners of the Martians.

One of the Martians moved toward Cavendish's prized egg box and Cavendish, with startling speed for a man of his size and especially one encumbered in a heavy suit and underwater, darted for the box at the same time. The Martian made it first and snatched it up triumphantly, and, at the same time, waved its weapon meaningfully at the man as if to berate him for his stupidity. Cavendish stopped short violently and stood still again, gnashing his teeth and glaring at the creature.

'It's mine,' he mumbled.

'Cavendish,' I said as calmly and quietly as I could. The man continued to stare balefully at the Martian and did not acknowledge my presence.

'Cavendish!' I repeated more harshly. The man looked slowly around, his eyes burned like fire.

'We must go with them, we have no choice.'

Cavendish's anger visibly subsided and we slowly began to move in the direction that had been indicated to us.

The landscape beneath the sea is not much understood by humanity. Perhaps, in some distant time, mankind will make its home underwater and enjoy the riches that lie under the waves. In the future, perhaps, great vessels not unlike *Nautilus* will prowl the depths and travelling through what is now largely unknown will become as commonplace as a walk in the countryside.

As it was, weighed down by the water in my heavy suit and being fed rubber-tinged air, I felt that we might as well have been on some distant planet rather than our own Mother Earth. This illusion was heightened by the dim darkness, the fish that darted here and there before us and by our monstrous captors who skipped along on their tentacles beside us as we walked.

The exertion of walking through the water soon began to tire me and my breaths came shorter and more laboured. The suit, despite the cool water temperature, made me feel progressively more hot and uncomfortable and the feeling of claustrophobia became near unbearable. The unceasing hissing of the breathing mechanism was like some torturous, diabolic sound specifically designed to drive one mad. Periodically, I had to fight illogical urges to tear my suit off and try to swim for the surface. Churchill marched purposefully along beside me but Cavendish fell behind from time to time. When he lagged behind too much, a Martian would prod him sharply with a weapon and the man would try to pick up the pace but the strain was obviously more for him in his condition than it was for me. I felt some pity for him then, despite what I knew of him.

On through this alien landscape we travelled. Here and there Martians skipped about carrying pieces of wreckage or at other tasks.

I wondered why they did not appear disenchanted at the destruction of the cylinder. It seemed to make not the slightest difference to their sense of purpose and they carried on as if all was well with them. What a hardy race they must be, I thought, they are beaten time and again and yet they continue as if their time as rulers of our world was imminent. I did not find this of any comfort in my predicament.

To my dismay, I soon found out the reason for their confidence.

After what seemed like hours of walking, but could only have been minutes, we came across a tall rocky outcrop. More Martians were gathered here bearing weapons, along with a few Remote Walkers, and, after some tenticular gestures between the two Martian parties, we were allowed to pass.

What I saw next made my blood run cold.

As we passed the rocks we came upon a huge construction. Dark, black and squat.

Like a huge spider, the thing crouched there. Martians and machines swarmed around this strange new thing.

We had destroyed the cylinder, but we had made a terrible mistake.

The real Martian base was very much intact.

Underwater base by Peter Fussey

CHAPTER 38
… Into the Fire

I am not ashamed to say that this latest horrible revelation nearly made me faint dead away. I thrust out a gloved hand and steadied myself on a nearby rocky outcrop.

All our efforts had been for naught and the greatest weapon we had, the submersible *Nautilus,* in which so much hope had rested, lay, a shattered ruin, on the seabed.

We had expended men and machines in our quest to destroy the Martians and, all along, they had sat smug and secure in this new monstrous edifice. Perhaps they had watched with what passed for them as amusement whilst many of our men died trying to destroy what was essentially an empty shell. I imagine that they hooted with glee as *Nautilus* was rammed into that shell whilst they viewed events from a safe distance.

I made a solemn oath to myself then that, if my fate was to die here, I would do anything I could before I met my maker to take at least some of those interlopers on our planet with me.

Shaking the cobwebs from my mind, I eyed one of the Martian weapons greedily but one soft word; 'No', crackling in my ears made me glance up.

Churchill was shaking his head slowly. The Lieutenant was, I realised, an amazing judge of his fellow man. He had seen the look on my face and immediately understood my intention. I could imagine him having a stellar career in politics under different circumstances.

I still lusted for revenge against the Martians, but something in Churchill's steady gaze made me see sense.

For now, I promised myself, I would go meekly with our captors but should chance smile upon me and an opportunity arise, I would seize it and do as much damage as I could.

So, what of this new horror?

As our party were escorted closer to this thing by our triumphant captors, I saw that it was indeed spider-like in general shape. Thick legs splayed out from around the distended black body of the machine. Green lights ringed the body and ran down the length of the legs. At what I took to be the front, a great green window could be seen.

To say the machine was big does not, by any amount, give it full justice. I imagined many hundreds of Martians could be housed quite comfortably within it. I hoped that there were not many hundreds of the monsters to crew it. I did not know, then, if this machine could actually move like its much smaller cousins, but it looked as if the legs could be mobilised. Great joints were visible and huge cables hung here and there. The legs themselves appeared to be much larger and sturdier versions of those on the Fighting Machines.

Movement for this thing would make sense, though and again I cursed these creatures for their ingenuity. A mobile base would make a formidable weapon indeed.

Soon we were underneath the machine and I wondered how we were to be transported into it. As we stood, a long tube extended out from a point underneath its huge belly and thrust down at speed into the sand. The Martians gestured that we were to go into this tube and we entered through a portal in one side. The tube seemed to be made of glass of some kind, or perhaps some other transparent material and I reached forward curiously and my glove touched the surface.

Small blue sparks danced around my glove and I recoiled immediately, although I felt nothing. I looked curiously at my hand as if it were alien to me. Cavendish stood nearby, looking up and around himself as well as his helmet would allow, his jaw open in wonder.

'My God!' he breathed.

When we were all gathered together, there was a sudden vague feeling of movement and I saw that the floor we stood upon was rising up the inside of the tube. I looked out through the clear walls and saw the ground seem to fall away. Feeling rather giddy, I set my eyes upwards and watched the bottom of the machine coming to meet us.

The journey took a very little time and, just as it seemed that we would be dashed against the metal above, a door slid aside, our platform moved past it and we came smoothly to a halt.

The inside of the machine was more impressive still than the outside.

We were ushered out of the tube by the accompanying Martians and into a large round room that I sensed was the very hub of this construction. Smooth walls lit with that eerie green glow surrounded us but set in at different points of them were doors leading to other areas.

Martians scurried here around and machines, not unlike Remote Walkers but with grappling arms and other unknown instruments attached, carried containers and machinery here and there.

A Martian, tapping me with a tentacle, distracted me from my observations. I looked at it sharply.

The creature gestured at my head. I did not understand its meaning and simply glared at it.

'Your helmet, Smith,' Churchill said. 'You can take it off. We are no longer in water.'

Of course. I had been so in awe of my situation that I had not noticed that we had come into a space full of air. I wondered how the water had been pumped out of the tube along the way but could not fathom it.

I saw that the Lieutenant was already starting to unfasten his helmet, so I fumbled at the clasps at my neck. Cavendish looked on as if we were quite mad.

'Come on, Cavendish,' I assured him. 'It's no trick.'

He stared a while longer then tentatively raised a glove toward his helmet. I started forward to help him but he waved me away.

I finished unfastening my own headgear and, lifting it off, took deep, gulping breaths of clean air, untainted by that interminable rubber smell, until my head began to spin.

The Martians gestured at us and we were on the move once more. Down many corridors we walked, goaded and prodded by our monstrous guards, until we reached another large room. I felt sure that I could not traverse these corridors alone as they all looked very much the same. I was reminded of the underground laboratories in London by this fact.

There were many doors set in the walls here, one was opened and we were prodded again until we entered.

In this room sat, by my count, twenty humans. All were soldiers and sailors from *Nautilus*. A few of them recognised us and glum faces brightened a little at seeing more familiar faces.

The door to the prison cell slid quietly closed behind us.

CHAPTER 39
Imprisoned

Our prison consisted of bare walls lined with benches that jutted out from them. Further inspection revealed that these benches were not so much attached to the walls but actually seemed to be part of them. I could perceive no visible joins and no means of support. It was if the whole room had been moulded, benches and all, at the same time and in one piece.

Sitting on one, I found that it actually seemed to give somewhat and mould itself to my shape. It was very comfortable but the feeling was strange. Where it touched my body, I felt warmth as if the thing was gently heated.

With the guards gone, one or two of the men already here began to question us about events outside. It seemed they had been taken prisoner early on in the battle in the sea and knew nothing of the demise of *Nautilus.* Their faces, eager for news, dropped at this revelation and several muttered that we were finished. A general feeling of gloom now hung over the assemblage.

It transpired, also, that the men in this room were not the only ones taken prisoner by the Martians. I was told that the other cells were also in this holding area and were served by the other doors I had seen outside.

The men told us, in hushed tones, of the fact that there had been others placed in this cell but some had been taken away, one by one, and had never returned. The reason for this was unknown, but I guessed that we would never see these poor souls again.

Churchill listened carefully to these conversations and asked questions here and there. Cavendish sat silently on a bench, eyes downcast and hands clasped in his lap. He showed no signs of registering anything he heard.

After a few hours, a buzzer sounded and the cell door slid open to allow entrance to a Martian pushing before it a long flat platform. This strange cart had no wheels, for, as my friend Wells has intimated in his novel based on my Wartime experiences, the Martians had not invented this most simple, to man at least, of innovations. The wheel, in fact, was as alien to them as their technology was to us. Instead, the trolley appeared to float a few inches above the floor and slid smoothly along when pushed. On the top surface of this contraption were large pans loaded with some sort of steaming, thick pink gruel that the attending Martian scooped, with a ladle, into metallic looking bowls. This food, for that was obviously what it was, was handed unceremoniously to all present in the cell. This task completed, the cell door slid open again and the Martian left, hooting softly.

I have found out since, on the investigations of our scientists, that this gruel we were fed seems to have been made from the dreaded red weed that covers the surface of Mars and very nearly covered our own. The Martians did not deem it suitable for themselves, it would appear, as blood met their needs better, but perhaps they had developed it, back on Mars, in experimentation on their own bipeds that they themselves used as food. It appears that the bipeds have a similar physiology to us, in many ways, and this gruel was found to cover our nutritional needs as well as theirs.

I sniffed at it carefully but could detect no smell. The others in the room, asides from Churchill, Cavendish and myself, had begun to take the food into their mouths greedily with a kind of thick metal tube that was attached to the side of the bowls and one of the men bid us follow his actions.

'Once you get used to the taste, it's really all right,' a soldier said. 'It fills you as good as a Sunday roast and you don't feel peckish until the next mealtime.'

I slowly took hold of the tube at the side of my bowl and pulled. It appeared to be stuck there by magnetism and came away easily. I pushed one end of the tube onto the unappealing looking slop in the bowl, gingerly put my mouth to the tube and sucked gently. Some of the gruel, after some suction had been applied, entered my mouth and slid slimily onto my tongue. I took the mouth away from the straw. The gruel had an odd bittersweet taste and I resisted the impulse to spit it out there and then. I swallowed.

After a few more mouthfuls, I grew accustomed to the taste and ate, or perhaps I should say drank, all that was in the bowl. My belly felt full and I lay back on my bench.

The rigors of the day and a full belly took their toll and I fell quickly asleep.

I awoke later, I know not how long had passed, disorientated and feeling vaguely nauseous.

Cavendish, I saw, was curled up silent and unmoving, like an overgrown child, on a bench with his back to us. I could not tell if he was asleep or not. A barely touched bowl of gruel lay discarded, upside down, on the floor beside him.

Churchill was speaking in low tones to a Corporal in a corner and they joined me as I sat up. Churchill informed me that, whilst I slept, another sailor had been taken away by the Martians. I had not stirred, it seemed, through all his imprecations, pleas and final calls for help that had punctuated his rough exit from the room. I thought then that perhaps the gruel was drugged in order to keep us captives docile. I certainly felt light headed and the slight nausea took some time to fade.

There was a plan being formulated, I was next told. Almost at a whisper, Churchill postulated that we could perhaps attempt an escape when the next meal was brought to us. It had been agreed, generally, that this was better than sitting here in this cell waiting for our turn to be taken away like the others. Churchill had somehow stirred within these men an arousal from the general feeling of inevitability of their fate. I hoped sincerely that the Martians did not have listening devices planted in the cell sophisticated enough to hear of this plan but agreed immediately that an attempt to escape may be our only hope.

The plan was simple, as sometimes the best plans are. When the door opened, several men would wait either side and attack the Martian as it entered. As there was no sign of any other Martians with it on previous visits, the men would grab its weapon and kill it quickly to stop it raising the alarm. Then we would attempt to fight our way out, hopefully gaining more weapons along the way. It was a desperate plan, to be sure, but better than sitting and waiting to be dragged away for God alone knew what foul purpose.

The plan settled, as best as it could be, we all returned to our benches and waited.

Later, Cavendish sat up blinking.

'Are you alright?' I asked.

'Yes fine,' he replied levelly, flashing an unconvincing smile at me. He got up and walked toward the door.

'Where are you going?' I asked, but Cavendish did not reply.

Reaching the door, the Knight of the Realm began knocking on the smooth door with all his might.

'I demand to be let out!' he screamed, suddenly red faced.

'Cavendish, no!' Churchill shouted.

'I am a representative of His Majesty's Government and demand that I am set free!' Cavendish continued, then fell silent and stared purposefully at the door before him.

After a few moments, the door slid open and a Martian appeared clutching a weapon. It waved the gun outwards and Cavendish moved forwards. The door slid shut again behind him.

'What the hell does he think he's doing?' a sailor asked. 'They'll kill him for sure!'

I could do no more than shake my head sadly.

CHAPTER 40
The Great Escape

Cavendish's departure and almost certain death did nothing to lighten the atmosphere in the cell.

Some of the men sat around in small groups muttering and cursing under their breath. Others tossed and turned fitfully on their benches.

A general air of hopelessness had settled over the group and I sat staring at the unmoving door.

Churchill tried to rally the men, moving around the cell readying the men for the attempt to escape that was planned. He gave me a reassuring smile and told me that this action gave us hope. Surely it was better, should the plan fail, to go down fighting rather than be slaughtered alone like an animal, he reasoned.

I had enough hatred left in my heart for the Martians for these words to inspire me and I nodded.

The wait drew on.

Later, the buzzer sounded and some men jumped from their bunks and stationed themselves rapidly on either side of the door, tensed like coiled springs. The rest of us sat, trying to look as despondent and cowed as possible, spread around the room in an attempt to allay any suspicions at the reduced numbers the Martian entering may have.

The platform laden with steaming pans appeared and we waited with baited breath. The attendant Martian entered and its saucer eyes widened in surprise as it was grabbed, none too gently, by the men at the door and it squealed as it was shoved bodily into the room.

The pans flew off the floating trolley as it was pushed aside and hit the wall with a crash. A small tide of pink steaming gruel spread over the floor.

The Martian dropped its weapon as it tried to right itself but went after it with lightning speed. Men followed and grabbed at its tentacles and pulled.

A furious battle ensued.

The Martian was immensely strong, like all its kind, and shook a man off with ease. The man careered backwards and hit his head, with a sickening crack, on the trolley. He collapsed like a rag-doll into the pool of gruel on the floor. A small puddle of blood spread out from his head and mingled with the pink mess that surrounded him.

Two other men pulled, with all their might and in opposite directions, at the creature's tentacles. The Martian squeaked in pain. One of the men pulling slipped in the spreading food on the floor and fell over on his back losing his grip on the Martian. The Martian snatched its limb back and used it to flick a sailor deftly away from the weapon that lay nearby.

I, suddenly filled with some kind of primal rage as I have never before or since felt, grabbed the ladle, that was to be used to dispense the food, from the floor and rushed at the Martian bellowing and brandishing the tool above my head with both hands. The Martian looked around and hooted with surprise but I was already upon it. I, without thinking, thrust the handle of the ladle, with all the force I could muster, deep into one of the creature's great black eyes. I fell to the floor, gasping.

Dark liquid jetted in a stream out from the Martian's damaged organ and it squealed sharply again. In its agony, the thing thrashed around wildly flinging the men grappling with it away.

Picking themselves up, the other men made to attack the creature again but Churchill shouted a quick command to cease. He carefully skirted the agonised monster and picked up the weapon, training it on the thing's head.

It seemed that my aim had been true and the Martian was mortally wounded, for soon its frantic movement slowed and it fell to the floor with a wet thump.

Its one intact eye glared at me accusingly, its tentacles waved and slapped around feebly, and, after a great shiver ran through its body, it lay still.

'Right men,' Churchill said, nodding with approval at me. 'Are we ready?'

The men, as one, answered to the affirmative.

The door was still open and, as a group we made for it with Churchill at the lead brandishing the Martian weapon.

As we got outside we stopped dead.

A large group of Martians stood in a tight semi-circle, pointing weapons at us.

This was not the only shock we had in store.

'You should not have done that, you know,' a familiar voice said from behind the group of Martians. 'I had to tell them you might try something like that.'

I gaped at an equally shocked Churchill. The Lieutenant's expression slowly turned to barely suppressed rage at this latest development.

We had been betrayed by one of our own kind.

Cavendish stood, grinning, very much alive and if he were back in charge of things.

CHAPTER 41
Treachery

All I could do was gape disbelievingly at the beaming Cavendish.

I had seen that he was capable of much deviousness and had seemed, of late at least, only to have his own interests at heart, despite his grand protestations that what he did was for the good of England. This new act was too much to take.

Anger surged up within me like a hot river of bitter bile.

'You dog!' I spat. 'You have betrayed your fellow men and for what?'

I moved toward Cavendish fists raised and hot faced but Churchill, despite his own obvious anger, leaped forward and held me back. I struggled against the unyielding Lieutenant's hold on me for a moment but eventually sagged and consoled myself with staring white hot daggers at the man, the many Martian weapons pointed at my head deciding the matter.

'Why?' was all I could manage to utter.

'You would not understand, Smith,' the Knight replied from within the safety of his newly recruited bodyguard. 'There are bigger things afoot here than anyone knows. Even I am just a pawn in a greater game, albeit a more well placed one.'

'You fool!' Churchill hissed. 'Do you really imagine that your new friends will think more highly off you because you have the ear of the Government? I'll wager that all the Martians see in you is a bigger meal!'

Cavendish's grin fell at this and his plump cheeks reddened several shades darker than was normal.

'I will not waste time bandying words with a mere Lieutenant,' he said disdainfully. He turned to me and struggled to affect a reasonable tone.

'Smith, you must see! You are a reasonable man! This is the best solution for us all. We must make peace with the Martians and I am the man to initiate such a historic peace. The British Empire will prosper as a result and we will be the survivors when the next invasion begins. Make no mistake, the Martians will return and in greater numbers. I can help you; join me in this effort I undertake for the good of our world '

'I will not be a mere pet of those things,' I answered as levelly as I could, staring straight into his beady eyes. 'I would rather die than assist you in this monstrous plan.'

Cavendish eyed me for a moment as if waiting for me to change my mind, then, seeing that my resolution was unbowed, he shrugged.

'You may come to regret those words,' he said, shaking his head sadly, and stalked away down a corridor flanked by two of the Martians. One of the creatures left facing us motioned for our unhappy group to return to the cell. Angry, but with no choice in the matter, we went back in.

So, our imprisonment continued but for how long I cannot say.

Churchill seemed to think we were in the cell for only two days, for me it felt no less than a week.

The feeding of the pink gruel continued but the Martians came to dispense it, in force now, emphatically waving weapons at us at the slightest movement from one of our group.

More men were taken away, as time passed, until our group in this cell numbered only ten.

Sometimes we shuddered as we heard the desperate struggles of those being removed as they fought for their lives, in vain I think, outside.

We did not see Cavendish again.

I tried to imagine how someone could do what this man had done, betrayed his own kind so that he could prosper. I was not fool enough to imagine that some humans were not capable of the most heinous act. I knew that many horrendous acts of barbarism by man against fellow man had been perpetrated, over the course of our race's history, in the name of greed, religion; or even both. Sometimes such acts were perpetrated purely for the enjoyment of it. Still I could not fathom the justification of the handing of all of humanity on a platter to a race of monsters for any reason. Such treachery was unheard of in the history of mankind. Did he imagine that he would become a Prince among men at the behest of those awful, heartless beings from so far away? King of the World, perhaps? Did he dream of sitting on some gilded throne, casually ordering the slavery or deaths of millions? What kind of Brave New World was this he envisaged?

In the quiet of what I took to be night, the time when all others in the cell were sleeping fitfully, I mourned for all mankind.

Sounds of a scuffle outside the cell awoke me from a restless dozing. At first, I thought it was just the sound of the Martians gathering outside and readying themselves to bring us our dreary rations. Then there was the unmistakable sound of gunshots, a muted explosion, and a bloodcurdling shriek, like that of a wounded animal. A, very much human, cheer followed this awful sound.

The door alarm buzzed.

The other men in the cell and I sat up. Now what was happening?

The door opened to reveal a familiar face.

'Hullo, mates!' the Sergeant said brightly, grinning from ear to ear.

CHAPTER 42
The Sergeant's Tale (i)

In our predicament and in my dismay, I had completely forgotten about my friend, the Sergeant and his brave commandos.

If I had, in my overwrought state, found the time to ponder his whereabouts, I should have thought him lost in the battle outside the cylinder with so many of his comrades. Or perhaps, I might have, with a glimmer of hope, considered him a prisoner somewhere else in this monstrous new base that we were currently captive within. Either way, the outlook for him would not, I am sure I would have imagined, been good. Perhaps as bad, if not worse in that cold unknown outside, as ours seemed to be in fact.

I did not find out the full story of what fate had had in store for my friend up to this latest meeting until much later. The Sergeant visited me at my home for what he called a 'jolly reunion of old chums'. Wells came, at my invitation, to this meeting as well; he could not resist meeting the man whose character he had written of in his own version of my experiences. The Sergeant and my literary friend were, to my surprise I admit, as old friends from the off. The Sergeant, though not being much of a bookish man had, however, read Wells' account of my story and had evidently not taken the least offence at his depiction within it.

We three sat by the fire, after a marvellous dinner prepared by my wife, sipping champagne, of course, and toasting old comrades.

It is then that I asked the Sergeant about events before he came to free us.

I made copious notes as he recounted his tale, as I knew I was to begin this work my esteemed reader now holds and I felt that his story may make an interesting addition to it. Wells sat quietly as the Sergeant spoke, but his eyes twinkled and his face bore a faint smile throughout, as if in appreciation of a story well told.

I feel that now is, at this point in my work, as good a place as any to recount the Sergeant's adventures in his own words.

'Well, my friends.' The soldier said settling back into his leather armchair and sucking on a fat cigar with relish. 'Where to start? I can't say I really had much in the way of schoolin' but I guess Smith at least knows I can tell a yarn and that is what I'll have to do.'

'Please,' I prompted. 'Just tell us what happened, no more, no less.'

'Well then, this is how it was.'

'We left Nautilus ready to fight and full of get up and go. Vim and vigour, even, my boys were straining at the leash to get back at the Martians and I didn't intend to hold 'em back, I can tell you.

We hadn't gotten far when all merry hell broke loose. The Martian buggers were everywhere and we saw that they had engaged our comrades near the cylinder.

Never in battle have I seen so much chaos and I doubt I will see its like again in my lifetime. It wasn't helped, I know, by our being underwater and those blessed suits we were forced to wear out there. It was like being in an oven after a little effort and breathing was tough. My boys bore it like the troopers they were, though, and I decided we should make a run for it around the side of the scuffle. If you remember, our mission was to blow the cylinder to blazes and, even though we hated to leave mates in peril, we didn't intend to be cut down before we could do it.

So, off we went as fast as we could, dodging and diving, watching out for Martians all the way.

It's funny, men were dyin' out there but one thing sticks in my mind. You know Glenn, quite the wag he is. Well, he started humming 'My old man said follow the van'. You must know it, that Music Hall ditty that everyone likes to sing along to.

Anyway, I thought, for a bit at least, it was quite the song for the occasion and some of the boys started to whistle or sing along with it. Quite what came over us I can't rightly say. I'm sure if Wayne had his accordion with him we could have led the

Martians, should we have met any there, in a right merry dance. A soldier's humour can be rough, as I'm sure you know, but the life can be much rougher and we find that the fun we make for ourselves helps keep some of the demons away, if you get my meaning. Some might accuse us of 'gallows humour', but we sees things in our work that a bloke ought not to and we have to lighten the load somehow or we should all end up in Bedlam being laughed at by the Toffs for a few pence.

Anyway, I soon thought better of it and told them best be quiet, as we didn't want to draw attention to ourselves if the Martians could listen in on us. Besides, even to us, it didn't seem right singin' what with what was goin' on out there and all.

We went around behind some rocks and watched the battle for a while and looking for a good route to our objective. One or two of the men wanted to take pot-shots at the enemy, to help our mates out, but I told them to hold fire in case we got spotted.

Then I heard the order to withdraw on my radio device and saw the men out on the battlefield try to get back to Nautilus. The poor blighters couldn't go anywhere as, by this time, the creatures were all around them. But they fought bravely to man, to that I can testify.

I saw the Martians round the survivors up like sheep and start to move them away.

Jameson was all for rushing out there and trying to rescue them for all the good it would do and he made no bones about it. Even though he knew, deep down, that the sensible thing to do was just what we were doing. We had to get to the cylinder and do our job. To try and help our comrades would have been nothing less than suicide and every man jack with me knew that. But a soldier's instincts are strong, my friends. We never leave a man behind unless there is no other choice. In this case there was none and we could do no more than sit and grit our teeth.

Then, just as we were about to move off to see what could be done, we were amazed to see Nautilus start to up and move. She sat there in the water for a bit, then moved quicker and quicker and slammed – Bam! – right into the cylinder. We ducked down behind our rocks as she blew to smithereens. We didn't know what to think. What was goin' on?

When things had calmed down a bit, we looked up and saw that the cylinder had a huge hole in it and we cheered and clapped each other, hard work underwater, on the backs. It looked like we wouldn't need to do our work after all.

Then Glenn said "Sarge?"

I looked around and saw a grim look on his face. He pointed slowly behind us.

One of the Remote Walkers, as that cur Cavendish – oh yes, I knew all about him and his new friends – called them, was just stood there behind us. Just lookin' at us with them strange metal eyes they have.

I figured then that we were sunk.'

CHAPTER 43
The Sergeant's Tale (ii)

My friend stopped telling his story for a moment. For effect, I have no doubt. As I have intimated before, the Sergeant was the sort who never tired of telling of his exploits, much, I found, to the delight of any audience he spoke before. I did not wonder that his orating skills led to many a free drink in the Hostelries he frequented. Wells and I waited for him to resume his tale whilst he grinned at us.

The soldier casually waved his empty glass at me and I took the hint, pouring him more champagne. He swallowed some of the effervescent, pale yellow liquid and smacked his lips with relish. Then, eyes bright, he took a puff of his cigar and continued on with his story.

'Well now, I'm sure you wonder how we got out of that pretty pickle. I can say it was by sheer luck and I don't mind admitting that. Sometimes even the best soldier can be scuppered by an 'appenin' and it was all I could do but stare at the machine, for a moment, as it carried on eyeing us up.

I was surprised, you can bet, when Dawson walked out from behind a rock just past the thing. Where he had been, I don't know, as I thought he was with us, but he stopped short and backed off a bit. The thing didn't know he was there but just stared some more at us.

I managed to catch Dawson's eye and tried to give him the idea he was to be ready. The soldier's mind is always at work, friends, and I hoped that Dawson would catch my drift. I saw him begin to creep towards the thing as quiet as a mouse would. I stepped forward a bit with my hands raised and motioned for the others with me to do the same. The thing jumped back a bit on those skinny legs they 'ave and I saw its weapon pop out from its head. We stopped dead and it started to move forward. Dawson took his chance and jumped on it, pushing against the water as hard as he could. There was a struggle, the thing was thrashing about with my mate Dawson clinging on for dear life.

The machine let off a shot, then another. The first shot narrowly missed Dawson, the other hit a rock, blowing it to tiny pieces. Some pieces of rock rattled off the helmet of my suit.

We jumped forward as one, I got my weapon and started beating the thing with the butt and the others copied me. We barely dented it.

Glenn grabbed a leg and pulled with all his might. The thing started to topple, all unbalanced already with the weight on its back. Dawson jumped clear before the thing hit the ground and we set to it, kicking and beatin' it with our weapons.

Then, I spied a sort of door in the back of its head and I started to beat at it with my gun. It wasn't easy, what with the thing wrigglin' around and all.

The panel flew off after a bit of work and my weapon butt went straight into the thing's head. Well, here was another surprise!

Some liquid came out of the head and the thing stopped wrigglin' just like that! It just lay there like some curious dead chicken in the butcher's shop.

"What the-?" Glenn said.

"It doesn't matter now," I told him. "The thing is dead. We must be off, lads, before some of its mates come lookin' for it."

We went off into the rocks as quickly as we could.

We found what looked like a quiet spot and took stock. Our mission couldn't be carried out and our way home was in a million pieces all over the seabed. So, what to do?

Then a thought marched into me head. The Martians had prisoners, lots of our mates that they were taking away. But where were they taking them to? The cylinder had been blown to smithereens, so where then?

"Here's a plan, boys," I said. "What say you for a spot of reconnaissance?"

"What do you mean, Sarge?" Glenn asked.

"Let's follow the blighters and see where they are taking our mates. Their cylinder is a mess so I don't think they'll be going there. So I say we find out if we can lend our pals a helpin' hand, eh?"

The lads all agreed in a wink so it was settled. We moved off in what we hoped was the right direction.

It didn't take long before we saw the last stragglers ahead of us. We rounded another set of rocks and watched as the Martians pushed the soldier and sailor prisoners onwards. We were going away from the cylinder now and we wondered just what was goin' on. We soon found out, all right!

We hung back a bit as we saw the massive machine the Martians had built as their new base. We watched the prisoners being herded into that weird tube and get sucked up into the belly of that horrible new thing. It was an uncanny sight; it looked like the men were floatin' up into the air, or should I say water, from where we crouched.

The base, as you know, looked like an oversized Handlin' Machine, as the boffins call 'em. After all the men had been taken aboard, we saw that the thing began movin'! Slowly, it went, its legs goin' up and down and carryin' the thing forward like some giant insect. I saw that there were little machines, no more than lights really, darting around it like crows flyin' around a dead animal. I didn't know if they had Martians in 'em or not but they moved at a fair clip and weaved about between the big things legs. It was a mesmerisin' sight.

The main body of the machine seemed to hardly move at all, so I suppose it had some sort of devices to keep it steady. Maybe it worked a bit like the suspension on a motor car, but that sort of thing leaves me baffled, as a rule, so I didn't take much notice of how it could have worked. I expect Cavendish's boffins would have had a field day. It would have been like Christmas for them!

The thing started to pick up speed a little and it was starting to get out of sight. It was time for us to do something! We needed a plan."

CHAPTER 44
The Sergeant's Tale (iii)

The Sergeant paused in his recollections once more. He waved his, empty, champagne glass meaningfully again with that usual mischievous twinkle in his eye. I sighed, as his seemingly unquenchable thirst meant I would have to leave the warmth of my drawing room (it was now November and the cold nights were drawing in) and venture down into the cold cellar for more 'essential' supplies.

As I passed the big leaded window in the hall I spied the moon, hanging pale and bloated in the clear, cloudless sky, amongst a glittering carpet of stars. I shuddered as I pondered the possibility that, on a distant red planet far away, somewhere amongst those friendly looking stars, monstrous beings may still be plotting another attempt to take our world from us.

When I had secured another bottle of champagne, I returned to the drawing room to find my two friends in deep and earnest conversation. All talk stopped at my approach, though, and my friends merely smiled at me as if nothing of importance had taken place. I did not, in the end, feel justified in asking the subject of their discussion, even though I felt sure that something had happened. I was not to find out the importance of that short exchange until years later, but that, perhaps, is for another time.

When all glasses had been refilled and fresh cigars lit, the Sergeant cleared his throat grandly and recommenced the story of how he had come to our rescue on the Martian base.

'Well, as I said before, we stood behind the rock watchin' the Martian base lumbering away from us. The only thing we could do was to follow it, so that's precisely what we did. Not much of a plan. I know, friends, but we were only five men and so we had to look for an opportunity. It moved quickly but we could move quickly too and we managed to keep close, but not so close as the little things flying around it could see us. Or so we hoped.

Wayne then told us the bad news. He only had an hour's air left in his tank. In all the excitement, we realised that none of us had checked the meters on our suits. The rest of us checked our supplies and found that we didn't have much more. That forced our hands a bit, as I'll bet you can imagine. We had two choices now,

We could get on board the base somehow or get to the surface and try and get more oxygen and maybe some friends to help us out.

We had a bit of a chat then and decided it would be easier to try and get on board the thing. Besides, all our mates were prisoners and we didn't think they could wait. It galled us to think of what could be happenin' to you all on board that thing, I can tell you.

Glenn, good, brave lad that he is, then suggested we just start firing at the thing in the hopes of enticing the tube down so we could get on board. Sometimes the most simple plans are the best, as any commander will tell you, so that's just what we did.

Nothing seemed to happen for a bit after the first volley of shots we fired so we loosed off more explosive harpoons at the belly of the thing. Then, the machine slowed and came to a halt.

We saw the elevatin' tube begin to come down. We could see there were about ten Martians in it and all we could do now was pray that we were quicker than them. As soon as the platform in the tube hit the seabed the Martians started to spill out and we picked them off through the door of the tube like rats in a barrel. Never have I seen a battle so short, one or two of the things were slippery and dodged about a bit, but my sharp-eyed boys took them down anyway. The last one managed to get a shot off which narrowly missed Thomas, but Glenn got him right through the glass in its helmet and it flopped over dead as a dodo.

We rushed onto the platform in the tube just before it started to go up again.

Now was the nervous part. We didn't know how much the things up there knew and whether there would be a welcoming party but by God we were going to have at them or die tryin'.

The trip up the tube seemed to take forever. We checked our weapons and smiled at each other even though we knew we could be marchin' straight into an awful death. But, if death was on the cards, a soldier's death it would be, gun in hand and with the smell of our enemy's blood in our nostrils. That was how fired up we now were.

The platform reached the top. Two Martians stood behind a console and one barely had time to squeak in surprise before I shot its eye out. The other didn't make a sound. We looked around quickly to see if there were any more but there weren't. I don't think I'll ever figure the Martian mind. Why there were not hundreds of the things waiting for us, I'll never know. Perhaps God was on our side after all.

We were in air now so we took of our helmets and stripped off our suits.

Now it was time to see what could be done.'

CHAPTER 45
The Sergeant's Tale (iv)

'So, there we were, well behind enemy lines and ready to fight,' the Sergeant continued. A log popped in the fire and we started a little in our comfortable chairs. The Sergeant stared into the crackling flames for a moment, then carried on with his tale.

'The entrance room was big and we saw that there were passageways leading off every which way. We didn't hang about for fear that we may lose any element of surprise we might have got. We picked the first passage we fancied and went off up it, weapons ready. A little group of Martians appeared out of a room and we engaged them. We were low on harpoons for our guns now and so we took great care with our aim. We still seemed to have surprise on or side and they all fell quickly, bar one that skittered off on like a scared rat. Thomas wanted to give chase but I stopped him. It was best, I thought, to stay together in this strange place. We couldn't afford, nor did we want, to lose a single man.

We knew now we didn't have much time. The thing that had ran off could warn its pals at any moment so we had to work quickly.

We picked up the weapons from the foes we had beaten, discarded our own, and set off again.

We started to search rooms along the way. Most were quiet and just contained machinery of one sort or another. In another a Martian was feeding. I don't need to tell you what that means. It looked around just in time to get hit by the weapon I held. I was surprised to find that this was a weapon I hadn't seen before. No beam came from it – that I could see anyway. I pointed the gun, pulled the trigger and the Martian squeaked and exploded in a mess of green guts. There's another toy to give the boffins happy dreams, I'll warrant.

We checked quickly if the poor man the thing had been feedin' off could be helped but he was beyond even God's benevolent hand. Too much of his blood had been supped and he was pale and fading fast.

"Where is everybody else, mate?" I asked him as gently as I could.

"Down the next passageway. Big room with doors with red switches," he answered with no little effort.

"Thanks, mate. We'll come back for you," I said, knowin' full well that this poor bugger had had it.

That poor young bloke even managed a smile at us before the last of his blood dripped out and he passed on to wherever good, brave sailors go.

"Come on, boys," I said to my men. "Time to get our pals out, eh?"

As we left that room, another small unit of Martians were walkin' by and we painted the walls green with their innards. They didn't even have time to get one shot off in reply.

I still couldn't believe that we hadn't been spotted and there weren't hundreds of them at us. Could our luck hold out? We couldn't take any chances and we were watchful.

We went into the next passage, the one, that sailor had told us of, and carefully approached the area where the prison was meant to be.

The door led to a big room, as you will remember, Smith. There were a lot of doors and all had a red switch on to the right of it.

Then, from around a corner at the end of the room came another load of Martians. We ducked behind some kind of machine that stood to one side just in time for some shots to sail over our heads. Some of these Martians were using Heat-ray rifles, whilst the others used the new kind, and a few black marks appeared on the walls above us.

We took it in turns to lean around the side of the machine and fire off volleys at the things as they dodged about this way and that. Drawing a bead on them was tough, I can tell you. Those blighters can move when they want to. One or two of them fell, though but one shot from the one carrying the Heat-ray narrowly missed Dawson leaving a great black burn on his arm. His flesh sizzled like bacon in a pan and he cried out, as well he might. He fell back behind the machine and let the rest of us carry on the fight.

I leaned around the machine again and took aim at the Martian with the Heat-ray. As I loosed off a shot it moved a bit, but not far enough.

The strangest, but luckiest I suppose, thing happened. My shot must have hit the Martian's weapon as it exploded with a bright flash. The Martian just had time to scream horribly as it and all its comrades were torn to pieces.

We could not resist letting off a little cheer then but common sense prevailed. We had no idea when there would be more of those fiends about, so we quickly got back to work.

We hurried to the first door and pushed the switch. A buzzer sounded and the door opened.

And that, my friends, is how we came upon my friend Smith."

The Sergeant sat back, satisfied, in his armchair and Wells nodded approvingly.

'A ripping tale indeed,' Wells said in his thin Cockney accent. 'One worthy, perhaps, of one of my novels, eh?'

We laughed long and hearty at this and spent the rest of the evening in talk of other, happier, things not concerning Martians or death.

CHAPTER 46
A Shocking Discovery

So, here we were, liberated from our prison on board the Martian base by the grinning commandos. The Sergeant stepped forward and clapped me heartily on the back.

'It's good to see you, my friend,' he said. 'Good to see you all alive and well!'

The men in the cell cheered our rescuers with great gusto.

'Shh! Come on, we have to move it," the Sergeant said his facing becoming serious for a moment. "I doubt we'll be left in peace for long.'

Surprised and thankful that we in the cell were, those words reminded us we weren't out of the woods yet. Churchill jumped up and growled.

'You heard the man. Let's move!'

The rest of us got to our feet and made ready to follow the grinning men at the door. Even Dawson, obviously in pain and gingerly holding his burnt arm, seemed of good cheer. Why, still very much in who knew how much peril, we could be so light of heart I cannot say. The commandos' disposition and devil-may-care attitude, I think, must have been infectious.

'What weapons do you have?' Churchill asked the Sergeant.

'Just these odd things," the man answered pointing to the rifle he carried. 'There will be a few scattered around this room that may work and we shall have to find more along the way for you boys.'

'What about the other rooms?' I asked. 'There may be others'

'Next stop,' the Sergeant winked.

We left the cell and went to the other doors. Sadly, there were no more than ten men to be found in those other rooms. The Martians had been taking men away from those cells just like they had from ours, we were told.

A few of the men picked up the Martian weapons that lay here and there about the room. Greetings were quickly exchanged and Churchill tried to get the men into some semblance of order.

'We may now have a fight on our hands, men,' he said. 'Our friends here report that they did not come up against as much resistance as they expected and that does not bode well. We can expect to meet many Martians before we leave this machine and it may not be an easy fight. That we have gotten this far, though, gives me hope and says much about the British spirit. We will do what we must to bring this monstrous machine, and the Martians that cower within it, to its end and if we can survive, so much the better. I say we must not allow the Martians to escape with this weapon and we must prevail!'

The motley gathering of men were visibly stirred by these words, and I include myself in that number. We moved off with a new sense of purpose.

The first passageway we came across was empty of Martians. The interior of the base could be, as I intimated earlier in this text, quite disorientating to move around. No signs, nothing on the smooth, glowing walls to give us any indication of where we could be in this place. We walked around, in silence and on guard, for a while trying to get our bearings. Those with weapons walked at the front and the rear in an effort to cover those who could not defend themselves.

We entered any rooms we found in the hope of finding any of our fellow humans who had been taken away but may still survive.

Most rooms contained strange machinery or were empty. One or two had solitary or small groups of Martians in them that were quickly despatched before they could raise the alarm.

In one large room, we finally discovered what had happened to some of those poor souls who had been taken away from the cells and it was more horrible than I could ever have dreamed.

As we entered, two Martians looked up curiously from a long bench they were bent over. Each was quickly sent to their doom with a well-placed shot from the invisible beam weapons and we could see the work they had been engaged in.

On the bench, a Remote Walker lay prone. Beyond that, an unmoving man was strapped down, his mouth open wide in a silent scream of terror. The worst realisation was yet to come.

The panel at the back of the Remote Walkers head was open. The man beyond had had the top of his skull sliced cleanly off and, instead of seeing the expected brain exposed, there was nothing but a red gaping hole. Blood dripped from that awful wound and fell to the floor with a slow pitter-patter.

It took no more than a second, and the sight of the blood smears around the rear panel in the Remote Walkers glittering head, to understand the implications of this scene.

A man behind me bent over and vomited noisily as he came to the same conclusions as I and, doubtless, the others who stood open-mouthed and suddenly pale in the doorway.

The Martians, with supreme and diabolic ingenuity, were using the brains of men to somehow control the Remote Walkers. Like cattle, we were not only being used as a source of nutrition, but the Martians could also turn other parts of us to equally good use. Man was being used as a weapon against his fellow man.

As we stood shocked, the legs of the thing moved a little and it tried to right itself. Slowly, painfully, it got to its feet and faced us. Did I detect an air of horror in that terrible thing's stance? Did it know what it was? Had it not been given it's instructions and still retained some part of its humanity? It began to clunk and clatter unsteadily toward us then stopped and merely stared with blank eyes, it's head cocked at an angle.

The matter was decided by Glenn who, face full of horror and pity, went quietly behind it. It did not even attempt to move or defend itself as Glenn smashed the butt of his weapon into the open panel in its head.

The Remote Walker's legs instantly folded and it fell to the ground with a crash, splashing small gobbets of gore onto the pristine, shining floor.

Utterly disgusted, our party quickly left the room.

CHAPTER 47
A Fitting End?

I tried, as we headed on through the Martian base, to forget the horrible sight that had greeted us in the Remote Walker room. I could think of nothing more terrible than to end up as a disembodied earthly brain imprisoned within an unearthly machine, forced, by some unknown means, to destroy any man that came upon it on sight. I did not want to contemplate the thought that these human brains may know full well what they were being forced to do, and were tormented by it, utterly compelled to carry out their evil orders regardless of their human emotions. Better to imagine, perhaps, that all humanity left the mind at the removal of the brain making the organic matter within the walkers nothing more than a form of complicated calculating machine. Either way, there was no time to dwell on this in our current predicament, but the idea of this awful thing happening to me haunts my dreams to this day.

Through more corridors we ran at a steady trot. The exertion was beginning to tell on me and, after a strange, inadequate diet and lack of proper sleep, my breath came in short gasps, I perspired as if standing in the hot summer sun in a winter coat and the muscles in my legs ached and complained with the stress forced upon them.

'Come on, mate,' the Sergeant quietly, said keeping pace beside me. 'We will be out of here soon. Keep it up!'

I noticed that, as a man in the peak of fitness, despite his leisure habits, he showed barely more signs of fatigue than if he was engaged in a leisurely stroll through the park.

'Get down!' shouted Churchill suddenly and we, to a man, scattered and fell to the floor with military speed. Guns were raised and fired by those that had them as a troop of Martians skipped lightly toward us down the corridor, dodging left and right with dizzying speed and firing their own weapons.

The beam from a weapon narrowly missed my head and I thrust my terrified face to the floor as a man behind me was splashed over an area twice his size. Some Martians fell twitching but another man near me died with a scream that chilled me to the bone. I looked up in time to see a Martian turning and casting its saucer eyes in my direction. I frantically groped behind me and my hand grasped the barrel of a weapon as the Martian raised its own. Just when I thought it was too late and I was to join the unfortunate dead, the Martian squeaked as a shot from Glenn's weapon severed most of its tentacles. The creature fell to the floor with a wet thump and I saw its eyes widen and heard it squeak again as it was instantly set upon, using fists and feet, by some of those who were without a weapon. Desperation can make even unarmed humans dangerous and the Martian's mewlings soon ended.

There were now two Martians left. One was despatched with a deadly accurate shot from Churchill, the other skittered away crazily, weaving left and right with deadly beams following in its wake, and hooting excitedly. A black mark appeared on the wall an inch above its head as it rounded a corner in the corridor and was gone.

The Sergeant breathed an oath. 'I think we'll have company soon, boys. We must pick up the pace!' The desperate search for an exit continued.

More rooms were quickly searched. One was a feeding room, not unlike the room we had seen in the cylinder on Horsell Common. Instead of Martian biped bodies lying discarded haphazardly and unceremoniously here, there were pale human figures lying motionless and drained of all life fluid.

As in the cylinder, the smell of corruption in this room made the bile rise in the throat. One or two men crossed themselves and muttered a short prayer for these poor lost souls and we quickly moved on.

The next room bore more than a cursory inspection.

In the centre of this large room was a long metal table like that we had seen in the Remote Walker assembly room. Machines that had flashing green lights and beeped and whirred surrounded the table at one end. From the machines, a complicated array of tubes exuded, they twisted and turned this way and that until they terminated in the thing that lay on the gleaming surface of the table. Some of the tubes contained a green fluid that seemed to be being pumped into the man that lay there.

Cavendish.

The Knight lay unmoving and appeared to be devoid of life. Tubes pierced his throat, his arms and several ended in the flesh of his bare legs.

The normal ruddy colour in his puffy cheeks had been replaced by a pale yellow hue. His heavily lidded eyes were firmly shut and his mouth hung open.

Cavendish was completely naked and his arms lay motionless at his side. The reason for his apparent death was brought to my horrified eyes as I saw his chest.

The flesh there had been cut cleanly and peeled back and was held open by large clamps. His ribcage had been broken open and his innards had been, it seemed, pulled out, as an untidy pile of glistening red offal had been placed in a metal dish that stood on a small table to one side.

I remembered Wiggin's talk of the devastation that had been committed on the prostitute Mary Kelly's body by the unknown killer, whom the press had named 'Jack the Ripper', fifteen or so years before, and this sprang instantly to mind as my eyes took in this terrible sight. But this was no senseless slaughter or some unfathomable blood lust. This was science at its most diabolical and inhuman. I had no doubt, though, that our own scientists had committed the same indignities to the corpses of Martians we had found in our laboratories after the war. Cavendish had probably overseen such butchery and was likely getting a bitter, posthumous taste of his own medicine.

Still, although my feelings on the subject of Cavendish had run hot of late, I thought that this was no way for any man to die, no matter what his crimes against common decency and humanity may be. I remembered suddenly that I had seen this type of procedure before. When the Martian in the Kensington base had touched my mind.

I moved closer to Cavendish's tortured corpse.

'Poor deluded man,' I muttered. 'I hope the end was quick for you.'

One of the men behind me, I did not see who, snorted at this but Churchill snapped at him to be quiet.

I lightly touched Cavendish's arm and opened my mouth to say a final farewell. His flesh felt cool and doughy.

I was about to speak when his eyes flew wide open and his mouth opened wider to let out a terrified gurgling scream.

CHAPTER 48
The Knight of the Living Dead

The scream that came from Cavendish's pain-wracked face tailed off into a strangled gasp and then he finally lapsed into quick, shallow panting. He struck me as alike a man drowning, every attempt at drawing air into the ghosts of his excised lungs causing him unimaginable pain and his eyes watered unceasingly as he stared wildly around him as if in search of some sort of redemption. Somehow, with all of his vital organs missing from his mutilated body, Cavendish was alive!

The group of men behind me stood shocked, and I turned to see horror on every face. No one appeared to know what to do and I doubted that anyone would find himself able to step forward to assist if they did.

Cavendish's pale arm shot up and grasped mine with a steel grip. I became strangely fascinated by the visible progress of the green fluid that was being pumped through the tubes into this poor man's body.

Was this fluid keeping Cavendish alive? Was it some sort of embalming fluid that gave life where there should be none? Did the Martians wish to wake the dead for some diabolic purpose, just as they had used our brains in their deadly machines?

Cavendish's head turning toward me prodded me from my reverie. The watering, bloodshot eyes locked onto mine and I again fancied that I felt for myself the excruciating pain this man must be enduring.

The mouth opened and a hiss emitted from it sounding, at first, like the rustle of leaves on a tree in a brisk breeze, but somehow I had the distinct impression that Cavendish was trying to speak. Stooping, whilst fighting the urge to turn and run from this horrible thing before me, I placed my ear closer to the Knight's mouth and tried to listen. The man's breath was heavily tainted with the sour odour of the grave.

'Ssssmiiiittthhh,' I could now hear.

'What is it, Cavendish?' I asked, as I could think of little else to say.

'You. Musssst. Lisssten,' he replied with what seemed like an almost superhuman effort. Between every word he took an instinctive attempt at a breath. How he could even attempt to speak, I do not know and yet speak he did.

'Tell me. I'm listening' I assured him.

His mouth was obviously dry but we had no water to give him and so we could only look on as he licked his cracked lips in an attempt to moisten them.

'I did not mean for things to end this way,' he finally managed. 'I was assigned to negotiate a peace for the empire. I had ordersssssss.'

His head fell back and his dry eyes gazed at the ceiling of this charnel house.

'Orders? From whom?' I asked as gently as I could.

'The Prime Minister,' he finally managed to gasp. 'He knew we would likely be destroyed if there were another attack from Mars … and it was decided … by the cabinet … that we should try … to ensure our survival in such an … event.' He stopped for a moment as the effort of speech obviously tired him greatly. His throat made strange gurgling sounds and he began gasping for breath for a moment as if in a panic. Finally, the noises subsided and he, with great effort, turned his face, his hair in disarray and framing his head like some untidy white halo, toward me.

'I did not agree with what I had to do … but I am a … a … patriot and un … ashamed to admit it,' he finally continued, foam flecking his mouth. 'I love my country and I would do … anything to protect her, no matter how the methods I need to adopt may … appal me. The old que … queen … once told me–'

The Knight suddenly stopped his dialogue and turned his face upwards, a beatific smile touching his face for a moment, as if some happy memory now occupied all of his thoughts.

'Cavendish, we will get you out of here,' I decided. I motioned for some men to come and help me, although I had not the slightest idea what to do.

'No!' Cavendish turned toward me again, the smile dropping like a discarded mask. 'I cannot leave here … now. Detach me from the machines and I will die as surely and as quickly …as … as if you had thrust a … d … a dagger … through my heart. I am … f … finished. You must escape … this place and warn them … the Government. The Martians intend to use this new base … for another attack on London and they will build … more. This cannot … be allowed to happen.'

'But what of your orders?' I said.

Pain twisted Cavendish's face once more, but he was not finished speaking.

'There cannot be any … ac … accord with these monsters. We are as cattle to them and they do not … not need our help to conquer our fellow man. How they have left me … shh … should be warning enough to anyone who tries to ally themselves alongside them. The world must prepare for their coming, for come again … they will!'

'We will warn the world, Cavendish,' I vowed.

'G … g … good man,' he gasped with great difficulty. His chest shook and he gritted his teeth as another wave of pain thundered through him. 'Now you must end … my torment. Please.'

With grim determination, I grasped the tube in his arm.

'Farewell, Cavendish,' I said in as steady a voice as I could manage.

I held his hand and he gripped it with surprising strength. He gave a small, pain-wracked nod and fixed his eyes steadily on mine.

I yanked at the tube and green fluid spattered out noisily onto the floor.

I grabbed at other tubes and pulled them. More fluid pumped out and lay in glistening pools on the table.

Cavendish's grip on my hand relaxed but his eyes remained locked on mine. It took me a few moments to realise that he had stopped panting and his ordeal was now over. I gently closed his eyelids and turned away.

CHAPTER 49
At the Heart of the Base

Cavendish's horrifying ordeal and merciful demise, at my hand, had had a sobering impact on the men. Much as some, including myself let us not forget, had hated him for betraying us, it was too easy to imagine oneself in that awful state; neither living nor dead, aware of every terrible atrocity that had been visited on your person and knowing, finally and with absolute certainty, that there was no way back to life as you had known it before. I would, as would any sane man I am sure, much rather suffer a burning, but infinitely quicker, death from a Heat-ray than endure this monstrous experimentation. I resolved that I would make my capture impossible, should the time come, and force the Martians to slay me instantly rather than have the facility to use me for any of their diabolical science.

A few careful but firm words from Churchill roused us all enough from our morbid thoughts to spur us on with our search for an escape route from this awful place we were trapped within. Weapons were readied once more and we left Cavendish to his final rest.

The corridor was quiet and empty and we made along it quickly but with great care, I trotted along near the front behind Glenn and Jameson, the Sergeant paced me and drove me on, breathing words of encouragement all the way. Being the only non military man present, and therefore not as fit and robust as the others, I felt a little ashamed that I was perhaps slowing the pace, but if this was the case, none of the other men made any mention of it. In fact I felt fully supported by them and, in the way that I was accepted by them, perhaps even as much of a soldier as they.

Our unit, then, trotted along these gleaming, glowing corridors, one after another. I felt thoroughly disorientated but

Churchill led the way with a purpose that demanded that we follow.

We saw no Martians for a while, until one unwisely peered out of a door, only to be knocked back squealing by a blast from Churchill's beam rifle.

In the room that the unfortunate Martian had died within, we found many more weapons and were surprised that it was not better guarded such as a similar human armoury would be. Perhaps these unfathomable creatures did not think there could ever be any threat worth guarding against in this, to them, their unassailable lair. To Glenn's obvious delight, we also found his pack that still contained the explosive that was to have been used to incapacitate the cylinder. It had been carelessly discarded in a corner of the room. He opened it and checked through its contents carefully.

'We can make some pretty fireworks with this, eh Sergeant?' he said satisfied, holding up his prize and grinning.

'Indeed we can, mate!' the Sergeant agreed with a smile. 'God willing, before this day is out, we shall put on a display that they will see and hear in the colonies.' He turned to the rest of the group. 'Everyone without a weapon can grab one now, I think. Help yourselves, boys!'

Now a force to be reckoned with, small but determined and every man armed to the teeth and ready for action, we continued on our way.

As the corridor we followed turned sharply to the right, we found ourselves facing a large silver coloured door.

We made ourselves ready with weapons pointing toward the room beyond and Churchill cautiously pushed the switch next to the door. The portal slid aside with a soft hiss.

A sharp squeal and an excited hoot in return alerted us to the presence of a number of our foe within this room and the air crackled with the discharge of weapons as a short but furious battle ensued.

One of our sailors fell decapitated before he had a chance to even cry out but we fought on with grim determination. The five Martians were hopelessly outnumbered and four fell instantly dead whilst the fifth squealed and writhed until, sickened, a man ended its existence with a shot from his weapon.

The huge room we had now secured appeared to be the engine room. It contained similar black machinery I remembered seeing at the rear of the cylinder at Horsell Common.

'Right. This place is as good a launching point for your display, Glenn,' Churchill said.

'Very good, Sir!' Glenn beamed. 'How long shall I set the timers for?'

Churchill pondered this for a moment. The clockwork timing devices on the explosives should theoretically have given us time to get away from this base before the engines, and hopefully the base itself, were blown to Kingdom Come by the high explosives. This, of course, depended on our ability to escape at all.

'Two hours, no more,' Churchill decided finally. 'That gives us a fighting chance at least, but we cannot leave it any longer lest this damned machine reaches its destination, wherever that may be. We have no idea where we are but I'll warrant we are not far from land. Hide the charges well, Glenn, and ensure that they are placed so as to do as much damage as possible.'

'I don't understand the workings of this engine as well as a human one but I shall do my best, Sir!'

Churchill nodded then turned to the assembled men. 'When Glenn has finished his work we shall see if we can't get off this thing, eh? I want four volunteers to stand guard here to ensure Glenn isn't disturbed. Meanwhile, the rest of the group shall carry on the search. There can't be much we haven't seen now.'

Wayne raised his hand instantly, as did Thomas. Two other men also offered to stay and Glenn set to work.

Churchill checked the corridor, found it devoid of signs of life, and led the rest of us on once more.

CHAPTER 50
The Control Room

At the end of a long corridor further on from the Engine Room we came upon another silver door. This one was open but began to close as we reached it.

'Charge, boys!' the Sergeant cried and we did just that. Another group of Martians, around ten or so, skittered backwards raising their weapons as we did so. Again, incredibly, we had surprise as an advantage and most of the Martians fell with a few well-placed shots from our weaponry.

A few, however, weaved out of and away from the melee and gathered in a small group at a far wall, seemingly refusing to fight. They stood in a tight circle, swaying to and fro, clutching their weapons tightly and pointing them outwards as if defending something.

Churchill shouted for all to cease fire, his eyes fixed on this little band of creatures. The men were confused, but were trained to obey orders and did so.

'What is happening?' I asked.

'I don't know,' Churchill answered. 'But my aim is to find out.'

For a few moments there was a tense standoff. Human beings faced creatures from far beyond our planet and, until recently, our imagination.

Weapons clattered in the hands of both sides and feet shuffled as warriors from both races fought the urge for battle.

I cast my eyes around the room and had an idea that this was the control room of the machine. Complex machinery lined one wall and, at the far end, a huge viewing window was set into another. I could see the undersea landscape passing by through this window, with silvery fish flitting by, and knew that the base was on the move. A large map sat on a platform in the centre of the room. It was there but I could see completely through it and I pondered how this could be. It did not appear to be glass as a soldier near to it was also studying it and pushed a hand forward as if to touch it. To his surprise, his hand went through it as if it were not there. It must have therefore been some form of projected image, although where it was projected from I do not know. Perhaps the platform over which it floated held the key but there were more important considerations suddenly brought to the fore.

The map showed what was unmistakably a photographic image of Southern England. Just off the coast of Brighton a small green light pulsed. If this green light was what I thought it appeared to be, there was no time to lose.

'Churchill!' I hissed.

'Yes, a moment,' he replied tersely, his eyes fixed on the group of Martians.

I held back further comment, for the moment, and looked again at this little group. The Martians were gathered round another Martian. It was similar to them, only some considerable amount larger and its glistening skin had a paler, greyer hue. It perched upon a small silver stool and its tentacles writhed around its great head. I was reminded, by the waving of these appendages, of hearing the tale of the Gorgon, Medusa, in Classics lessons as a boy.

Its great, black, watery eyes locked onto mine and held my gaze.

A piercing pain inside my head warned me that this creature was trying to enter my mind. I must have given out a sharp cry as the pain began as all eyes turned to me.

'Smith?' I distantly heard Churchill ask.

'It …' I said with difficulty. 'It is trying to communicate.'

Images flashed before my mind's eye now. An opulent building in which this creature, or one similar, sat. Tapestries lined the walls, seemingly showing episodes of Martian history. Smaller Martians attended to this creature's needs as it waved its tentacles emphatically at some form of screen and I had the idea I was looking at how things had been on Mars before the invasion. An arid-looking landscape of red rocks came next, across which a Fighting Machine stalked. Great fields of the Red Weed swaying in the Martian breeze lay beyond that. Finally, I saw, in a huge construction like a zeppelin hangar, the building of a giant cannon and a cylinder being lowered into it. I almost felt the thunderous report as this device was fired and, with a massive spurt of green flame, the cylinder was ejected into space.

I became aware that I was being shaken.

'Smith, don't let it read your mind!' Cavendish was saying. Cavendish?

My vision cleared a little and I saw it was Churchill, not Cavendish who shook me. I have often, since pondered on this illusion but have failed to come up with an explanation.

I tried then, to stop the probing. I built a wall in my mind, brick on brick, with which to close my thoughts off from this creature. As I did so, much to my relief, it appeared to work. The pain faded and my head cleared.

'Are you all right?' Churchill asked concerned. I could see that, beyond him, soldiers were shuffling about nervously. They wanted to kill this creature and its entourage and get away.

'I think I know what this creature is,' I said finally, images and feelings still strong in my mind. 'It is the Supreme Commander of the invasion force. The closest approximation I can come to is that it is named the Overlord.'

'What does this … Overlord … want?' Churchill asked.

'It wants to live,' I answered simply.

'I'll bet it does!' the Sergeant said hotly, stalking toward us. 'I say we put it out of its misery and get off this base before it becomes so much scrap metal!'

Churchill simply glanced at him and something in his eyes stopped further words before they left the Sergeant's already open mouth.

'This creature may be useful to us,' Churchill said after a moment.

'Useful how?' the Sergeant asked, his face twisted with frustration. 'The only good Martian is a dead Martian!'

'We have what could be the enemy Commander in our grasp, Sergeant. How can we let this opportunity slip away? If, as Cavendish has said, the Martians plan to invade again, we can learn much about their possible tactics from this creature. It may give us an advantage we may not have without it.'

'I do not agree!' the Sergeant said bitterly. 'We know how tricky these things are. It will try to be away at the first chance it gets! Kill it now and we save ourselves a job later, I say!'

'Kill it now and we are no better than they are. When the time comes, it will be brought to account for its crimes. Besides which, it can perhaps aid our escape. It lives and that is an order. Do you understand?' Churchill's burning eyes bore into the Sergeants, as if daring him to disobey.

There was a tense pause and then the Sergeant nodded, deflated. I had an idea, then, of the greatness in the Lieutenant that would, I was sure, see him rise to bigger things in years to come.

'Sir,' the Sergeant said quietly.

'Right. Men; all eyes on the prisoners. One move to escape and you shoot to kill.'

The men, who had been watching this exchange, nodded their affirmation and levelled their weapons at the Martians.

'Now then,' Churchill said. 'Let's see if we can't stop this thing, eh?'

CHAPTER 51
The Martian Gambit

Churchill took in his surroundings and, after a glance at the map screen, came very quickly to the same conclusion as I. This monstrous machine was headed on a course toward London, presumably across the South of England.

We, and the men not watching the Martian prisoners, gathered in a hurried conference to discuss the next move.

'We appear to be headed toward the South Coast. Why did they just not bring this thing to land at the mouth of the Thames?' I asked, puzzled. 'Surely it would have given them a better chance of surprise, as they would have less distance to go to be in London?'

'Perhaps,' Churchill pondered. 'They mean to sweep away any resistance they find in the South on the way. With a machine like this it would likely take much more firepower to halt than we have in any one area. The terrorist actions have spread our forces a little thinner than I am comfortable with. We were watching for an attack from Mars itself, and we should have, we hoped, had enough warning to prepare for that. What we did not consider was that the Martians had a weapon as potentially powerful as this. In fact, we have no understanding just what capabilities this machine possesses. At any rate, I am supposing that they are banking on the idea that, with resistance in the South crushed, there would only be one major front to cover at the North. With the approach of this thing, there would probably be a mass exodus of people to the North from London, which would hamper any potential attempt at a counter-attack from there. I don't even think the Martians are especially concerned about surprising us. Their aim here and now is to pound London into the ground once again, and I think that this machine is quite capable of that. With London incapacitated again, the United Kingdom would be in turmoil once more.'

'Do you think that our attempt to destroy them has forced them to take this action?' I wondered. Was this a last ditch attempt by the remainder of the invading forces to do our country's infrastructure some serious damage. To soften us up again for the next force who would surely someday come?

'Perhaps,' Churchill nodded slightly. 'Or we could have just sped things along somewhat. All that matters is that we make sure that this plan of theirs does not come to fruition.'

'Amen to that, mate!' the Sergeant said. A glance from Churchill reminded him of his place. 'Sir,' he added quickly.

We inspected the machinery that lined the walls, in hope of finding some way to halt the progress of the base. It would be better that it, God willing, exploded harmlessly out to sea rather than on land where innocent people could be harmed. Even if we could not escape, many lives could be saved if we could stop this thing before it got inland.

A soft hooting made me glance around to where the gaggle of Martians sat watching us curiously. I may have been mistaken, but I could have sworn I saw amusement in some of those saucer-like, glinting eyes.

I did not have the physical symptoms that heralded an attempt at a mind probe from the creatures and, therefore, had no basis for the feeling I got then. The distinct impression I had was that we were wasting our time.

There was another hoot from the Overlord as if to confirm this thought.

Churchill was pushing a lever but there appeared to be no effect. His frown deepened when I addressed him.

'I do not think we can stop it.'

'What? Come on, one of these levers or something must control this thing,' the Sergeant said.

'I think it already has its instructions and it will follow them,' I struggled to put my feelings into words. 'It must have the capability to control itself without intervention from the Martians. I feel that it can think for itself and act on whatever situations it comes across.'

'A self controlling machine?' Churchill asked.

'Yes,' I answered. 'I feel it has a form of brain and a sort of intelligence. To all intents and purposes a living creature made of metal!'

'That's preposterous!' the Sergeant scoffed.

'Look,' I said wearily. 'I don't know how I know this, but I do and that is that. I tell you that I would swear that this thing can move of its own accord and we cannot change its course.'

'Then we must make sure that this … metal creature … is incapable of reaching its destination,' Churchill said grimly. 'We must kill it.'

'Surely the explosives my boys are planting, as we speak, will stop its heart,' the Sergeant said confidently.

'I hope it is as simple as that. We must try to warn our forces, though, just in case.'

The green light on the map screen was dangerously close to land now.

CHAPTER 52
A Call to Arms

The seriousness of the situation called for immediate action. As the machine we stood in neared the South Coast, many lives on land were at risk.

'I wonder if this machine has radio equipment of some kind,' Churchill mused.

'Would they need such a thing?' I asked. 'I mean, Cavendish assumed that the Martians communicate generally via telepathy. Then there are the calls we heard from the tripod machines during the invasion. Cavendish, I remember, once likened them a language in itself. He thought that imperceptible, to us, differences in the calls could mean that many messages could be transferred between machines.' An image of Cavendish's ravaged body flickered across my mind and I shook my head as if it could physically dislodge the unpleasant thought from my mind.

'We don't know for sure that they do not use radio,' Churchill answered. 'Our technicians, I know, scanned the frequencies we can operate within to listen for any anomalous signals when the terrorist actions began, but they may have more sophisticated equipment than we do which could explain why we found nothing. But I have to admit, I cannot see anything that look remotely like the sort of thing we need.'

I cast my eyes across the identical looking pieces of machinery at the wall. Nothing looked anything like radio equipment I have ever seen, either. 'So what do we do?'

'We could use our own radio,' Churchill flashed a rare smile. He called a sailor over who was carrying a bulky pack on his back. He must have picked this up in the armoury where the explosives were recovered.

'Is that equipment working?' the Lieutenant asked the sailor.

'Seems to be, Sir!' the fresh-faced lad answered after placing his pack on the floor and flicking nimble fingers expertly over some dials and switches. The harsh hiss of static echoed around the room.

'Excellent! Get to work. See if you can't raise some sort of human contact outside of this infernal machine, if you please!'

'Aye, Sir!' The grinning sailor flicked an exaggerated salute at Churchill and resumed his ministrations on the radio.

For a few minutes there was the disorienting hiss of static and little else. The sailor plugged a headset into the device and the sound of static was cut short.

The Sergeant paced to back and forth like a restless tiger in a cage, casting the occasional glare at our Martian prisoners. Churchill stood staring out of the viewing window, hands clenched behind his back. From time to time he rocked forward on his toes.

The door to the control room opened suddenly with a swish and many guns flicked quickly toward it. A grinning Glenn entered with the soldiers who had stayed with him.

'All done, Sir! Timers set and … hullo!' He was staring at the Martian Overlord and his would-be guards.

The Sergeant shook his head slightly as if to stop the red-haired soldier asking any more questions.

'Erm … yes. Sorry for the delay. Got into a bit of a scuffle back there with some of those fellas,' he nodded towards the Martians. 'Seems there still a few of 'em about but the ones we met didn't have a hope.'

'Good job, mate!' the Sergeant said. 'How long we got?'

'About an hour, or thereabouts. Hid the charges pretty well, I think. Even if they get to know about them, I set some little surprises for anyone who wants to mess with my work.'

'That may not be enough time,' I said looking out of the viewing window. 'Look!'

Through the window, we could all now see that the window, and therefore the top of the base, was leaving the water. We were coming onto the land!

'Radio?' Churchill snapped.

The sailor was crouched on the floor with the headset on, his tongue flicking around his mouth with concentration.

'Yes!' he said finally. 'I have something … HMS Cavor, stand by for a communication from Lieutenant Churchill of the expeditionary force. What? Yes, there are still some of us alive. No time to explain. Lieutenant?'

Churchill snatched the headset from the sailor and clamped one earpiece to his ear. He took up the microphone and spoke.

'This is Lieutenant Winston Spencer Churchill of the expeditionary mission which began aboard Nautilus.' He listened for a moment. 'Nautilus was destroyed; some of the force still remain.' He listened impatiently again. Finally he snapped. 'Look, much as I would be pleased, under less urgent circumstances, to give an official debrief, the situation is not over and there is no time! Well, if you would care to contact land perhaps you could ask them to look out to sea off Brighton. They will, no doubt see an enormous machine emerging from the sea. I am aboard that machine! No, I really doubt they could miss it, it's very big and looks very odd. YOU can see it, now? You thought it was Nautilus and followed it toward land? Well, let me put this simply, this object must be stopped at all costs. If you are able, begin bombardment immediately and warn any land forces that can be mustered. Thank you.'

Churchill let out a deep breath and handed the headset to the sailor. He looked round the expectant faces of the men.

'You gentlemen might want to brace yourselves,' he said finally.

At that, an explosion rocked the base.

CHAPTER 53
A Way Out

The control room shook in the blast from *Cavor's* guns, throwing the unprepared, despite Churchill's warning, to the floor. If the base had not taken a direct hit, the aim of the gunners, for the first salvo, was close enough to the mark to make them proud of their deadly work.

As the base continued to rock with the force of the bombardment, I glanced at the Martians and saw them skittering around clumsily like overexcited dogs on a highly polished stone floor. The Overlord grabbed, with some of its tentacles, at the stool it perched upon to steady itself.

The Sergeant grabbed onto the nearest machine and clung on, managing to keep on his feet. Churchill seemed, like an old oak in a light breeze, to be barely moved. One sailor, as he fell, hit his head, with a sickening crack, on another machine and fell to the floor moaning.

I had, on some primitive impulse, thrown myself to the floor at Churchill's warning and only found myself sliding a little across the shiny surface on my rear.

'I think perhaps we should make good our escape now, if we can,' Churchill grumbled. 'I shouldn't like to be on board when she goes, eh?'

The men picked themselves up and grabbed for weapons.

'What about them?' The Sergeant nodded slightly toward the Martians.

'They are coming with us, as we discussed before,' Churchill told him, his face allowing no further disagreement.

'Sir!' the Sergeant said simply and stalked toward our unwelcome, and now weaponless, guests. As he reached them he affected a strange pigeon English of the type an Englishman abroad might use on a local man he met whilst in a foreign territory. I was aware that this could have appeared comical in other circumstances.

'Okay you boys come with us, yes?' he said slowly. 'Any mess with us and we bang-bang!' He pretended to fire his gun at them and they backed away, eyes wide. 'You be good Squids, we no bang-bang, ok?'

Squids. This was, I had heard, supposed to be an entirely derogatory term dreamt up by some wag to describe the Martians, in a similar way that natives of other countries under our Empire had nicknames given to them. It is unknown where this term stemmed from but the general populace were catching on to it, even some of the lower illustrated dailies, after the invasion, had begun to refer to the Martians in such a way. It is, I have found, so typically human for one race to mock another in this way, perhaps as a way to help banish any mystique they may have about them. I feel, however, that I shall leave further musings on such things to commentators on the human condition much more qualified than I.

The Martians watched the Sergeant with great curiosity as he paraded around miming that they were to go with us and behave. At the end of this absurd and untimely pantomime, the Overlord let out a soft little hoot. The Sergeant assumed that this meant that they would behave and appeared satisfied.

'See!' he grinned, turning to me and tapping his head with a calloused finger. 'They can understand all right! No need for them to poke around in the old noggin, eh?'

Churchill cast his eyes heavenwards and then mustered the men.

'Come! We must be off!'

So, a strange procession left the control room, the Sergeant and his commandos at the front, the Martians, who seemed to have understood the Sergeant's mimes after all, in the middle. Then came Churchill, myself, some more of the men. The man who had hit his head was supported by one of his comrades and, with a few others, took up the rear.

Another explosion rocked the base but we were ready this time and no one fell. Sparks flew from somewhere within the door mechanism and it closed shut, jerkily and emitting a high-pitched screech, behind us. The search for freedom continued.

We travelled another corridor, so like the others we had already passed through. This corridor appeared, though, to head dead straight through the base and I wondered where it led too.

The Martians wobbled along with us but occasionally received a sharp jab from a human-held weapon for no apparent reason. When they invariably turned to look at their tormentors with wide eyes, they were generally rewarded with angelic smiles that hid evil intentions. Still, they received far better treatment than we would at their hands and they should, perhaps, have been thankful for that.

The corridor seemed endless but finally and totally unopposed, came back to where we had started in the base initially. The tube room! I realised that we could have found the control room much earlier had we used the correct corridor! The thought did not have long to linger in my head.

As we entered the tube room, another fight began.

CHAPTER 54
Of Fight and Flight

The waiting group of Martians fired instantly as we entered, killing three men instantly.

Our group scattered every which way and men found whatever cover they could.

The air crackled as energy laced the air as we battled for survival. Our Martian prisoners made their escape, bunched together around the Overlord and hooting shrilly. They headed toward a group of their comrades at the other end of the room.

'Get back here, you damned Squids!' the Sergeant yelled, letting off a few quick volleys with his weapon. One of the Overlord's guards fell limply to the floor, like a deflated balloon, but the others hurried on. The Sergeant took aim again at the fleeing enemy, but a dark patch appeared on the wall close to his head and he ducked down cursing.

Another missile blast shook the base and men and Martians alike staggered here and there. A few weapons clattered on the ground but were quickly snatched up and aimed and fired at the wielder's foes once more.

When the shaking of the base had abated, I saw the Overlord and his entourage disappear from sight behind a group of other Martians. Churchill grunted angrily but soon gathered himself back together.

'We have to find a way off this infernal machine!' he shouted above the noise of battle. 'Keep fighting, but keep your eyes peeled for something we can use.'

The tube, I saw, was surrounded by more Martians who were calmly taking shots at us. To go that way and try to escape down the tube would be suicide. We needed another way.

More Martians fell to our weapons but it seemed that more simply appeared from nowhere to take their place. Worse still, two Remote Walkers suddenly materialised and also took up the fight. I remembered all too well that these were once human beings but I roughly pushed that awful thought aside and tried to hit one with my weapon.

'Here!' Thomas shouted. He pointed towards a row of doors at one wall.

'What is it?' I asked.

'I think they may be just what we need,' the soldier replied, ducking as a shot crackled over his head.

'How so?' said Churchill, making his way, crouching to avoid a shot in the back, over to the young soldier.

'I saw the head Martian and his cronies leg it into one of these things, Sir!' Thomas pointed now to similar doors at the other end of the huge room. 'I didn't see them come out again.'

Churchill frowned. 'Well, they could lead anywhere. But I don't know if we have a choice. We are outnumbered and our escape is blocked.'

He thought, only for a split second, then came to a decision. 'Let's see what's what then. Fall back!'

The remaining men fell back as ordered, firing all the way and cutting down Martian after Martian. I dashed along, too set on survival to be afraid, with them.

The doors were all closed but each had a switch next to it. Churchill, still crouched, experimentally pushed the switch next to the closest door. The door swished open.

Beyond the door was a large space. It reminded me, instantly, of the back of a troop carrying carriage, as I had seen some of these at Holy Loch.

The inside glowed with that same eerie light that the Martians always seemed to utilise in their décor. The room was lined with what I could only assume, from their appearance, to be seats of some kind. These 'seats' were deep and reminiscent of half of a scooped out melon. A viewing window, darkened, was set into the far end of this room and in the centre of the room a bank of machinery sat.

'What is this?' Glenn breathed from behind me.

'The way out,' Churchill said and glanced at me. I nodded as I had a sudden inkling that Churchill was correct.

The Sergeant looked a little puzzled but, despite that, barked orders to our comrades who were, still crouched and fighting for their lives, nearby.

'Come on you lot, get yourselves in here!'

The Sergeant stood to one side inside the door, Churchill on the other.

'Covering fire!' the Sergeant yelled and, as the men desperately tried to make their way towards us fired his weapon in short accurate bursts at any Martian he could see. I skipped into the room and attempted to help, although my aim was far less true than my friend's. Nevertheless, I managed to disable or kill a few of the creatures. Our enemy began to surge forward, firing wildly toward us as if they guessed our intentions.

'Come on, boys!' the Sergeant yelled. 'Get in here and I'll be buying the beers in the pub tonight!'

More men entered, Glenn, supporting the sailor who had been injured in the control room, entered and, dumping his charge unceremoniously in one of the seats, joined us at the door, weapon raised. Soon most of the men were inside with us now, only two men remained outside; Dawson and a sailor who's name I did not know.

'Let's go!' the Sergeant yelled.

The sailor stood and quickly made his way toward us. Dawson also stood and, firing off one last shot turned toward us and began to run. The fair-haired man made it halfway to relative safety before a Remote Walker stalked out from behind some machinery and regarded him curiously.

'No! Run, mate!' Glenn shouted a warning.

As if time had been slowed down, we saw the young soldier glance quickly behind him. His face full of horror, he tried to pick up speed, dropping his weapon in the process.

The walker followed his progress with its blank eyes for a heartbeat or two more, and there was a whoosh and Dawson was dead before his charred body hit the ground.

Before anyone could retaliate, the door slid quickly shut.

'Will the door hold them off?' the Sergeant asked whilst laying a hand gently on Glenn's shoulder.

The soldier fired at the switch with his weapon and was rewarded with a shower of sparks. The green light next to the switch blinked once or twice, then went dark.

'I think it will now,' he said bitterly, a lone tear for the loss of his friend quivering at the corner of his eye.

'Get into a seat,' Churchill said. Then, gently: 'There will be time to grieve for our comrades later. These creatures will soon get their comeuppance.'

We sat down gingerly in the seats and settled back.

Churchill was still standing and looking at the bank of machinery in the centre of the room.

'If I am right …' he said brushing his fingertips over the switches. 'There!'

There was a low hum that seemed to fill the room and Churchill went quickly to a nearby seat.

Men glanced around in alarm as straps emerged from out of the fabric seats and, snakelike and as if with a mind of their own, encircled each man snugly. A soldier let out a small shriek then sheepishly looked around at his comrades.

I tried to move but found myself securely fastened with only my head mobile.

'What?' someone said simply, as the hum rose in pitch.

There was a rattle, a vague thump and then a building sense of movement.

I looked toward the viewing window and saw lights outside flash past at seemingly breakneck speed.

There was a sudden sinking feeling in my stomach as the escape room was ejected out of the base and into the open air.

CHAPTER 55
Down to Earth

The escape room rocked wildly on its axis as another shell from *Cavor* must have burst nearby.

'Hang on!' yelled the Sergeant.

One did not heed his words, and, as the explosion tossed the escape room around, there was a sharp crack that reverberated around the room followed by a strangled cry. I saw the sound came from a man opposite me and, as I looked, his face turned pale. His eyes rolled back in their sockets until only bloodshot white showed and his tongue lolled out of his mouth. A thin trail of silver drool trickled slowly onto his chest. Whilst the seats we were secured into would give ample support and comfort to their intended Martian occupants, the design obviously did not allow for human physiology and left the head unsupported.

In the shock from the blast, the poor man's neck had snapped back and broken and it had been the end of him. That the man had come so near to freedom and had died so needlessly was so typically and bitterly ironic that, once again, I wondered if we were nothing but playthings in the hands of some malevolent god.

The room settled and seemed to fly straight for a short while. Through the viewing window, I saw a darkened sky pinpointed by tiny stars. Along what I took to be the horizon, I noticed lights of an earthly, rather than stellar, variety in the distance. This could only mean we were headed toward land.

'Where is this thing going?' someone asked.

Churchill shook his head, 'I have to admit, I cannot say.'

'We are in a strange Martian craft and we don't know where it is going?' I asked incredulously, turning my head toward the Lieutenant whilst being careful to keep it as straight upright as I could.

'Escape was the best option, I thought, given our predicament,' he replied with a trace of annoyance in his voice. 'I did not anticipate being held prisoner in a blessed chair!'

'Then we really are in the hands of the gods,' I said under my breath.

Soon, the craft slowed and I felt a vague sense of falling. There was a slight bump and we appeared to have landed.

'Well we appear to be down in one-,' the Sergeant began, when there was a rattling noise as something was loudly pitter-pattering against the outside shell of the room.

'It's raining?' I said, but a quick glance at the viewing window appeared to contradict this. The noise stopped.

There was silence for a moment then the straps that fastened us to the chairs suddenly and quickly snapped back and we were able to move once more. The man who had succumbed to a broken neck slumped deeper into his chair and his head flopped forward. He looked as if only asleep.

Churchill went to the door at the rear of the room and pressed the door switch. It, to my surprise, began to open a little but, thanks to Glenn's, then timely, shot at the switch, would not open all of the way.

The door snapped closed, but started to jerkily open again. The pitter-pattering from outside started once more and something zipped past my head and hit the far wall. Men ducked as they realised what was happening.

Churchill dashed to the gap in the slightly open door.

'Dammit! Whoever's out there cease fire!' he shouted angrily. 'This is Lieutenant Churchill! Stop firing at once!"

The pitter-pattering stopped abruptly.

'Now, for the love of God, come and help us with this door!'

After some organisation, a party of the men outside brought crowbars and levered the door open so that we could exit our strange conveyance.

I found myself on solid ground for what had felt like weeks. I took in air tinged with the slight tang of salt and savoured every breath as if it were the finest wine.

Beneath my feet was sand and it transpired our craft had landed on the seafront.

Disorientation set in for a short while. After the events and locations of the previous days, standing quietly on this earthly beach with a soft, salty breeze ruffling my hair felt quite surreal. The cries of gulls soaring above my head sounded alien and the noise of the nearby waves breaking was like the roar of some mythological beast.

A soldier came and touched my shoulder gently.

'Ok, mate?' He asked kindly.

'Yes,' I said, mentally shaking the cobwebs from my brain. 'Yes, I am very well.'

'Sorry about the welcome and all,' he said apologetically. 'We thought you was Squids in that contraption.'

I smiled at him to let him know that all was forgiven and glanced around.

Churchill was talking animatedly to another officer nearby. The Sergeant stood, arms crossed, with them.

Soldiers milled around looking out to sea, pointing. Nearby, a gun crew attended to their weapon that was pointing the way we had come. As I watched, the gun boomed, the muzzle flashed and a shell flew out over the waves. More soldiers marched quickly over the dunes toward us in a steady stream.

I looked out to sea. I gasped as I saw the base, towering above the waves like some great black cloud. The green lights along its length pulsed and flashed and the smaller lights we had seen below the surface danced around it. Just beyond, a ship sailed at full speed toward it, guns blazing. The shell from the gun on the beach exploded harmlessly in the air between them. The base had, it appeared, broken off from its course to engage *Cavor*.

The small lights flew, like a swarm of angry bees, at *Cavor* and fired off some sort of light weapons, the dark sky now became criss-crossed with green beams. On the ship sped, but small fires sprung up from areas all over the deck. Tracer rounds reached out from the ship and some of the small lights dropped from the sky as they were touched.

'God help all who sail in her,' the Sergeant breathed beside me. Together, we watched the conflict in awe, like small boys at a firework display.

The base stopped moving for a moment, its great front end pointing toward the ship that threatened it. *Cavor* fired off another round and an explosion made the base appear to waver for a moment. Then, a great, wide beam of red light, more terrible and powerful than anything I had ever seen, flew from the nose of the machine and *Cavor* was vaporised instantly, leaving nothing but a great cloud of hissing water. It was if she had never been there.

A few cries of dismay came from the assembled men.

'Did you see that?' the Sergeant said. 'My God!'

The enormous machine stood still for a moment, as if admiring its handy work and an almost deafening cry, louder by far than any I had ever heard, reverberated through the air and shook the ground at my feet.

'ULLLAAA!!'

Men around me clamped their hands to their assaulted ears. Truly, this sound was almost as terrifying a weapon as any the Martians had ever brandished before.

The machine, having shown it's earthshaking pleasure with its handy work, slowly turned and began lumbering toward us again. Towards land. Towards London. Waves crashed around its great legs in dazzling white spray.

'Everybody get ready,' the officer who had been talking to Churchill said. 'Here it comes!'

CHAPTER 56
'We Shall Fight Them on the Beaches …'

With the passing of the plucky ship *Cavor*, the huge Martian base continued its slow, methodical progress towards its objective.

There was frenzied activity on the beach as more soldiers spilled over the dunes and took up their places.

The officer approached his horse that was placidly grazing on a tuft of grass at the edge of the sand and mounted. The horse whinnied and tossed its mane as if annoyed at being disturbed at its repast, but obediently set off down the lines at a trot. The officer clung on with one arm and pointed out to sea with the other, shouting orders as he went.

There was the sound of motors from beyond the dunes and soon two Heat-ray cannons were wheeled onto the beach by teams of soldiers who sweated with the exertion, despite the cool night air.

Next, a unit of five human Fighting Machines wheezed, clanked and thudded into sight. A small gaggle of white-coated scientists followed nervously behind these clumsy machines watching them closely. It seemed that this new technology was still not trusted enough for it to be allowed to operate in the field without the attendance of these oddest of chaperones. The scientists were, quite obviously from the way they fidgeted and mopped their brows, wishing they were safely in the company of their blackboards and test tubes. When they spotted the base stomping relentlessly toward us, though, their jaws dropped and hurried discussions took place. The allure of new scientific wonders was strong, as it had been to the late George Cavendish, and, temporarily at least, compelled them to forget their fear. They shuffled forward slowly, like a flock of chattering white geese, to gain a better view.

'We have to delay it,' Churchill said loudly, trying to make himself heard over the noise of the general activity and the periodic booming reports from the guns that now lined the beach. 'It will not be long now until the charges do their work and, with luck, stop this thing once and for all. It is imperative that this machine does not get inland. God be with us all!'

One or two soldiers crossed themselves and muttered prayers to their makers. Weapons were shouldered and aim was taken. The beach guns fell silent, waiting for their target to come nearer. A deathly quiet settled over the scene, broken only by the clatter of nervously hefted rifles and the occasional nervous whinny of officers' horses.

'Wait for the order!' Churchill barked. By previous arrangement, it seemed, this honour had been bestowed upon him only.

As we stood silently, the base drew silently nearer. In the light of a pale moon I could see more white spray kicked up as its huge, thick black legs propelled it through the water.

The small flying machines, which had disappeared somewhere into the base after the demise of *Cavor*, re-emerged from behind it and headed towards the waiting men.

Churchill saw this and yelled: 'Fire at will!'

Rifle shots sounded from along the human lines like the pops and crackles of logs on a fire.

The small light machines swooped down from the sky, firing their beams at targets in their path. A beach gun took a direct hit and exploded in a ball of fire, flinging the men surrounding it, like broken, smouldering rag dolls, in all directions.

A man staggered away from the scene, screaming and aflame, until some of his comrades threw him down and rolled him in the sand.

The Heat-ray cannons were hurriedly brought to bear and the air in front of them wavered as their deadly beams reached for our attackers. One, two then three of these machines were caught in the blasts and fell from the sky, showering men below not quick enough to flee with white hot shards of metal.

The base was now emerging onto the beach and towered ominously above us. An enormous metal foot came down and smashed a small cluster of gaily-painted bathing huts near the water's edge to splinters.

The huge machine halted suddenly as if pondering its next move.

The beach guns spoke again and again and puffs of smoke erupted around the bottom of the base. They seemed to have little or no effect.

The small machines continued their assault and men were struck down all around by their weapons.

Then, the glass tube emerged quickly from the bottom of the base and planted itself with an enormous thud in the sand.

'They are coming out!' the Sergeant shouted from nearby.

Through the tube we could see a large troupe of Martians descending, clutching weapons. The platform reached the sand and the creatures spilled out as soldiers surged forward, shouting battle cries and firing wildly, to meet them.

So began The Battle of Brighton.

Brighton Battle by Peter Fussey

Aftermath by Peter Fussey

CHAPTER 57
Blood, Toil, Tears and Sweat

The opposing forces, rushed, the men bellowing and the Martians hooting, head long toward each other and met with an audible crash.

Too close for rifles or other such weapons to be used, a vicious hand to hand battle began in the moonlight on that small area of beach beneath the dark looming shadow of the base.

Humans brandished bayonets and used them to deadly effect, stabbing at saucer eyes and slashing at groping tentacles. The Martians utilised their brute strength and long knives with sharp, wavy blades that glinted in the light from the pale moon. I had never seen them use these weapons before but they used them to deadly effect.

This was no ordered battle with a definite plan. This was an undisciplined melee, a desperate struggle for supremacy and survival on this sandy, damp battlefield.

The cries and squeals of the wounded and dying from both sides rang across the night air as we stood and watched this horrendous spectacle from a little way up the beach. The smell and sight of blood awakened something primitive within me and I, despite myself, wanted to be part of this conflict. I wanted to assist in the destruction of these interlopers who dared to sully our land once more with the stench of their very existence. I wanted to rip and tear at these creatures and send them to whatever hell they went to after they expired.

The Sergeant must have seen me fighting with these instincts as he gently laid a hand on my arm.

'Your chance may yet come,' he said quietly. The feelings dissipated somewhat at this, but bitter bile lurked at the back of my throat.

The battle raged on, limbs and extremities thudding to the sand at regular intervals. Gruesome set pieces flashed across my eyes as this carnage continued.

At the edge of the conflict, a Martian tried to crawl away with four of its tentacles missing. A small group of men followed it then, like a pack of cats toying with a mouse, stabbed at it as it tried to escape. They, mad-eyed, slashed and stabbed until it moved no more.

A man was grasped by two Martians and pulled, screaming pitifully, literally in half, his innards falling to the floor in a wet heap. Another had his head twisted off by thick, rope-like tentacles as if the creature was unscrewing the lid of a jar. A fountain of blood, black and glistening in the darkness, gushed into the air and the man's limp body was flung unceremoniously to one side.

Another charging soldier was set upon by three hooting Martians and his limbs were sliced cleanly off by the weapons they held. The man's twitching torso lay flopping about on the surf and his pitiful cries floated through the air toward me.

A Martian had its eyes stabbed out by a man already covered in green blood and fell away squealing.

Whilst this horrendous battle on the sand was fought, the beach guns kept up their salvos and the Heat-ray cannons took shots at the base. Very little damage appeared to be done by this but, like a great beast annoyed by the constant attentions of mosquitoes, the machine finally showed its displeasure.

The great red beam lanced out from the front of the machine, suddenly and without warning, and sent a trio of guns to oblivion. The sand on the beach was turned to scorched glass at its touch and men and weaponry simply disappeared in a great cloud of smoke.

'Fall back!' Churchill shouted.

The remaining forces began to retreat a little, still firing, but two of the human Fighting Machines clanked forward, belching smoke from their exhausts and began to shoot their Heat-rays at the base.

'What are they doing?' I cried.

'Buying us some time,' the Sergeant replied. 'Look!'

A platform was descending within the tube and, swaying excitedly on it, was another large group of Martians.

The Fighting Machines concentrated fire on the tube and it shifted slightly from its position. Something must have broken within it as the platform fell to the ground too quickly and the Martians, unsupported now, squealed as they fell. One or two attempted, I could see, to cling onto the smooth walls of the tube but it was to no avail.

The glass inside the tube was painted sickly green with their blood as they hit the sand at tremendous speed and a few broken bodies spilled out of the portal.

'Yes!' cried Glenn. His smile dropped, however, when the base's deadly beam reached out, like a thunderbolt sent from a malevolent god, again and wiped the Fighting Machines cleanly from existence.

The Sergeant gathered his men, Thomas, Wayne and Glenn together.

'We need to delay this thing a bit longer, eh boys?' he said. The men nodded as one.

'Smith, you will stay here!' the Sergeant said. 'Glenn, you stay with him.'

'But-!' I began. I wanted desperately to be part of whatever they had planned.

'No!' he reiterated. 'Look, mate. Things aren't going to well. We are just going to keep this thing busy for a bit. As I said, you may yet get your chance. But for now, stay out of it. Someone will have to tell the world about this fight and you should be that man. Stay here and, if you can, survive!'

I nodded but still wished for a part in this plan, whatever it was.

'Good man!' the soldier said and gave me a friendly clap on the arm. He chanted his now familiar mantra: 'When all this is over, I'll see you in the pub for drinks, my friend! Oh, and you're buying!' With that, he turned away.

The men turned and ran over to where the remaining human Fighting Machines were crouched, unmoving on the beach. A quick discussion took place and the scientists in attendance showed their dissent with red faces and waving arms.

The Sergeant prodded one in the chest with a finger and shouted something in his face. Finally, the man shook his head, resigned and in no position to argue, and waved at the machines drivers to dismount.

The three commandos hopped quickly into the cabins, the glass canopies slid shut and the engines roared into life.

In a cloud of smoke and fumes, the three machines clattered and stomped down the beach toward the base.

'Don't worry mate! They'll be fine,' Glenn said at my side. But he could not hide the concern in his eyes.

CHAPTER 58
Their Finest Hour

During the skirmish on the beach, the small flying machines had taken many losses but had wrought havoc among the human forces. They soared above the battlefield at a blinding speed, stopping briefly and suddenly to take a shot at this or that human soldier or beach gun and then, when satisfied at the results, zipping away again to find another target. They were, however, easy to disable with a single rifle shot, I gather this was because of the lightness of the armour required to facilitate the high speeds they could maintain. But, despite heavy losses, they were still a major contributing factor to the severe depletion of the human forces we now faced.

A little way down the beach I saw one following the officer who had been with us earlier. His horse's mouth was flecked with foam and its eyes were wide with terror as it galloped madly toward us, the officer clinging desperately to its back.

The machine buzzed around them as they went, the small beams that lanced out from its nose narrowly kicking up puffs of sand around them.

The officer drew his sabre and frantically swiped at the machine, but it was too fast and the horse's course too erratic for him to take effective aim. The metal threat dodged his clumsy attempts at dislodging it from their course.

Finally, a lucky shot from the machine sliced a leg clean off the horse and it tumbled, with a scream that sounded terribly human, head over tail snapping its neck. The officer was thrown clear only to land in a heap of the burning wreckage of a beach gun emplacement.

His cries and writhing as he was turned, in an instant, to a ball of flame, mercifully, did not last long.

The machine that had ended both these lives began to zip away to search for more game, but it was felled by a clean shot from Churchill's rifle.

'We must do something!' I shouted, sickened at the death and destruction around me.

'We are doing all we can!' Churchill replied, grimly. 'We can only delay them now and hope that the explosives do their work.'

Beneath the base, the melee continued. It appeared now that the Martians were gaining the upper hand despite heavy losses to their group.

The men fought bravely but they must have seen that the game was nearly up as some of their number, desperately tired and streaked with blood, tried to retreat. The Martians, seemingly indefatigable, had other ideas and ruthlessly chased them. Some they cut down with their wickedly sharp blades or others they simply tore apart with their tentacles. It seemed there would be no prisoners, on either side, in this conflict.

I followed the Fighting Machines containing the three Commandos as they moved up the beach toward the base.

As they neared the giant machine, they split up and advanced on different paths. When they were within range of the battle, their Heat-rays flashed and cut down some Martians that had scattered at their approach.

The human machines did not join in the struggle beneath the base, however. The battle was so dense that they would have been in too much danger of hitting human comrades as well as our foe. They simply picked off some small groups of Martians that skittered about on the periphery and then concentrated fire at different areas of the underside of the base.

A shot from one machine rocked the top of the access tube and a small explosion was the reward.

The soldiers who stood nearby me shouted with glee as sparks and bits of molten glass and metal rained down from the tube. The Fighting Machines, rather than present sitting targets, clanked to different positions and resumed their attack.

The first sign that the base began to move again was that the tube suddenly leaned over at a crazy angle. It appeared that it could not, because of the damage to it, be retracted and, as the base's mighty legs began to propel it forward once more, the tube was pushed over. It came away in a shower of sparks and fell to the sand, crushing some unfortunate combatants, both man and Martian, who were engaged in a struggle for life nearby.

'It's moving again! We have to stop it!' Churchill shouted and men ran forward brandishing weapons. Soon, only Glenn and I were left as all had surged forward and a last desperate attempt to stop the machine began. I wanted to go forward and do my part, too, but Glenn forcibly held me back.

Suddenly maddened, I punched him squarely on the jaw and he fell back surprised. I ran forward after the rest, the pain in my hand unnoticed in the heat of the moment.

I picked up a discarded weapon on the way and began firing wildly at any target I saw. I felled two Martians in my anger and a light machine that stopped to target me got a bullet for its pains that brought it to the ground.

I halted for a moment, exhausted, and saw the Fighting Machines standing in a wide triangle targeting the gaping hole where the tube had been. More explosions resulted and men and Martians scattered from debris that rained down upon them.

The base moved on and I saw a leg begin to come down. Directly in the path of its descending metal foot was a human Fighting Machine. The driver, Thomas I was close enough to see now, frantically pulled at the control levers and smoke poured from the machine as the engine was gunned. The machine began to jerk forward but it was too late. The last sight I saw was Thomas mouth open wide with terror and his hands thrust out to the glass as if to fend off the enormous foot as it crushed his machine into the sand.

In another machine, I saw the Sergeant's face contort with anger and grief and he fired his Heat-ray, with renewed vigour, at the huge machine.

I heard exultant howls and looked over to see Martians looming over the dead bodies of many men waving their knives and weapons like banners. Then Churchill and the remaining soldiers reached them and, screaming defiance, took up the fight.

Churchill himself blocked blow after blow from a big battle-scarred Martian and stabbed it in the eye. In its death throes, a tentacle from the creature flailed out and knocked him out cold.

Then, as I despairingly saw the last of the men fighting what seemed to be a losing battle, there was an enormous muffled explosion.

The base was now perilously close to the beachfront houses and any civilians who had stopped, at what they thought was a safe distance to watch the battle, ran away screaming.

An ear splitting screech followed the explosion and the base rocked forward on its massive legs. It carried on a little way, a foot smashing a house to a pile of rubble, but there was another explosion and it stopped suddenly, another leg poised mid-air.

Flames and smoke belched out from the tube hole and more, smaller explosions followed. Small flaming shapes fell from the hole and I realised that these were the bodies of Martians caught in the blasts. They fell to the sand and burned merrily.

Another shape shot out from the side of the base. It was an escape room but it was aflame and it streaked, like some erratic comet, straight toward the sea. It hit the surface at a steep angle and broke apart, flinging its howling occupants at tremendous speed to their deaths.

Explosion after explosion rocked the wounded base now and the glass at the viewing window erupted out into the night. More Martians were thrown clear with flames following them.

There was another screech and the base began to topple over.

Glenn had reached me and had begun to remonstrate with me for hitting him when the explosions had started. His harsh words were forgotten and he whooped with joy at each explosion as the base slowly tore itself apart.

'It worked! It worked!' he repeated dancing around like a man possessed. Even I had to smile, exhausted physically and mentally as I was, at this man's joy at the outcome of his work.

The base fell to the ground with a metallic crash crushing more houses over a wide area. Two of its legs came off and more explosions followed, blowing more houses to pieces with their ferocity.

The wreckage burned for four days.

CHAPTER 59
The Tide Turns

As the base crashed to the ground the Flying Machines, as one, dropped to the ground. The base had controlled all of them, through some means and, with that method of control gone, they were nothing but useless hunks of metal.

The remaining men, at seeing this, carried on the fight with renewed vigour. The Martians, for their part, seemed to have had some of the bravado suddenly taken out of them with the destruction of their greatest weapon and some tried to escape the battlefield. One made it to the water's edge but was cut down by the Sergeant's Heat-ray. Through the glass of the machine's cockpit, I saw my friend cast a weary 'thumbs up' in my direction.

The struggle continued for a while but the humans soon began to turn the tide in their favour and the methodical killing of the creatures from Mars began.

Glenn pointed suddenly further down the beach.

'Well lookie there!' he said.

I followed his finger and spotted an escape room lying on its side in the sand.

From it, in the light of flames that billowed out of what had, until recently, been a beach gun nearby, I saw two Martians crawling away. They were heading toward another escape room that was hovering just above the sand a short distance away.

'Come on, Glenn!' I said and ran toward a small group of horses that huddled at the dunes. I had ridden a horse before in my youth and I jumped onto one taking the reins quickly. Glenn jumped up onto another and, nudging the nervous horses with our feet, we galloped off down the beach.

The wind ruffled my already dishevelled hair as we went and sand periodically got in my eyes but I could still see that, at the door of the intact escape room stood the Martian Overlord. It was waving its tentacles at its fallen comrades to hurry towards it. As we approached, I saw its eyes widen and I vaguely heard it squeak. The tentacle waving grew more emphatic, then. This thing evidently wanted to be off.

I let go of the reins, clung onto the horse as well as I could with my knees, and raising my rifle, fired at the creature. Aiming was difficult with the speed of our gallop and some shots pinged harmlessly off the walls of the craft. Glenn took up the shooting too and the Overlord's frantic state became more apparent. It danced and skittered about the entrance, hooting loudly.

We came, then, upon the crawling Martians and my horse reared without warning. As I was flung from its back, the horse stamped and trampled on one of the creatures into a bloody pulp. The wind was knocked out of me by the fall and I lay stunned on the sand for a second or two. Glenn pulled his horse around and came to where I lay.

'Go … on!' I said desperately trying to catch my breath.

'What?' Glenn said, dismounting and reaching down to help me up.

'That's the Overlord, you fool!' I shouted angrily. 'It's getting away!'

'Oh!' Glenn said simply. His face suddenly took on a look of surprise and his eyes rolled back. A small trickle of blood ran from the corner of his mouth and dripped onto his collar. He fell forward onto his face, a harpoon protruding from his back.

I spun round looking for the source of this missile. A Martian stood nearby trying to reload its weapon. I groped for my weapon and raised it. Just as the Martian got me in its sights, I fired. The Martian dropped to the sand, lifeless.

Again I looked to where the Overlord's craft stood and saw it begin to rise from the sand. The creature's eyes widened as I took aim and fired. The bullet sped toward the creature, then there was a small gout of blood as one eye ruptured. The Overlord fell back squealing. As the door to the craft began to close and it rose higher into the night sky, I saw tentacles drag the wounded monster away from the opening.

There was a clanking behind me and I turned to see a Fighting Machine stalking up the beach. There was a wave of heat above my head as the machine fired at the dark retreating shape of the escape craft. The shot clipped it and it wavered in the air a little. Small pieces of molten metal dropped to the ground as the craft shot suddenly up into the air then moved forward, at amazing speed, away over the land and out of sight.

'No!' I shouted in frustration and fired volley after harmless volley at the thing. The chamber of my rifle clicked empty and I let it fall to the floor. The Overlord, if it still lived, had escaped.

The canopy of the Fighting Machine opened and the Sergeant sprang out.

'Are you alright?' he asked.

'No!' I said angrily. I could say no more and sank, bitter and exhausted, to the soft sand, my head in my hands. I sobbed, then, for all those who had died and for my inability to stop the creature that had directed all the carnage the Martians had wreaked on Earth.

CHAPTER 60
Cleaning Up

The Sergeant waited for a few moments then held a rough hand out to me.

'Come on, friend. It's time to leave,' he said gently.

I took my hands from my face and looked at him for a moment.

'Yes, we must go,' I said wiping my face, wet with tears, with the back of a grubby hand.

As he helped me up, I said: 'Thank you.'

'What for?' he asked, with a puzzled expression.

'For coming to my aid.'

He dismissed this with a wave of his hand. ''S what mates is for!' he said flashing a quick, warm smile. 'Us comrades got to stick together!'

We walked toward the Fighting Machine. Glenn's unmoving body, the harpoon in his back pointing straight up to the heavens, lay nearby and we stood above him for a moment. The Sergeant's face grew grim and he bowed his head and placed a hand on his breast over where his heart lay.

He muttered a quick prayer and, despite my not being the religious sort, I joined him in a quiet 'Amen', when he had finished.

'You were a good man, Glenn, and a good mate. Let's hope you are drinking a toast to us in heaven!'

'Trying to get rid of me already, Sarge?' a muffled voice said.

The man's body twitched and he laboriously turned his face towards us. He cursed with the pain of the movement but spoke again.

'You're not angels,' he said breathlessly. 'I don't see any wings.'

The Sergeant hurriedly knelt down to him and laid a hand gently on his shoulder, a single tear of joy trickled down his face.

‘Glenn! Don’t move, mate!’ he said, his voice a little choked.

‘It hurts a bit,’ Glenn managed between laboured breaths. ‘How’s it look?’

The Sergeant regarded the harpoon. ‘You’re looking like a pole without a flag, but it doesn’t look like it’s in too deep. You’ll be fine!’

Glenn gave a small painful grin. ‘Good. Me missus would kill me if I didn’t come home.’ He chuckled a little, but the effort turned it into a hollow cough.

‘Easy, mate!’ the Sergeant said. ‘This is no time for jokes. Maybe in the pub when you’re better!’

The Sergeant stood up and waved his arms at the men down the beach.

‘Hey there! Medic needed here! Hurry up!’ he shouted loudly enough for the gods to hear.

Three men soon hurried toward us, two carried a stretcher and one had a medical bag slung over his shoulder.

With Glenn checked over and gently laid, face down, on the stretcher, we bid him a quick good-bye and the Sergeant climbed back into his Fighting Machine. The machine was gunned into life again and set off in a cloud of black smoke that nearly choked me.

I found my horse chewing on some grass as if nothing had ever happened to it. The only sign of anything unusual were the gobbets of Martian flesh clinging to its hooves and a small wound down its flank. I stroked its mane calmingly, mounted and we trotted behind the machine back down the beach toward the battlefield.

At the battlefield, Churchill was standing puffing a great cigar. His head was bandaged but he appeared to have suffered no other ill effects.

A little way off, I saw Wayne’s Fighting Machine clanking wildly after a fleeing Martian. The creature weaved this way and that but it was only a matter of time and soon it ran no more.

A few men stood, weapons raised before a small group of cowed looking Martians. Things really had turned for the human forces whilst I was in my futile pursuit of the Overlord. More soldiers had come over the dunes to join the fray and soon the enemy had been overpowered.

Now a small band of the creatures were all that was left of the force that seemed about to overwhelm us.

I briefed Churchill on what had happened with the Overlord while he listened attentively.

'What are you going to do with them?' I asked Churchill, meaning the Martian prisoners.

'Classified,' Churchill replied, winking.

'What?' I asked. I had a terrible feeling that I knew the answer. 'You intend to hide them away somewhere, don't you? They are too dangerous! You know what happened before and there already some of them free!'

Just then, an important looking, rotund man fought his way through the gathering crowd of civilians that had gathered at the edge of the beach. This crowd was being held back by a cordon of soldiers, but the man flashed some papers in the face of the officer there and was let through. A small weasely-looking man with bright black eyes kept pace just behind him.

The important man looked so surprisingly like Cavendish that, for a moment, I was lost in thoughts of all that had gone before since I had first met the Knight in my drawing room so long ago. I came back to myself when he approached and I got a closer look at him.

The man had the same red face as Cavendish, the same white moustache draped across his chops. He even dressed in a similar manner.

'Are you Churchill?' he rumbled. The voice was so alike the dead Government man's and to such a startling degree that I began to doubt my sanity.

'I am he,' Churchill said around his cigar.

'I am Sir James Cavendish,' the man huffed. 'My brother was in charge of your operation.'

'May I say what a good job he did of it, too, Sir,' Churchill said, without a trace of irony. 'A great man indeed.'

Cavendish's face coloured a little darker at this but he said nothing else for a moment. Finally, his eyes moved to the huddled band of Martians that stood a little way away, their human guardians watching them like hawks.

'I am here for the prisoners. We have much to learn from them,' the man said.

'You do?' Churchill asked, slowly taking the cigar from his mouth.

'Quite so,' Cavendish said impatiently. 'Your answer?'

Churchill looked at his cigar for a moment and rolled it between his fingers. He looked at me, straight in the eye and barked one word.

'FIRE!'

There was a series of sharp cracks from behind him and the Martian prisoners all fell to the sand. Their executioners moved quickly in and bayoneted them to make quite sure they were dead.

Cavendish's face coloured purple.

'I'll have you court-martialled for this!' he said barely containing his anger. 'Every man jack of you will swing!'

Churchill regarded him as a boy might watch a fat spider crawling across his wall.

'I had orders from the Prime Minister himself!' Cavendish ranted.

'And I had orders from the King!' Churchill retorted. Cavendish's mouth flapped in that gaping fish look that his late brother had often adopted. He gathered himself together, span around and stalked away, nearly knocking his little weasely attendant over in the process.

Churchill turned to me and winked.

'As you said, Smith, they are too dangerous.' He moved off to direct the cleanup operation as the first rays of a new sun began to peek above the horizon.

EPILOGUE

I would like to take this opportunity to bring a sort of closure to this tale, for now at least. Here, my esteemed reader, is a brief summary of events immediately after the Battle of Brighton.

The cleanup operation took many months. The destruction that the Martian base machine, and its attendant Flying Machines, had wrought on the town of Brighton cost many thousands of pounds to put right. Incredibly, despite the loss of hundreds of human soldiers in the fighting, only twenty civilians were killed in this fiercest of battles. Ten of the dead were in a small hotel on the seafront that was directly in the path of the falling base, why they had not been evacuated during the battle is not clear. The cowardly owner of this establishment, who rather cannily *did* make good his escape, leaving those supposedly under his care to their own fates, was brought up on charges of negligence of the most heinous kind and was hanged, to the general approval of the populace, for his trouble.

Many services of thanksgiving were given in churches up and down the land, particularly in the South East and London, the primary targets, that the death toll had been so astonishingly low.

A few Martians had gone to ground in the area but it is thought that all were found in the following days and were despatched on sight. The Martian Overlord's escape craft was, to my chagrin, never discovered but was last seen, careering erratically and trailing smoke and flame, heading North over the Highlands of Scotland. I pray that the thing eventually crashed and the monsters within were obliterated on impact.

Scientists swarmed over the wreckage of the base and tried to salvage what machinery they could. The papers, at the time at least, were told that the explosions had damaged everything too badly to gain anything from what had been found. I, knowing how these things went in my dealings with our leaders, thought that this may not have been too close to the truth.

Events were, as they always have been, toned down in the press. No mention was made of the mission in *Nautilus*, but it was alluded to that Sir George Cavendish had died a hero, in the defence of the realm, leading an attack on a Martian stronghold. Little mention was made of the many brave men who had died with him, although some, including Thomas and Dawson received the Victoria Cross posthumously. Glenn made a full recovery and enjoyed a solid career in the military. The Sergeant marched proudly into the palace, one fine summer day, to receive the DSO from the King himself. He brought it to my house to show me one day and said he felt that I should have received one too. He never tired as before, in his frequent visits to my house, of telling the tall tales of his previous exploits, but sometimes, when the subject of the mission aboard *Nautilus* came up, his face took on a haunted look and the subject was turned to lighter matters. One does not, I have found, face demons and come away unaffected.

As for Churchill, he did not receive any punishment for his disobedience in killing the Martian prisoners. It seems he did, indeed, have the King's blessing for his actions and, instead of a trip to the gallows, was offered a Knighthood. Churchill politely declined as he felt that such an honour was above him, such a man as he is.

I, for my part, went home as quickly as I was able. My wife's face was all I wished to see now and, a few days later, I fell gratefully into her loving arms.

So it was that, after all the death and destruction I had seen, came my own moment of joy.

I was, one day, tending the roses in our little garden on a warm day, with nary a cloud in sight in the wide blue sky, my wife returned from town after having gone on 'some errand'. She stood at the gate, simply looking at me for a while, her skin pale and her complexion flawless, and I thought I had never seen anyone more beautiful and that my love for her would last forever and, perhaps, past that.

'John, my love,' she said in a clear, gentle voice as she closed the gate behind her. 'I have some news.'

I put down my clippers and went to her.

'What is it?' I asked, concerned. 'Are you all right?'

She looked at me again with watery blue eyes.

'John,' she said steadily. 'I have visited with Doctor Pegg today. He says that you are to be a father.'

'Can it be true?' I asked as a wave of happiness that almost hurt washed over me. Her slight smile and the love that burned in her eyes told me that it was. 'But that's – that's absolutely the best news a man, any man, can have!'

We tearfully embraced then and, when I thought I could bear to let my darling wife go, just for a moment, I took her hand in mine and led her into the house.

Meanwhile, the rumblings of jealousy and resentment over British power grow louder in Europe. The people of the continent yearn for the wealth and power that we enjoy and strikes and rioting are common amongst these disgruntled peoples. Still the foreign governments, that we do not control, do nothing against us but protest in the strongest possible terms.

Across the British Empire, human Fighting Machines and other technologies are increasingly used to crush the growing insurrection amongst the subjects under our care. The more radical papers tell stories of the ruthless brutality and the stony hearts of those who are at the head of this, our new Rome, and there are those organizations within our own society that vocally, but anonymously, abhor such incidents.

Wealth and power are the aphrodisiacs that drive our leaders and they are not afraid to wield either to keep what they have accrued.

It is the fear of the technology that we apply with such vigour that keeps our nearest neighbours in check and us safe and aloof on our small island. For the time being, at least.

Across the wide, cold gulf of space, it is now, as I write these words, certain that the Martians are plotting anew. The Sergeant, on one of his visits, soberly told me that there has been new activity detected on that arid planet. The Crystal Egg had been recovered, its box slightly burned but the Egg itself unharmed, and scientists gaze into its depths constantly. Huge machines now crawl across the arid surface of Mars and the denizens of that eerie red globe hop excitedly about the Egg's line of sight. Our enemies will, I feel sure, make adjustments to their original flawed calculations and turn their brilliant, ruthless minds to a foolproof plan for our destruction. The next time they come, there will be no mistakes.

Our British Empire of Steel, like all great Empires over time can, I am sure, not last forever unopposed. Whether this opposition originates from our envious neighbours on Earth, or from equally envious creatures from a distant red planet is, ultimately, of no consequence.

One day, I fear, the citizens of this small, green island will once again be routed and the world will, this time, surely follow.

THE END?

Martian Montage by Peter Fussey